SILVER BEASTS

Book One in the Mapmaking Magicians Series

EMMA STERNER-RADLEY

SIGN UP

Thank you for purchasing Silver Beasts.

I often hold sales and giveaways, to find out more about these great deals (and what I'm working on) please sign up to my mailing list by clicking the link below:

https://www.subscribepage.com/emmasternerradley

To my wife Amanda,
who lifts me so I can reach for my dreams. (And the cookies on the top shelf.)

A big thank you to my sensitivity reader for my characters that are POC, Nick Campan. Secondly, I have to thank my critique partner Niamh Murphy and developmental editor Jessica Hatch. My third thank you goes to the diligent Cheri Fuller for copyediting and proofreading. And the fourth to Miira Ikiviita, Dee Powell, and Frances Craig for pointing out the typos that escaped us all. A fifth thank you goes to Hatti Bailey for the illustrations.

And of course great thanks to May Dawney, Carol Hutchinson, Kyla Rede and the beforementioned Miira Ikiviita for supporting this story on Patreon.

A last gigantic thank you goes to my family for patiently putting up with this weird, know-it-all, sensitive, city-loving lesbian who has vexed them for years.

As always, in memory of
Malin Sterner
1973-2011
Who never liked fantasy books but who would've read this one anyway.

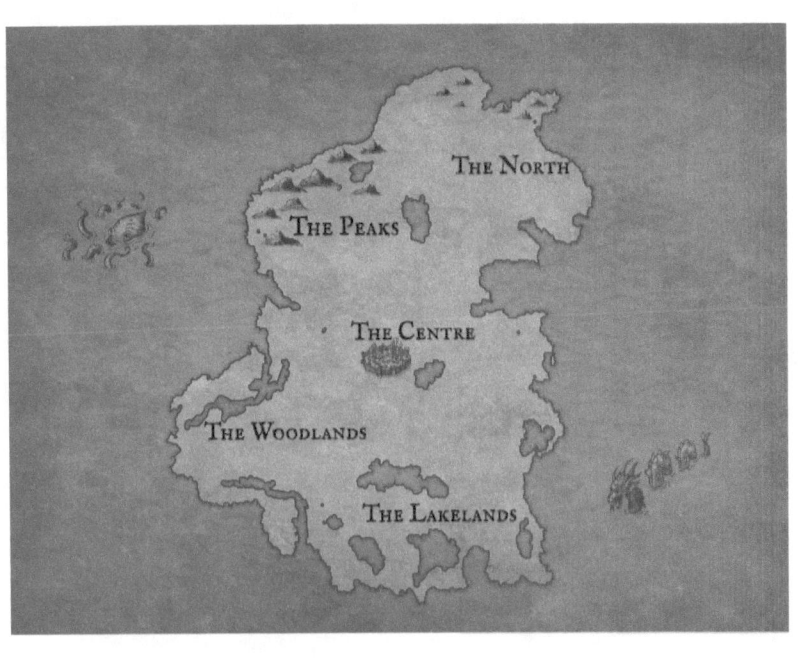

Chapter One

AVELYNNE, BEFORE IT BEGINS

Today, Countess Avelynne Ironhold *had* to keep her nerve. Everything depended on that.

Sadly, staying calm was easier said than done, especially when the clanking of swords and neighing of horses outside the castle walls unsettled her. Up here in the Peaks, which was all cloud-touched mountain tops, all should be peaceful. No such luck, though. Not even here, behind the thick walls of Ironhold castle.

She moved away from the window and rubbed her temples, admitting to herself that her lack of patience with the noise might be due to stress and a guilty conscience.

Never mind. It was too late to tell the truth now. This was bigger and more important than her. Lives might be at stake. She would have to go to the Hall of Explorers and make the best of it.

There was a shout from one of the combatants in the courtyard. Avelynne turned to her maidservant, who was closest to the source of the clamour.

1

"Myllie? Would you mind shutting the window? The chaos out there is getting worse."

Myllie looked annoyed but obeyed while mumbling, "Yes, Countess." The maid dawdled, in her usual unhurried manner, to unlatch the window. She screamed as a flash of silver whooshed in.

Avelynne's blood froze. The shout from outside… it hadn't been about the swordfight. It must've been a warning that a particularly bold and large silver beast was circling the castle. Why hadn't they killed it?

Myllie cried out again and ran for Avelynne's four poster bed. She crawled under the covers and lay there squealing. Avelynne couldn't say why. They both knew that a silver beast would bite through the bedding as easily as it did skin and flesh.

Avelynne was still as a statue. Like everyone else, she had received training on what to do when a silver beast attacked, but hesitation kept her actionless.

The fiends' magically thickened skin was hard to pierce, and that same armour made them difficult to render unconscious. Knocking them out was still the easiest solution, but how?

The beast circled the room, as if choosing which of them to attack first. It made that incessant, eerie clicking sound they always did. It grew louder and louder. She examined the fiend's every move and aspect. It must've been a wasp before the mutation of Cavarra's insects into silver beasts, as it was still wasp-like. Now, however, it was the size of Avelynne's foot and had sharp metal wings and knife-edge fangs in its mouth.

She was sluggish in the icy grip of fear, but her thoughts were all the quicker.

Act now! Subdue it. Kill it. Or at least call for the guards!

It spun mid-flight, its unbreakable wings cleaving through the air with a heart-stopping sound as it headed for her. It was in no hurry. Had these things developed a pleasure for taking their time and savouring the hunt?

Warring plans on what to do still kept her immobile. Run? Scream for help? Fight? If so, how best to do it? What could she use? What good could she possibly be? She would unquestionably choose the wrong course of action. She always did.

It came yet closer, those keen but somehow lifeless insect-eyes trained on her. As if practising biting off chunks of her flesh and bone, its mouth opened and shut, making the razor teeth gleam in the light from the window.

She wasn't moving. Why wasn't she moving?! This thing could rip her face to shreds with the beating of those blade-like wings. Before it took bites big enough of her body for her to bleed out from the injuries. She had heard they liked to devour eyeballs, especially from dead prey.

Every flap of those unforgiving wings brought the beast nearer. Every panicked heartbeat in her chest made her more unsure of what to do. The beast fixed its gaze on hers. One of its silvery wings caught the sunlight and the flash blinded her for a moment. The sight made a memory from Avelynne's childhood come flooding back.

That silver beast. Its left wing had reflected the sunlight the same way. When it crawled towards that sweet, still, cold body... Ready to bite. Tear. Wrench. Eat. Ready to defile the one Avelynne had loved most. The person she had needed most.

Rage and hatred for these monsters made Avelynne snap out of her immobility.

She screamed her throat raw for help. No one replied. Even if they had heard her, they wouldn't make it before she or Myllie had been maimed. The scream had however made the beast halt. It hovered now. Then its jaw began to open and snap shut faster, as if she had angered it. It was done flying slow. It tore towards her.

She reminded herself to not hold her breath. She had to act before it was too late! Myllie was in her care, she had to defend her.

With a faltering cry, Avelynne threw a stream of magic at the creature. It wasn't as powerful a volley as she would've liked, in fact, it was more of a foolhardy discharge. She groaned. The first rule of fighting silver beasts with magic was that you had to throw enough of it to incapacitate the creature. Or shape the magic stream into something which could bind the beast. Small amounts of magic would only serve as food for it. Like now. She squeezed her eyes shut and clenched her jaw, trying not to cry with frustration.

She could hear what her parents would say.

Typical Avelynne Ironhold. Your magic, like you, has disappointed us all.

They would be right. Instead of defeating the intruder, the magic pressed against the silver beast until the wasp-like creature began lapping it up, making the fiend swell with the power and its skin glow even brighter with magic silver.

While the beast was busy feasting on her failed attack, Avelynne picked up a bronze jug of water from the dresser and tossed it at the creature. The water splashed through the air and, through a stroke of luck more than skill, the heavy jug hit the creature with the clank of metal against metal.

The silver beast fell but was clearly not incapacitated for long. It shook itself off, fluttered its magically strengthened and sharpened wings, and then took flight again. Avelynne scrutinised her bedchamber. There must be something else she could throw! That mirror on the wall? No, too far away. The tapestry behind her? No, not heavy enough. That book on jousting her father had gifted her? No, not big enough to do real damage.

If you'd only acted right away, you could've incapacitated it with one big volley of magic. Hesitating has once again worsened everything, you useless fool, she berated herself.

There was an urgent knock at the door. "Countess Ironhold? Are you all right?"

She recognised the voice of the vice-captain of the guard. The supreme captain, a woman who frightened the living daylights out of Avelynne, must be busy guarding her parents. Never mind, the vice-captain would do! She loosened a breath from her aching lungs and called, "No! There is a silver beast in here. Come in and kill it!"

The door opened with a crash and the large man scanned the room with wild eyes until he spotted the beast. It was by the wall next to him. In his left hand was his spiked iron shield, bearing the Ironhold emblem, and he swung it with all his might towards the creature. It smacked the silver beast's head into the wall. He didn't let it recover but used his big frame to smash it with the thick shield again. The second blow shattered it against the wall with a sickening crack. Wisps of magic escaped the silver beast as it fell to the ground and died with an unnatural squawk. A smell of infected pus filled the room, as always when a silver beast's insides were exposed.

With a deep bow and a mumbled apology for letting the beast live long enough to enter the castle, the vice-captain gathered as much of the stinking, broken silvery corpse as he could and left with it.

Not a word of farewell, of course. People rarely spoke to Avelynne. She suspected that her parents had decreed it, and later pushed the point even further after a certain disastrous love affair she'd managed to steal from her uneventful life. The Ironholds seemed to simultaneously think everyone was below her and that she was below everyone.

Avelynne couldn't make it out. She only knew to keep quiet, obey, and try to predict their every expectation of her before it arose. How that forced behaviour wore her down, it grated on her, like an itch under her skin.

Thank the stars she was leaving.

A spell later, Myllie was still shaking and Avelynne remained on high alert. Nevertheless, nobles and their servants knew how to get on with procedure. Right now, they had to pack.

"Countess? Do you think one portmanteau and this small trunk will be enough? Shan't you be needin' more than this if you're to be away for two years?" Myllie asked as she opened said trunk.

"No. The Hall of Explorers will provide bedding, washing supplies, study books, and any weaponry I might need."

"What about clothes, Countess?"

"I'll get clothes for my training and, when I'm done, they'll provide armour imbued with special oils to protect against magic damage." She paused to look around the bedchamber. "All I must pack are my favourite drawing implements and some mementoes to make my room at the academy my own."

"Armour and weapons," Myllie muttered while playing with her blonde braid. "I can't believe your parents are lettin' you go, Countess. Don't they fret for your safety?"

"I'm sure they worry about losing their only heir. However, the prestige of their child being chosen for the second wave outweighs that, it seems."

"Well, I am glad I'm only to be goin' as a companion."

Avelynne smiled at Myllie, who kept packing. The paperwork that had been sent to her family when Avelynne was chosen suggested a servant or trainer to come along as companion. She had picked her only confidant, Myllie, who had agreed to go with some reluctance. The friendliness between them was, Avelynne feared, rather one-sided from her direction.

Avelynne picked up a hair clip and murmured, "I suppose I shan't need this anymore."

Myllie shrugged. "I wouldn't say that, Countess. Your hair may be shorter now, but I reckon it might still be long enough to put up. Sort of."

On her mother's orders, Avelynne had her hair cut shoulder length yesterday. All to appear "ready for physical endeavours" in her mother's words. It wasn't vanity that had made Avelynne want to keep her long hair. It was the fact that it was so like her grandmother's. The same glossy, fine strands and the same dark crimson, almost black, as her grandmother's before it greyed. It had been a wearable memento of the only person who ever loved Avelynne.

It still is. You have plenty of it left, she consoled herself as she ran a hand through it.

The only problem was that its flatness—which had made it look smooth and mysterious when it hung down to her hips—now merely made it look thin and flat. Another thing to make Avelynne feel inadequate.

She handed the hair clip to Myllie. "I don't believe I can wear this properly anymore. You keep it."

Myllie's face brightened. "Really, Countess?"

"Of course! It will suit you."

"Thank you ever so much. I'll wear it when we leave. Me lookin' lovely will make Errold cry his heart out that he ever let me go."

Avelynne curled her lip. "That brute never deserved you."

"Eh, perhaps not. He did, however, deserve to lose his job as the armourer's apprentice and end up a stable boy again. Strange that it happened right after I told you how I caught him with that milkmaid, Countess."

"Strange indeed," Avelynne said with a wink.

"Ha! I knew that was your doing, Countess."

Avelynne smiled at her and they returned to packing.

Placing a few quills and her favourite stylus in a leather pouch, Avelynne shivered. Today she'd begin her journey to the Hall of Explorers, the prestigious academy set up to save them all. Most other eighteen-year-olds would be getting married and then either be starting work or gaining an apprenticeship. Some scholarly inclined would be training as physicians, clerics, magicians, or studying the law. Avelynne would be one of those who studied further, however her subject would not be medicine or law but expeditions to find new lands. Ones without that which plagued them here in Cavarra: those vile silver beasts.

They had been lucky up here in the Peaks. Due to the rocky terrain and volcano eruption, the silver beasts with wings reigned up here. That had saved the Peakdwellers from the huge numbers swarming over the rest of the continent of Cavarra with its three-hundred million people. *That* was the problem which had led to the silver beasts. The beasts started out as various insects living off Cavarra's crops and flora but were also drawn to magic in the same way some insects are drawn to light. As the humans over-farmed the land and the scarce food filled human and livestock bellies, the insects began living off magic, to the point where they now preferred absorbing magic as sustenance. It made them grow hard skin, the silver colour of magic, and to evolve. Most of them still resembled silvery bugs, albeit ranging from the size of her palm to the size of her head.

The beasts filled every hidden nook and cranny of homes. They stole food, ate pets, and scared horses. They'd bite you for no reason, taking a chunk of flesh to eat, and they bred fast. So fast. Plaguing all of Cavarra. That was why Hall of Explorers had been founded. Well, that in combination with the lack of food, not only the crops and flora but the decreasing livestock who tried to live off the scarce remaining resources too. It didn't help that the sea life was being overfished either. No, they needed new fertile ground to settle on before Cavarra died under their feet. Or the silver beasts evolved further and grew large as men.

"Countess? D'you want me to wrap this little mirror in paper for protection?"

"Um, why don't you give it to me. I'll pack it in the portmanteau, we might need it close at hand for the journey."

"Yes, Countess."

Avelynne packed the mirror, which her grandmother had left her. She stared at the portmanteau. She still found it so hard to believe she was actually going. That she was doing something this monumental and dangerous. That after finishing their training, she and the others of the second wave would be captaining a newly built longship, with men and women trained as sailors at their command. Exactly as the first class of students, known as the first wave, were to do before them. No one knew what they would be facing out there.

What everyone did know was that the second wave would begin their lessons next week. Avelynne's secret simmered under her skin, poisoning her little by little. She clenched her fists, cursing her parents for making her carry this burden.

And curse me for agreeing. What else could I do, though?

She swallowed hard and placed a couple of books in the trunk.

Myllie watched her, brow furrowed. "I was thinkin'. D'you reckon there'll be trolls and goblins on the land you find? If you do find land. Maybe it's all endless water?"

Avelynne hugged her arms around herself. "I certainly hope not, Myllie."

"Oh, I didn't mean to scare you, Countess. I'm sure it'll

all be fine. At least you won't be fightin' the silver beasts like we who stay'll have to."

"True. Neither will you while you're safe with me at the Hall of Explorers. It's in the Centre, with the King's castle, remember? They say that any silver beast that comes near there is killed in mere moments."

While closing the lid of the now full trunk, Myllie grimaced, struggling with the trunk's lock. Avelynne laid a hand on it and, with magic, forced the bolts securely in place. Myllie watched the silvery light emanating from Avelynne's hand with her usual awe. Obviously everyone had magic, but Myllie's was weak and she had always been thrilled to watch Avelynne use her stronger abilities.

My abilities are not likely to be the strongest ones at the Hall of Explorers, though.

"Thank you, Countess."

"You're most welcome."

She observed Myllie move over to the portmanteau to pack parchment, so her mistress could draw during their long journey.

Myllie knew her shameful secret, of course. Avelynne couldn't bring her along without awareness of the thorny situation they were in.

The maid noted her frozen form, met her eyes, and casually said, "It'll be fine, Countess. You're real clever. You'll figure it all out."

Avelynne nodded with a forced smile that was only for Myllie's benefit.

She knew for certain that this was going to take more than cleverness.

Chapter Two

HALE AND SABINA AT THE HALL OF EXPLORERS

Hale's chest smarted as the sword slashed at it. He watched a line of blood slowly appearing next to his line of chest hair. He couldn't help it, a thrill coursed through him at the sight of the dark red streaking his tanned muscles.

He looked back up when he heard the words, "Ha! That'll teach you to spar bare-chested, lad! No one wants to see nipples unless they're undressing a lover. Put a tunic on. Or are you afraid to sweat in your new, pretty clothes?"

Hale's trainer and mentor, Ghar, had already begun mocking him for his new Hall of Explorers uniform. Well, uniform was not quite the word. They'd get their tailored leather and mail armour and doublet later.

For now, he had been given a student's plain garments: a leather jerkin with the Hall of Explorers emblem, a few tunics - some short and some long, three pairs of trousers, plenty of undergarments, and a pair of sensible, light boots. All in the Hall of Explorers colours: black and light brown with dark green details. There were fancy names for those colours, he remembered, but who could be bothered with that?

The clothes would suit well for studying and training, Hale admitted as he looked down at the trousers and shoes he'd agreed to wear. He wanted his real uniform, though. The full-body leather along with the protective mail vest would look great with his hard-earned battle scars. The number of which would grow if he didn't let this new cut on his chest heal. He could keep picking the scab off, so it would scar up, like he did with the cut he got on his forehead last month. Not to impress anyone, of course. Simply because Woodsfolk had scars. Ones from battles with wild boars or falling from the tops of the trees during bird hunting season.

Hale would be the most scarred of them all. He would make them proud. Then they'd no longer see the malnourished orphan he had been. They'd see the eighteen-year-old he was now. If not tall, then at least of average height. Strong but lithe, enabling him to climb as well as he lifted things. Well-read and quick to learn. Respected and liked. He had worked so hard, much harder than the others. And fate had awarded him with a place at the Hall of Explorers. One of the four in the second wave of explorers. One of the eight chosen ones to map unknown worlds.

No wonder he'd been so eager to get here that he and Ghar had arrived far earlier than they were expected, their carriage pulling up at the gates before the sun had even risen. Still, it had given them extra hours to spar, something which had been sorely needed after the sedentary eight-day-long carriage ride from Whispering Willows, which was in the heart of the Woodlands. Now, he was finally here. He had made a name for himself.

Hale took a proud breath, stood to his full height, and thrust his shortsword against Ghar at an unexpected angle. It almost hit home, and his trainer laughed while saying, "not bad for an overgrown child with naked nipples. Imagine what you could do if you were fully dressed and focusing more on the sparring than this fancy academy and that gleaming future of yours."

Hale made another move, side-stepping an apple tree with ease. "Jealous, old man?"

"Of someone who's going to brave the waves and whatever beasts can be found in other lands?" Ghar dodged. "No thank you. I'll stay here where it's dry and I can get a nice bit of oakenberry pie to eat by a cosy fire at night."

"Soon there'll be no oakenberries to be had. Not unless I find us new land where we can grow them away from the silver beasts."

Ghar dipped his sword and fixed Hale with a glare. "You and the others. Do not forget that you're not the only one chosen. The first wave, and the other three in your group, all worked equally hard and are as skilled as you. Perhaps even more so."

Hale lowered his blade as well. "True enough. They're not Woodsfolk though."

He had meant it as a way of pleasing his mentor, of sharing something familiar with him in this new place where the sparring grounds were overlooked by people in tall buildings and the sun shone too hot without a canopy of trees above. Ghar didn't seem to see it the same way.

"No. But the Lakelanders, Peakdwellers, and North-erners are all as brave and clever as we are."

Hale rolled his eyes. "I know. The people of all four counties are needed to make up the exceptional power of Cavarra," he intoned. Showing that he remembered the information pounded into every child's brain as well now as he did at the age of six.

"Exactly. Don't forget it, lad." Ghar's brow furrowed. "We both know that sometimes your enthusiasm and confidence comes off as cocky. And upon occasion," he lowered his voice, "your temper flares and you say silly things you don't mean. Don't frighten off the three people you'll entrust with your life. You'll have not only the years here together, but who knows how long out there. In unknown waters and on strange lands."

Hale tightened his jaw. "I'll be mindful of that."

Ghar gave him a smile. "Good. Then raise your blade again. Let's see if you can actually hit me this time."

Hale chuckled and gripped his sword tighter. He took the right stance and engaged his muscles while softening his knees for a fluid strike.

As his mind calculated the jab, he saw something out of the corner of his eye. Something large and white. Moving far too fast and quietly to be a sheep, horse, or cow. He lowered his sword. "Wait, Ghar. What's that?"

It was a giant, powerful feline. White with a few faint grey stripes. His jaw dropped, and he whispered, "a real Snowtiger."

Running behind it was a lass about his age. Her hair was as white as the tiger's and she moved almost as quietly as it did.

"Must be a Northerner," he mumbled, as much to himself as to Ghar.

If her thick tunic and serious appearance hadn't given it away, walking in with a creature who only existed up north settled it. The Northerners were the only ones who travelled with a predator, anyway. For protection, hunting assistance and, Hale assumed, for company.

Hale felt a smile tugging at his cheeks. This lass must be one of his group. He'd be teamed up with someone who had an actual Snowtiger! He stopped himself from doing a little dance of excitement. Now he just had to hope that she was friendly. What is more, that she'd let him wrestle the lethal animal, which she was currently crouching by and stroking. From what he could hear, she was scolding it for running ahead without her.

He strode up to the lass and her tiger.

"Hello! I'm Hale. One of the new recruits."

Her brows knitted. "Good morrow. Your name is *Hale*? As in being healthy?"

"Indeed, I try to live up to the name," he said, flexing his muscles. "Is that a real Snowtiger?"

"If it isn't, he's been doing an excellent job of impersonating one," the lass said and stood. "He's called Kall and I'm Sabina Rosenmarck. I didn't catch your family name?"

"I don't think I gave it," Hale said, busy staring at the animal. "Woodsfolk don't have much use for them."

"Woodsfolk, huh? So your family name will be something like 'tree' or 'bark,' I gather?"

He looked at her, trying to decide if she was mocking him. She didn't look like she was. Her face was grave, but her eyes seemed friendly enough.

"It's Hawthorn, actually. Can I pet your snowtiger?"

Sabina fidgeted with her long braid. "He has a name. But, aye, you can pet him. If he likes you."

Hale bent and slowly ran his hand over the animal's back. The fur was so dense that Hale didn't feel the skin underneath. The snowtiger sidestepped and Hale immediately took the cue and removed his hand.

They stood in silence as the feline seemed to hesitate. Then it retreated from Hale with its ears pointed back. He accepted its decision, turning to Sabina instead.

"Such an excellent animal! Back home, I once had a red jungle falcon I trained to hunt for me. I had to sell it to afford a new tunic and a dagger."

A crinkle appeared between her white brows. "Sorry to hear that."

"It's all right. It wasn't as brilliant as your companion is."

They watched the prowling snowtiger for a spell until Sabina glanced down to the sword behind Hale. "That's a beautiful one-hander. The hilt is Northern, you can tell by the snowflake carved into the brushed steel. The fancy blade, however, looks like it comes from the Peaks."

He shrugged. He hadn't picked it for its smithing, but how it felt in his hands. And the fact that Ghar for some reason was always worse at parrying attacks from smaller, quicker weapons. "I don't know anything about its origins. I took it from the weapons rack over there. It did the job. Shame it's kept blunt for practice sparring, though"

Sabina hummed. "I'm more of an axe-wielder, but if I do pick a sword, I prefer twohanders. No one expects a woman, especially a young one, to wield a huge greatsword.

By the time they've finished sniggering, I've pointed it at their throat and made them yield."

"Ha, I like that! Remind me to be careful if I see you picking up a greatsword."

"No need, we'll be on the same side," She said with the briefest flash of a smile. "So, you started sparring as soon as you arrived?"

"Yes. I figured I might as well. They scanned me and my mentor here for silver beasts and then told us to wait in this courtyard until all four of us had arrived. I had to pass the time somehow."

"Spending it practising was a sound plan," Sabina said, inclining her head in appreciation.

"Thanks. And you…" He looked to where she and the tiger had come from. "You've been walking the edges of the courtyard? Checking the premises and how far you could go before the guards stopped you?"

She gave that slight bow of the head again. "Exactly. I thought I might get better acquainted with my new home. *Our* new home."

"Good thinking," he said, trying to give the same dignified bow of the head. He wasn't sure he'd pulled it off. Maybe he'd just looked like he was copying her and, to make matters worse, doing a bad job of it. He sniggered to himself. Never mind. She could think what she wanted of him. He knew his own worth.

Something flew right above them. Both their heads snapped up to see what it was. Hale relaxed. It was only a crow heading for the apple trees.

"Strange isn't it?" He said quietly. "That there are no silver beasts here, I mean."

"Aye, it'll take a while to get used to that." She was stroking the tiger's big head now and it was leaning into her touch.

"His fur is so thick," Hale said, staring admiringly. "Won't he struggle with the mild climate here in the Centre?"

"At first, yes. But they adapt their fur to the temperature. Kall's body will simply assume it is summer and he'll start to shed. Give it a few weeks and he'll be accurately dressed. Unlike you."

The last words had been said with the faintest hint of a smirk and a finger pointed at his torso.

Hale straightened. Had his scarred and sculpted chest impressed her? He decided he'd like it if it had. She seemed a clever and practical person. No nonsense. She had a severe but striking sort of beauty and more importantly... she had a snowtiger. What else could you want in a woman?

He gave her the broad smile which always made the lasses back home giggle. He ran a hand over his chest, wiping away the dried blood, while saying, "I'm guessing a treat for the eye will have been a nice welcome, huh?"

To his surprise she made a sound which was a little too close to a snort for his comfort.

"It's good to see that someone I'll be teamed up with is in impressive physical shape," she said. "Other than that, I take no more pleasure in your naked chest than I do the view of the attractive buildings or the trees. It takes different shapes to *treat my eyes*, as you put it."

He tried to process her words for a second but to no avail. "What?"

"I prefer women," she snapped. She touched her braid again and didn't meet his eye.

Hale's mind came to a screeching halt and tried to re-orientate. He knew that the practise of loving one of your own gender was more common up in the North and in the Peaks than in the two southern counties. He couldn't remember if he'd ever met someone like this. Although, surely, he must've?

He scrambled for something inoffensive to say. "Uh. Aha. Well, here's to hoping the other two recruits are not only skilled fighters and thinkers but also attractive women-folk, then."

Her body language seemed to thaw, the stern face softening. "Hm, maybe not. We have two years of gruelling lessons and then an important and dangerous mission. The last thing we need is to be distracted by beautiful women."

He laughed and, as he did, he found the snowtiger coming closer to him and sniffing his leg.

Hale studied the animal's signals as all Woodlanders were taught. He extended his hand and when the tiger had sniffed it and its ears stood happily erect, he petted the feline's big head.

"Did you bring the snowtig... I mean Kall, instead of the one person we are allowed to bring?"

"Aye. I have more use for him than I do a servant or a sparring partner. I can clothe myself, but I cannot be without my hunting companion and protector. I've had him since he was a cub."

Hale nodded. "Sound choice."

Sabina inclined her head, and her lips twitched into a wide smile.

Pride swelled in Hale's chest. He hadn't pushed his first fellow second-waver away. Even better, he had made the snowtiger like him! Now he had to figure out a polite way to ask if he could wrestle it. That could probably wait until at least day two.

Chapter Three

THE CARRIAGE RIDE

Avelynne and Myllie sat on opposite sides in the carriage. Facing each other but not speaking, both busying themselves with whatever pastime they could find. Avelynne watched the landscape through the glass-less window, feeling the breeze on her face.

How many miles had they travelled now? This was the sort of thing Avelynne needed to learn. Distances. Measuring. Making and remembering maps.

They set out from Ironhold Castle to the Hall of Explorers a fortnight ago. How far had her mother said it was? Around 600 miles from home to the Centre, which held the Hall? Travelling light in a sprightly carriage, stopping at inns only for the darkest hours and the occasional meal, they could traverse 30-40 miles a day. All depending on the weather, road conditions, and how fresh the horses were, of course. She rubbed her forehead when she thought about the tedious journey. At least she'd had gotten a lot of drawing done. And reading. Thank the stars she had brought study books. She had to learn fast.

She watched Myllie from under her lashes. The maid had struggled for things to do. A couple of romance books and some knitting. Bored sighs and complaining about the bumpy ride. The occasional flirtation with the carriage driver who was twice her age and married, but happy enough to flirt when he thought Avelynne couldn't hear them. The rest of Myllie's time had been filled with questions. So many questions. It had begun on the morning of day two with a conversation about silver beasts.

Avelynne was watching a flock of small but particularly sturdy silver beasts whizzing about outside. The carriage driver chased them off with a volley of magic, making them careen away and switch prey to a flock of sheep who all ran for shelter.

"Look at those vicious fiends."

Myllie followed her gaze. "I know. We can't stay on Cavarra with those sodding monsters. It's only a matter of time before they grow bigger and kill us all off."

"Mm. Hopefully the first class of students, the first wave I mean, will find new lands for us when they travel out next year."

Myllie put her knitting down and sat forward. "Seems strange to trust our future to people so young, if you don't mind me sayin', Countess. You in the second wave are eighteen, so they must be nineteen now, right?"

"Yes. King Lothiam wants the leaders of the expedition to be eighteen when they, well *we*, sail out."

Myllie scrunched up her face. "Why? If you want a set of learned mapmakers to lead a team to go explorin', why have 'em so young?"

"The king chose that age as he believes eighteen-year-olds are in peak physical condition. The lack of a proper diet is affecting the population, making people grow weak and ill. So, he wants the healthiest of us to be trained and then set sail."

Myllie sat back. "Health's not what all them tests you had to take were about though?"

"No, the tests were to determine who was the best in skills needed to explore, create maps, liaise with foreign people, and fight possible enemies. Therefore, they tested the magic, geography, drawing, arithmetic, swimming, fighting, and orientating skills of each county's eighteen-year-olds."

"I see," Myllie droned, playing with her blonde locks in a bored manner.

Avelynne had told her all this before, but Myllie wasn't much interested unless the conversation involved handsome boys, juicy gossip, or herself. She asked questions but never remembered the answers.

Which explained why, on a warm afternoon on day five, Myllie shouted over the sound of the carriage clattering over the particularly rocky road, "d'you reckon there'll be dragons and sea monsters, Countess?"

Avelynne put down her drawing parchment. "Pardon?"

"When you go explorin' after you're done at the academy? Might be there's creatures in the seas? Or, um, or wizards that turn into huge fish and eat whole boats."

"There *might* be, however we—"

Avelynne was cut off by Myllie who had warmed to her topic. "I've heard tales of men tall as mountains, Countess. Oh, and magic users who can shift into animals and change things, like turnin' a plain goblet into a sceptre with rubies and all!"

"No one has ever ventured far enough to see such marvels. The fishermen who travelled away from Cavarra's shores only got far enough to find dead seas and dangerous currents," Avelynne said, remembering the ten other times she had explained this to Myllie. "These tales have been made up. Usually by people who wish we could use magic for more than moving and manipulating objects. Or by bards who want more colourful yarns to sing about."

Myllie sniffed, braided her golden tresses demonstratively, and then said she was going to have a nap. Avelynne returned to drawing, glad for a respite in the questions, but still wishing she could have more normal conversations with Myllie. The easy, give-and-take ones that friends always had in novels.

Although, Myllie wasn't a friend, Avelynne reminded herself. She was paid to put up with Avelynne and tend to her. She was a job to this woman and nothing more. She had to remember that. She also had to answer the questions to save her travelling companion from boredom.

On day eight, there had been many rapid queries about clothes and dresses, Avelynne had patiently described her student clothes and her future armour for the fifth time. On day eleven, the topic for the questions had been titles, which had started with Myllie dropping her romance book down next to her on the seat.

"Blimey. This book is all flowery words and such. Would you like it, Coun—" Myllie cut off mid-word and got that faraway look that signified she was about to launch into one of her rapid topic changes. "Will the tutors and the other three students of the second wave call you 'Countess'?"

Avelynne squirmed. "At the Hall of Explorers? I hope not."

"I see. I didn't know how common titles were in them other places," Myllie said while stretching.

Avelynne's stomach spasmed. Titles. The Peaks was governed by the Grand Count, Avelynne's father, which made Avelynne's mother the Grand Countess. So yes, Avelynne had to lug around the heavy title of Countess. It singled her out and made her sound superior. She hoped she could simply be *Avelynne* at her new home.

"They have their own titles," Avelynne replied. "The Lakelanders have a Duke and a Duchess. The Northerners have a Baron and a Baroness. The Woodsfolk only have a Warden. The sole title we all share is the one of our King. Oh, and I don't want your book, no. Thank you, though."

Myllie picked up the romance book again and with a grimace dove back into reading it.

Avelynne thought about King Lothiam of Cavarra. Yes. He, and the queen – if the king had not had her beheaded – was one of the few things Avelynne would have in common with her new... What was she meant to call the others who'd been chosen for the second year of Hall of Explorers? Fellow recruits? Students? There would be four of them, one from each county. Avelynne would be the only Peakdweller.

Well, except for the Peakdweller who had been sent last year, his companion and any academy staff from the Peaks. And the Queen, if she was still alive, Avelynne mused.

She had been a lady from one of the finer areas of the Peaks, before the king picked her out, married her and one day... decided she was unfaithful and ordered her executed in an excruciating and public way, with a blunt execution-er's axe and an audience larger than the one which had attended her coronation.

Avelynne took a tighter grip of her bag. At the Centre, she would be under the control of her tutors first and fore-most, then the Hall of Explorers officials, a council set to govern the academy. However, leading all of them, was the king. He would be only a short walk away in his royal castle. She had never been allowed to meet him when he visited the Peaks, but she had heard the sharp comments from her parents after his royal highness visited. She had also heard how no one at court had been surprised at the cruelty of the Queen's beheading. With unease coursing through her, she put him out of her mind.

Yesterday, right before the sunset, Myllie had inter-rupted Avelynne's studying with a new line of questioning. One she had already asked weeks ago when Avelynne was accepted into the Hall. "D'you reckon the other students'll be highborn like you, Countess?"

"I should think not. The spots are given out on merit, not status."

"Right. Also…" She chewed her lip.

Avelynne put all her warmth into the smile she gave her maid. "Go ahead, Myllie, speak your mind. I'm not my parents, I shan't shout at you."

Myllie's gaze flitted to the window. "I've been wonderin' what our new home will be like, Countess."

Avelynne tucked her arithmetic book away. "Well, long, long ago the Centre was measured out to be the middle of Cavarra, straddling a corner of each of the four counties.

The Centre contains the king's castle, complete with vast grounds. On the edge of those grounds, they built the Hall of Explorers two years ago."

"Is it simply a big house, then?"

"As far as I've read, the Hall of Explorers is made up of four large connected structures. It's got living space, which will include the servant quarters and the student quarters, so we won't live together I'm afraid. Then there's lesson rooms, kitchens and such." Avelynne stopped to think. "There's also a vast library and the grand hall after which the academy was named."

"I see."

They both gazed out the window. The scenery was so different. No mountains or herds of reindeer. Leafed trees where the Peaks had pines. It was lusher here and more humid, but so strangely flat. Had it been this flat when Avelynne had passed through here to go to the Lakelands with her parents? Everything seemed so different this trip, as if she was seeing it all for the first time.

Needing to break the silence, Avelynne picked up the conversation again. "The Hall of Explorers also has a court-yard for fighting lessons, both with weapons and magic. Oh, and apparently, we can practice our mapmaking skills in the grounds between the Hall and the king's castle. Under strict supervision, of course."

Avelynne reeled the facts off fast, revealing how closely she had studied the paperwork the Hall of Explorers sent when she was chosen.

She'd have to know every detail and appear confident if she was to keep her secret. If she was to hide that she didn't belong.

Inferior. Liar. Imposter.

The words rang through her skull. Avelynne pinched her lips tight and swallowed over and over again.

She was happy to have her thoughts interrupted by noises outside. There was neighing of horses and shouts of men. Myllie and Avelynne peered out. Four men, all in the scarlet and gold colours of the king, rode after a person fleeing on foot. It was a skinny man in rags. He was screaming, mostly profanities but Avelynne picked up the words, "he can't treat us like this! Everyone knows he's evil, but no one dares speak." Soon followed by, "I have a right to tell the truth!"

The men in the king's livery caught up with him, of course. The lead guard, judging by his armour, reached down from his horse and grabbed the man by his dirty shirt-collar, bellowing, "you have no rights, peasant. Not unless we give them to you. Now shut your mouth before we do it for you."

The skinny man, who looked like he hadn't eaten for days, screamed more obscenities in reply.

The guard spat in his face and then shoved him into some thornbushes by the road. The others laughed. Avelynne tried to see what would happen next but three of the men blocked her view with their large, glossy horses and all their immaculate, shiny armour.

The lead guard turned his horse, swaggered close to their carriage and greeted them with a hand resting on the bejewelled pommel of his sword. "Well met, ladies. My apologies for the unpleasantness. This man is a crook, a murderer, and a liar. We will see he gets his due punishment. Travel on and don't let this disturb your journey." Then he grinned and saluted.

Avelynne gave him a brief nod and sat back out of sight.

As the carriage drove on, Myllie clapped her hands. "Dearie me, wasn't he handsome with that fine armour and that there broad jaw? Why did he salute us?"

"I assume he spotted the Ironhold emblem on the carriage," Avelynne replied. Unease crept under her skin at the thought of this brutal man feeling that they were connected. That she was someone he should salute. Someone he could share that conspiring, cruel grin with.

They drove on for a short spell. Avelynne closed her eyes and thought about drawing. Or reading. Anything that soothed her and pushed the unease of her future out. They were almost there, she needed to be calm. She imagined the crinkle of parchment and the comforting smell of books. Long rides in cheerful sunshine. Resting in a warm bed on a cold, rainy day.

The carriage slowed, and the driver called out, "Hall of Explorers, Countess."

We're here. No turning back now.

Avelynne ignored her dry mouth and shaky knees as she gathered her bag and smoothed her hair. No matter what it made her, imposter… liar… She would do what she must. For her people and for her parents, who relied on her to get this one thing right. She could not allow herself to fail.

Chapter Four

VALUABLE LESSONS

Hale and Sabina stood chatting in the courtyard still. Judging by the height of the sun, and confirmed by the far too ornate sundial, the morning was growing late. Hale looked to the gate. Their official paperwork had told them to arrive at the Hall of Explorers this morning. Where were the other two? Had they not been as eager to get here?

Sabina and he had been comparing tales of how nature tested you in their respective counties, a pastime he had observed in adults all his life.

"Tropical storms are worse than snowstorms," Hale said.

Sabina cocked her head. "Do you think so? My parents always said that the cold killed more often than the heat."

"It's not about the heat. Anyway, Northerners aren't nearly as tough as you think. You're only hearty because you have to put up with the cold. It's not like you prove any bravery by having to put another fur on."

Sabina's head snapped back to the centre. "First of all, that was condescending and shows your lack of understanding of a cold that cannot be fought with more clothing. Secondly, please tell me you're not one of those."

"One of what?"

"Competitive people," she said. "Especially, those who keep the old rivalries of the four counties alive? That's for our parents and grandparents. We're here to give Cavarra a new future. I'd hope that included our generation not bothering with infighting."

Hale was about to ask who in the name of the shitting silver beasts she was to lecture him but stopped. Ghar's words about not losing his temper or offending the other second wavers repeated in his mind. He took a heartbeat to calm and then said, "You're right. We'll leave that for the old folks. We have enough to handle, what with silver beasts and how our elders ruined Cavarra and now sends us to find new ground for them to use up."

She nodded with a smile and Hale congratulated himself on pulling that off.

Someone else, however, was faring worse with containing their temper. Over by a doorway, a bearded lad was shouting at a clean-shaved one, who gave as good as he got. Their voices rose so that Hale heard the one with the beard say, "I lent you my book on waves and currents last semester and now it's mysteriously gone but you didn't lose it? Who in the name of snow did, then? Some thieving gnome?"

The other lad spat on the ground. "You didn't lend it to me at all, you toesack! You refused to let anyone borrow your books, as always!"

A woman wrapped in a green cloak, despite the warm morning, strode up to them.

"Gentlemen. Calm. This is unbefitting for educated, civilised people like yourselves. You are first wavers, future heroes of Cavarra and the king. Act. Like. It. Go inside and discuss this with your head tutor."

They went in, glaring daggers at each other. The woman turned and spotted Hale and Sabina. She came over, passing Ghar who gave her an appreciative glance.

The woman moved with purpose, had a sharp nose, a kind smile, and an honest face. Good attributes in Hale's book.

"Good morrow. I'm Tutor Atha Santorine. I assume you're both part of the second wave?"

"Aye," Sabina said and introduced herself and Hale.

She gave them both a smile. "Welcome to the Hall of Explorers. I shall be teaching you about the sea, both in a practical and theoretical fashion. I shan't be your head tutor, though. That will be Tutor Hason Rete." She pointed to a bald man standing by the apple trees, speaking to a boy with a broom. "He is an excellent man and an experienced academic. You're lucky. He's fair but takes no nonsense. I fear Tutor Elya Hathleen, who is a skilled scholar and head tutor for the first wave, is laxer. Which is why you just saw two of the first wave shouting in the courtyard like brawlers at an inn."

"They certainly didn't seem to get along very well," Sabina said.

Tutor Santorine clicked her tongue. "No. Friction comes when you pick four driven, competitive youths from different cultures to live in close quarters and have demanding schedules. Also, they are in their second year, which means they will now have rigorous tests on their first year of lessons. I assume that is not helping."

She was sneering in a way which made Hale think she wasn't feeling as understanding of their behaviour as she sounded.

"Anyway," Santorine said. "I must get back to double-checking your curriculum this year. As soon as the other two newcomers have arrived, expect Tutor Rete to call you in for your introduction. I shall meet you all at dinner in the Great Hall tonight."

They said their farewells and she left. As she strode off, Sabina whispered, "Now I've met all our tutors except Tutor Rete. So far, they all appear reasonable. Tutor Myle and Tutor Hathleen both seemed a little wishy-washy but kind enough. Tutor Rogan... well, you'll see when we encounter him tonight."

Hale was about to ask what she meant by that when his attention was taken by the sound of a carriage. Either his unusually astute ears were playing tricks on him or there was another one not too far behind. They both sounded like big contraptions and Hale could only hope that whoever this Lakelander and Peakdweller were, neither would be stuck-up, rich city folk.

"Let's go wait by the gate," he said to Sabina and took off running.

He was pretty sure he heard her mumble, "you could *ask* if I wanted to." Followed by a hoarse little laugh and the footfalls of a lass and a snowtiger.

Chapter Five

ELEKSANDER AND AVELYNNE ARRIVE

Avelynne stepped out of the carriage, clutching her portmanteau. Behind her she heard Myllie and the carriage driver chatting away. Flirting again, by the sounds of Myllie's crooning. Why was romance and flirtation every-where? She was so tired of it.

She ignored them and took in her surroundings. They had gone through the grand gate to the Centre earlier today but were now faced by a smaller gateway, leading to her new home.

Her insides fluttered and the hair on the back of her neck stood up, if that was due to the excitement or the fear of being discovered as a fraud, she wasn't sure.

A large carriage stood next to them. It was as grand as her own but beautifully painted in pale blues. The horses were chalk-white. *Lakelander colours*, Avelynne realised. That explained its splendour. Even a poor Lakelander tended to be richer and more sophisticated than anyone from the other counties. Not to mention better educated. Inferiority heated her cheeks.

A young man with a multitude of long braids tied with a ribbon stood next to the carriage. He was wearing Lakelander blues as well and appeared well built, although it was hard to tell since he slouched terribly. A woman was looming behind him with a hand on his shoulder. Her skin was as light as his was dark. Avelynne had always envied the difference in appearances and skin tones down in the Lakelands and the Woodlands. It made for much more interesting contrasts in the populace than up in the Peaks and the North. The light-skinned woman, a little older than them by the looks of her, was casting glances at Avelynne. She said something to the youth and he turned to Avelynne too, revealing a beautiful face with a hesitant, crooked smile.

He ambled towards her and, when he arrived, shuffled his feet for a moment. "Hello. My name is Eleksander Aetholo. I'm one of the new recruits."

"And I'm another one," Avelynne quipped in her friendliest tone. "I'm Avelynne Ironhold, from the Peaks. It's a pleasure to meet you!" She intentionally skipped the title to not sound haughty. They'd all hate her enough when her secret came out, no need to make it worse.

"You there," a man shouted at them. "Have you both been searched?"

"Searched?" Avelynne asked.

The man frowned. "Yes, for silver beast eggs?"

"No?" Eleksander croaked.

The man frowned. "Well, why do you think you've been stopped outside the gate? To admire the view? Take all belongings and companions you brought along over to the station here. We'll check you for eggs and for any small silver beasts lurking in your belongings and clothing."

Myllie walked past Avelynne with the trunk in tow. Avelynne made haste in gathering her portmanteau and followed Myllie to the checking station. It had the simple banner of the academy flying above it, black cloth with a ship in light brown, no *khaki* she corrected herself, on it. Above it was the academy's motto in emerald green. Those were the colours she'd be dressed in for her time in the second wave. It all felt so real now. Nowhere to run.

When she turned to see what had become of Eleksander, he was inspecting an embroidered silk cloak and then tossing it back into the carriage before retrieving a gleaming bronze trunk and three satchels.

Avelynne's attention returned to the checking station. A woman was running her hands over the air surrounding Myllie, her hands glowing silver. So, they checked you with the use of magic, that made sense. Any lurking silver beasts or eggs would react to the pull of magic, glowing and reverberating.

When Myllie was cleared, the female magician and a male counterpart opened Avelynne's luggage and searched through them item by item. By the time it was her turn to be searched, she heard the footsteps of the two Lakelanders behind her.

"What happens here?" Eleksander asked.

The question was possibly not for her, but Avelynne wanted to calm him so she answered. "They check you with magic to see if you have traces of silver beasts or their eggs on you." The gatekeeper started running her hands along the outside of Avelynne's dress, a hairsbreadth from touching the garment.

"See?" Avelynne said to Eleksander, nodding down to the gatekeeper's hands.

"Ah, that doesn't seem too bad," he replied.

She smiled as reassuringly as she could. "No, I cannot feel it at all."

The gatekeeper gave a curt nod. "You're clear. Please proceed inside."

Avelynne and Myllie obeyed. The gates opened with a crash, revealing a sunlit courtyard inside. It was stone paved with a few grassy areas, giving plenty of empty space for outside training. In the courtyard's centre, stood a sundial decorated with what looked like some sort of sea monsters peeking out of waves. Surrounding the large open space were severe-looking buildings in unblemished dark grey stone. Avelynne spotted several sets of target dummies and weapon racks against the walls. The buildings weren't as beautiful as the king's castle, which they had passed en-route, nor the smaller Ironhold castle where Avelynne had spent her life. These structures were sturdy, new, and fit for purpose. It was a place to learn your craft and hone your skills.

Avelynne tightened her grip on her portmanteau.

"Should we try to find the entrance, Countess?" Myllie asked.

"No, let's wait for the Lakelander we met outside. Like me, he appears to need an ally."

Myllie put the trunk down with a muffled groan. Avelynne inspected her and the luggage. "Is it too heavy for you? Should we switch?"

Myllie gave her a look. "Countess, I'm used to carryin' water, heaps of laundry, and trays from the kitchen. You're used to carryin' only your woes and some drawing thingies. Perhaps I should continue shiftin' the heaviest object?"

"Fair point," Avelynne said with a self-deprecating laugh.

A voice came from behind them. "Did you wait for us? Thank you."

Avelynne caught Eleksander's shy gaze. "No need to thank us," she replied. "They say there's safety in numbers. Besides, I shall be going everywhere with you for the foreseeable future, so I might as well start now."

He smiled from ear to ear, lighting up his brown eyes and making them glint in the sun. He had such finely chiselled features that Avelynne found herself aching to draw him. The thought prompted something else in her mind. "Oh, if you're a student here, you must be adept at drawing. Did you bring any materials?"

He blinked a few times. "Yes. I brought quite a few."

"Excellent! You Lakelanders have the best inks. I'd love to trade some with you."

His smile grew back into its full splendour. "Gladly."

That was when Avelynne heard Myllie yelp. Then the maid whispered, "Someone brought some sort of monster cat here. That can't be allowed, Countess. We'll all be gobbled up!"

There was a large feline appearing before them, but it was no monster. It looked like a creature Avelynne had only read about in books about the North. They were common up there. What were they called? Snowcats?

"By all the waters, it's a Snowtiger," whispered Eleksander reverently.

Avelynne snapped her fingers. "Ah, yes, that's what they're called. My, it's so elegant. Calm yourself, Myllie. If it's allowed in here, it must be safe."

A girl followed step with the snowtiger, holding her hands up in apology. "Aye, he's very safe. I'm so sorry he rushed towards you like that. Kall usually heels to me but ever since we arrived, he's been on edge and scurrying about. I think perhaps he feels my unsettled nerves."

"That is quite all right. We are all tense, I believe," Avelynne said while studying her. The young woman wore an intelligent expression and a long, practical braid of white hair. Her tunic was tight over healthy curves and lean muscles.

A cruel part of Avelynne's mind said, *now this is what a Hall of Explorers recruit should look like. Not like you.*

Another person appeared. A young man this time, but he was just as muscular and straight-backed as the woman. Which was clear since he was naked from the waist up. His unbelted trousers were drooping, revealing a tan line and stomach muscles reaching down to a place Avelynne shouldn't contemplate.

She wondered if Eleksander's flowing, oversized tunic was concealing a physique as perfect as these two had. She groaned inwardly as she realised that she already knew it would.

The bare-chested youth held up a hand in greeting. "I'm Hale. This is Sabina. Two of you must be our fellow recruits?"

His gaze scanned Avelynne, Myllie, Eleksander, and the latter's companion.

Avelynne went to answer him but found herself distracted by his eyes, they were so pitch black they resembled deep wells of ink.

Instead, it was the woman with Eleksander who answered. "I'm just the companion to Eleksander Aetholo." She pointed to him. "He is the chosen recruit from the Lakelands. He beat all the others in this age group by large margin. In *all* the subjects."

Eleksander moaned. "I'm not that good at all. Please excuse her boastfulness. She's my older sister and likes to show me off like some pet in a competition." He smiled at his sibling and then bowed to the newcomers. "It's a pleasure to meet you both. And the boisterous Snowtiger. May I introduce you to the Peakdwellers' chosen recruit, Miss Avelynne Ironhold." He held out his hand, palm up, towards Avelynne.

"That's *Countess* Avelynne Ironhold," Myllie amended. She then missed Avelynne's pained noise at the mention of her title because she was busy adding, "And I'm her maid. We ain't used to predators stalking courtyards."

The last sentence was said in a disdainful whisper.

Avelynne's stomach dropped. She waved a hand, trying to find the words to mend the injured situation. "There's no need for the title! We'll all be together here for the next two years. And after that, it'll only be the four of us in charge of a large, complicated longship so—"

"You four and a band of rough sailors and some physician," Myllie interrupted.

"Yes," Avelynne said. "Thank you, Myllie. Anyway, my

point is that perhaps formalities should be disposed of between us?"

There were smiles and nods all around so Avelynne gathered the courage to step close to Sabina. "And, for what it's worth, while we're unused to having a predator as a companion, I know it is a common custom up north." She cast a glance at the animal. "Your Snowtiger is simply magnificent. I'm sure we are all eager to draw it."

"Draw it and perhaps one day wrestle with it?" Hale said.

Sabina looked from Avelynne to Hale. The Snowtiger was close by her side now and following her gaze.

"I don't know about wrestling him. But he does make a good drawing model. I must have hundreds of sketches of him."

"Can I see some one day?" Avelynne asked.

Sabina played with her braid. "Aye, why not?"

"So, the second wave is made up of two lasses and two lads?" Hale said. "Good! All efficient teams need balance."

"Unless someone in the group doesn't count themselves as either of the genders," Eleksander suggested tentatively.

Hale wasn't deterred. "That would make for an even more diverse group. Nature always works better when there's diversity. I remember reading that in cases when—" He cut off, staring at the centre of Avelynne's collarbones. "Wait, is that a silver arrow? If so, that's a great piece of jewellery."

Avelynne put her hand to the necklace, wishing she didn't have to disappoint him. "No, it's a quill, I'm afraid. My grandmother gave it to me when I fell in love with drawing."

A bell tolled. The sound came from above the door to the largest of the surrounding buildings.

They all moved towards it and a wiry, bald man appeared in the doorway.

"Good morrow, second wave. I'm Hason Rete, you will refer to me as *Tutor* Rete. I've been assigned as the head tutor of the second wave. I will also be tutoring you in the subjects of magic and how to orientate yourself." He paused to shade his eyes from the sun. "Throughout the day you will meet your other tutors: Atha Santorine, Coth Rogan, Elya Hathleen, and Ithikiel Myle. They are all the best in Cavarra in their individual fields."

"May… I ask what those are?" Eleksander asked, fidgeting with his sleeve.

"Of course. Tutor Rogan will train you in the fighting arts, everything from archery to staves. Tutor Hathleen, who is head of the first wave, is in charge of arithmetic and geography, while Tutor Myle shall train you in drawing and mapmaking. In fact, he is right over there," Rete said, pointing to a youngish man scurrying toward the gate with parchment in one hand. "Finally, Tutor Santorine, besides being a dear friend of mine, is the leading scholar on the sea. She has braved travelling on the farthest venturing fishing boats. She will be tutoring you in swimming, using the new nautical instruments, and how to sail."

"Thank you," Eleksander mumbled.

"You're welcome. Nevertheless, before you're introduced to them or have any lessons, I shall be handling your introduction to the Hall of Explorers." Rete turned to the people behind the students. "May I ask the companions to take all belongings and luggage inside? There will be servants there showing you where to place them. Then you will have your own introductions to your tasks and positions here."

Eleksander's sister, Myllie, and an older man with the same golden tan as Hale, began picking up bags and carrying them in one by one.

"My companion is this Snowtiger," Sabina said. "Should I carry my own luggage up and join the rest of you later?"

The tutor shook his head. "No need. I shall have a servant take your belongings up. Your feline may come with us into our introduction instead. After all, knowing where the servants' uniforms and quarters are shan't do the animal much good."

Striding out with large, soundless steps, so unlike the discreet, anxious moving of Ironhold retainers, a manservant emerged and took a large case in rugged leather from Sabina.

Tutor Rete clapped his hands together. "All right then. Gather yourselves and we shall head inside and get you situated in a lesson room."

Chapter Six

THE SECOND WAVE

Hale quickly replaced his sword and pulled on his tunic as the tutor led them towards the door. The short tunic fit a bit tight. At least that meant it wouldn't get caught on things or flutter in the breeze, creating noise and giving away his position. On arrival, the outfit had been handed to him in an embossed leather satchel. One which he now spotted the two new arrivals carrying, still filled with their new garments. Obviously, they weren't as curious about the new outfits as he and Sabina had been.

The lad – Eleksander was it? – wore light-blue. Was that silk or something fancy like that? Must be from a rich family. His outfit was not as lavish as Avelynne's, though. She appeared every bit the Countess her servant said she was. He took in her long, lowcut, tunic which was the same colour as her hair, reddish black, like a thick pool of newly spilled blood. Over that she wore some kind of sleeveless gown in dark green with silver lacing and details in the fitted waist. Was that called brocade? He'd read that in a book once. He shrugged, embarrassed to be spending time thinking about swanky clothes. Still. This lass. She moved like water. He had never seen anyone like her before.

Nor had he seen buildings this winding nor this stark. As soon as they were inside, they were led to a room off the first corridor. Hale clenched his jaw in frustration. He wanted to see the four structures framing the courtyard. To know them inside out. Surely talking could wait until he knew his surroundings?

The room the tutor led them into was less gloomy than the corridors, mainly due to the many arched windows. There were only two wall decorations. On the far side of the room was a large map, showing Cavarra and what little of the waters around it that fishermen had travelled. On their end hung a set of large parchment papers, scribbled full of text. The tutor pulled them off the rough nails while saying, "Be seated, please."

Hale counted four short benches, each with a desk in front. He picked one by an open window. The others sat down too, Avelynne picking the bench next to him.

While the tutor placed pieces of unused parchment on nails in the wall, probably to write on during future lessons, Hale inspected the other students. He was physically the fittest. Good, that was a start. If he could use his strength and flexibility to help his team, he could make them like him. Respect him. Maybe even see him as a leader. He nodded to himself, liking the look of them all. They all had intelligent, clear eyes and appeared healthy. Although Avelynne was thinner than the others. He shrugged, maybe she'd been ill recently. Or perhaps it was the thin mountain air that made the Peakdwellers reedier? The fact that she was short couldn't be helped, of course. She had pretty features, with the usual elegantly narrow eyes of the Peakdwellers. She also had those sweet little dips in the cheeks when she smiled. Were they called dimples? Hopefully she was as skilled as she was comely. His gaze moved to the next bench. No problem there, Sabina was sure to be an asset to any team.

He craned his head to view Eleksander next to her. A Lakelander, of course. That dark skin was only common amongst his own people and the Lakelanders. In fact, it was a colour Hale had always wanted himself, hating how his lighter skin burned in the sun when his friends' skin didn't.

Hale cracked his knuckles while deciding that Eleksander was as pretty as Avelynne. His black braids were certainly longer and more plentiful than Avelynne's tresses.

Hale ran his hand over his hair which had been trimmed to a light brown fuzz on his scalp. Much more practical. Nothing for an opponent to pull in a fight, or a braid to get stuck on a branch.

The tutor asked if everyone was comfortable and could see him properly. The two lasses and Hale all answered loud and clear. Eleksander only shifted in his seat. Considering where he was sitting, he couldn't have a very good view. Why didn't he say that? Ask Tutor Rete to stand more in the middle? Or move his desk?

Hale concentrated on Rete. The bald man adjusted his high collar and then clasped his hands behind his back. "I shall start with some general information. First, you will be sharing rooms throughout your time here. This is to get you used to living together in close quarters, as you will while you explore. For ease, it will be womenfolk in one room and menfolk in the other."

He waited, probably to see if there were any questions or comment.

Hale didn't care how they lived. He was used to traveling around and sleeping however his group managed to camp during the hunt. Up in the trees if it was bird season, in one huge, linen tent if it was boar season, and so on. As long as the doors weren't locked around him, he'd be fine.

No one else had any questions or comments so Tutor Rete continued.

"You have all been issued sets of student's garments. Treat them well and wear them always. They will suit both intellectual and physical endeavours and ensure you all look alike. It'll get you used to the idea of constantly wearing your uniform."

Hale watched the two who hadn't changed into their new outfits. They were both peering down at their clothes and squirming. He noticed Sabina picking a long hair off her jerkin. Had she changed right away because her Northern clothes had been too thick for the balmy weather or did she, like he, want to get right into their new life?

Rete spoke again. "What you haven't been given on arrival are your compasses. Like the four recruits before you, you have been awarded a compass each. The king had them specially made and engraved with your name on the back. Do not lose them. Using them will save your lives and they can also be used as proof that you have attended the Hall of Explorers."

Hale jumped forward in his seat. "A compass?! When do we get it?"

The tutor smiled. Hale wasn't sure why.

Rete held up a hand in the air, making it glow with

magic. "I don't see why you can't have them right now." He moved his hand as if it was picking objects up and sending them off to each student. From the other side of the room, the silvery strands picked up four compasses and delivered them to each recruit.

Hale marvelled as the magic dropped a compass into his outstretched palm.

It had a copper casing and was cold against his skin. He lifted it, testing its weight. The needle moved around the plain, simple wind rose as Hale turned the compass. It was mesmerising. Did they have these in the other counties? Was he the only one in the room who had never seen one? He had a faint memory of hearing that compasses were used when building large constructions and creating the Cavarra map, currently behind his back. But hadn't the Woodsfolk created most of that map? How had he never seen one of these?

He shrugged. What mattered was that this one was his. It was useful, reliable, and through that, utterly beautiful. He closed his fingers around it and squeezed.

"Turn it over," Avelynne whispered.

He did and saw two lines engraved in the metal.

Hale Hawthorn

Second Wave

His breath hitched. He beamed at Avelynne who returned the smile.

Tutor Rete appeared in front of him. "Nifty little things, no? Invaluable to us ever since their invention a decade ago. I sometimes wonder if the Hall of Explorers and the first wave would have come about unless we had these."

"Will we meet them before they sail?" Hale asked.

"The first wave? Hard to miss them," Rete replied. "They occupy the same buildings as you. However, their bedchambers are in the other end of the living quarters. They have a room each as they are three females and one male. It was seen as unfair if the boy was the only one who got his own room."

"The room splitting here seems unnecessarily gendered," Eleksander mumbled.

Rete didn't hear him. He merely pulled up his collar and added, "Also, you will have a gruelling study schedule while theirs is even worse. You will all be too busy to socialise with each other."

"Will we start off with all the subjects right away?" Sabina asked.

The tutor turned to her. "Certainly. I and the other tutors will train you in swimming, fighting, magic control, and how to navigate on water, which includes using your compass, the ship's built in sundial, and obviously your nautical instruments."

As he spoke, Sabina nodded with a clenched jaw. Hale watched her taut body language. Did she ever relax?

Rete carried on. "And, of course, mapmaking skills. Which means: arithmetic, drawing, and geography. In short, you'll have classes in each subject every day. Only the evenings will be free. We start off with the basics and by the time two years have passed, you'll be experts ready to lead your sailors like an army and find us a new world. You will navigate by the stars as easily as you climb a tree to escape an attacking wolf."

Eleksander gathered attention by clearing his throat.

"May I ask why we need to rely so much on our mundane skillset?"

Rete's forehead furrowed. "What do you mean?"

"I mean that I know we need those skills to fall back on when our magical energy is depleted, but surely what we need to have as our first defence is our magic?" Eleksander said in a timid tone of voice.

"Not necessarily. Not always. You must think about what you do. Measure every action." The tutor looked grave. "We Cavarrians are not skilled at that. After all, we caused the silver beasts."

"Through over-farming the land and gobbling up all the insects' food, yes we know," Hale monotoned.

"Not just through that, Woodlander," Rete said coldly. "Also, due to our use of *magic*. The human population grew and grew, with us all using magic every day, and the beasts love magic. Thus, it was our fault in two ways." He held up a hand in a stopping gesture, "We must ensure we don't make the same mistake in the new lands. We must spread out more, eat only what we need. Additionally, each family can only have three children a piece."

"And we must make sure we don't bring any silver beasts or their eggs with us to the new lands," Sabina added.

The tutor gave her an approving smile. "Exactly."

Hale saw that Eleksander was slumped in his seat, fiddling with his sleeve. Clearly their tutor noticed too as he addressed his next words in the Lakelander's direction.

"Your magic *is* important, you are right in that. You will be expected to use it. I know from your test results that your magical energy is particularly strong, Young Master

Aetholo. But it does still run out, does it not? Like the rest of us, you become exhausted if you do too much magic?"

With pursed lips, Eleksander nodded.

"Consequently, you will save your strength whenever you can. Keep your magical energy stored up for if you encounter dragons, harpies, or unfriendly natives."

Eleksander's head shot up. "Tutor Rete, with all due respect, should you put human beings inhabiting a land, that we plan to trespass in, in the same sentence as monsters?"

The room fell silent, all attention on Eleksander. He'd been so unsure before. Now he seemed ready to pounce on their tutor, knuckles whitening in clenched fists on his desk.

Rete fixed him with a serious gaze. "Of course not. Slavery and colonisation were strictly forbidden in Cavarra's accords decades ago. That is why they made the Hall of Explorers motto, 'To Explore. Never Exploit,' when it was founded."

The heavy silence spread though the room, filling every corner and crevice. Eleksander and Rete maintained eye contact.

Eleksander blinked first. His tense body slumped. "Sorry. Injustice is the one thing in the world I cannot stand. And slavery is the highest form of it."

Confusion muddled Hale's mind. Then his old lessons poured back into it, filling it with righteous rage. Their history was indeed filled with slavery and colonisation, right up until their lifetime. Throughout Cavarra's long history, there had been several occasions where one of their homelands had been owned by the others. Power—and through it, slave owning—

shifting back and forth. He threw a glance at Sabina. Well, all except the North, which had never been taken due to its fearless warriors and the icy landscape that none of the others were equipped to handle.

Hale bristled. He rarely understood why people were so quick to take offence at things but now he regretted that it wasn't he who had reacted like Eleksander had. That *he* had not been the one to call out their tutor and stand up against this outdated, shitty concept.

Rete cleared his throat. "That is quite all right. I did not mean to compare any people you might encounter with what you call 'monsters.' Nor do I think any dragons or such beasts that you might find will be monsters either." He paused. "I believe that what you find is just as likely to be good as evil. Which is why you will treat them *all* with respect until you know their intent."

"With respect *and* without meddling in their affairs?" Avelynne asked.

"Of course," Rete stated. "We will only take lands that are uninhabited by intelligent beings. And even in the case of unintelligent beings, we will take our responsibility to not have a negative effect on their lives. We must learn from our mistakes here on Cavarra. Be they the ones we committed against the land and its animals, or those we committed upon each other."

They all murmured their agreement.

"Enough on that for now," Rete said. "Your classes will begin tomorrow, giving you a day to settle in and get to know each other. Perhaps even try for some extra sleep after your journeys."

Avelynne blew out a long breath and Hale echoed her relief.

"Go ahead," Rete said. "Follow the corridor to the adjoining building, down to the chambers with your names on the door. Your belongings should already be waiting for you." He stood back, hands clasped behind him. "When the dinner bell tolls, you must make your way to the Great Hall, which named our institution. You cannot miss it, it's in the middle of the building opposite this one. I shall see you there, combed, washed, and wearing your new outfits."

They all got up. Eleksander stopped to hold the door open for everyone. When Hale passed him, he slapped a hand on the boy's stomach and said, "I'll fight you for the best bed."

"I'll give you first pick," Eleksander said, with a lopsided smile.

Hale smiled back and walked out. He was relieved that he had felt some iron muscles in the other's stomach. He only hoped the lad had as much iron in his heart. And that they could find something to eat; his stomach was grumbling.

Chapter Seven

WOMEN

The door closed behind Avelynne and she dropped the satchel containing her uniform down by her feet, right next to where her trunk and portmanteau had been left. Her gaze moved from all her things to scan the small, simple room.

There's a risk I might have overpacked.

There was a faint scent of something fresh and sweet in the room, probably coming from the open window which faced the apple trees.

Sabina turned to her with a slight smile. "Since we are to be roommates I should introduce myself with my *full* name. Apparently, Hale doesn't give much heed to family names. I'm Sabina Rosenmarck."

"A pleasure. As Eleksander mentioned earlier, I'm Avelynne Ironhold."

Sabina extended her hand and when she figured out what she was meant to do, Avelynne shook it. Clearly there was to be no more bowing and curtsying. Thank the stars!

"Sorry that my hand is a little cold," Sabina said with a

grimace. "My mother always says, 'cold hands – warm heart.' Whatever that means."

"I've heard that saying. I hope it's true, sharing a room with someone who's warm-hearted sounds like a good start. Speaking of which, can you believe that the affluent Hall of Explorers only afforded two rooms for their new recruits?"

Sabina laughed. Her voice was husky but not low in pitch. Like that of a young woman with a sore throat. She didn't look ill, though. In fact, despite her paleness, she looked in rude health.

"Aye, all that nonsense about getting used to living together," Sabina rolled her eyes, "surely then all four of us should be in one room?"

"I suppose they don't want us becoming… amorous."

"Well, then they shouldn't have put me with a girl," Sabina said with a scoff.

"Pardon?" Avelynne took in the words. "Oh! You prefer women?"

"Aye, but don't worry, I'm not going to sneak into your bed all of a sudden." She smiled disarmingly and Avelynne chuckled.

"I wasn't worried you might. Now, your Snowtiger on the other hand…" she trailed off with a grin.

"Call him Kall," Sabina said. "He'll like you more if you call him by his name."

"Of course, I do apologise, Kall," Avelynne said with a bow to the animal, who was busy washing his paw.

"He won't sneak into your bed either. He finds beds too warm in this mild climate. Until he's gotten used to this temperature he's certain to sleep on the floor."

"Will you join him?"

"I just might! I'm not used to this much sun!"

Avelynne took in the pink flush the sun had put on those on those milky cheeks, seeing the truth of the words.

"Not much room here. I'll have to do my more strenuous exercising outside, I think," Sabina said as she moved her leather case out of the way. "I hope you won't mind not having your own space? I come from a family with eight younger siblings, so I'm used to never sleeping alone."

"I've never shared a room. Not unless you count when I was ill, and a servant slept in the bedchamber in case I needed anything."

Sabina examined her. "Servants. Bedchambers. You really are a Countess, then?"

"I'm afraid so. But not here. Here I'm a student like you. I'm just Avelynne."

Sabina lifted her head. "Then that is how I'll see you."

Avelynne saw only truth in those blue eyes. Things seemed very simple and straightforward with this woman. It made Avelynne's secret feel even darker and dirtier.

"Thank you," she murmured.

"No need to mention it. We all begin a new life today. A life together."

Avelynne broke the eye contact. "True. We do."

She took in her new room. A sizable, vaulted window let sunlight bathe two beds, two dressers, and a table with some cloths and a tall jug of water for ablutions. Smooth stone walls with only a few hooks and a candle sconce to keep them from being totally bare. The latter and a small chandelier, both made of utilitarian iron, would illuminate the room after sunset. She'd have to ensure she had candles on hand.

It wasn't the opulence Avelynne was used to, but somehow that was exciting. Could she thrive if she no longer had all the luxuries she had grown accustomed to?

Sabina joined her and remarked, "I see the rooms are as modest as the rest of the building. I would expect maps on the walls at least. Or diagrams of our nautical instruments or longships. There's not even a fireplace in here."

"No. Thank the stars we get plenty of blankets." Avelynne pointed to the pile of wool blankets on the nearest bed.

"Aye. You know, I'm glad it's not extravagant like a castle, or I should feel out of place, but this does look a bit like a prison cell," Sabina paused to put her hands on her hips, "I wonder if the first wave students have these sparse rooms too or if they're afforded something more inspiring?"

"We'll have to ask. Anyway, is there a particular bed you would like?"

"No, go ahead and choose which one suits you."

"Thank you," Avelynne said and placed her new satchel on the closest one. She had to get her outfit unpacked. It was all in there; the full list of garments the admittance paperwork had said she'd be getting. She ran a trembling finger over the Hall of Explorers emblem embossed into the brown leather of her new jerkin.

After a moment, she noticed Sabina patting down her trousers and tunic.

"What are you doing?"

"I read that the full armour we get later is filled with pockets for navigation instruments, daggers, parchment, and, of course, our compass. These, however, don't seem to have any pockets."

Avelynne carefully checked along Sabina's sides and finally found openings hidden in the flexible fabric of the trousers.

"There," she said while pointing to the back of Sabina's hip. "They're a little farther back than normal. And from the looks of them, not very big."

Sabina grimaced. "That's unhelpful. Oh well, at least I can put the compass in there now."

Avelynne reflected on her own compass, which was stowed safely in her dress' pocket. "Where is yours right now? We must keep them close at all times."

Sabina's cheeks reddened. "It's safe. Just not in a very ladylike place. Turn around while I fish it out."

"What?" Avelynne squeaked. Her mind was coming up with a few unlikely hiding places but nothing useful.

Sabina grunted with embarrassment. "Fine, I'll tell you. I wedged it under one of my breasts. I've seen my mother do that with keys and other important small things."

Avelynne, who was less well-endowed and so unable to wedge anything under hers, gaped.

Sabina reached in under her tunic and, in her own words, "fished it out." All while muttering, "I'll have to get some strips of fabric to tie these down or something. Especially for fighting and training." She yanked her tunic back into place. "Northern garments are built to keep them fixed in place, these are not. Probably tailored by men."

Avelynne tried to not seem taken aback at the frank conversation about bodies. "I see. I'm sure we can find you something to secure them comfortably with. I wager my maid could alter your tunic to the way your regular clothes were tailored, if you'd like?"

Sabina's mouth twitched into a brief smile. "I like the use of 'we' there."

"As you said, we all begin a new life today. A life together."

"Aye, but I can't see Eleksander casually skipping along to find a way to bind my breasts."

Avelynne mulled that over, considering the new acquaintance. "Actually, I think he would do it. Although he might die from embarrassment as he did so."

Sabina chuckled. "I hope he's made of sterner stuff than he seems."

"I'm sure he is. You saw the force and fight in him when the subject of colonisation came up. I think he has hidden depths."

"True enough. He must have if he was chosen. Those tests were gruelling, and all four of us were the best of all the eighteen-year-olds in our county. We deserve our place here."

At that last sentence, Avelynne quickly looked to the door. "Uh, I-I don't know where our companions went; we need Myllie to help with the bosom situation."

Sabina patted Kall who had been pacing the room but now stood by her side. Good, she clearly hadn't seen Avelynne's reaction then.

"All right, let's go find your maid. Hopefully Kall will win her over this time."

"I wouldn't get my hopes up," Avelynne said.

Myllie had promised to make the adjustments to Sabina's garments without hesitation. She had, however, not been any fonder of the snowtiger.

Obviously sensing this, Sabina took her leave at the earliest opportunity. When she and Kall headed back to their bedchamber, Myllie frowned in their direction and whispered, "Unnatural to walk around with a deadly creature like that. Can't she at least have it on a leash?"

Avelynne leaned against the doorframe to the laundry rooms, which weren't in the basement as usual, but on the first floor, allowing sunlight to illuminate the lye-stained stone of the walls and floor.

"Northerners often have companions, Myllie. The animals are trained from birth to stay with their human and take orders as if their life depended on it. They're safe. *Kall* is safe."

"If you say so," Myllie muttered.

"Thank you for helping."

Myllie folded the four tunics she was going to alter for Sabina. "It's all right. Bein' on the rounder side of body shapes myself, I know her struggles."

"Mm," Avelynne said.

She watched Myllie work as she always did: slowly, humming off key, without a care.

Avelynne envied that beyond belief. She clenched her hands into fists, her fingernails digging into her palms. "Oh Myllie. The others... they're all so much fitter than I am. Probably smarter and more skilled too!"

"Don't be silly, you're fit and clever enough to keep up with the best of 'em, Countess."

"That's very kind of you to say," Avelynne said halfheartedly. She tried to keep her voice from quivering as she added, "Anyway, how are you settling in? Do you like it here? If not, you can always go home. Merely say the word."

"Nah, it seems fine here. Plenty of nice people to work with," Myllie leaned in with a conspiratorial grin, "many of 'em handsome men."

"You should have plenty to do then," Avelynne said with a forced laugh.

"Certainly. And I'm not the only one. Those boys you're teamed up with, they're awful handsome too. Well, the tall one with the braids is handsome. That crooked smile of his is dazzlin'. The other one, the Woodlander, has more of that sexy, powerful feel." Suddenly Myllie seemed to forget that her employer was in the room. She was squeezing a tunic in her hands and staring into space. "Those scars and intense eyes of his make him dangerously delicious. Like he's pulsatin' with energy or something. And his shorter stature works better for smaller women like us from the Peaks." Myllie bit her lower lip. "But then, the tall one is so big and pretty. He'd have the kind of embrace you'd like to get lost in. Well, I s'pose it comes down to what sort of lover you're in the mood for, Countess."

Avelynne looked away to hide her blush. "That is inappropriate, and you know it. I'm not going to get romantically involved with either of them," she thought of Sabina, "or anyone else. I am here for much too important reasons and will rely on these three far too much to risk it all for love."

Myllie looked sheepish as she whispered, "It wouldn't have to be love, Countess. It could be something… temporary and more physical."

Avelynne stomped her foot. "What is this nonsense? Why does no one value friendship anymore? Why am I expected to seduce every non-married person my age I come across?"

Myllie shrugged. "You're eighteen. Most girls your age will be takin' a spouse and settin' up a home."

"Well, I'm not. And you never answered my question! What's wrong with friendships?"

"Nothin'. But someone with your taste for bedplay might find friendships a little... wishy-washy after a while, Countess?"

"Do not make assumptions regarding my tastes, please. Oh, I do not have time for this." Avelynne turned to leave. "Thank you again for your help and I'm glad you're settling in well."

In the corridor on the way out to the courtyard, she passed one of the Hall of Explorers' rare decorations: a tapestry showing a knight kissing the hand of a princess. Behind him was a crude likeness of a ship, which was actually a rowing boat depicted ten times larger.

Avelynne muttered, "With a mission like ours, we need to focus more on proper ships and learning how to navigate deadly seas than romance."

Chapter Eight

MAGIC AND MUSCLES

After shutting the door with his and Eleksander's names on, Hale inspected his roommate. Would he snore as badly as Ghar did?

"Do you always do that?" Eleksander asked.

"What?"

"Stare so brazenly? We're all curious of each other but the rest of us only sneak subtle glances."

Hale leaned against the wall. "That's not my style."

"It's true, then," Eleksander murmured. "Woodsfolk don't care much for social niceties."

"It's true that we don't *play games*," Hale said, putting some severity in his voice. "We don't have time for that. We have animals to hunt and wildlife to try to look after. Not to mention all the cursed silver beasts trampling at our feet."

There was a twitch in Eleksander's pretty face.

"Not a fan of our silvery little friends?" Hale asked.

"Friends?" Eleksander spat. "Vicious little monsters. They're growing larger and bolder in the Lakelands. Last week, one of them—" He cut off and swallowed visibly before forcing out the words, "bit off an infant's legs. One after the other. It happened so fast that the baby's family had no time to stop it."

The way Eleksander's voice wavered and broke made Hale wonder if he had known the baby in question. Or perhaps he was always this soft-hearted? Silver beasts maimed and harmed on a daily basis. If you took it this badly, you'd go mad in days.

"They've got to be stopped," Hale said gruffly. "Have you heard that the king's physicians are looking at poisons? Gasses, tinctures, and even ointments. Ones to kill them off but not harm us."

Eleksander nodded grudgingly. "Yes, but they're not getting anywhere, are they?" His tightly clenched teeth were suddenly bared.

Good. There IS iron in that soft heart, Hale thought.

"No, but they will. Meanwhile, we'll do our bit by finding new lands where Cavarrians can start over without the beasts. That's our task. That's how we help. Focus on that."

Eleksander stood straighter. "I will."

"Good lad," Hale said, slapping him on the shoulder. He regretted the gesture when the other reeled backwards. He'd have to be gentler.

Something whizzed past their window. Hale had time to wish he had his weapons with him before he realised it was only another crow. Obviously, he didn't *need* weapons. He could slay silver beasts with his magic and muscles. Especially the flightless ones. Nevertheless, a blade in his hand would make him more comfortable.

He crossed his arms over his chest. "It's so strange to –"

"What is?" Eleksander asked right away.

Hale gave him a look. "I was getting to it. Give me a chance."

Eleksander gave a diffident smile. "Sorry."

"I was going to say that it's strange to be here without any silver beasts. Not having to sleep with one eye open in case they sneak into your tent and bite your toes off. Not having to fend them off every time you eat. Or, worse, when you do magic and they swarm like mad."

"Yes. It'll be quite the welcome change."

There was a quick rap at the door. Just one, and then the door opened. Hale smiled as he recognised Ghar's informal way of treating the custom of knocking.

He came in and greeted Eleksander with a nod and a smile. Then he switched his focus to Hale.

"Here's the things you wanted to bring, lad," he handed Hale a burlap satchel. "Now, all the things you *didn't* feel you needed but you will—like Woodlander clothes, your training mat, and pressed leaves from the tree you were named by—I'll keep. When you need them, come to me and I'll hand them over."

"Mm-hm," Hale grunted.

"That was all I wanted to say. Are you both settling in all right, lads?"

"Yes, thank you," Eleksander answered. Hale gave another affirmative grunt.

With a grave expression, Ghar observed them for a moment. "The word amongst the servants is that they put you in rooms together to keep you from touching yourselves. I reckon that'll lead to nothing but trouble. Give each other some privacy so you can relieve your pressure.

And make sure to tell the lasses to do so as well. It's not natural to try to curb people's natural needs like that."

Then Ghar left without a farewell.

Hale caught the Lakelander coughing nervously. Perhaps they didn't speak so openly about matters of the flesh? Hale hefted the satchel in his hand, unsure of where to put it. It only contained his favourite dagger, the roll of bandages that he always carried, and two books: one with exercises for keeping a body fighting fit and one listing all Cavarra's plants and how edible or poisonous they were. The room's two dressers were probably for clothes, right?

He spotted iron hooks by the door. With the use of magic, he levitated the satchel across the room, past Eleksander and onto the nearest hook. He could've gone over there and hung the bag up, of course. But where was the fun in that?

Eleksander's gaze followed the satchel's ascent and then continued taking in the room. "Not many decorations or amenities here. I should have liked a desk or room for a bath, so we didn't have to go down the hall for proper ablutions. Still, this room has everything we require, I suppose. Speaking of furnishings, have you chosen a bed?"

"I'll take this one," Hale said, picking one with his usual decisiveness despite them being in equally good positions. Then he remembered that he was meant to be charming his fellow recruits. "Unless that's the one you want?"

Eleksander shook his head, sitting down on the opposite bed. "I'm fine here. It actually seems a tad longer which works well for my height." He leapt up. "Not that I'm saying you're short! I'm merely freakishly tall."

Hale tried to appear unaffected, but he did find himself

trying to stretch a bit taller. "Relax. I know what you meant."

In the ensuing silence, Hale shoved his hands into his pockets while Eleksander scratched the back of his neck and stared at his boots.

"Anyway, can't hang around here. We need to go explore!" Hale said. He clapped Eleksander on the shoulder again, gentler this time. "Come on. The courtyard is surrounded by all these buildings. Since I wasn't allowed to explore when I arrived, I began sparring without having found out what was in them all. I noticed one was a stable but the others… who knows! Let's go claim our new home!"

"Yes! The information they sent us said that the buildings were," Eleksander held up four fingers and started to count them off, "Servant quarters–which has rooms for the servants and workers. That's where the laundry rooms and kitchens begin too, continuing all the way into the structure which also houses the Great Hall. Then the buildings are broken up by the gate, of course. We're in the one that houses all the students and tutors and has the library!" He held one finger up, most likely trying to remember which building he had left out. "Ah, yes, the final one has the classrooms, a room where the tutors convene and, at the corner, the small stables you mentioned."

He dropped his hand and grinned. "But knowing that is not the same as seeing it with our own eyes, is it?"

"Exactly!"

Eleksander grabbed the satchel. "Let me just get into my student's garments."

"Good lad. Hurry up," Hale said, stretching.

"I will." While unlacing his long, ornate boots, Eleksander examined his bundle of tunics and then raked his eyes over Hale's body, his eyes lingering a little longer than Hale would've expected. "Is that, um, one of the short tunics you're wearing?"

Hale couldn't figure out why Eleksander seemed so embarrassed suddenly. "Yes. Now come on! We might have time to go for a run later if we don't dawdle."

Eleksander laid out one of the short tunics for himself while asking, "You don't sit about, do you?"

"We'll have lots of time to sit in most of our lessons. Let's move while we can."

"I cannot argue with that," Eleksander said while taking his trousers off. "I look forward to going for a run later, maybe asking Avelynne and Sabina along. It'll be nice to work off some of the stiffness of the journey over here."

"Lakelander, this promises to be the start of a beautiful friendship."

They grinned at each other.

Chapter Nine

THE GREAT HALL

When the dinner bell finished tolling, Avelynne was hurrying towards the Great Hall. She tugged at her trousers where they were tight against her thighs. Clothes like these had only been for sparring or riding back in Ironhold castle. She found that she didn't much miss the long dresses. Well, not right now anyway.

Despite that it wasn't fully dark outside, the corridors were lit by sconces. The flames danced against the walls from the draft of her and Sabina rushing past. Drawn on the stone walls were signposts of a sort, arrows and names of the rooms painted in white, tidy letters.

Thank the stars, or we'd be terribly lost.

Avelynne was a step or two behind Sabina and Kall. The Northerner seemed to want to lead the way and Avelynne didn't mind. If Sabina wanted to keep playing the big sister like she had back home, she was more than welcome to.

In front of them were a bulky set of rounded wooden doors. Sabina stopped by them and turned to Avelynne with surprising glee. Sabina had so far been serious and dignified, but now her eyes twinkled, and her rosy lips twitched into a wide smile.

"Do you want to do the honours?"

Avelynne shook her head. "No, you open it."

"As you wish."

With a soft grunt, Sabina heaved open the doors and Avelynne was happy she'd let the stronger woman do it. Now she knew that when it was her time to open them, she must apply force and try to make it look like it was easy. She had to pack some muscle on. Before anyone noticed how suspiciously weak she was.

The doors parted, revealing a vast, oblong gallery. Now Avelynne understood why the whole institution had been named after this one hall.

The grandeur started with the high, wood-beamed ceiling and the many copper chandeliers. Everywhere else, the chandeliers had been simple and made of iron. These were polished and well-crafted copper, looking surprisingly like her compass. Along the stone walls banners were hung, each one displaying the colours and emblems of the four counties, as expected. What took Avelynne's breath away for a moment was that these banners were studded with gemstones and gold and silver thread, making them gleam and twinkle. Fixed on the walls between the flags were ornate axes, broadswords, and several kinds of polearms. On the far wall hung the banner of the king. It was obviously larger than the others and its gilt threads and rubies caught in the firelight, demanding attending. Beneath that was one of the biggest fireplaces Avelynne had ever seen.

She heard Sabina gasp and realised that she wasn't paying attention to the walls but what was right in front of them, a long table with benches on either side. The table was set with polished pewter plates, tankards, cutlery, and candelabras with long scarlet candles. There were bowls with dried rose petals and spices, filling the air with warming sweet scents.

If the rest of this academy was meant to seem modest and disciplinary, this hall was the celebration of the hard work they had put in to get here. And the hard work they would do in the future.

Avelynne switched her footing back and forth at that thought. But it *was* true! She had worked so hard to earn her place here. She had doubled her efforts in every subject, sparring until she was all bruises, and reading up on her arithmetic and geography until her eyes ached. Luckily, her magic had always been quite strong so that hadn't needed as much work.

Her thoughts were interrupted by Tutor Rete coming over to greet them.

"You found your way then, ladies. Excellent. I'm glad to see the garments all fit. They suit you."

"Thank you," they said in unison.

Tutor Rete glanced behind them. "Have you seen Eleksander and Hale?"

"No," Sabina replied. "We've only been in our room and down in the servant quarters, finding some... spare clothing and speaking to the staff here. Everyone has been most helpful."

Rete clasped his hands behind his back. "I would expect no less. The Hall of Explorers have highly trained employees, from cooks to stable boys. You will be well looked after.

Not to mention well fed! Wait until you see the feast we have planned for you."

"A feast? When so much of Cavarra is starving? The Centre truly does live better than the rest of us," Sabina muttered quietly.

"What was that?" Rete asked.

Avelynne stepped in. "She said it sounds lovely."

While she too bristled at the injustice of them being fed better than the rest of Cavarra, she didn't want to start trouble on their first night. Besides, she was famished. Her uneasy stomach hadn't allowed her to eat much throughout the journey or her time here.

Rete's reply was cut off by the sound of thundering steps along the corridor behind them. He quirked an eyebrow at Eleksander and Hale who all but landed at his feet as they halted their run.

"I, we, I…" Eleksander stopped to catch his breath. "We're sorry we're late. We got lost between the armoury and the stables."

Rete gave a deep belly laugh. "Well, that is a terrible start to your career, getting lost while *exploring*."

They all laughed, the young men with some difficulty. Even the impossibly athletic Hale was struggling to get his breath back.

Sabina whispered, "They must've run like silver beasts from a lightning storm. Remind me to ask them what they found later," into Avelynne's ear.

Behind them, four adults walked in. They were, as Tutor Rete, dressed in emerald green cloaks bearing the Hall of Explorers emblem.

They must be the other tutors, Avelynne realised, craning

her neck to get a closer look as they all took their seats by the fireplace. The two women left an empty seat between them. Probably for Rete?

"Do we sit down now too?" Hale panted.

"No, not yet. Wait for the first wave of recruits to take their places," Rete said, pointing to a group that were skulking behind the doors. They were whispering to each other while peering over at the younger students.

"The first wave," Eleksander murmured. Avelynne understood his reverent tone. These were the only people who knew what was in store for them. The only people who would undertake the dangerous mission before them. They were so broad-shouldered and confident. Would she ever look like that?

Rete called over to the older students, "Stop staring like wolves sizing up bear cubs. Go sit down. The food will be getting cold in the kitchens."

With nonchalant expressions, the first wave took their seats next to the tutors. They spoke to a woman with frizzy, blonde hair. Avelynne guessed it was their head tutor, the one who taught arithmetic and geography.

"Do you remember what the name was of the arithmetic and geography tutor?" she discreetly asked Sabina.

"Tutor Hathleen," Sabina replied. "That's the blonde you're looking at. The scowling muscle-mountain with a neck like an ox is Tutor Rogan, the fighting instructor. I bumped into him right when I arrived this morning. He has the manners of an ox too."

"Come along," Rete said to the second wave. He indicated seats to the left. Sabina sat first, then Avelynne, Hale, and, Eleksander on the end. Kall curled up by the door and began to wash, looking like an overgrown housecat.

One of the tutors, a long-nosed woman with a charming smile, said, "well, well, the ever dawdling Hason Rete and his new flock has finally joined us. Welcome. Let's eat!" Then she banged a small gong.

"Did you hear that jesting?" Sabina whispered, just loud enough to be heard over the ringing. "You can tell Santorine and Rete are friends, can't you?"

"Sabina and I met her this morning," Hale said, a little too loud to be discreet. "Seems competent and fun. I can't wait for her lessons on the sea and sailing. I bet she's braved some dangerous waves in her time."

As the last reverberations of the gong rang out, the open doorway filled with servers carrying trays. Avelynne had grown up surrounded by servants and servers, but even she couldn't figure out how these men and women appeared so fast and silently. She surveyed them with awe as they floated in and placed filled bowls, platters, and jugs on the tables.

Hale peered into the jug which had been placed by him and said, "Red wine, I think."

"The smaller jugs have cherry wine," Rete said. "The others contain water. I recommend being careful with the wine. Save your heads for everything we intend to fill them with tomorrow."

Sabina grabbed one of the big jugs and poured her tankard full of water. Avelynne glanced around, unsure of it they should've waited for someone to serve them, like she was raised to do.

"Help yourselves," Tutor Santorine said kindly, probably having picked up on Avelynne's uncertainty.

"Thank you," Avelynne mumbled.

Hale stacked his plate with various meats and vegetables. Sabina followed his example. She muttered, "I miss bread. Stupid silver beasts eating all the grain," before sampling a chicken wing.

Eleksander leant forward and with raised eyebrows caught Avelynne's gaze. With a shrug he reached past Hale to hand her a plate of buttered beets. She took them with a smile and a gracious nod, wondering if perhaps she should've been housed with the more similar Eleksander. Guilt made her grimace. She was being unfair to the lovely Sabina, who had been nothing but friendly. Besides, she could probably use a companion who pushed her along. Eleksander now poured Hale some water, positively beaming with joy as the black-eyed Woodlander thanked him.

Perhaps we have been perfectly matched after all.

Conversation soon filled the room, and so did constantly replenished plates of food. The feast was as generous and delicious as Rete had intimated. Avelynne was relieved to overhear the first wave discussing that the servants always ate the substantial amounts of leftovers, ensuring nothing went to waste.

When the last courses were brought in, Avelynne barely had room for the stewed, honeyed oakenberries dowsed in thick pouring cream.

"There," Hale said through a mouthful. "This treat should finally put some weight on your rattling bones, Peakdweller."

His tone and choice of words sounded rude to her, but Hale had been making friendly conversation with her all night. Now Avelynne examined his obsidian eyes, which reflected the candlelight, trying to gauge his intent. He smiled and poured some wine into her empty tankard. Avelynne decided that he didn't know the cut of his words or his tone, so he was neither mocking her or had guessed her secret.

"I don't think honey and cream will give me the sort of weight I require. I need muscle, not fat," Avelynne replied before sipping her wine.

"That's why I served you extra of the spiced pork earlier," Sabina said, still chewing. "We'll get your muscles bigger than even this Woodlander's ego."

There was sniggering from Eleksander and spluttering from Hale.

Avelynne put her hand on his arm. "Nothing wrong with a big ego, as long as it can be backed up with the skill and strength it portrays."

"Thank you!" Hale said. "I knew you Peakdwellers were nice people. Unlike *others*." He cast a dark glance at Eleksander and Sabina but then chuckled.

Avelynne drew in a deep belly breath between her own laughs and marvelled at how good it felt. Had she been taking shallow breaths ever since she set out for the Hall of Explorers? Now she filled her lungs as she listened to Sabina and Hale discuss how quickest to get Avelynne built like an ox. All while Eleksander interjected that maybe she was stronger than she appeared and was merely wiry like Tutor Rete. The latter was said in a whisper. Unnecessarily, since Rete was busy arguing over lesson plans with the other tutors.

Avelynne sat back and enjoyed her wine, revelling in her

relaxion and the relief from her secret being pushed to the back of her mind. Perhaps she could get through this after all.

The only moment to take her out of her first taste of calm was when a female server caught her eye and held it. It looked like the young woman mouthed, "Be wary." And then, when she'd poured a first wave student some more cream, the words, "Do not trust them." Or was it, "Do not trust *him*?"

Avelynne shook off the thought, certain her anxious mind was inventing things to worry about. She wouldn't allow it tonight. She had wine to drink, new friends to talk to, and then sleep to catch up on.

Chapter Ten

FIRST LESSONS

Hale woke up on his back and didn't recognise the ceiling above him. It wasn't lush tree tops, a starry sky, or the bright fabric Woodsfolk used for their tents. All he saw was tarred, grim, rosewood beams. He huffed a breath out through his nose. Being boxed up like this was uncivilised.

"Eleksander? Are you awake?"

The Lakelander rubbed his eyes with his knuckles. "I am now.

"Can you remember what Rete said would be our first lesson?"

"Magic casting."

Hale put his hands behind his head as an extra pillow. "Good. That's bound to be outside. I'll get some fresh air and sun on my skin."

"It might help that cut on your torso heal," Eleksander said between yawns.

"Oh, you noticed that, did you?" Hale said, flexing his chest muscles.

Eleksander gave a non-committal sound, turning so he was no longer facing Hale.

With a snicker, Hale let his eyelids close. Someone was sure to wake him when it was time to eat.

———

Finally. Their first lesson was about to start. Hale had washed, shaved, eaten, and dressed. He even had time for a few stretches out in the morning sun. Now, he wanted to begin.

Except, the others hadn't arrived. Only he and the barely awake Eleksander were present. Hale breathed in the crisp, almost chilly morning air.

A table had been placed in front of the sundial in the courtyard's middle. He ran his fingers over the objects laid out on it. A crow's feather, a dagger, clay shards, and a bag containing what appeared to be sand.

"I gather we're to mend the broken clay thing. But what they want us to do with the rest, I have no clue," Hale grumbled, closing the bag of sand.

Eleksander stifled a yawn. "If you wait, you'll find out. I'm sure Tutor Rete will be here soon."

A lass, in the unusual yellow that the Centre's employees all wore, crossed the courtyard carrying a wicker basket. Hale recognised her. It was Avelynne's companion, the one who feared snowtigers.

"Good morrow," Hale said. "I'm glad to see someone else up and already at work."

She stopped and for some strange reason, bobbed into a curtsy towards him and Eleksander. "The countess is awake too, despite being bone tired after sneakin' out to practise her swordsmanship long after sundown. I left her to her breakfast in the Great Hall, havin' laundry to get on with."

"I'm sure plenty of people are up," he paused for emphasis and a companionable smile, "but not necessarily *working*."

He was shocked that people like Eleksander and Avelynne didn't do their own laundry. He and Ghar took turns washing their clothes. If he asked Ghar to do all of it, he'd get his head bitten off!

The lass giggled, then grew solemn when Hale's gaze flitted over the laundry basket. "I spotted blood on the Countess' sleeve," she said. "Can I ask… I mean, could you tell me… I wouldn't want to speak outta turn…"

Her beating about the bush was wearing on Hale's patience. "Come on, what do you want to ask?"

"Be nice," Eleksander whispered to him through almost closed lips.

Her sweet, solemn mask slipped to show displeasure for a moment and then she griped, "I meant that when you leave, all the fightin' and the dangerous plants and such. Won't you be needin' some nurses to patch you up?"

"When we sail? Sure, a physician will join us. Although, only one. We're to travel with only essential persons. If we find land, the next expedition will have plenty of scholars on board, though. Like scientists of all kinds to note and categorise any flora, fauna, and population we might come upon."

Hale expected her to ask further questions but instead her gaze fixed on the objects on the table.

He stepped closer to it. "Odd selection of things, isn't it?

We were discussing what we're meant to do with them for our magic lesson. What do you think?"

Her forehead furrowed. "Me? I'm sure I wouldn't know. Nor should I be guessin' at such things."

Hale tilted his head. "Why not?"

She glowered at him as if he was slow-witted. "I'm just a maid."

"There's nothing 'just' about that," Eleksander piped up. "It's a good profession."

She frowned. "I meant that all I need worry about is cleanin' and lookin' after the countess. Besides, I'm rubbish at magic. I can barely float parchment pieces around. And when I do manage it, I'm knackered for a fortnight!"

"Float?" Hale snapped his fingers. "Ah, levitate! I bet that's what the feather is there for. Clever lass."

Colour rose high on her cheeks. "I didn't do nothin'. You figured it out."

"Well, I *might've* figured it out. We don't know yet," Hale said, weighing the feather in his hand. "Let's try levitating it, though. Maybe you're better at it now than you used to be? Come here and I'll show you."

He heard her shuffling her feet before she asked, "what's your intention?"

The question made his head jerk up. She made it sound like he wanted something not… innocent. What intention would he have but curiosity and wanting to pass the time? Was he missing something here?

"To try something out?" He said, confused. "We're here and so is the feather. So, why not?"

She bit her lip through a sudden smile. "All right then! I reckon the laundry can wait."

She put the basket down by the table and stood next to him. A little closer than necessary, but maybe that gave her some sort of moral support.

"Great," he said. "Now, what you want to do is focus your energy on the feather."

Her face was the very picture of concentration. "Um. All right."

"When you feel your magic taking shape within that focus, see yourself, in your mind I mean, lifting the feather with your magic."

"Yes, that's what I were taught. Never did me much good, though. It rarely worked, I mean."

Hale shrugged. "Things change. Skills can evolve with time. My trainer Ghar always says that he was bad at magic as a child, now he's as good as I am."

"I see," she replied and began staring at the feather. Her face scrunched up and her lips pursed as if she was trying to blow it away.

After a moment, there was a flash of silver at the base of the feather but that was all. Hale searched for words. He had been so sure that she could at least shift it a little.

Eleksander stepped forward. Hale had almost forgotten that he was there.

With a shy smile, Eleksander said, "Sorry, what was your name? Mollie?"

She stopped focusing on the feather and answered, "Myllie, if it pleases."

"Right, *Myllie*, my apologies. Perhaps if you started off with not attempting to lift the feather but merely moving it somewhat? Envision the feather being covered in the silver of your magic and then," he moved his fingers in the air, "being transported the tiniest bit."

Myllie ran a hand over her brow. "I think I might be too tired, milord."

He held up a hand. "No need to call me that. Avelynne is the only one with a title."

Hale was scuffing the tip of his boot on the cobbles, annoyed with himself for not asking the lass' name or starting with something small.

Myllie blinked her long eyelashes a few times. "Surely you're some sort of lord? Your voice, clothes, and the carriage you arrived in, they're all so—"

Whatever she was about to say was cut off by Avelynne coming over to greet them and ask what was happening.

Hale watched Myllie curtsy to her mistress but also give her a smile, one which Avelynne returned, making those dimples appear again.

"Hale was helping Myllie practise her magic," Eleksander explained. "With the use of the objects laid out for our lesson today."

Sabina and Kall joined them with their usual inaudible steps. She was biting off large mouthfuls of an apple. The tart, fresh scent of green apples infused the air, making Hale's stomach growl.

Hale considered the apple trees by the stables. They were filled with crows.

"How did you pick that without disturbing the birds?" he asked.

"Actually, they didn't seem to care one whit; they watched me and Kall without a trace of fear."

Avelynne put her hand on Hale's forearm. "Thank you for helping Myllie."

"What?" Hale drew his attention away from the apple trees. "No need to thank me. She couldn't do it anyway, so I failed."

He didn't wait for replies, too busy striding over to the nearest tree. Could he pick apples for all of them without disturbing the crows? There was a shiny, little one at the top which Avelynne would probably like.

He heard the others talking quietly behind him and, from the corner of his eye, saw Myllie pick up her basket and leave. He grabbed hold of a low hanging branch, noting that the crows did indeed not care.

Strange.

He was about to start pulling himself up into the tree when he heard the unmistakable voice of Tutor Rete call, "Leave the tree alone, Hale. We are about to start our lesson."

While the tutor was busy depositing a set of large metal boxes under the table, Hale rushed back to stand with the others. Avelynne tut-tutted at him and winked. That wink made his stomach flutter.

"Good morrow. Gather round this table," Rete said. "Now, I'm sure you have noted that it has certain objects on it."

They all nodded or hummed their agreement.

Sabina offered Avelynne her apple. Without taking the fruit, Avelynne leaned close and took a tiny bite of the white flesh. Her hand was now on Sabina's, holding the apple in place. The flutter left Hale's belly, replaced by a souring sensation. *He* should have had an apple for her.

Rete leaned his tall frame over the table, both hands flat between the objects. "With the use of these items, I want to assess your magical abilities. We will warm up with some levitation. Lifting this feather should be easy for you considering you passed the choosing tests for the Hall of Explorers." He straightened up. "However, levitating the feather and the dagger at the same time, followed by flitting them about in different directions and using different movements, that might provide a bit of challenge."

"And the other objects? What is in the boxes you brought?" Sabina asked.

Rete's eyes glittered. "You'll see. First, the feather. Who wants to start?"

Hale stepped forward.

"Of course, Young Master Hawthorn," Rete said with a smile. "Your task is to levitate the feather and then the dagger. Make them tumble around each other and when I give the word, throw the dagger at the target by the gate and soar the feather towards the apple trees."

Hale squinted towards the gate. Sure enough, there was a wooden square with a silver beast drawn on it. He'd seen it before and assumed it was target practise for archers.

Then he turned to the tree he'd been about to climb. The crows in it stared at him with grim calm.

"So, the point is to forcefully hit the silver beast drawn on the board and to gently touch the tree without scaring the crows," Hale muttered while still surveying the tree.

Rete fixed that constant high collar of his. "Well done, you sussed it out. Some of the first wave used to fail frequently at this, sending the wrong object at the wrong target. Or using the incorrect amount of force for the task, the feather flying hard and the dagger hovering. Hence why the crows here don't frighten easily, they're jaded."

Hale didn't need to know anything else. He planted his feet, cleared his mind, and levitated first the feather and then the dagger. They felt different in his mind and he tried to keep them separate. This was two tasks, not one. That was all.

"Good. Now tumble them around," Rete said.

Hale did so, making the two strands of magic touch as the objects danced around each other in the air. It was harder to separate them in his mind now. He clenched his fists and focussed harder. The objects kept tumbling, but Rete wasn't telling him to let them loose. Everyone seemed to be holding their breath. Hale was tiring, partly due to the use of magic siphoning his energy, and partly at the strain of keeping the two uses of magic separate in his mind. He was growing impatient too. It was time to act!

Then, a flash of yellow in one of the windows distracted him. Great. He now had to redouble his efforts to maintain this shitty task.

Moments passed in taut silence. Hale wanted to check if Rete had become distracted too and forgotten to give the order to let loose, but he needed to focus on keep the heavy dagger and the light feather in the air. He had to be ready to send them in the right direction with the correct amount of force.

He heard his pulse throbbing in his ears. Louder and louder. Still, not a word from Rete. It wasn't until sweat began to bead on Hale's forehead that Rete shouted, "Now!"

Hale acted. The dagger flew true and hard and hit the board with a thump. When Hale checked on the feather, however, it had landed an arm's length away from the trees. His heart sank.

"Chin up," Rete said. "I've seen much worse first attempts. We will be doing this, and similar exercises, until you can tickle the crows with the feather while carving your name in the wooden target with the dagger. Who's next?"

Avelynne stepped forward, fiddling with her silver necklace. Her skin was suddenly paler than usual. Hale dismissed it with that she was probably afraid of doing worse than he had.

She levitated the objects, tumbled them, and on Rete's command, launched them. Both the dagger and the feather flew through the air like arrows from a bow. The dagger hit the very edge of the target. Meanwhile, the feather struck the nearest apple tree, the tip actually wedging into the bark! The crows all looked down at it and cawed with what sounded more like inconvenience than fear. Humming with amusement, Rete used magic to dislodge the feather and dagger and return them to the table.

Then it was Sabina's turn. She was a picture of concentration and calm throughout the task. The dagger was soon buried in the belly of the sketched silver beast. Nevertheless, she made a mistake too, sending the feather straight up into the air. It then wafted down to land at her feet and she shook her head at it as if it had disappointed her.

"All three of you have at least thrown the dagger correctly, showing that you have respect for lethal objects," Rete said. "Now, Young Master Aetholo. Your turn."

Eleksander took his place by the table with his lips pressed together. He performed the task and... achieved it flawlessly. The dagger hit home, and the feather brushed the tree bark as if caressing it.

Hale was about to congratulate him, but then saw that flash of yellow from the corner of his eye again. Its brightness stood out against the grey and dark green surrounding them. This time he could take a closer look. There was something, no *someone*, moving in one of the windows. He squinted and saw a thin figure, probably a woman, watching them. She'd obviously been there at the start of the lesson and had now returned. Noticing him, she quickly stepped out of view. He shook it off. It was most likely Myllie bunking off work to sneak a peek at Avelynne's progress.

"Excellent work, Eleksander! Now, let's have some more tests so I know where your strengths and weaknesses lie," Rete said.

He made them all mend the broken clay bowl and separate it into five shards, then ten, and finally mend it again. After that, they used the sand to form a perfect square on the table, followed by dissolving the grains of sand again and replacing them into the bag. Not leaving behind a single grain. They all managed, although Avelynne became agitated and took a surprisingly long time with the sand.

Rete clapped his hands. "You all seem drained now so that will be enough for today. You have a drawing lesson soon. However, I will show you one final thing before you go," he said. Any joviality in him was replaced with severity.

"Young Miss Rosenmarck asked what was in the boxes I brought. It's time I show you." He hefted the first box onto the table. "In here is what you'll fight when you have all mastered the trick with the dagger and the feather."

He pulled up one side and, with the screech of metal against metal, it rose to reveal bars. Beyond those bars shone silver. Silver that moved. Hale leaned in with bated breath. It was two silver beasts! Large ones at that. They were climbing over each other inside the box and making the clicking sound they were known for.

Almost under his breath, Hale said, "Shit."

Eleksander's nostrils flared. "You allowed *silver beasts* into the Centre?"

"And such big ones?" Avelynne added in a stunned murmur. "One is the size of my head and the other is not much smaller."

Rete held his head high. "We have only four silver beasts here at the Centre. Two are kept for experiments up in the castle. These two are here for our students to practise on. You are right in that one is bigger, Young Miss Ironhold. But that is only because it has—"

"Wings," she interrupted.

"Exactly. You should be familiar with that version from up in the Peaks. As I said, when you have mastered the feather and dagger task, you will fight these two. However, to display your mastery of magic you are not allowed to kill or badly injure them. Only stun them and place them into the second box."

Hale winced. So that was what it was all about. He had been killing silver beasts since he was knee high. But defeating them without burning, suffocating, piercing, or otherwise damaging them long-term, that would take control. Precisely like the feather and dagger test, he realised. He had spent so many years growing the force of his magic. Now he knew he should've been growing its precision. Oh well, it was a new challenge and that was always a good thing.

Rete closed the hatch with a loud clank. "Now, go to the Great Hall and drink some honey milk to regain your energy after the magic use. Then Tutor Myle will come fetch you for your next lesson."

As they headed inside, Hale could swear he saw that flash of yellow again. Was Myllie still watching them? Surely, she'd be bored by now? He gave it all of a moment's thought before he was distracted by Sabina jostling Eleksander while shouting congratulations and the Lakelander smiling in response. Hale hurried to catch up with them to add his praise for the other lad's magic skills.

Chapter Eleven

THE NOTE

It was near a fortnight later when the first summer rains fell. The sound of it hammering the window pane woke Avelynne. Untroubled by her new wakeup method, she yawned and stretched. Kall stretched as well, watching her from the floor with his keen, turquoise eyes.

Unsure if Sabina was asleep, Avelynne whispered, "Morning kitten."

Over from her bed, Sabina laughed quietly, her voice even raspier than normal from sleep. She rubbed her face and said, "I bet he'd love that you call him that. It means he can get away with behaving like a spoiled baby."

Avelynne reached her hand out and the snowtiger edged forward until he was close enough to lick her fingers with his coarse and strangely dry tongue.

"He *is* a big kitten," she crooned. "He should be spoiled."

"He's not. You'll make him into a terrible beast if you don't stop," Sabina said, the softness in her voice belying the sternness of the words.

Avelynne arched a defiant eyebrow at the other woman, who chuckled and muttered, "Fine. Spoil him. But if he attempts to sit in your lap and eat of your food, I shan't stop him."

"Suits me," Avelynne said before yawning.

Sabina propped herself up on one elbow and observed her roommate. "How did you sleep?"

"Better than usual, actually," Avelynne said, marvelling at that she'd only had *one* nightmare. "I suppose the days of constant training and lessons, not to mention getting used to the new surroundings, has caught up with me. I was never a good sleeper but last night I slumbered like a dormouse nestled in warm moss for most of it."

"Aye, it's probably exhaustion. You do push yourself harder than the rest of us. I see you reading geography books until the candle burns out." Sabina grinned as she added, "or perhaps it's Kall's calming presence."

Avelynne contemplated the possibility of her improved sleep being due to being away from her parents and reminders of the secret they made her keep.

She settled for saying, "Probably. Or yours. Your loud breathing is soothing."

"Hey! Are you saying I snore?"

"No. If that was what I meant, that would have been what I said. You don't snore, you breath deep and loud. It sounds like the waves on the coast of the Peaks. Slowly ebbing and flowing, constant and safe."

Sabina slumped back down, frowning at the ceiling. "It's nice that you think of the sea as something safe. Where I come from it's all lethal ice floes in winter and in summer... chilling, gigantic waves that will force you out and take your life away in the blink of an eye. Beautiful but deadly."

"Sounds like a frightening place to grow up," Avelynne said softly.

Sabina faced her, those usually sky-blue eyes flashing as dark as the winter seas she had spoken of. "You can't be frightened. Instead, you become cautious, sensible even. However, you still have to defy the harsh sea, the piercing cold, the howling winds, and the long sun-starved days of darkness." Her forehead furrowed. "Most of all, you cannot cower away from the fields and mounds of dense, unforgiving snow."

Avelynne thought about the snow back in the Peaks. There it was only heavy on the mountain tops; everywhere else it was a few fingers deep and soon turned into slush and ice. Snow was an inconvenience, not perilous. "So, you attempt to avoid the elements?"

Sabina scowled. "No, that was what I meant by that you cannot cower away from it. The cold sneaks into your clothes, no matter how many furs you wear. The snow blocks your front door. The ice coats the waters that has your main food sources. So, you defy it by adapting and surviving. For example, you drill through the ice of the lake to be able to fish."

"Oh."

"The elements were there before you and will be there after you. Consequently, you try to live with it. You move with the seasons and adapt whenever possible."

"Do you miss it? The North, I mean."

Sabina hummed. "I miss parts of it. I miss the celebration of warmth, the camaraderie, and the richer food and drink. I miss my family." She brushed her thick mass of hair behind her shoulders before adding, "However, I don't miss frost on my eyelashes. Also, it's a lot quieter and calmer here, with kinder, sweeter company." She smiled. "Not to mention that I only need to be responsible for myself and Kall. I'm not being woken by some child screaming about having wet the bed or needing breakfast immediately."

"Eleksander says that Hale constantly talks about the next meal. So in their bedchamber there might be shouts about needing breakfast," Avelynne said pointing towards the door and the young men's room beyond it.

Sabina laughed, that raspy voice making it sound warmer and cosier. Avelynne basked in it, as well as in the joy of having amused her.

"Hale is always shouting about something," Sabina said, her voice now serious. "He frustrated me the other day in the courtyard, cawing loud and endlessly about how he had out-sparred me."

"Mm. At some point we'll have to ask him to be more careful with his words."

"I already have. He only laughed at me. So, I'll leave that up to you in the future. You and Eleksander are better at getting through to him."

"I'll try, then. As soon as a good moment arises."

Kall yawned and Avelynne followed suit. She sat up and stretched, wrenching the last sleep out of her constantly training-fatigued muscles. As she did, her necklace got stuck in her hair.

"Careful there," Sabina said. "It amazes me that you can sleep with jewellery on. Must be the nobility in your blood;

I can barely wear trinkets when I'm awake without hurting myself. Or losing them."

Avelynne disentangled the silver quill and placed it back against the hollow of her throat. "It's just out of habit. I've worn it since I was twelve."

"That's a long time." Sabina chewed her lower lip before adding, "Did you say someone gave it to you? Pardon my forgetfulness, but I think that was on our first day, meaning it's been weeks. And, well, I was quite nervous that day."

"We all were. And yes, that was when I told Hale that it was a quill, not an arrow like he thought, and that my grandmother gave it to me."

"Oh yes, because you loved drawing."

"Mm," Avelynne said, playing with the clasp of the chain.

"It's a lovely gift. I thought you nobles wore jewels and fancy gold, though. Not such simple things?"

"My grandmother knew I didn't like ostentatious objects."

Sabina tilted her head on the pillow. "She clearly meant a lot to you."

"She was…" Avelynne let her hands drop into her lap. "The only person I never had to fight to please. She loved me for who I was, even if I was sad, frightened, or in a bad mood at the time."

"You mean your parents didn't?"

Avelynne gave that a moment's thought. "They loved me when I was what they needed. Unobtrusive when they were in the room. Entertaining when they were bored. And of course, pretty when they wanted me to charm some local lord. Or lady."

Sabina gave a disgusted scoff. "I may have come from a poor family with more children than rooms." She paused. "And my parents might have robbed me of my childhood by making me look after my siblings, but at least they love me."

"I think my parents believe they love me. And each other."

"Well, if that's how they treated you, they're wrong." Sabina propped herself back up on her elbows again. "What's more, they missed out on a lot by only wanting to see certain sides of you. From what I've seen, you're great no matter what mood you're in." She smiled a little. "Actually, I like it when something bothers you so much it breaks through that veneer of civility. I want to see every mood you've got. Bring it on," Sabina said, laying back down and clasping her hands behind her neck. Her face was still turned to Avelynne, though, smiling from ear to ear now.

Avelynne adjusted her hair, trying to hide her embarrassment. "Thank you."

"No need to thank me. I'm only being a decent human being."

There was a noise outside, probably a servant bumping the door. Avelynne might've dismissed the sound, but the flash of silver got her attention. Magic was being used to push something white under the door. Why not simply slide it under? The only reason she could think of was that the messenger didn't want to be seen delivering it.

"Sabina, something's been pushed in under our door."

Avelynne got up, adjusting her nightdress before stepping over Kall's big paws. She picked up the piece of parchment and saw its scrawled words.

Your mission isn't what they say.
Be careful with who you trust. Take nothing as truth.

Sabina sat up. "What is it?"

Avelynne hurried over to her and handed her the note. Sabina read it while Avelynne sat down on the edge of the bed.

Sabina's gaze found hers. "What do they mean by 'Your mission?' Our future as mapmakers?"

Avelynne spun her silver quill between her fingers. "I suppose so. It's the only mission we have."

"And what does 'take nothing as truth' mean? Isn't that a peculiar sentence structure?"

"More importantly, who wrote it?" Avelynne let the necklace drop to her chest. "I wonder…"

Sabina sat closer. "What?"

"A servant at our first dinner in the Great Hall, she mouthed something to me. Something along these lines. I thought I imagined it because I," Avelynne stopped herself from saying anything about guilt or fear, "I was tense."

"Now, however, you think it was real."

"Yes. Perhaps," Avelynne said, staring at the door. "Either way, we have to take it to Tutor Rete."

Sabina chewed her lip. "I'm not certain we should. It said to be careful of who we trust."

"You don't think we can trust Rete?"

"I don't know," Sabina muttered, clearly deep in thought.

"Then what do we do?"

"I think we should keep it to ourselves for now, only showing the boys. Then, we heed the note's warning and stay careful and vigilant."

"Mm," Avelynne said, fussing with the edge of Sabina's blankets.

"Avelynne. Don't let it upset you. It's probably just a joke or perhaps an unhealthy mind at play. Did the servant who mouthed the warning look unhinged?"

Avelynne tried to recall that night. "She looked… anxious. Whether that was due to what she was warning me of or fear that someone would catch her warning me, I couldn't say."

Sabina put her hand over Avelynne's, stopping her fingers from fidgeting with the blankets.

"It'll be all right. I promise you. Let's get washed and dressed, then we'll break our fast with Eleksander and Hale. After that we'll sneak away somewhere to tell them what's happened."

Avelynne took her hand and squeezed it. "Yes, of course."

As per their quickly settled routine, while Avelynne got ready, Sabina stayed in bed, no doubt luxuriating in not having to make breakfast or change sodden beds.

When finished, Avelynne checked her reflection in the small mirror her grandmother had left her. Getting ready without the aid of a maid had taken some adjustment, but now Avelynne found she preferred it this way. It was nice to handle your own affairs, even though she was blessedly not alone. Mere steps away was someone who had become a good friend. One who always laid with her back to Avelynne during the ablutions, to give her some privacy.

Avelynne watched Sabina's sculpted back, covered only by a thin nightdress and her long white hair, with the urge to touch the perfect curves and planes of her. Instead, she watched her breathe. Such slow, steady breaths. In a world where nothing was certain, Sabina was so solid. So strong. So safe. Not to mention warm-hearted and beautiful. She was so utterly, powerfully female that it took Avelynne's breath away.

In the most private and cordoned off corners of Avelynne's mind, there lingered a wish that Sabina would turn to sneak a peek as Avelynne took her nightdress off. She undressed while rolling her eyes at herself.

A surprising side effect of being out of the isolated Iron-hold castle, and the watchful gaze of her parents, was that Avelynne was now surrounded by three people of her own age, each uniquely interesting and charming. They all made her feel appreciated and sometimes even desired. She enjoyed how easily they could all give each other attention and even tentative flirtations, without adults judging or getting involved.

She sighed. And, how wondrous all three of her fellow students were. So smart, so talented, so kind. So, well, *enticing*. Eleksander's pretty features, Hale's strong body, and all of Sabina's magnificent... Avelynne stopped herself as she realised that she was standing frozen by the water jug, staring at her friend with lips parted and heartbeat elevated.

With a grimace, she returned to getting ready. She had an education to think about, a secret to keep, and now these strange warnings to contend with. Attractive fellow students could not be at the forefront of her mind.

Breakfast finally finished, Sabina convinced Eleksander and Hale to join them out in the empty courtyard. The rain had stopped but the air was still heavy with moisture, making the courtyard smell of wet cobblestones as well as the usual scents wafting from the stables and the open windows to the laundry rooms. When they were certain they were not being watched, Avelynne retrieved the note from her pocket and showed it to Hale and Eleksander.

They asked the same questions that Sabina had. Avelynne could only reply with similar questions, before telling them about the server at their first feast in the Great Hall.

Hale furrowed his brow, making a faint scar dip into his eyebrow.

"What are you thinking?" Eleksander asked him.

"I'm thinking that during our first lesson, the magic exercises out in the courtyard, I kept seeing the unusual shade of yellow the servants wear from one of the windows. I thought it was Myllie but…" he paused. "Whoever it was constantly ducked out of eyesight and watched us for much longer than needed. There was something unnerving about it. And trust me, I don't get unnerved easily."

"Could it have been the server I saw at the dinner? Thin, tall young woman? Dark blonde hair?"

"Could've been," he said. "She was far away. I can't be sure."

A window opened above them and Tutor Rete shouted down, "What business have you here? You should all be in your arithmetic lesson with Tutor Hathleen."

"Aye, we were just heading there," Sabina lied.

She drew them away, and as they headed inside, whispered, "I don't think there's much we can do now. We need more to go on. This is probably all some prank on the new students or the work of a madwoman. Either way, stay vigilant and let's keep each other informed."

They all agreed.

"And if anyone sees a tall, thin lass in yellow who acts strangely, try to talk to her!" Hale added. "Now, let's get our arithmetic class over with. After that, Eleksander tells me we've got our first introduction to the navigational instruments we'll one day use on our ship. I can't shitting wait!"

"Or refrain from cursing," Sabina chided with a twinkle in her eye. "I have to admit to being excited too, though."

Just like that, they were on to a new subject. Avelynne reeled at how easy conversation flowed with these three. She put her hand on Kall's steady head as they walked and tried to focus only on Hale nattering on about astrolabes.

Chapter Twelve

RAINSTORM AND INK

Hale stood by the rain-spattered window in his bedroom, arms crossed over his chest. Eight days. Eight shitting days of constant downpours, which were not even warm like back home. No, they were cold and in the form of incessant tiny drops that you couldn't avoid even with the best clothing. Granted, it had also been eight days of interesting lessons and getting to know his fellow recruits better. He was proud of having already gotten quite close to the three of them, all in different ways. Sabina as someone he admired, Eleksander as someone he could trust and Avelynne... He swallowed and closed his eyes.

There was something about her. The way she checked up on them all. The way she always put others before herself. The way she had no idea how captivating she was. Avelynne's charm had so far stopped every burgeoning argument between the three of them and her beauty, well, it kept stealing Hale's attention.

He opened his eyes again. Thinking about Avelynne

wasn't enough to lift his spirits right now though. Not when they were up to eight days of non-stop rain.

He stomped his foot at the hampering weather, glad no one witnessed the childish behaviour. Eleksander had gone for a run in some of the quieter corridors at the back of the building with Sabina. Normally Hale would've loved to join them, but he was too infuriated by the fact that they couldn't run outside. He watched the rainstorm fill the sky. It was ruining the usual calm of twilight. The evening birds sang, as if trying to compete with the pitter patter, but he could barely hear them. These summer rains were as severe as the monsoons in the Woodlands but lasted longer. He was used to putting up with downpours for a few hours and then being fine. Here, the rain had made itself comfortable and decided to drown them all by the looks of it.

Frustrating as silver beast shit.

There was a knock at the door before he heard Avelynne saying, "Hale? May I come in?"

He loosened his arms and turned. "Of course."

She entered with her usual, fluid movements. Her dark hair was behind her ears and her leather jerkin in her hand. His palms grew hot and damp. The white Hall of Explorers tunics suited Avelynne so well and he was glad she wasn't wearing her jerkin to cover it. He had a flashback to how she'd looked on that first day, her elegant and colourful dress outshining everything here. Like a single, bright flower against grey rocks.

He shook his head.

What in the name of the shitting silver beasts! Since when are you interested in what lasses wear? Focus on why she's here. Does she need anything?

He opened his mouth to ask but she got there first. "I hope I'm not interrupting," she said. "I was growing too tired to read and the rain sounds were giving me a headache. So, I thought I'd come here to speak with you instead?"

"Great! I'm standing here grumbling about the rain. I could use the distraction. Ghar always says that whinging gets you nowhere, that it's a waste of breath and time."

"He seems like a clever man. I've only spoken to him a few times, but I like him. May I?" She pointed to the bed. Eleksander's bed. Hale wasn't sure what she meant for a moment.

"Uh? Oh, sit down? Sure."

Gracefully, she moved a pile of books and sat. She barely made a dent in the bed. She couldn't weigh much more than a wet cub.

"Thank you. So, how are you, Hale? Apart from angry at the constant rain. Are you missing your family?"

Hale hesitated between sitting down on the bed next to her or on his own on the other side of the room. As if sensing his thoughts, she patted the spot next to her on the bed.

He sat, at a respectful distance. Then he cleared his throat. "Ghar is the closest thing to family I have. My parents died when I was little."

She jumped. "Oh! I'm so dreadfully sorry! I shouldn't have—"

"No, it's fine. It's not something I bring up, so you weren't to know. I don't remember them. Ghar has told me how they died. Snakebite. He also said that shortly after, that snake was swarmed and eaten by a flock of silver beasts. I guess there is some fairness in this world, huh?"

She examined him. "You speak of it so casually."

He fastened his gaze at a point above her head. "As I said, it was a long time ago."

Slowly, she placed her hand to his cheek, probably to lower his head and get eye contact. It took him a moment to understand that, though. And sadly, it was long after he had flinched away from her touch.

At his lightning-speed withdrawal, Avelynne drew in a sharp breath. "I must apologise once more, I didn't mean to—"

He interrupted her again. "No, I'm sorry. It's just that… I'm not very used to being touched like that. So, um, *softly*. A friendly punch on the shoulder or slap on the back, yes. Maybe even a quick roll in the bushes. But not… like that."

She tensed. Why? Was it because of the "roll in the bushes" thing? Did she expect him to be a virgin? He recalled hearing somewhere that the people in the other counties sometimes waited to take lovers until they were older than twenty. Woodlanders had little time for waiting. After all, you could very likely be eaten, poisoned, lost, or starved to death by tomorrow.

"Ah. Perhaps the touch was inappropriate?" Avelynne asked anxiously. "I'm only used to the way we Peakdwellers often punctuate our dialogue with touch. Or at least the ones at Ironhold castle. I, well, I wasn't allowed much contact with others."

Hale forced his useless tongue to speak. "No. I mean, no, it wasn't inappropriate. If I'd had a family, or even a long-term lover…" He trailed off, hoping she'd understand the rest.

Moments passed. The rain filling the silence.

He took her slim wrist between his thumb and fore-finger and lifted it back to where it had been before he flinched away. When she opened her hand, he leaned into it, placing his cheek against her warm, dry palm.

Her frame relaxed, and those dimples appeared, framing a glittering smile.

Why was his mouth so parched? He tried to swallow to fix it.

"I," he began in a hoarse whisper. "I can't remember the last time someone touched me like this."

"Not even those lovers you rolled with in the bushes?" Avelynne asked with a tentative smirk.

He snorted. "No. Woodsfolk lasses tend to be less gentle than even Woodsfolk lads. They take what they need and then get back to what they were doing. Unless you wed each other, of course."

She nodded, as if something had been confirmed. Then she breathed out, the sound like winds through the trees. He wouldn't have heard it unless he was paying such close attention to her. But how could he not? That velvety hand on his cheek, that gentleness in her eyes. He remembered a word he had heard somewhere a long time ago: spellbound. That was what he was.

"I suppose I'm rather used to being touched," she said. "Myllie, and the other maids, were forever primping and doing touch-ups. Pulling my hair that way and the dress the other." She let her hand drop into her lap. "Then there were my parents, pinching my cheeks to make them rosier, slapping my stomach to remind me to tuck it in, placing a hand at my back to lead me towards some awaiting aristocrat in need of charming."

He grunted with ire, but she carried on as if she hadn't heard him. As if she was just realising these things herself. "All to ensure that I was the face of the House of Ironhold. The prize daughter to adorn the public events and act as a lure for rich merchants hoping to secure a highborn bride." She smiled as if it didn't wound her but even Hale could tell that the smile was fake. He tried to find the right words to say. To explain how shitty that was. He couldn't say shitty. Unfair? Degrading? Ridiculous? It all sounded wrong in his head. In the end he had to settle for, "You're free from that now, though. I mean, you won't only be an ornament or someone's bride. You'll be an explorer! A brave mapmaker who's venturing out to find us all a new home."

"True! Although, I suspect that my parents expect me to return to them when we've found new land. Still with perfect nails and a girlishly trim figure. Ready to act as lure, or what was it you called it, ornament?"

"I'm sorry."

Her eyes went wide. "Don't be! I'm incredibly fortunate. I have lived a life with plenty of food, fine clothing, parents to keep me safe, and servants to cater to my needs. I should not complain."

"Doesn't matter much if no one touches you with nothing but love and tenderness in their intentions, does it?"

Avelynne stared out the window, seeming to watch something far, far away. "My grandmother used to do that.

She used to play with my hair and let me rest my head in her lap."

"She doesn't anymore?"

"She passed away."

"Ah. Sorry."

"Don't be. She had a long life and left few regrets. We should all be so lucky."

"Yes. Hopefully we'll all die old and content. And not on a ship fighting off some four-headed sea serpent."

She laughed. "You strike me as the sort of man who'd rather die with a sword in his hand and a monster to fight, than in a soft bed."

Her laugh injected joy into his bloodstream. "You've got a point."

Silence returned, or as much of it as the rain would allow.

Hale couldn't resist. He moved closer. He didn't know what he was intending with that, other than a need to be close to her. To see her. To get to be in her sphere, feeling the warmth emanating off her skin, the glow of her very presence.

Avelynne must've noticed because she sat back a little and put her hands tightly in her lap. "I wonder if the others have had our problem."

"What? Who?"

"Sabina and Eleksander, of course," she said as if it was obvious. "I wonder if anyone touched them with love."

His head spun from how quickly their intimacy had been shattered, but he hurried to carry on her line of conversation.

"Um, I suppose so."

She gave a curt nod. "Yes, I should say so. Sabina comes from a close, Northern family with lots of children. All needing to huddle for warmth, no doubt. Besides, friendly touch comes easy to her, she must be used to it."

"Yes," he said feebly.

"And Eleksander has that sister who dotes upon him. So much so that she agreed to come here and act as his servant. Even though she doesn't have to. I mean, she washes his clothes. It's not like Ghar does that for you. Or Kall does that for Sabina."

He sat up straight, trying to look casual. "No. True."

Silence again. The rain sounded less like pitter patter now and more like grains of sand pelting the window. Or perhaps that was only in his mind.

A knock and a creak from the door signalled Eleksander's arrival. He was shouting his farewells to Sabina and wiping sweat from his brow.

He startled when he saw Avelynne and Hale on his bed. "Uh. Hello?"

Avelynne stood. "Good evening, Eleksander! So lovely to see you. I've been chatting with Hale to drown out the noise of that rain. Did you have a nice run?"

"Yes! Or rather we did until Sabina barrelled straight into Tutor Myle! He dropped an inkwell. Such a terrible mess! She's gone to get cloths and soap to help him clean up. They said they didn't need my help so I, um, left."

"Probably best," Avelynne said quickly.

Eleksander tugged at his damp tunic. "I needed to clean up. You know what my people are like when it comes to hygiene."

"Yes, no one bathes as often as Lakelanders. Plus, the exhaustion must have you ready for bed," Avelynne agreed. "I, on the other hand, have lots of time and happen to be an expert on cleaning up ink. I'm always dropping my drawing supplies. I shall go lend them a hand."

As she opened the door, she gave them a fleeting smile and said, "See you both tomorrow. Goodnight."

Hale stood. He tried with all of his might to think of something to make her stay, to entice her to keep talking to him. His mind was as blank as a fresh leaf. He had to settle for murmuring, "Sure, goodnight. Thanks for the visit."

She nodded and quietly closed the door.

Thanks for the visit? What a sad excuse for conversation.

From the corner of his eye, he saw Eleksander pull his sweaty tunic off. Was it his imagination or was the other lad casting meaningful glances at him?

"Something the matter?" Hale asked, a little harsher than intended.

"No. Only making sure you're all right."

"The rain is annoying me, otherwise I'm fine."

"I see," Eleksander said, soaking a washcloth.

"I don't do well with being cooped up."

"I know." The Lakelander began washing.

"I'm… I'm going to train for a while."

Without further explanation, Hale began shadow boxing. Aiming blows at the words "thanks for the visit" that he saw in the air before him. And at Avelynne's parents for treating her like that. And at his own parents for leaving him in as feeble a way as death by snakebite.

He couldn't wait for this day to be over. He wanted it to

be morning, so he could sit down to breakfast with Avelynne. And the others, of course. Surely, it wouldn't rain then. He'd be able to be outside without huge drops thrashing his skin and eyes.

Most of all, he wished that his blows into the empty air weren't so… useless.

Chapter Thirteen

HEARTSBANE

Avelynne was surprisingly alert for the day's first lesson. For once, she hadn't been plagued by nightmares. Not that she could remember at least. Kall was sitting next to her chair, staring at her expectantly. She put her quill down and stroked his warm head.

Sabina smiled at them both. "He's going to plonk himself next to you forever if you keep feeding him pieces of chicken like you did this morning."

"That's what Eleksander said too, right before he took the chicken away from me," Avelynne admitted.

"He's a clever man, our Lakelander," Sabina said affectionately. "Where is he, by the way?"

"He wanted to finish his tea. I'm sure he'll be here soon," Hale said.

He was trying to make his stylus stand on its own on the desk. Without any luck. Still, the way the tip of his tongue poked out when he concentrated was cute.

Avelynne had made faces while concentrating as a child. Her mother had taken to pinching the sensitive skin at the side of her neck with her long nails whenever Avelynne grimaced. The Grand Countess claimed it was to stop Avelynne "from becoming even more unattractive."

Funny. She hadn't dwelled on these things so much in the Peaks. But here, so far away and in such different circumstances, memories flooded her mind.

Once, at the age of seven, Avelynne had protested against the pinching. That had led to her being locked in her room for a little over ten weeks, without company or any other food than vegetables and water. Everyone was told that she had a contagious disease and could not come out. After that, Avelynne had very rarely stood up to her mother or father.

She remembered what her grandmother had said whenever holding her tongue became too hard for Avelynne. *One day, sweet blossom, one day you shall be a full-grown woman and you can do as you please and tell your mother what is what. For now, abide and learn how not to treat others.*

With a bang of the door, Eleksander rushed in, barely breathing. "Guess who I just saw!"

"Who?" Avelynne asked.

"I'm pretty sure it was the servant! The one who mouthed the warning to you."

"Tall, thin, and with dark blonde hair?" Avelynne asked.

"Yes! She entered the Great Hall right after you left. She must've thought I'd gone with you. She's definitely avoiding us. As soon as she spotted me, she took off! That's why I think it was the servant you talked about. I followed her for a while but lost her in the winding corridors."

Hale banged his stylus down. "Shitting silver beasts."

"Language!" Sabina growled at him.

He held his hands up. "Sorry, but we were so close."

The door opened again, this time to allow Tutor Rete to stride in with his usual purpose.

"Good morrow, second wave."

"Good morning," they answered.

He was about to say something else when there was a knock on the door. He answered it and was given an old-fashioned scroll by a servant.

"One moment," he said to his students and unrolled it.

His face went from neutral to vexed in seconds. Avelynne tried to see what the scroll said but spotted only one thing: the king's seal.

A vein in Rete's forehead began to throb. He grimaced and tore the scroll in two before placing it in the pocket of his surcoat.

Avelynne caught Sabina's eye and saw her own surprise mirrored.

"Let us get on with the lesson. You may wonder why I asked you to be inside for today's magic lesson. The answer is simple. We're going to study a text by Cartitia Nox on the correct breathing during magic use. Then, and only then, will we practise what she teaches."

"Breathing?" Sabina queried.

Rete took his usual posture, hands clasped behind his back. "Yes. We all know how depleting magic use is. By practising mindful breathing, you can preserve your energy to squeeze in a few more moments of magic use. These breathing techniques can also be used during combat and," he smirked at Sabina and Eleksander, "when you run around the corridors and want to be able to quickly get out of the way of oncoming tutors carrying inkwells."

Sabina coughed to hide her laughter and Eleksander gave the sweetest smile of embarrassment.

Out of the blue came a chilling shriek. Avelynne couldn't pinpoint where it came from but noticed that Sabina and Hale were both staring towards the window.

Without a word, Rete rushed out, his surcoat flapping behind him.

The four of them sat there, sharing uncertain stares.

"He... didn't say we couldn't come along," Avelynne ventured.

As if this was the permission they'd waited for, they all got up and followed Rete out. Kall soon overtook them and, as they came outside, Avelynne saw him sniff the air and make a turn towards the servant quarters. They followed him and when they arrived at the doorway, they saw Rete leaning over something and placing his surcoat over it. It was only when they got closer that Avelynne saw a pair of legs, dressed in that special yellow of Hall of Explorers servant's clothing.

"What... I mean who is it?" Sabina whispered.

Rete turned to them with a perturbed expression. "You came after me?" He sighed. "Of course. You are to be explorers, I should have known you'd follow. It's one of the servants, Thomey. He's worked here the full two years of this institution's existence. He will be sorely missed."

"What happened to him?" Eleksander asked.

Rete put his hand to the doorframe with a pained expression. "He's ingested something lethal. Probably not here though, he must have crawled from one of the rooms." Rete gazed down at the still form under the coat. "From the look of him, it could be heartsbane. I've seen it before. It gives the symptoms Thomey is displaying and is slow acting, which explains why he managed to crawl out here and cry out."

"Heartsbane?" Avelynne asked.

The tutor nodded gravely.

Avelynne hesitated. She hadn't wanted confirmation on what he'd said, she had wanted to be told what heartsbane *was*. Did she dare enquire? Would they think it strange that she didn't already know?

Finally, she decided on who to subtly ask. "Eleksander, what is that?"

"Heartsbane? It's an herb," he whispered back. "It used to be given, in small doses, to quieten hearts that beat too fast, back then it was known as heartshelp. However, it was soon discovered that if you take too much, it continues to slow your heart for hours until it finally... stops it."

"Oh," she said, trying to keep her gaze off the covered body.

He put an arm around her, also averting his eyes. "Exactly. That was why they changed its name and stopped giving it to people."

Rete stood. "I'll have to send someone up to the castle to fetch the physician, not that she can help poor Thomey, but someone has to decide what to do with him. You should all go have some water to calm your nerves and then return to the lesson room. If you wish, you can start to read Nox's text on breathing. I will join you soon."

"As you say," Sabina said in subdued tones.

She clicked her tongue and Kall followed her. As if summoned by the click, the other three traipsed after her too. Avelynne nearly tripped over her own feet in her daze.

A death. Here. She thought this would be the safest place in Cavarra.

Hale leaned closer to the rest of them. "Do you think he took the heartsbane himself? Or was he poisoned?"

"Don't be absurd," Eleksander hissed, a little too emphatically. "Why would someone poison a servant? He must've suffered from a speeding heart and against his physician's advice still taken the herb. Or perhaps he was trying to end his own life. Either way, that herb tastes foul. You cannot sneak it into someone's food or drink."

"Good to know," Hale said.

Sabina opened the door for them and in a low voice said, "Rete is right. We need to take a moment to collect ourselves. Then, we get back to work. We'll hear more about that poor man when they have information to give us. Come on, in you go."

They all obeyed. Avelynne was last and after Sabina had closed the door behind her, the Northerner took her hand and whispered, "It's all right. I'm sure it was an accident."

Avelynne squeezed her hand. "Of course."

That evening, Avelynne's bed creaked as she fidgeted to find a more comfortable reading position. She turned a page and groaned at the book. It was a fairy tale that had been read and loved by many, nevertheless Avelynne found the embossed calfskin it was bound in more impressive than the story.

I should've borrowed that book about mountain-climbing adventurers from Eleksander instead.

However, romantic fairy tales had seemed a better idea after the gruesome shock of the death.

There was a knock on the door and then Myllie came in, without waiting for a reply as usual, a habit that drove Sabina mad. Luckily she was out playing with Kall in the courtyard.

"Good evening, Myllie."

"Hello Countess. What are you readin', there?"

"It's meant to be about a young princess having to take back her throne from a devious goblin. Except, so far it's more about if she should fall in love with the roguish stable boy or the handsome duke."

Myllie chuckled. "And you do so hate a love triangle."

"Yes. I don't know why writers have to do it."

"Ha! Personally, I like 'em. Oh, and the answer has to be the stable boy. He's sure to show her a better time than some dusty nobleman. No offence."

Avelynne sat up. "Myllie, you are hopeless."

She didn't admit that she'd just been wondering why the princess had to choose. Maybe she could have them both. Or neither. That way she could get on with defeating the goblin before the end of the cursed book!

Ignoring the comment, the maid picked up one of Avelynne's tunics and grimaced. "Countess, do you know you've gotten tiger hair on all of your clothes? *All* of them."

"Yes, and I have apologised for that several times," Avelynne murmured, tucking hair behind her ear. "Can we change the topic, please?"

Myllie sat down on the edge of the bed, suddenly wide eyed. "Yes! Perhaps we can talk about that poor man, Thomey. You saw the corpse, didn't you?"

This was the first time in days that Myllie had wanted a longer conversation. The first time in a long while that Avelynne held her interest.

"Yes. Well, the legs at least," she answered, her stomach turning. "And can we not call it a corpse? It sounds awful."

"Of course, Countess. Is 'body' better?"

"I suppose so," Avelynne said quietly.

Myllie leaned in and said, "I heard it wasn't suicide! Nor an accident. The other servants say that he wasn't ill or feelin' sad. The head cook claims it was a crime of passion. Meanwhile one of the stableboys is sure Thomey was some sort of spy for the king and got found out! Such a spectacle!"

"Do you have to be quite so excited about this? It's awful."

Myllie's lips pursed. "Mm. As you say. I should be gettin' down to the laundry anyway." She left the room with a deep bow, something she hadn't done for years.

I shouldn't have reprimanded her.

With a hand on her uneasy stomach, Avelynne dropped the book and went to the window. In the courtyard, Eleksander and Hale had joined Sabina in playing with Kall. They took turns throwing or kicking a ball to him and he batted it back, looking more like an overgrown kitten than a one of Cavarra's most vicious predators.

Sabina and Hale were both shouting things over at Eleksander, seeming to compete over who could make him laugh the most. His laugh was as infectious as it was rare. He tossed the ball towards Kall, but as he was laughing so hard he rolled it off course and Kall had to hunt after it. Avelynne noted that Eleksander wasn't slouching now, he was moving and standing to his full height and width. Like this, his shape was as impressive as that of the powerful snowtiger. They were all laughing now, to the point where all three were wiping their eyes. What was the joke?

Avelynne wrapped her arms around herself. It wasn't only the physical distance that separated her from them. Her cursed secret marked her as different as it sunk her into self-loathing and fear. How could she ever deserve to be with them? She took a shaky breath and closed her eyes. She couldn't watch them anymore, couldn't let her mind drone on about how she wasn't one of them, but had been left with no choice but to pretend. Her duty was to keep the Peaks safe. No matter how that made her feel.

Fraud. Liar. Inadequate.

With sluggish movements, she returned to her book, fairly certain that the princess was going to choose the dusty duke.

Chapter Fourteen

THROWAWAY

Hale noted a new bruise on his arm. Did he get it during sparring? Or last night when they played with Kall? He left the bruise alone. Its origins mattered not. What did, was what was happening now.

They were at their desks, waiting for Tutor Myle to arrive for their cartography lesson. Maps. Maps. Endless maps. Hale was growing impatient with drawing markers and calculating distances, and that was before he even had to prepare for tests on his knowledge in year two! All this painstaking practise before he could brave the seas and find something to actually map.

The upcoming lesson might not be very diverting, but their current conversation was.

It started sad, with talk of Thomey's death, dealing with shocks, and who had seen a dead body before; everyone but Eleksander had. Now they were discussing other things they had or hadn't experienced.

Hale had just made them all turn queasy by describing

how he'd learned to use vines to leap from tall tree to tall tree when he was five.

"Sounds dangerous but fun," Sabina said. "Say, have any of you ever had blue rash?"

Avelynne made a face. "Is that the little blue, raised bumps that itch something terrible?"

"Aye, the very same," Sabina said with a grin.

Avelynne's grimace deepened. "Yes. I had them six years ago. I was so covered I could've been bathing in blue ink. I've never experienced such a burning itch before or after."

Sabina pointed to Avelynne. "Oh, speaking of blue ink! We should have a moment before Tutor Myle arrives, fancy fetching that ultramarine ink you wanted to borrow for the lakes on your maps? It's in our room."

Avelynne peered around, as if expecting Myle to be hiding in the pile of firewood or something. "Yes, as long as we make haste."

"Come along then, I'll show you. Hale, Eleksander... We'll be right back."

With that the two lasses stole away. Hale watched them go with grumpiness souring his stomach.

Eleksander sat back with an amused expression. "Any particular reason you look like a knight whose armour has melted?"

Hale quickly tried to think of a reason for his bad mood which didn't make him sound like a jealous lover or a nipper not allowed to play with the other children.

"I suppose I'm not looking forward to another couple of hours drawing maps."

"Why not?"

Hale shrugged. "I'm bored of it. Also, I suspect I'm not as good at it as the rest of you."

"Nonsense. You're far too hard on yourself."

"That's the only way to excel."

"Not if it means you never allow yourself to rest. Or never allow yourself to accept that you cannot be perfect," Eleksander said with a delicate smile.

"You're near perfection in all our lessons," Hale countered, unable to keep irritation out of his voice.

"In these subjects, yes. However, I was terrible at history and grammar. I'm fortunate that our education here happens to focus upon the subjects I've always excelled at."

Hale poked at that new bruise on his arm. "Sure."

"Don't do that."

"Do what?"

"Shut down. Look at me, Hale. It's only us here."

Hale connected their gazes. "So?"

"So, I think I know what's bothering you."

Hale gave a dead scoff. "Everything bothers me at one point or another."

"That's not true. Yes, you have a temper, but you take a lot of joy in things. Your enthusiasm and love for what interests you makes you radiant."

"Lad, did you just call me... *radiant*?"

Eleksander cleared his throat. "Never mind that. What I mean is that you keep being too hard on yourself, both regarding lessons and your embarrassment over your temper. You expect too much of yourself."

Hale crossed his arms over his chest. "Well then, Young

Master expert. You said you knew what was bothering me, before. Let's hear it."

Eleksander hesitated. "As you wish. Do you recall an evening about a week ago when neither of us could sleep due to the loud rainstorm, so we laid there chatting in the dark?"

"Sounds like quite a few nights lately."

"True. However, during this conversation you mentioned your childhood. Growing up without your parents or any set guardians."

The memory clicked into place. He'd been so sleepy that night and words had trickled out far too easily. "Sure, I was raised by all the adults around me in Whispering Willows. As much as they had time for. The rest of the time, I sort of raised myself. What about it?"

Eleksander bit his lip. "Well… There was a throwaway comment about wanting to prove to everyone in the Whispering Willows that you were going to be someone great and important one day. That you were more than an unwanted orphan. Remember that?"

Hale scratched the back of his neck. Had he really said that? Had he really admitted to that?

He tried to loosen his shoulders and look at ease. "Right. Sure. You know, I'm impressed you remember that."

"I try to remember everything about you, and do quite well at it. Maybe more than I should." Eleksander paused to run a hand over that good-looking face of his. "Anyway, that comment seemed important. I think it indicated that you're trying to prove your worth. You want to demonstrate that you deserved the parents that life took away from you. That you deserved unconditional love, from people who weren't random citizens showing charity by giving you some of their time, but who were, well, *yours*."

There was a muscle jerking in Hale's jaw. He couldn't still it. It twitched faster and faster. "That's, um, deep. I'm really not that complicated, you know."

Eleksander's features saddened. "Yes, you are. What's more, I think that throwaway comment explains why you're so hard on yourself. You're trying to prove to everyone around, and I'm including yourself in that, that you deserve to be loved and wanted."

Hale forced a laugh. He had to break the seriousness. "Pfft. Who'd waste precious emotions like that on a hopeless oaf like me?"

"I would."

Hale's laughter halted. He sat there, without a clue what to answer.

"Let me c-clarify," Eleksander stuttered. "I mean that I want you on my team. In my life. As my friend. Although, I believe I shall feel even stronger for you in the future as we live together." He smiled a little. "And you know… eat, train, sleep, study, and then the tiny chore of operating an untested ship in unchartered waters and, therefore, risking our lives together!"

"Not to mention trying to make sure Kall doesn't eat us if we run low on food stores," Hale added.

They shared a chortle at that before Eleksander rounded up with, "I've never met anyone like you and I want to get to know you. You don't have to work yourself to the bone to earn that, just being *yourself* makes me choose to be around you."

Hale averted his gaze, unable to maintain eye contact

for a moment longer. He'd never thought that this academy would give him friends that would say something like that. If he was honest, he'd never thought anyone would say something like that to him anywhere. Did people from the other counties always speak of their emotions so easily? And after only a *couple of weeks*? Avelynne, Eleksander, and Sabina all appeared able to do it without feeling as if the words were skinning them alive. How did speech like that simply leave their mouths as if they weren't baring themselves with every syllable?

Maybe it wasn't about different cultures. Perhaps Hale had simply had the fortune of entering into a team of people who were abnormally loving and kind. He had no idea how he'd deserved such luck. Nonetheless, he would make the most of it. He'd protect these warm-hearted people. He'd carry them through the harshest storms and biggest waves if need be.

He forced his useless brain to find some words for the now clearly anxious Eleksander.

"Talking about wanting me like that. I... Wow."

Eleksander fiddled with his earlobe, gaze down on his boots. "It's not such a big deal, really. I suppose," He tugged his earlobe harder, "I suppose witnessing what happened to Thomey—seeing how death can strike at any time, no matter your age or health-levels—it's a reminder to say what's on your mind and in your heart. Before it's too late. Especially for us who have such an uncertain future."

"Still. I'm blown away. I didn't know you were..." he trailed off, trying to find words that weren't too sappy.

For some reason, the other lad panicked then, so Hale hurried to finish the sentence. "... such a great friend."

Eleksander relaxed visibly. What had he thought Hale was going to say just then? Strange.

Hale reached out and slapped him on the arm. "Even if you are a spoiled, soft-hearted Lakelander-coin-bag who's far too tall and big for his own good."

Eleksander guffawed. "You *had* to make it into a joke, didn't you?"

Hale held his arms out wide. "I told you. Hopeless oaf."

"I wouldn't have you any other way."

The door opened and the lasses returned, winded and giggling. Avelynne held up the inkwell with a victorious squeal.

Eleksander laughed again. "Honestly, I have never met anyone who made such a fuss over ink."

Avelynne and Sabina barely had time to return to their desks before Tutor Myle came in, adjusting his cloak and primping his pretty hair.

"Apologies for my tardiness. I had to send a missive by carrier pigeon and the cursed animal wouldn't behave for me. Fetch some parchment and let's begin with our lesson."

They did as he asked. Hale moved automatically, his body doing what he expected it to as always. His mind, however, was on Eleksander's words. How much could that soft-hearted... no... *perceptive* lad read into his behaviour and speech? Hale stared at the other's broad back, wishing he could see through the Lakelander as easily as Eleksander saw through him.

Just then, Eleksander turned a little. Their gaze connected again. Hale was hot and cold at the same time. He had to fight not to crumple the piece of parchment in his hand.

There was something strange about being truly... seen.

He brushed the whole thing off and focused on his parchment. There was work to be done.

No matter what Eleksander said, no matter what that sweet-hearted dreamer thought of the world, Hale had to improve. He had to be the best at this and their other subjects. He must put more blood, sweat, and tears in. He had to try until he either excelled or died trying.

Chapter Fifteen

DAGGERS AND LIMITATIONS

Avelynne shut her eyes against the late night's harsh winds. Sabina and Eleksander had gone to bed while Hale played cards with that gruff mentor of his, Ghar, in the servant quarters. The only one out here in the windblown courtyard was Avelynne. She saw no other way to get some practice in without witnesses to her ineptitude.

Luckily, the armoury hadn't been locked, allowing her to fetch two daggers. She had considered swordplay, archery, spear-throwing, or even working on her axe work. However, she was mindful of the clatter that came with fetching the bigger weapons. It was silly of course. No matter what weaponries she chose, there was a big chance someone would hear or see her, but at least then she would've gotten a throw or two in before anyone could stop her.

Now she weighed the two slim daggers in her hands. They had the Hall of Explorers emblem on the hilts. They were also heavier than they had any right to be. The latter detail however, was sure to be all in her head.

She fixed her feet and summoned her magic. It enclosed

one of the daggers and she used it to propel the blade at a training dummy some distance away. It found its mark but only with a very small margin.

Avelynne whinged up at the stars. They merely twinkled back in infinite silence.

She took the correct grip of the other dagger and this time threw it by hand towards the dummy. That was even worse. She missed and hit the stone wall behind it. The noise seemed to echo through her bones and fill every part of her with shame.

With the use of magic, she retrieved the two knives. She squinted hard at the dummy, not because of the dim lantern light, but to focus to her fullest ability. This time she would do better. She steadied herself, tossed one of the daggers and actually hit the target! However, the throw had not been powerful enough to penetrate, meaning that the weapon simply smashed into the dummy and fell unto the flag-stones below.

Another clanging noise. Another bout of shame.

She looked around but found no prying eyes or laughing spectators.

Thank the stars I picked the training dummy furthest away from the gate, she mused. The gate was always manned by guards, who tended to be both vigilant and jeering.

She grabbed the remaining knife and held her breath as she launched it. It hit the dummy but only at the very bottom of it. Avelynne wanted to scream. Instead she looked up at the stars again until she was calm. Then she retrieved the daggers by the use of magic.

She was about to make another attempt when she heard voices. Not the unruffled, weary voices of the guards, but loud and brash male voices that sounded too cheerful for the quiet courtyard. It was Tutor Rete, Tutor Myle, and Tutor Rogan. They were stumbling about the vast space as if drunk or dizzy. Considering the laughing and the late hour, Avelynne assumed inebriation was a more likely choice.

Spotting her, Rogan shouted out, "What are you doing there?"

"Good evening. I'm only practising a little," she called back, hoping they wouldn't be angry that she smuggled out the knives.

Rogan clutched his tree-trunk of a middle. "Ha! What's the point? You were not built for physical endeavours. I cannot say what you *were* built for, come to think of it."

During his taunt, he and the other two had come closer. Myle, who seemed the worst for wear of them, wore a pitying expression as he slurred, "Drawing. The young Countess excels at that! Perhaps you should keep to that, dear?"

Avelynne clenched her fists. "I believe I need to master all the subjects to pass the tests in year two. Surely you won't let me sail at the end of my education otherwise?"

That gave her pause. What would happen if one of them failed their tests? Or if they were slain or taken seriously ill? No one had mentioned that. Strange. She knew that the plan was to constantly train more students to have several teams to fall back on if need be. Otherwise, why would there even have been a second wave? Or indeed the third wave, which would begin lessons next year. However, she'd never considered what would happen if an individual was taken out of play. Would the second wave sail without her? Was the idea to have four of them so that if some failed or were lost, there would still be a mapmaker captaining the mission? Now wasn't the time to enquire, considering how drunk these three were. She was sure to be told in lessons when it became relevant.

With lumbering movements, Rete corrected his high collar. "Don't listen to these louts. We have been entertained by the king up at the castle and had a little too much of the fine, royal wine. We should have followed Atha's example and left early."

Atha? Oh yes, Tutor Santorine.

"Well, you seem to have had a good time," Avelynne answered, as politely as she could.

"Yes, yes. Never mind that. Heed my advice, don't listen to these two. Practising is what will improve your skills." Rete stopped and observed her for a moment in a comical squint. To see through his alcoholic haze, no doubt. "You know, I believe what *you* need, even more than practice, is confidence and conviction."

Rogan scoffed but Rete spoke over him. "You can have as much aim and technique as you wish, without the conf-conw-conviction to drive your arm and the confidence to believe you will strike true, you won't improve much."

Avelynne didn't know what to say to that. She would happily have more confidence and conviction, but how did you get those things? Were others simply born with them? Or did they somehow acquire those skills?

"Yes. Yes. Confidence and conviction are both needed for explorers," Rete slurred up to the stars. He really was inebriated.

Avelynne scrambled for a reply. "I'm sure they are. I shall try to be the exemplary second wave student everyone at the Hall of Explorers, and King Lothiam of course, expect me to be."

Rete's gaze snapped to hers. "The king? Oh, that imperious swine cannot always get what he expects. What he *wants*."

"Here we go again," Myle said with a nervous titter. "Too much drink always makes you indiscreet in regard to the king, Hason."

Rete's eyes, still trained on Avelynne, flashed. "Do not be one of those who follow orders blindly. Question things. Stay true to yourself, girl, and don't give those who abuse and plunder what they want. Or what they expect of you."

Avelynne took a step back. She couldn't understand how they'd gone from drunken discussions about her dagger throwing to… whatever this loaded peculiarity was.

"We cannot always get what we want. Not the king. Not I. Not the Hall of Explorers officials. Not you. Dear Thomey certainly couldn't. Poor, beautiful Thomey," Rete mumbled, eyes glazing over.

He was about to say something else, but Rogan yanked on his sleeve. "Come on Hason, no more railing against the king or this barmy treasonous babble. You promised us some of your secret stash of booze."

They wandered off, leaving Avelynne bewildered. Then she remembered her parents' drunken ramblings after tournaments and revelries throughout the years and dismissed Rete's strangeness. She had to focus on her daggers. She'd give herself two more throws. Then she had to sleep. Then she had to give up.

Chapter Sixteen

FRIENDS AND MAGIC

Days passed without any new strange occurrences. That had relaxed the others. Hale, however, stayed vigilant. Partly for his own sake, but more due to feeling responsible for his new team. Not because they couldn't look after themselves, but because they had come to mean so much to him.

Meanwhile, the lessons were getting harder by the day. He couldn't imagine what they would be like when they broke for Winter Solstice in a few months. For now, the start of autumn lingered right out of reach and Hale wished he'd be allowed to see the slight shifts of nature happening each and every day, instead of being cooped up here.

At least he had finished his morning meal and was on his way outside for another magic lesson. By now, they'd all managed the dagger and feather test. Rete said that it had taken the first wave students almost twice as long to master it.

Hale laid the pride aside and focused on what this meant. Today they would surely get to fight the silver beasts!

"What are you smiling at?" Eleksander asked as they strode towards the entrance to the courtyard.

Hale put a hand on the taller lad's shoulder. "I think Rete's going to let us battle the silver beasts this morning."

Eleksander's shoulder tensed, something which had never happened before when Hale had touched him. In fact, he always relaxed into any touch Hale offered. More than that, he'd sought out physical closeness whenever possible. This tensing was new.

"Filthy fiends," Eleksander growled. "The best thing about the Centre was that I thought it devoid of the little monsters. They plague our nation and the Hall of Explorers keep some as *pets*?"

"Hardly as pets," Hale squeezed his shoulder, "More like target practice."

"Yes, but we're not allowed to kill them."

Hale blinked at the rage in Eleksander's voice. "No, if we did, they'd have to find new silver beasts for every lesson. Besides, we're meant to learn control, Lakelander. To incapacitate instead of killing. It'll come in handy when we meet creatures in new lands."

Eleksander's jaw looked set like a sprung trap. "Tolerance and control are necessary when we meet others, since we don't know if they're friend or foe. Silver beasts are foes."

"True," Hale mumbled, letting go of his shoulder.

He wasn't sure what to say. The weeks here had brought him close to Eleksander, but he still hadn't found a way to handle it when the other lad became like this. On subjects as colonisation or the silver beasts, his friend would become unreachable in his ire. Hale never had the right words to calm him, only Avelynne could achieve that.

Avelynne.

She may be weaker in most of their classes, especially arithmetic, but she was far better at manoeuvring all of their strong personalities. She always knew what to say. When to give someone their time alone or when to offer support. Or hugs. She was excellent at those. That amazing blood-red hair of hers smelled of night blossoms and her body softly slotted into any embrace.

"You're smiling like a deranged ape again," Eleksander sniped from his side.

"Sorry. Only thinking of the new friends I've made here."

Eleksander huffed a breath out through his nose. "Ugh. A certain one more than the rest of us, I'd wager."

"What do you mean?"

"Never mind." Eleksander pointed out into the courtyard. "Rete and the ladies are already out there, let's hurry."

They picked up the pace and were soon out in the pallid morning light.

"Good morrow. Nice of you to tear yourselves away from your breakfast," Rete said with a sniff.

"Sorry for the delay. That apple and cinnamon compote was far too delicious to scoff too quickly," Hale joked.

Sabina moaned, and Rete looked unamused. Eleksander was still sulking. Only Avelynne braved a smile at his comment.

"Be that as it may, Young Master Hawthorn, we have work to tend to. As you all mastered the task of the dagger and the feather last lesson, I have stayed true to my word and brought the silver beasts for you to fight."

Avelynne gave a small gasp, making Eleksander place a hand on her lower back.

Rete ignored it and continued. "I do not need to point out the large amounts of trust I am putting in you. There has never been a silver beast loose in the Hall of Explorers."

He locked eyes with each one of them in turn. The tension filled the courtyard, pressing against the sides of the buildings.

Hale's gaze was pulled to the metal box on the table. Was it moving ever so slightly? Surely it was too heavy for the creatures to knock over?

Excitement rushed in his blood.

"Remember the rules: you render it unconscious or trap it in place," Rete said. "You do not kill it or maim it beyond recovery. What would you say are ways to achieve that, students?"

Sabina was staring at the box as well as she murmured, "Knock the beast about until it passes out."

Rete inclined his head. "That is a viable solution. As long as you only use magic. I don't want to see you kicking it or getting your snowtiger to swipe at it. Any other suggestions?"

"You said it yourself earlier, Tutor Rete. We can trap it," Avelynne said.

"Exactly, Young Miss Ironhold. Use your magic to make a cage to enclose it in. Or perhaps a rope to bind it to the table."

"It's *Countess*, actually," Sabina whispered so only the four students could hear it. Avelynne playfully slapped her on the hip.

Hale had to admit that it was a pretty good impression

of Myllie. And it was nice to have some of the tension broken. If only he'd have thought of that.

"Are we all still paying attention?" Rete asked.

Ignoring the question, Eleksander said, "what if we hit it too hard and it accidentally dies?"

The way he was staring at the metal box made Hale doubt that any death would be an "accident".

"That depends on if I deem it a true accident, carelessness, or… something else," Rete said, clearly thinking along the same lines as Hale. "But I am certain we will have no such mishaps. You are a clever and magically talented group, I have faith in you. In fact, I believe you to be more promising than the first wave. Obviously, do not tell them that."

He didn't look as if he was joking. In fact, he seemed to be wanting to say something further but stopping himself. Huh. What could that be? He would have to ask Avelynne later.

"Now, unless there are more questions," Rete said, pausing. "I should like my first volunteer to step forward."

Eleksander advanced. "Let's get this over with," he said through clenched teeth.

"As you wish," Rete said. "As this is your first attempt, I shall let only one beast out at a time. Remember, one of them flies."

With that, he pulled up the box's side and then the cage bars in quick succession. In the blink of an eye, one of the silver beasts forced itself out. Rete shut the box behind it with a snap.

The beast crawled fast along the table's surface, making

its eerie clicking sound and baring its needle-teeth. No wings.

Good. Save the trickier one for me!

Eleksander waved his hand and a flow of magic emanated from it, swiping the huge silver beetle off the table and onto the ground. It landed on its back and flapped its legs around in the air for a moment. Then it was on its feet again. Had Rete stealthily turned it? Or could they right themselves now?

It scurried towards them, attracted to Eleksander's magic. Or perhaps ready to retaliate.

Eleksander flung another silvery burst from his hand and this time it was forceful enough to toss the beetle towards the closed door behind it. The creature smacked into the wood and then limply slid down.

Hale saw Eleksander raise his hand again, ready to give the beast another dose. Possibly a lethal one? As subtly as he could, he reached over and put his hand on Eleksander's arm.

It worked. The Lakelander dropped his hand and took a deep breath. Hale gave his arm a squeeze and then let go.

Rete stepped over, carefully. He had a bottle of water and now he poured some on the beast. It awoke and headed towards Eleksander again. Its maw opened and worked soundlessly, unless you counted the sound of the spiky teeth snapping together. Was that what their clicking sound was? No, of course not. Hale had heard them make that unnerving sound even if one was lucky enough to knock their teeth out. It was something deep inside the beasts, clicking and tinkling.

"Now would be a good time for the next student to have a try," Rete shouted.

Despite having wanted a go at the winged beast, Hale didn't hesitate. He extended a hand and made his magic form a rope. With circling motions from his fingers, he bound the magic around the struggling fiend until it was still. It bit at the magic, trying to devour the silvery energy. But Hale kept up the flow of magic from his fingertips, overwhelming the creature and squeezing it in place.

"Good work, Young Master Hawthorn," Rete called. "It's defeated. Now, I have a second box here, place the beast inside it."

Hale transported the squirming, clicking beetle along the ground. It almost ate through the magic twice, and he had to redouble the squeeze of the magic to take the beast's breath away enough to stun it. When it was inside the box, Rete shut the flap and gave Hale a smile.

"There we are. That one can have a little rest now to recover. We'll let the ladies handle our flying friend."

With that, Rete turned to Avelynne. "Flying silver beasts is all you have in the Peaks, is it not? This should make you feel right at home. Would you like to start?"

Avelynne hesitated and Hale began thinking of ways to help her without anyone noticing.

Then she cracked her neck. "I'm ready," she said, raising her hands while staring wildly at the box.

Chapter Seventeen

FIGHTING THE SILVER BEASTS

Avelynne tried to keep her breathing steady and her outreached hands even steadier. Everything would be fine. She could get through this without revealing her secret or making a fool of herself.

Her hands trembled.

Rete once more opened the box. This time a streak of silver took to the skies. Avelynne's gaze followed its ascent towards the apple trees and their rotting fruit. Did it desire a snack, or it was heading there to escape? Either way, the crows were not amused, they cawed at the bigger creature, spreading their wings and parting their beaks as if ready to attack. Could the fiend be aiming to eat the crows?

All silver beasts had started as insects of some kind, beetles, cockroaches, spiders. By the look of it, this one must have been a butterfly, no wait, a *moth*. Now it was a large mass of razor-sharp teeth, hard skin, and destructive metal wings.

Avelynne tensed her muscles, trying to ignore that she was overheating. It seemed wrong to attack something that wasn't assaulting her. She reminded herself that it was only a matter of time before it came for her.

Hurry!

The eyes of the others burned on her skin and time was slipping away. She launched a shapeless volley of magic at it. It missed. Her pulse picked up a little more.

She tried again and this time the fiend turned in mid-air, drawn to the magic. Now she could hit it and she didn't miss her chance, with a scream she launched so much magic at the beast that the courtyard lit up and the creature was slammed into a tree. The silver beast dropped to the ground, motionless.

Finally.

Avelynne sank to her knees. That had taken as much energy as when she'd last gone for a long run with Sabina. No, much more. With the panic and adrenaline leaving her body, she wished for sleep. For a moment, her eyes fluttered closed. Then they flew open when she heard a terrible sound she had heard before: a silver beast gorging itself on magic.

This was always the risk of battling silver beasts with magic. It was the easiest way to fight them as it took a lot for weapons to penetrate that thick silver hide, but these animals lived off magic as much as they did food. What is more, if they managed to ingest the magic, it made them stronger. And sometimes… bigger. Before Avelynne's eyes, the limp beast sucked the magic in and glowed almost white before swelling. It wasn't much, only a few fingers of girth in either direction. Nevertheless, it made a difference. The beast would now be bigger and that meant it was probably more powerful. Sharper bite, thicker skin, more energy. While she, well, she was weaker.

Avelynne wanted to shriek but lacked the energy. She had spent all this time at the academy trying to keep her secret, but now it would spill out. And her lifeblood with it.

Don't be ridiculous. Your tutor won't let you die.

Avelynne lifted her heavy arms and extended her hands. She had to fire more magic at the fiend before it got back up and went for her. Her hands trembled worse than ever.

No, Rete won't let you die. It takes a long time before a silver beast kills a grownup, even a weakened one.

Nevertheless, accidents happen. Limbs get bitten off. Faces get mauled beyond recognition. Her trembling spread to her heart, the very core of her seeming to quiver.

If it bites the column of the throat… will it kill me before Rete can intervene?

She glanced to him.

He bored his eyes into her, "Get up, Avelynne. I know you're tired, but you will feel worse after months at sea. You need to learn to fight under the toughest conditions. One day you might face a kraken or an army of foreign soldiers. A silver beast, even if it is high on fresh magic, is nothing in comparison. Stand up. Take your stance."

Shakily, she got to her feet. Her body was heavy, as if she was moving through treacle. She had to summon up some energy from somewhere. She couldn't let them see what she was really like. She had to fight. But how?

Her brain didn't seem to keep up with her eyes, she saw Sabina step towards her and Hale shifting his footing, as if in slow motion.

Wake up!

The panic was setting in, meaning that the adrenaline was pouring into her blood. But it wasn't enough to clear her exhausted mind. Her body thrummed with the wish to fight or flee but her anxious brain struggled with making decisions. She shook her head to clear it but only made herself dizzy. When should she strike the beast? And how? Another volley of unprepared magic? Or that rope thing that Hale had done? What would be best? What was Rete expecting her to do? Why was everything suddenly so confusing?

The beast was crawling around on the ground, still groggy, still glowing with magic. It clicked menacingly with every step.

Do something. Anything!

Its teeth glowed white as well. Were they growing too? Were they sharpening? Soon, the creature found its footing and it seemed enraged.

One heartbeat of silence. Then it flew right at Avelynne.

Chapter Eighteen

A DIFFERENT KIND OF FIGHT

Hale gritted his teeth with burning frustration. Wasn't there a way he could make Avelynne fight? Make her react faster? Wake her up!

The beast was all but upon her. Rete's hand was raising, as if to intervene. Hale's gaze flitted from Avelynne to Rete and back again.

Come on Avelynne. Try again!

His heart seemed to be in his throat and his hands clenched into such tight fists that it hurt. Avelynne's eyes were unfocused and her hands barely held up in defence.

At eye level now, the silver beast opened its mouth and those knife-point teeth were exposed. Avelynne yelped and…

Sabina stepped into the silver beast's path and thrust a large stream of magic towards it. The magic shaped into a cage with thick, silvery bars around the beast, enclosing it. The beast tried to bite at the magic, but every time it did, Sabina shook the cage and it lost its grip.

Hale wanted to roar and clap his hands. Then he saw

Rete's stern face. Was Sabina going to get in trouble for intervening? After all, Avelynne *had* defeated the beast. It wasn't her fault that it managed to revive itself by eating up all that residual magic. That was just bad luck.

Hale was distracted by the beating of hooves from the gate. A man called, "Make way for the king!"

The man was a flagbearer, flying the scarlet and gold royal banner high and proud. Behind him, doublet-clad riders surrounded a thickset man on the biggest Woodlands stallion Hale had ever seen. Seeing the horse of his people made his chest ache with homesickness. Its auburn coat gleamed even more than the gemmed and gilt livery and saddles of the king's following. The whole showy entourage stopped at the entrance of the courtyard. The king was helped off the sleek stallion and then strode towards them with two of his men at his heels.

"Ah, I see I am late to the show," he boomed. "Seems this litter of young explorers have already attacked their first foes successfully."

Hale followed his gaze up to the beast that Sabina still held caged in the air. The words "show" and "litter" niggled at Hale. He noticed the others, Rete included, bowing. After a moment, he remembered that he had to do so too. No one in the Woodlands would bow or curtsy to their Warden. He or she was merely someone that was elected to speak for the Woodsfolk, not one to be worshipped or fawned over. The King of Cavarra was different. Ruler of all, and *everyone*, he saw. Hale bowed, hiding his pursed lips by staring down.

Distracted by her bowing and the shock of meeting her king, Sabina nearly lost control of the silver beast. Hale heard it chewing at its cage and abandoned his bowing. The beast was squirming and getting noisier by the moment.

Rete reached out with his magic, grabbed the creature and then quickly boxed it up. There was a look on the tutor's face. Was that disgust? Dislike? Of what? The silver beast? The king?

The monarch held out his meaty hands. "So, you are the second wave? I have seen your names and backgrounds on paper, but it is always different to see people in the flesh."

He raked his hooded eyes over them individually. "You all appear to be strong and hearty young people. Good, that's what Cavarra needs. More importantly, it's what your monarch expects of you."

Hale didn't know what to say. None of the others replied either. From the corner of his eye, he saw Eleksander supporting Avelynne.

"Such a shame I missed the little tussle," The king said. "Oh well, I'm sure you get to play with the pests again soon enough. And after that, you can all go show your villages how you deal with these beasts."

King Lothiam guffawed, and his men soon joined in.

Hale muttered, "We know how to deal with them. We just don't have a private army and the most advanced weapons and magic users in the land to do it for us. Like you do."

The king's eyes flashed. Then his face split into a cruel grin. "Oh my... Listen to the snapping little Woodlander mutt," he bellowed. "Perhaps you should go chase a rabbit for your esteemed ruler's dinner and leave silver beast fighting to civilized men."

The king and his entourage cackled once more.

Hale stopped dead. *What did that sniggering satchel of shit just say to me?*

His brain whirred, trying to come up with something to say or do when royalty taunted you. Unsure of what he was going to do, Hale surged forward.

Sabina put her hand on his chest to stop him, but her face mirrored his own irritation at the king's words. The same emotion seemed to fill the snowtiger, since Kall's tail began to swipe and his ears went back as he kept his keen eyes on Lothiam.

The king coughed, stopping his guffawing. "Anyway, I shall leave you to draw pretty maps and play with your navigational toys. Make me proud, little ones." He pointed to Rete. "Tutor, you will contact the court well in advance the next time the second wave engages in any form of combat. I want to see what they are made of."

"Of course, your Majesty," Rete answered.

The king was helped to mount. The stallion, fine-boned and trim to be able to cope with Woodlander climate, neighed at how clumsily the wide man plonked himself down on its back and forcefully tugged the reigns.

Hale wanted to spit at the lack of respect for the graceful animal.

Lothiam turned his horse around, narrowed his eyes and said, "I also came to deliver a verbal decree from your king and master—you work for me first, not Cavarra. You never question my orders. You are the arrows I shoot out into the world. And where you land, I will have staked a claim."

"Unless it is already populated, of course," Rete said, wearing a smile which seemed too subservient to stick to his face.

The king faced him and they shared an uncomfortably long look. Rete did not look away. In the end, it was the king who chuckled out the word, "Naturally."

He dug his heels into the sides of the horse and took off towards the gate with his following, including the pointless flagbearer rushing to keep up. Rete walked after them and spoke to the guards manning the gate.

The four students were left alone. Hale shifted his weight. His palms were itching. Avelynne was safe. He hadn't helped her, though. *Sabina* had. The palms itched more. King Lothiam was... what? Why was he so infuriating? Where did he get that beautiful horse? What had that windbag said? He had called him a Woodlander mutt. Surely, he wasn't meant to have to stand that without retaliation?

But you did.

"Well, he was unpleasant," Sabina grumbled.

"Yes," Avelynne said drowsily. "I remember my father calling the king the 'Monarch of arrogance'. I thought it was because my parents always hated paying the court's tithes. Now I wonder if the epithet wasn't right on the mark."

"Sounds about right," Sabina agreed.

Eleksander rubbed his chin. "This may sound paranoid but do you think... he could be what the servant was warning us about? Could he be the one that the note told us not to trust?"

Hale put his hands to his head. Why were they were talking so quickly? He couldn't keep up. His heart was still racing, bile lined his throat, and he had the strange urge to run after the king and knock him off that horse.

"I don't think so," Sabina said. "I doubt King Lothiam could be dangerous to us."

"Why?" Eleksander asked.

They were being so loud. Hale wanted to cover his ears.

Sabina waved her hand dismissively. "First of all, we are to do his bidding, so why kill us? Secondly, he's all bark and no bite. Spoiled nobleman with milk instead of blood in his veins." She scoffed. "He doesn't fight, half because he doesn't know how to and half out of fear of bloodying his clothes. He's a buffoon, because only a brainless buffoon would distract someone who's trying to keep a silver beast contained."

"King Lothiam showed plenty of bite when he had his queen beheaded. Or when he ordered that massacre on the whole Bronzeforge clan because two of them had conspired to take the throne," Avelynne said.

Eleksander nodded. "Yes, and all the Lakelands talk about how the king rooted out the rebellious groups in our cities and imprisoned the people involved for life. With their families, children included."

"Aye, but he stayed by his cosy hearth, making his guards and liegemen do the dirty work. Back in the North, everyone says that it's his Northern advisors who think up his most forceful moves," Sabina said in a confrontational tone. "They say that without those advisors, he'd simply stay on his golden throne and whinge. Having met him, I believe them. He's a wealthy, overgrown child who can't fight. Like I said, he almost made me lose control of the silver beast. What sort of fighter would do that?"

In the distance, Hale could still see the dust being kicked up by the hooves. They must be halfway to the castle by now. The king was gone. It was too late for Hale to do anything about the mocking. And whatever this niggling sensation was.

Sabina kept talking about how the king made her lose focus. On and on and on. Her voice was tearing at Hale's overwrought mind.

"Don't feel too ashamed of losing control of the beast," he heard himself snarl, gaze still where the king had disappeared. "A friend of mine back home always said womenfolk are more likely to be distracted and drop your fighting edge. Maybe because you don't have the *bone and bag* to protect, like we menfolk. It keeps us focused, I think."

Everyone fell silent, staring at him. Hale twitched back into attention, wondering if their reaction was due to him using the slang for the male genitalia.

Sabina growled deep in her throat. "That piece of assumption about womenfolk, as you call us, makes no sense. The fact that my reproductive organs are on the inside doesn't mean I'm easily distracted or careless."

When he only watched her, she added, "In fact, it proves that I take care to place vulnerable, important stuff tucked out of sight, featherbrain. Besides, the parts of my privates that I care about are on the outside."

Still distracted by fierce feelings he couldn't explain or stand to endure, Hale had to think about the female anatomy for a second before he realised what she meant. Then he spotted her vicious glare, aimed straight at him.

Why was she angry about their conversation? Didn't she see that there were bigger things happening here?! Wasn't she furious about that shitbag of a king? "Calm down, Sabina, no need to get so emotional! I'm not saying you're not a brilliant fighter who'll make an excellent mapmaker. Women are usually fiercer fighters, no matter what their level of focus is."

He thought that would clear things up, but they were all still gaping at him, so with his heart still pounding, he carried on speaking. "I mean, we all know that even with your hands tied behind your back, you could survive years longer than delicate Eleksander in the wild, and he's a lad. So, calm down."

He heard Eleksander suck in a quick breath as he staggered back.

Sabina clenched her fists. "Really? Not only are you talking like a sexist toad, you're also going to attack both me and Eleksander in the same breath? You are in fine form."

Hale stepped closer to her. "What? I'm not being sexist! I know for a fact that women are as good as men, better in plenty of ways. Nor am I attacking anyone or being in any particular *form*. I. Was. Just. Talking!" He stopped when he realised he was shouting and lowered his voice. "You are all far too sensitive, and more so today than normally. Perhaps because meeting that silly arse who calls himself our ruler unnerved you?"

"Stop. Wait, wait," Avelynne said before Sabina could retort. "I think we were all shaken by the king's appearance and his terrible behaviour. Especially you, Hale."

His blood seemed too hot for his body now. "Me?"

Avelynne put a calming hand on his forearm. "Yes. You're not accustomed to having to be subservient, it's not in the Woodlander nature and certainly not in yours. It brings out your temper and makes you say things you don't mean. Not to mention that we're all worn and testy after the silver beasts fight and the drain of magic use."

He pulled his arm away from her cool but far too clingy hand. "Be subservient? What the shit are you talking about? All I know is that you lot need to grow thicker skins."

Sabina's eyes flashed. "Oh really? You're going to tell us what we *need* to do? How *we* have to change?"

"Yes," he grunted. "Because my way of handling things is better than yours. I can't be bothered tiptoeing around your feelings. I have better things to do!"

Sabina turned to Eleksander. "Do you still think he can't help it? That he is one of those people whose mind isn't built to understand social interaction?"

"No. Not anymore," Eleksander mumbled with a crest-fallen sigh.

Sabina's gaze snapped back to Hale. "Me neither. I think his mind works like ours, he's just a boorish overgrown boy who would rather take his temper out on other people than stop to inspect his own behaviour."

Hale took a step closer to her. "Who are you calling an overgrown boy? You're the one getting hurt like a crying baby."

"Let's not allow this to escalate," Avelynne said. "Why don't we all go get something to eat, take a deep breath, maybe walk off some nervous energy?"

The silence was as heavy and hard as rocks, pressing down on them. On him.

Eleksander slowly shook his head and walked off towards the Great Hall.

Sabina stayed frozen to the spot, a muscle in her sharp jaw twitching.

Avelynne brushed her cheek, calming the twitching muscle. "Sabina. Please? Go ahead and I'm going to have a talk with Hale."

Thawed by Avelynne's words, Sabina gave a curt nod and followed Eleksander.

It was impossible for Hale to stand still, he shifted his weight from foot to foot and flexed his biceps. He hadn't done anything wrong! Or had he? What had he said? It was all a blur. A frustrating, confusing blur that made him want to kick or throw something!

Avelynne gave him a sad look and he stopped moving.

A moment passed. Hale counted his shallow breaths.

"Fine," he said with a sigh. "I'm listening."

Chapter Nineteen

DEFENCE

"Fine," Hale said. "I'm listening."

His body looked even more corded with muscle and pulsing veins than usually as he stood there tense and ready for attack. Or was it for defence?

Either way, Avelynne had to decide how to tell him what the problem was without making him more confrontational. She tapped her fingers against her leg as she weighed her words.

There were a lot of people like Hale, ones who said things on impulse in the heat of the moment and then didn't apologise, assuming that their words would soon be forgotten, not etched into hearts and minds. People who themselves didn't mind an insult or a rough joke and therefore didn't understand why others were hurt or angered. Both her parents were like that. Each of them, at different moments, told her what Hale had just told their friends: "Grow a thicker skin."

As if it was that easy. As if a sensitive person could just decide to stop being sensitive. And—she squared her shoulders as she came to a decision—it shouldn't have to be that way. Should the so called "thick-skinned" people of the world really be forcing the thin-skinned to change simply because they couldn't show enough compassion to alter their behaviour? Their convenience of not having to think before speaking surely couldn't be more important than a thin-skinned person's right to their own personality and feelings?

She tapped her fingers faster. How could she make Hale understand that? He never meant any harm and she didn't want him to have to second guess his impulses. But... he would have to unless they wanted moments like this to be a weekly occurrence.

She stilled her fingers and steeled her nerve. "Hale. You find Eleksander and Sabina too sensitive, right?"

"Yes," he growled. "Sabina gets irritated and Eleksander gets sad. For a mere comment in passing! They know I don't mean anything by it. I can't even have a shitting conversation without stepping on someone's toes!"

"All right," Avelynne said calmly. "Well, they're different than you. Things that don't bother you, hurt them."

"I know. But I can't tell what'll hurt them, because they're too sensitive. Which can't be good for them! All I do is talk like I would to my friends back home and–boom– I've offended someone." He scratched his forehead so hard he left red lines. "In the Woodlands, my friends would laugh it off or tell me to shut up. Maybe one or two people have been pissed off, but then they've just avoided me. No problem!"

"I see. Well, we can't avoid each other, Hale. We will study together, live together, then explore and survive together." She let that sink in before adding, "Your friends back home were all like you?"

"Pretty much, yes."

"Your friends here are different. I don't know why. Maybe due to traumatic pasts. Or because they were born this way. Perhaps their academic inclinations or creative natures lead them to be like this. Or rather, *us* to be like this."

"Us? My comments don't hurt you," Hale said.

"Actually, I… get hurt too. I've simply learned not to show it. My parents told me to grow a thicker skin. I couldn't do that, but since I wanted to please them, I pretended I had."

Hale's face fell into a grimace of absolute horror. "You pretend with me, too?" he said, low and hoarse.

"I wanted you to like me. I wanted…" She chewed her lower lip. "To seem like you, strong and carefree."

His frame softened. "You are strong, Avelynne."

She liked how he said her name with such warmth. His black eyes glittered in the light, full of tenderness and a desire to understand, and she wished she could pour her explanations right into them, instead of having to use clunky words.

"You can be sensitive and strong at the same time," she replied. "That's what I'm trying to tell you. You see Eleksander and Sabina's thin skins as something they need to overcome, while your behaviour is the correct one." She held up a finger. "But you forget, in a world like ours where there's so much cruelty, selfishness and even starvation, everything grows harsher. Being sensitive is hard and takes a strong person."

He was staring at her, a crinkle between his dark eyebrows. She tried to smile, to not appear like she was lecturing him.

"Sabina and Eleksander don't stay thin-skinned because they're spoiled or weak, Hale. They stay thin-skinned because that is who they are. Who *we* are. We have empathy with others, feel things deeply, worry about people, and dwell on things in-depth." She reached out and tugged his calloused hand into her own. "It makes us thin-skinned and, in the case of Eleksander and I, perhaps not as quick to act as you. But it also makes us peaceful, tolerant, and able to see other people's points of view. These are things that will come in handy as we meet other populaces and creatures, right?"

Hale dropped his gaze. "I suppose so."

"Your straightforwardness, toughness, and tendency to not get hurt easily will come in handy as well. In fact, it's good that you have a personality different from ours. It means we can learn from each other and have different perspectives on the situations we face."

He brightened a little. "It gives us the advantage of diversity."

"Exactly." She interlaced their fingers while blowing out a long breath. "However, it doesn't solve the problem. The three of us are sensitive, we know that and we're aware that it makes things complicated for you. Because of that we've given you leeway plenty of times throughout these past weeks but today—"

"I crossed the line. I don't know why I said all that nonsense." He ran his free hand over his face. "I need to find a way to not let my emotions control what pops out of my gob."

"I think you might want to try, yes. Otherwise we'll never relax and trust each other completely. I think we need some sort of compromise. You do your part and we'll do ours."

"Agreed," he said. "You keep cutting me some slack whenever you can and I'll... hm. What's my role in the plan?"

Avelynne thought it through. "Firstly, as we said, try to watch your words. Secondly, you could apologise when you overstep, then we know that you didn't do it on purpose and that you don't think less of us."

"Think less of you?"

"Yes, that you don't think us whingy and thin-skinned," she searched for the right words, "If we don't feel attacked, we're more likely to be able to just brush your comments off without getting hurt. Does that make sense?"

"I guess it does. And I never thought any of you were weak." He squeezed her hand tight. "I never want you to think that!"

"Thank you." She smiled, and this time it didn't fail. "Great. Then we have a plan. This way, we'll know that you don't think we need to change who we are to make your life easier. Then, we can attempt to take your comments as they were meant—without malice."

Hale sucked his teeth. "I'll try. But I don't really know how to watch my words. It'll be a long process."

"I know. And we'll help you along. Just as long as you tell Sabina and Eleksander that you don't think there's anything wrong with them. Then they'll be less defensive."

Looking down, he murmured something.

"Pardon?" Avelynne asked.

"I said, can you teach me how to apologise properly? I had no parents. So, I was raised by whatever adult happened to be around but mainly had to figure things out myself. Apologies weren't high on the list of priorities, you know?" His scarred forehead furrowed. "Besides, the Woodsfolk aren't much for unnecessary words. Even if the rest of the world find them necessary."

Avelynne squeezed his hand back. "Gladly. Perhaps, in return, you can explain what some of your comments meant, so that I'm no longer hurt by them? So, I understand how you feel and think?"

"Of course. I'll do that for Eleksander and Sabina too."

Avelynne watched their entwined hands. His so much bigger, the skin tanned and coarser. There were large veins pulsing with life on the back of it. Avelynne was struck by how powerful that hand would be if he wanted it to, and how gentle it was being right now. How gentle *he* was being. How he wanted to learn and to improve.

Her heartbeat picked up and she was suddenly aware of how close he was. And how he smelled, earthy and fresh. She moved her fingers, caressing his.

Then another realisation struck her.

He's not the only one who wants to improve.

Improving in all their subjects, by extra training and reading until her eyes ached every evening, wasn't enough. Her heartbeat grew even more rapid. She would have to dare be as vulnerable as Hale was right now. She would have to tell her new friends, or rather her new family, her secret. Even if it did risk starting a civil war back in the Peaks.

Shards of images tore through her mind: infighting devastating the villages nestled between the proud mountains. Cousins burying arrows in each other's chests. Decades of war and turmoil causing trade, decency, and kindness to crumble. Children getting caught in the crossfire or being used as hostages.

Those images caused shooting pains in her temples. No. She had to stay silent.

She retracted her hand. "Well, I'm glad we had this talk, my friend. Thank you for listening to me and for being open to change. I know that's not easy."

"Thank you for wanting to help," Hale said. He kept throwing glances at his hand. It still stayed open and abandoned between them.

Avelynne had to get away before she became too honest. Before she looked into those dark, passionate eyes and told him everything. Before she poured her heart out to him.

"We should join the others, get something to eat to regain our strength, and then head to our next lesson," she said, tucking some hair behind her ear.

"Yes! Food. Always a good idea. Come on Peakdweller, we still need to feed you up."

Avelynne couldn't stop a chuckle. "Fine. Lead the way."

When they entered the Great Hall, Sabina and Eleksander were seated at the corner of the long table. Sabina was slathering a piece of pork with apple sauce while Eleksander was mid-conversation. Avelynne picked up the words, "I wish there was someone we could tell. Not just about the note but about that servant who mouthed the warning. I mean we —"

They both turned and froze as they saw Hale.

Avelynne noticed him tensing next to her. Then he began spitting out words at great speed. "I'm sorry. Shit. I'm not good with apologies, but I'm so sorry. I didn't mean to sound sexist. Or cruel. I…" he paused, scratching the fuzz of hair at the back of his neck. "I admire you both so much and regret anything I said that wasn't kind. You're great. You're just different from me, especially you Eleksander, and I don't always understand that."

He stood back and looked pleadingly at them.

Eleksander was about to say something, but Sabina put a hand on his arm and spoke up instead, "Thank you for that apology. I know you don't have those narrow-minded beliefs, you were talking absolute nonsense due to your distress. I've got to ask, though, do you still expect us to 'grow thicker skins', Hale?"

He winced. "No, I don't want you to grow anything. When I said that, I, um I suppose I meant that I wished my words didn't hurt you. But as they do, I'll try to think before I speak." He made eye contact with both of them in turns. "And hopefully in the future, you'll be sure enough of my high opinion of you to ignore anything I say that's, you know, shitty."

Sabina returned to preparing her pork and said, "Fine. I like you and I know your heart's in the right place, even if your brain goes out your ears when you're upset. So, if you say you'll try to be respectful, then I'll take the apology and move on."

Hale nodded gratefully to her.

Avelynne sought Eleksander's gaze. "It's acceptable to want some time to think about all of this, you know," she said to him.

The Lakelander shook his head, making his braids dance. "No. I think I know Hale best of all of us, he means no harm. Like Sabina said, if he's attempting to think before he speaks, I'm certainly willing to give him the benefit of the doubt."

Avelynne breathed out, relief relaxing her every muscle. Hale must've felt the same as he roared, "Phew! Thank goodness for that. You're both better people than I am." He reached out a hand. "Now, stop hogging that apple sauce, Northerner."

He took a seat and Sabina threw the jar to him. Avelynne sat next to Eleksander, who gave that crooked smile and rolled his eyes.

When they'd eaten, Eleksander wanted to go out and get a quick breath of fresh air before they headed to their next lesson. Hale followed him. Avelynne heard him tell Eleksander that he was so impressed with how he'd handled the silver beast and ask for tips.

"Well done," Sabina said, sneaking some meat down to Kall.

"Do you mean for finishing my pork?" Avelynne said innocently.

Sabina pursed her lips and raised her eyebrows at her, making Avelynne laugh. "Fine, not food related. What then?"

"Well done on reaching out to Hale. Eleksander would have let him off the hook too soon and I would've shouted at him. You, well, you clearly managed to make him understand."

"I think he already understood a great deal. It's hard for him to change his first impulse, though."

"No one wants him to change who he is. We only want him to alter his behaviour somewhat," Sabina said while scratching Kall's chin. "He'll always speak his mind and be blunt. We only want him to attempt to see things from others' perspective enough to know there are things he may not want to be blunt about."

"I know."

Sabina moved her penetrating gaze from Kall to Avelynne. "Sometimes I wonder if there is anything you don't know. Or take care to learn."

"Well, I am worse than you in every single subject so that seems a silly thing to wonder."

"Avelynne, I didn't mean the sort of knowledge that can be taught." Avelynne jolted at how serious Sabina sounded and how that seriousness was echoed in her piercing eyes. "I meant the knowledge of how people work. How the world works. You seem more mature than many other eighteen-year-olds."

"Thank you. So do you and…" Avelynne lost her words as she spotted something new. "Purple."

Sabina flinched. "What?"

"There's purple in the centre of your eyes, surrounding the pupil. The rest is blue, save for that violet circle."

"Why in the name of the silver beasts are we suddenly talking about my eyes?" Sabina said with a kind chuckle.

Avelynne bit her lip, holding back her own laughter. "I'm sorry. I find eyes fascinating. For years I struggled with how to draw eyes, so I began studying them to learn. Now I can't seem to stop." Avelynne sipped some water, more to busy her self-conscious mind than out of thirst.

"Uh-huh. Does that mean you've been staring at all of our eyes? Or just mine?"

"Oh, I'm getting to know the eyes of our group very well. Hale's are black as obsidian, mysterious and deep. Eleksander has those big eyes in the warmest, sweetest brown. And you, I used to think your eyes were sky-blue. Now, in this light and this close, I can see that sliver of purple."

Sabina licked her lips while her pale cheeks coloured. Then she broke eye contact and gave an embarrassed smile. "You see everything as if you're drawing it. When I think of your eyes, I only think of how kind they look and perhaps that beautiful, narrowed shape. I suppose I think more about how your eyes make me feel than their colour."

"And how do they make you feel?"

Sabina smirked. "Not going to tell you."

"Fine," Avelynne said in a pretended huff. "Anyway, my eyes are iron grey. Which is probably where my ancestors took the name Ironhold from." She lowered her voice into a teasing tone and added, "You know, if you'd take the time to notice exact colours, perhaps your drawing and sketching would be of better quality."

Sabina held her hand to her chest in theatrical distress. "You vicious little vixen! Be careful or I'll get Kall to sleep on you."

Avelynne couldn't help it, she raised a flirty eyebrow. "Is that meant to be a threat? Because I'd love to cuddle that *beautiful northern beast*."

If Sabina noted the double meaning, she didn't let on. "Yes, but if Kall sleeps on you, you'll be as flat as a piece of parchment in the morning!"

Avelynne giggled. "Good, it'll get me out of our first archery lesson. Anyway, we should go, I'll be flattened like a piece of parchment by Tutor Rete if we're late for our 'orientating with a compass' lesson."

"True," Sabina said and stood with her hand indicating that Avelynne should walk first.

They left with Kall walking between them and their hands resting on his head. It made Avelynne smile that Sabina's little finger was tentatively touching her own.

Chapter Twenty

LIKE AN ARROW THROUGH THE HEART

The next morning Hale weighed a longbow in his hand and watched the sun, currently buried behind clouds, illuminate it in eerie grey light. The bow was well-made and from a nice cut of yew. Despite the solid craftsmanship of the weapon, he grunted at it. He was a good marksman but preferred close-range fighting. Staying far way and shooting arrows was a Lakelander's game. He gave another grunt. Would archery really be that important on their mission? He'd ask Avelynne what she thought. She usually had answers.

Out of the blue, an arrow flew past him.

"Don't look like a rabbit faced with a snowbear; I wasn't aiming for you," Sabina called, pointing to the target behind him. She had struck right in the bullseye.

She was smiling, and he grinned back, happy that she wasn't angry at him anymore.

"That'll teach me for standing by the target," he shouted back.

He used his magic to yank the arrow free and levitate it over to a safe landing spot by Sabina's feet.

She picked it up and strode towards him. "You've been preoccupied all morning. Everything all right, my friend?"

"Yes. I've got some things on my mind."

Some things. That wasn't a very nice nickname for the frustratingly charming Countess Avelynne Ironhold, he mused with unease prickling under his skin.

As if knowing he was thinking of her, Avelynne appeared. She was adjusting her jerkin, pulling the leather tighter. He couldn't blame her, it was getting chillier and the cloudy morning nipped at his nose and cheeks.

Eleksander came after her, walking with Tutor Rogan. The burly man was saying something about stance and Eleksander was nodding. His body language was uncertain, but then that wasn't unusual for Eleksander. That uncertainty also wasn't unusual for anyone speaking with Tutor Rogan, whose rudeness was almost as immense as his body.

Behind them, a horse neighed as it was led out the stables.

Sabina leant against the sundial, turning to watch. Hale joined her in time to see four well-nourished and perfectly groomed horses being brought out and saddled.

Avelynne appeared at his elbow. "Hello you two. Beautiful horses, hm? They're for the first wave. They're all riding to the coast to have their introduction to their future ship."

Hale flinched. "It's been finished?"

"Apparently," Avelynne said.

Hale crossed his arms over his chest. "Those lucky shits."

Avelynne gave him a reproachful look, softened by a smile. "Mind your tongue."

"Or what? You'll slap it with yours?" He said, waggling his eyebrows.

A smirk played on Avelynne's rosy lips. "I think slapping your face with my hand would be more efficient. Unless you enjoy roughhousing, Woodlander?"

"Anything that involves your body and mine connecting sounds like a good idea to me, pretty Peakdweller."

Sabina groaned at them, but he ignored her, mentally patting himself on the back. *Yes! That's how you do it. Your flirting game is back.*

With a seductive hum, Avelynne ran her fingers through her hair, sending a waft of its sweet scent towards him. He breathed it in, feeling it quickening his pulse.

Sabina cringed. "Can we get back to the first wave and what they're doing?"

Avelynne's smirk evaporated. "Yes, of course. I overheard the first wavers talking about the vessel. One of them said the sails had been attached and everything. Apparently, it's three times the size of normal Cavarra ships."

"I should think so," Sabina said. "I mean, it's not going to be fishing off the coast or delivering goods from port to port. It'll be battling sea monsters and the elements! Not to mention that the first wavers and all their sailors will be living on it for years."

Hale looked around as he picked up a quiver and fastened it to his back. "Always struck me as odd to have a seafaring academy landlocked. Surely a port town would've been better?"

"I'd say that it was because the king wants to keep an

eye on us," Sabina said with a scoff. "But we all know it's for political reasons. The institution has to be in the middle of Cavarra, so it doesn't sit in any one county and cause the other three to start a war."

"Mm," Avelynne agreed. "Just as we mapmakers have to be one from each county. Otherwise, they could've simply educated one captaining mapmaker and be done. Perhaps have a second, in case the first one perished. But certainly not four of us."

Hale scratched his chin, registering that he forgot to shave this morning. "One captain would make sense, I guess. Maybe someone with more experience, like someone older. Perhaps a fisherman who already knew the seas."

"Don't be silly, mere fishermen don't have enough education to be entrusted with such a vital mission," a gruff voice said behind them.

They turned to see Tutor Rogan glaring at them from underneath bushy eyebrows. "We need clever but unoccupied minds to fill with information, and young, healthy bodies that can take some punishment out there. That's why they don't send someone qualified, like *me*. It has to be expendable youths with flexible minds and bodies. Like them," he nodded towards the four first wavers who were mounting their horses. "Through daily lessons for over a year they've been sharpened like expensive rapiers and will only improve to acceptable shape in their last year. Then they sail east. The next year, you sail west."

One of the first wavers added something to her saddle bag. She didn't seem anxious or weighed down by responsibility. She was all *vigour*. Hale stiffened his spine. He was going to be like that too.

Tutor Rogan scoffed at his own words. "Which is a worrying thought as you're all piss-poor in my eyes. I know Rete keeps telling you how much better than the first wave you are, but personally I believe he's only flattering you to keep you trying to improve."

He cracked his knuckles. "Anyway, it's my unenviable job to try to prepare you for fighting anything you find on foreign shores or in the dark depths. Firing arrows at it seems pretty foolproof. Everyone, pick up a quiver and a bow."

Sabina and Hale, already kitted out, stepped back, letting Eleksander and Avelynne take a quiver each. While Eleksander spoke to Rogan about bows versus crossbows, Avelynne stared at the selection of bows that were differently strung and in varying sizes.

"Choose one that's not too long," Sabina whispered.

"Exactly. You want one that'll sit well in your tiny frame and be easy to draw," Hale said in the same hushed tones.

"Are you hinting that my size makes me weak, Young Master Hawthorn? Surely not after all those push-ups you've made me do," Avelynne replied. But her tone lacked her usual teasing. And she was avoiding eye contact.

"Only saying that you should pick the weapon that best fits your build, *your royal Countess-ness*," he said, hoping he wasn't offending but instead making her at ease.

She gave him a watery smile. Sabina picked up a smaller, older bow and handed it to Avelynne. "This one looks like it'll bring you luck. Not that you need it. Simply relax and focus on your target. Let everything else fade away."

Eleksander joined them. He let his hand hover over every bow until he chose one in treated elm.

"Interesting choice," Hale said.

Eleksander lowered his head so his braids covered his face. "I suppose I wanted a change from regular yew bows."

"Hey, no need to explain," Hale said, squeezing the taller lad's shoulder. "You shoot with what you want. After all, you're a Lakelander, you'll be excellent at this."

Hale spotted Tutor Rogan watching Avelynne, examining her grip on the bow. Or was it something else he was checking for?

"Let's start. I don't have all day," he grunted. "Ironhold, you go first. Aim at that target board. I'm not expecting *you* to be able to get anywhere near the bullseye but at least aim for the inner circles."

Hale puzzled at Rogan's disparaging comment but got distracted by the first wavers and their entourage riding off. Was Rogan right in that they were better than them? Or was Rete correct when he said that the second wave were the ones to watch? When Hale's focus returned to his group he realised he'd missed something Avelynne had said.

"No. Someone else won't go first," Rogan barked at her. "In all my classes, you never go first, and you never excel. Rete tells me that your magic skills are good and apparently you're talented at map drawing, but in everything else… you're slowly improving."

He stepped so close his chin was almost touching her forehead. It made her have to bend backwards to keep eye contact.

"There are two problems with that, Ironhold. One, that it's happening slowly. Two, and more importantly, that you need to improve to catch up with your fellow students at all! You should've been exceptional at all these subjects on arrival. Let's have no more trouble from you. Take your aim and fire."

Avelynne lifted the bow. She held it correctly and took the right stance, so she had clearly done this before. Although, from the look on her face, Hale guessed that she hadn't had much luck with it.

She nocked the arrow and took her aim. Hale saw her arms shake at the tension of drawing the rigid bowstring. Or perhaps it was nerves?

She released the arrow and it sailed towards its mark. With a twang, it hit the edge of the target. Not even in one of the rings.

"Pathetic! Again," Rogan bellowed.

Avelynne obeyed. Her arms shook even worse now and she gave a high-pitched whimper as the arrow took flight. This time it struck into the outmost ring. Hale winced. He would've hit the bullseye and he had seen Sabina do it earlier. Eleksander rarely spoke of his accomplishments but he was brilliant at all their subjects. And he was a Lakelander, they'd invented archery for shit's sake. Even on a bad day, Hale couldn't see any of them missing the mark by this much. Twice. There was a tightness in his throat. How could he help her?

"It's windy out here today," he said.

"Yes. Exceedingly windy," Eleksander immediately agreed.

"There's only a slight breeze," Tutor Rogan replied, steel in his voice. "Fire again."

Avelynne lowered her bow and her gaze. "I don't see

much of a reason. I fear I was never very good at archery. I'm better with staves. Or axes."

Rogan scoffed. "Yes. Better. But you're not excellent at either of them."

"I'm not used to being in competition like this," Avelynne said, a little too fast and too shrilly. "Nor the gruelling schedule of lessons. It makes me anxious, which makes me unable to show my true level of skill."

"Perhaps that's the problem. Sadly, I'm not convinced," Rogan said, his nostrils flaring. "I'm a Peakdweller too, remember? I know that intense study is common for us. Moreover, I know how brilliant our young are. I can see no way that you were the most skilled eighteen-year-old this year. Not when I've heard from my brother how the son of the Forgeborn family easily excels at all the subjects we teach here."

That's why he spoke to her so informally and so rudely, Hale realised. *He knows who she is.*

Avelynne dropped the bow with a clatter and pinned her arms against her stomach.

"I-I cannot... I," she stammered. Her eyes went wildly from all of their faces to the gates leading out of the courtyard.

Before Hale had time to react, she took off running. She was heading for the gates, like a hare sprinting for the opening of a cage, but then she shifted left and went into the nearest building. The servant quarters. Was she going to see Myllie?

Hale hung his bow over his shoulder and began to follow her.

"No," Rogan snapped. "You're not excused. I need to assess your bow skills, Woodlander."

Eleksander took a tentative step forward. "You've seen and approved of my skills when you caught me practising the other night. May I go after her? Only to fetch her back of course," he said to a sceptical-looking Rogan.

"Fine. Return quickly," the tutor said.

Eleksander rushed into the servant quarters while Hale dragged his feet back the others. He picked up Avelynne's bow and heard Sabina whisper, "She'll be all right."

He nodded to her as he stood, then took the proper stance and nocked his arrow. He tried to focus completely on the target board. An impossible task with that tightness in his throat getting worse. Caring this much about someone was awful.

Chapter Twenty-One

SECRET SPILLING

The stones of the servant quarters building were cold. Avelynne leaned into them, pushing her forehead against the wall as if she could enter it and disappear.

Useless. Weak. Pathetic.

Someone cleared their throat behind her. She turned to find Eleksander. He was slouching even more than usual, and his hands were deep in his trouser pockets.

"Are you all right?" He asked.

"No." She squeezed her eyes shut.

"No. I suppose you're not. What I meant to ask was, can I help?"

When she didn't answer, he said, "At least let me hand over your compass. It fell out of your pocket when you ran."

He felt closer now. She could smell the expensive soap he used and which his sister washed his clothes in. She held out her hand and he placed the compass in her palm. Its weight was unbearable to her now and she winced.

With the softest touch she'd ever known, Eleksander's

fingertips brushed her cheek. Her eyes flew open and she saw his beautiful face locked in a frown.

"Avelynne. Something is on your mind. Something more than failing in lessons. I see it, always hidden by your smiles and your willingness to please. But it's there, keeping you apart from us, and it's clearer now than ever. Could you confide in me? Do you want me to fetch Sabina instead?"

His voice was so gentle. She was tired to the core. Tired of hiding this. Tired of keeping secrets from the three people she now cared the most about. What good did keeping the secret do, if she was failing anyway? The words filled her mind and then her mouth, aching to come out. The poisonous secret needed to be lanced out. She let go of her last barrier and let the words bleed out of her.

"I've been lying. I never deserved my compass or the place in the second wave that it represents. I cheated to get into the Hall of Explorers. Or rather, my parents did, and I let them."

He didn't move the warm fingertips that still rested on her cheek. In fact, he looked frozen. "What?"

"I wasn't the best in my year. In fact, my mother told me I was only the third best. But who knows, I could have been fifth or seventh. She lies, I'm afraid," Avelynne said with shame. "What I do know is that the two best Peakd-wellers born the same year as I were a Forgeborn and a Bardsley. The two warring families in the Peaks."

He retracted his hand and murmured, "I've read about them. They're the ones that have been starting wars with each other for generations."

"Yes. Other than us Ironholds, they're the richest and most influential families in our county. They constantly compete in everything. If it wasn't for my parents keeping them in check, they'd start warring, with the leadership of the Peaks probably being their spoils."

She rubbed her forehead where a headache was beginning to spike.

"So…" Eleksander prompted.

"So, when the winners of the tests for who got chosen for the second wave came up at pretty much a draw, and the winners were from these two families, my parents knew they couldn't pick one of them to go. The Forgeborns and the Bardsleys would never accept if the other family's child was chosen. They altered the results that were handed in to the Centre's officials."

"Aren't the results double checked somehow?"

"Why would they be? It's in the Peaks' best interest to only send their best student. Not only for pride but because the fate of Cavarra hangs in the balance."

Eleksander's expression darkened. "True. It's important that only the best received that spot. That the deserving winner was chosen."

She grabbed the sleeve of his tunic. "I know I wasn't the best candidate and that no matter how I try to study and to practise to make up for it now, I can never be as good as the two who got better results." He looked like he might argue but she couldn't stop. She gave a mirthless chuckle and added, "You know, sometimes I lay awake and worry that maybe all of this was more about my parents' ambition to send me here than the war between the Forgeborns and Bardsleys."

She let go of his sleeve and added, "Either way. They told me that if I didn't go, and it came out who had actually been the winners, war would break out. Neighbours killing each other. Trade stilling. The few remaining crops being trampled during battles. No one having time to stave off all the silver beasts."

Eleksander was silent for a long time. Then he murmured, "You had to come."

Avelynne swallowed a sob. "I felt like I did. I tend to do what my parents expect of me, even when it makes me miserable. Except, in this case, it was so much more than that. I couldn't be the cause of war." She paused to catch her breath. "Coming here seemed the right thing to do, despite the lying and cheating. I comforted myself with the knowledge that I would study myself to the bone to catch up and deserve my spot. Not that any of it was much comfort."

"That explains all the books you've taken out of the library. And the late-night fighting practise." Eleksander ran a finger over his lips, clearly digesting all of this. "Did you have to keep this as a secret, though? Couldn't your parents have been honest with the officials?"

She shrugged. "They said that the Hall of Explorers wouldn't care about Peaks squabbles. That they and the other counties would laugh at us while we tore ourselves apart."

He hesitated. "What about you? Couldn't you have been honest with me, Hale, and Sabina?"

That one was harder to answer.

"I... thought you'd hate me. And that you wouldn't keep the secret."

He couldn't meet her eyes. "Well, I'm not sure we should keep it. I, and all of Cavarra, will be putting our lives in your hands. In my case, quite literally as we will need to defend each other on our travels. You should be the *most qualified* person. And you shouldn't keep important things from your team."

She swallowed something jagged. "I know."

"It's been weeks. You should've trusted us enough to tell us by now. Perhaps it isn't the right thing to do to keep your secret, but I, for one, would keep it if you asked me."

"You would?"

"Yes. All the waters help me, I would," he said.

"Why?"

"Because I believe you're a good person, Avelynne. I've spent my days and evenings with you. I've seen you exhausted, seen you triumphant, seen you comfort others. I think I know enough about you to give you the benefit of the doubt and keep your secret. At least until something shows I shouldn't."

"You're so kind," Avelynne mumbled in the direction of her feet.

"I'm simply doing what I think is right—keeping someone on the team who I believe fits well with us, works hard, and is willing to sacrifice to maintain peace and look after her people. You cheated and lied not because you wanted to be chosen, but because you wanted to keep bloodshed and catastrophe away. I can understand that."

Avelynne's eyes welled up. "Thank you for saying that."

"It's true. Referring back to that you work hard... that cannot stop now." His voice was graver now. "Your lack of skills is showing, and someone might catch on. You need to be better, immediately."

"I'm trying! I study until my eyes ache, I train whenever and however I can. What else can I do?"

"You can be trained by someone. I need to practise anyway, why don't we study and train together? I can teach you everything I know. Well, except drawing, you're better than me at that."

She blinked away the tears. A countess should not cry in public. "Really?"

"Really. You…" he rubbed the back of his neck. "You'll have to earn back the trust you broke by keeping secrets, though. Luckily for you, I forgive easily. As long as you don't abandon me, then all bets are off."

She wasn't sure why he had turned so serious on that last point, but she nodded, full to the brim with gratitude.

"However, I don't know how you should handle Sabina and Hale," he said with a wince.

"Neither do I. I'll think about it."

"Good. It's awful to have to carry something so big and dangerous like this secret around alone. They can help you. Until then, *I'll* help you. In any way I can."

Avelynne couldn't stop herself, she rushed him and threw her arms around his wide torso. He made an "Ouf" sound as she knocked the air out of him but then he slowly wrapped his arms around her.

The smell of that soap filled her nostrils as she leaned into his chest. He began to rub circles on her back and whisper that everything was going to be all right, that she wasn't alone. That was what set her crying unconsolably. Soon her tears were soaking the front of his tunic and she still couldn't stop. The more she shook with sobs, the tighter he held her.

A moment later she managed to croak out, "Sorry for crying all over you."

"Oh, don't apologise. It's only saltwater. I've always preferred it to sweet water anyway. Smells fresher when it dries."

She chuckled but it sounded more like a sob.

"We'll figure it all out, Ave. Tonight we'll start working on your archery. With some tutoring and some confidence, you'll be hitting that bullseye in no time."

"Did you call me Ave?" She said between sniffles.

"Um…" He hesitated. "I suppose I did. Is that all right?"

"Only if I can call you El."

"Hm. No. Sounds strange to me. My sister calls me Sander, though."

She sniffed again, wishing she had a handkerchief. "Then I'd like to do that too."

"Go ahead," he said with a warm smile.

"I promise I'll regain your trust. And work harder than you have ever seen anyone work. Both to earn my place here and to make it worth your time training me."

"I know you will. I wouldn't be offering to help you if I didn't believe in both those promises."

All out of words, she nodded.

He wiped her cheeks with his big hands, so much softer than Hale's. Then he said, "Let's go find you a handkerchief and a glass of water. Then we must hurry back to Rogan before he screams the walls down. I don't understand why he's so hateful towards us. I overheard the first wave complain to Tutor Hathleen that he was awful to them too. Still, he shouldn't be allowed to ruin your day."

He put his arm around her and led her toward where she knew his sister's room was.

She cursed her snotty nose as she had to sniff again. She tried to ignore it and focus on calming down with every step they took. "Isn't it strange to have your sister work as your servant?"

"Not really. I would never treat her like a servant, nor does she feel like one. If she'd done better at her tests and been chosen for the first wave when she applied, I would've gone as a servant, or *companion*, for her. We Aetholos prefer to rely on each other if possible."

"Your sister applied to the Hall of Explorers too?"

"Yes, and Ellenaria was close to getting in."

Avelynne subtly wiped her nose. "Ah, so brilliance runs in the Aetholo blood?"

"Oh, we're not related by blood."

"What?"

He quirked one of his shapely eyebrows. "Have you not noticed the glaring difference in appearance and skin tone? We can hardly have the same birth parents."

Avelynne felt more useless than a broom in the desert. All she could reply was, "Oh."

He laughed. "There you go, I don't know all about you and you don't know all about me, but we're getting there. Now, let's freshen you up and get you back out in that courtyard."

She nodded again and leaned into him as they walked.

Chapter Twenty-Two

EVENING SWIM

Hale flinched in his library chair as he realised that it must be six weeks since the second wave started lessons at the Hall of Explorers. He counted on his fingers and confirmed it. Stars above, how many days of nonstop lessons would that be? His brain seemed to ache with how much information he was stuffing into it each day. Unless he cooled his brain with something fun and relaxing soon, it would boil in his skull.

Although, he wasn't the one studying the hardest. Ever since their arrival, Avelynne had put them all to shame in that regard. Hale pressed his lips together when he considered that all her extra training lessons and library trips had been done with *Eleksander* lately. Why had she suddenly chosen him for constant company? She'd been happy to do her extra work alone for the first few weeks.

At least tonight they were all studying together.

It was only an hour after supper, and yet the library was quiet. The first wavers were still at the harbour, getting to try out their ship in the fresh ocean air. They must be cooler than everyone left here at the Centre, where a bout of surprisingly hot weather had drifted in.

Left wilting in this stuffy building were the second wavers, trying to catch up on some map studies.

Sabina and Avelynne were sitting close together, looking into the same large book of maps of the North. Sabina was explaining it all while Avelynne took notes. Hale tried to focus on his own books and drown out their beautiful voices mingling as they discussed glaciers and hot springs.

However, he couldn't help noticing Sabina point to a big mountain range and say, "You'd like it there. Plenty of mountain goats and incredibly pretty women, exactly like where you come from."

Avelynne's mouth fell open in a way that was surely meant to indicate shock and reproach but ended up being far too erotic. Why did she have to draw attention to her wonderful mouth all the time? It made Hale's knees weak.

Avelynne said, "Are you implying I'm a mountain goat?" before shutting her mouth and pursing her lips.

Sabina laughed and gently leaned her head against Avelynne's. "You know very well what I was implying you were. Or are. Oh whatever, you're confusing me!"

She moved away from the smirking Avelynne and Hale saw pink creeping into her Northernly white cheeks. He understood the sentiment. He understood a lot about Sabina.

Avelynne caught him looking and smiled over at him, dimples in full view.

"Hale? Are you all right?" she asked.

"Huh? Who? Uh, yes. I'm fine." He closed his book

with a thump. "I need to get out of here, though. We're missing all the autumn leaves changing."

"You mean you want to watch the leaves on the apple trees?" Sabina asked in a sceptical tone.

"Of course not. I don't mean I want to sit in the court-yard, playing with my toes and staring at the same five trees! I want to get out *there*." He pointed towards where he knew the gate must be.

Eleksander frowned. "We're not allowed to roam outside the Hall of Explorers without a tutor present."

"I know that, soft heart," Hale said, taking care to make his tone friendly. "But if we only go to the lake for a quick dip and look at the scenery, and then come back… we're not going to get lost or in trouble, right?"

He meant the lake by the king's castle, the one they had their swimming lessons in. It wasn't far away. Surely, they'd dare to come with him there?

Avelynne massaged her shoulders. "I could do with getting into the water and giving my muscles a stretch," she said. "That strenuous spear fighting lesson this morning has my muscles feeling like knotted pieces of strings."

"Aye, a cooling dip would be nice. Especially as it's weirdly hot for autumn," Sabina whinged. "One quick swim. Then we come straight back here. No dawdling or breaking the rules further."

"As you say, older sister," Hale teased.

Eleksander sat biting his thumb nail. "We could ask Rete to accompany us. Say that we want extra swim practise?"

"Sure. And he could say no. In fact, he probably will," Hale replied.

Avelynne brushed a stray braid away from Eleksander's face. "It'll be fine. I shan't let us get caught. Besides, if they did catch us, the worst they could do is make us attend more lessons in the evenings. Which isn't that different from sitting here staring at maps."

He gave her a shy glance. "You don't think they'd, well, cane us or something? My father warned me that academies outside the Lakelands can be more… physical."

"The only place you can still beat students is the North and the Woodlands," Sabina muttered.

"Even there it's rare, though," Hale agreed.

Avelynne cupped Eleksander's cheek. "If they did hurt us, my parents would have them tried for brutality. The Grand Count might not be a doting father, but he wouldn't allow anyone to injure or challenge an Ironhold without consequences."

Slowly, Eleksander nodded. "All right, Ave."

They smiled at each other.

Hale drummed his fingers against the table. The sudden feeling that he and Sabina weren't needed here niggled at him. Avelynne and Eleksander hadn't even looked away from each other when he and Sabina were speaking. Also, the nicknames that they'd been calling each other for weeks, *Ave* and *Sander*, yes, that bothered him enough that he wanted to throw things.

Sabina stood and replaced the book on its shelf. "Let's not dally then. The sooner we get going, the sooner we can sneak back in. I assume you mean to climb the servant quarters building and get out that way, Hale?"

He gave her a thumbs up, wishing he had the sort of

friendship with her that Avelynne had with Eleksander. At least he hoped that friendship was the right word.

"Exactly," he said. "We can't go via the gate; it's always manned and soon they'll ring the bell to signal the locking of the gate. But no one'll expect us to climb over a building."

"And as the building housing the servant quarters has the thinnest width, and the easiest roof to climb and traverse, it's a good choice," Sabina confirmed with her sage nod.

"Splendid. Let's go then," Avelynne said, already halfway to the door.

Finally, they had snuck out and scaled the uneven stone wall and the roof with its tiles of fired clay. Avelynne had made the climb with the happy whisper of, "I bet I couldn't have done this a few weeks ago!"

The only one unable to scale the building had been the snowtiger, but Kall had simply walked out the gate and gone around. The guards had either not cared or not dared stop him.

Their walk down to the lake was now turning into more of a run, energy spiking in their bloodstreams as they dared to escape.

It was growing dark, the skies above painted in dim blues and dark purples. Hale spotted the moon, and elbowed Avelynne while saying, "Look at that full, fat yellow ball. It thinks it can hide in those clouds and leave us in the blinding dark."

"Ah. Well, it is sorely mistaken. Young Master Hawthorn wants his fresh air, changing leaves, and his moonshine. Nothing will stop him."

He was about to reply, but Avelynne's attention was taken by Kall nuzzling her hand. Damn animal.

The banks surrounding the lake were crawling with creeping vines and thorny bushes. They stuck to the path and then took care as they undressed to only their long tunics.

From all corners, there were glances sneaked as the clothes fell away. Sabina and Avelynne made jokes about this being the closest to being in dresses they'd been for weeks. Like him, they didn't appear too uncomfortable in their scant clothing. In fact, there was a hum of excitement emanating as much from them as from himself. It was only the four of them here in the dark. Why would they be shy? Eleksander was a different story. As the two lasses discussed whether or not Sabina should undo her braid, Eleksander turned to Hale and murmured, "This tunic only barely covers my... modesty."

Hale clapped him on the back and whispered back, "Are you bragging about the size of your modesty, brother?"

Eleksander opened and closed his mouth like a fish, making Hale laugh and say, "It's fine, just don't stretch your arms up high until you're in the murky water."

"You're right, I suppose. I'm going to hurry in." Eleksander ran for the water, holding his tunic down.

He laughed with abandon as he splashed into the water. This was clearly where he felt at home, half submerged like some water god of old. He began swimming and Hale understood where he got those broad shoulders. Hale grunted, lamenting not having grown up surrounded by lakes and the sea.

As the moon came out from the clouds, Avelynne appeared and followed Eleksander into the lake. Hale chased her, making her giggle and squeal. Sabina sighed theatrically as she slowly strode in after them all, ignoring their calls to hurry up. She ordered Kall to stay by some bushes and the snowtiger happily began washing, occasionally checking on his mistress.

Hale luxuriated in the water licking at his skin and soaking his tunic. He dove under the surface and didn't come back up until his lungs protested. Suddenly he wasn't so disappointed with the freakishly hot weather, the water was a perfect temperature.

Avelynne seemed to think so too, she cupped her hands and scooped some water up to pour over her neck and shoulders. Her necklace glinted in the moonlight, the water trickling off it onto her drenched, clinging tunic. She showered water over herself again, smiling as if she didn't have a care in the world. As if she knew some divine secret.

Such smooth, graceful movements. How can she be real?

Avelynne caught him staring and misunderstood his gaze. "Want some too?" She asked.

He nodded, words escaping him.

She dipped her elfin hands in the lake and brought up water that reflected the yellow moonlight. Then she poured it over his neck, throat, and shoulders. When the water was gone, she placed her cool hand on the back of his heated neck.

"Is that better, my warm-blooded Woodsman?"

She blinked her black, silken eyelashes a few times and Hale's heart drummed in time to their movements.

"Much," he whispered hoarsely.

He was almost certain that her smile was flirtatious. He tried to return it, but she looked away since Sabina had finally joined them. Avelynne immediately turned to splash water at the other lass. Over and over, until Sabina's mane of loose hair dripped with lake water. Sabina responded by grabbing Avelynne and clamping her arms down. Hale watched as Avelynne laughed and pretended to try biting Sabina's nose to get free. They were so tightly entangled. Like lovers.

Then Eleksander splashed water at him, catching him right in the face. That was all it took. A full-on water fight was on.

Soon they were all as soaked as if they'd been under water for hours. Eleksander's braids had escaped their hair tie and now hung down his shoulders.

Avelynne grabbed a couple and ran them across her fingers while sighing, "I'm so jealous. I miss having long hair."

Sabina had been floating next to them but now stood, tossed her soaked shock of hair and said, "You can have some of mine. I have far too much."

Avelynne took a handful of Sabina's hair in her free hand. Her gaze flitted from the black braids in her left palm to the white tresses in her right. Reverently, she said, "So different and yet so lovely."

Hale changed his footing. The soil at the bottom of the lake suddenly bothered his feet. Had it gotten stickier? Soggier? The water wasn't even that nice anymore.

As the moon momentarily hid, Sabina turned her head to kiss Avelynne's fingers. "Your hair is wonderful too. It doesn't have to be long to be beautiful, you know."

"No, but it should be thicker. Mine is so flat," Avelynne whinged.

"Fine, not flat," Sabina amended.

Avelynne smiled at her, gifting Sabina with the sight of those dimples. Right then, the moon came out to illuminate her face, as if it was taunting Hale with the beauty of that smile being awarded to someone else.

Stupid moon. Stupid sandy lake bottom. His patience was wearing thin. He kept quiet, as to not say something cutting. He remembered his talk with Avelynne and recognised that he was losing his temper. He should analyse what he was feeling and act accordingly. Be sensible. But that was so boring. So much work. Why should he have to bother with all that?

Maybe he should do a headstand to impress them instead? Distract them, especially Avelynne, from the silly topic? Distract them from what looked like flirting and excluded him and his short hair. Yeah, that was what he'd do. A headstand to show his superior bravery and strength.

He focused back in. They were still talking about stupid hair! He'd had enough of this nonsense. "Long hair won't be useful on our mission," he snapped. "It'll get stuck and be smelly and tangled. You'll get lice and other things living in it. If you three don't cut your hair before we set sail, I'll do it for you."

A beat of silence.

"Ha! I'd like to see you try, you big bully," Sabina said.

She was smiling but there was an edge to her voice. Eleksander wasn't smiling at all, he was looking down.

A voice in Hale's head, one that sounded a lot like Avelynne's, told him that this would be a good place to stop. The perfect time to explain and smooth things over. However, that voice was drowned out by the words now spilling out of his mouth, "Maybe I'll do it when you sleep. You'll wake up, finally hygienic and sensible-looking."

"What?" Sabina snarled.

"Yes," he thundered. "You'll look much better. Not like the shittingly vain, silly ladies who dance at parties you resemble now! I bet you'll thank me, then."

Hale actually felt the wonderful evening being ruined. It was a sensation of icy water being poured down his spine.

He ached to put all those words back into his mouth. But they were out there now, floating on the surface of the lake like oil on water. Now he knew why he should have bothered to analyse his behaviour and think of the others.

Shit. Being sensible and bored would've been better than this.

"Hale," Avelynne sighed.

Now he felt even worse.

Eleksander cleared his throat. "I didn't know you thought I looked like that. Sorry to hear it. Anyway, we should get back. We're not allowed to be here."

He walked out of the water and began trying to pull his trousers on, struggling with them against his wet skin. Sabina gave Hale a glare and left as well. Hale wasn't sure, but he thought he heard her tell Eleksander something like, "You're perfect the way you are. Don't listen to that arse."

Hale saw Avelynne glide through the water towards

him. "This is exactly what we spoke about," she said. "You did it again, this time due to jealousy, I think. Nothing to do about that now. However…" She waded even closer. "You can learn from this, so it doesn't happen again."

"Mm, I suppose."

She put a hand on his shoulder. "Furthermore, this is a brilliant time to practice apologising, especially to Eleksander. He worships you and he worries about what you think of him. Try to mend the wound you caused."

Hale swallowed hard. "Shit. I will. I'm sorry."

"I know. So do they. However, it doesn't solve the problem."

He took a shaky breath. "I know. I'll talk to them."

"Good." Avelynne let go of his shoulder and headed up to the banks without another word.

He wanted to stay in the water but heard Eleksander mutter that they couldn't leave him here alone. Even when so hurt, the Lakelander was trying to keep him safe. It made the guilt burn in Hale's stomach all the more.

When they got back to the Hall of Explorers, he told them to go to bed and that he'd talk to them—and apologise—after he'd had a moment to collect his thoughts.

They all wandered off, Sabina with her arm around Eleksander's waist.

Hale watched them go, his mind a wasp's nest of thoughts. Was Avelynne right in that he'd spoken out of jealousy? Was that what made him unable to keep his tongue? No, not just that. On some level, he'd been conscious that he was doing wrong and that he should stop. He hadn't wanted to, though. Had his own sense of fun and ego been more important than their feelings?

He banged his fist against his head.

Shit. Shit. Shit.

He needed to speak to someone who knew his mind and behaviour better than he did. He had to go find Ghar. His mentor had known him since he was a snot-nosed, lonely, little orphan with something to prove; he'd have answers.

As Hale headed towards the servant quarters hoping that Ghar hadn't decided on an early night, he heard words whispered fast from an open window.

"Silver like magic. Silver like the young countess' necklace. Silver like the beasts."

Hale stopped. "Silver like the young countess' necklace?" Was that about Avelynne? He stopped and pricked up his ears.

"Look for the silver. Silver like magic. Silver like the young countess' necklace. Silver like the beasts."

It was a woman's voice and the accent sounded like his own. The hairs on Hale's arms stood up.

"Hello?" He said. "Is someone there? I, uh, didn't mean to eavesdrop."

"Oh. Now you listen? When I try to warn you, you ignore me," the voice hissed. "You carry on romancing each other, burying your faces in dusty books, playing at magic, and fighting with pointy sticks."

So, this was their anonymous note-writer? Hale clenched his fists. "That's not true. We've been watchful and careful of who we trusted. Maybe if the warnings we got were a little less vague... Maybe then we'd take more action."

There was a desperate laugh. "What action, young mapmaker?"

"I don't know," Hale snapped. "That depends on who it is we can't trust! We could get someone to help, right? I could send a letter to the Warden. I hear your Woodlands accent, you know the Warden can be trusted."

"I don't trust anyone anymore. The whole system is twisted. Why do you think they want you mapmakers so young? So impressionable?"

"Because of our flexible bodies and minds and that we have handled the lack of a varied diet best. Also, we're not busy fighting the silver beasts."

Another shrill laugh. "That's what they tell you. What they tell all of us." The voice grew quieter, as if it was moving away from the window. "Don't trust him. He's your biggest danger. He will twist you."

"He? Who's he?"

"Silver like magic. Silver like the young countess' necklace. Silver like the beasts," the woman's voice uttered, so far away that Hale had to strain to hear it.

He'd had enough of this. He jumped so his hands could grab the window sill and pulled himself up and in. The room was empty. It was a clean and modest space, much like the room Ghar had farther down this corridor.

Hale ran to the door and scanned the corridor. No one there. He snuck along it in both directions. Trepidation crept along his skin; he wouldn't be allowed in this building without a good reason.

Everything was dark and still. All the doors to the bedrooms were closed. The whisperer must have hidden in one of them. But which one? Hale couldn't yank open every door and search for her, he'd wake dozens of sleeping servants and workers. Besides, who knew how heavily punished he would be when he was caught? Biting his tongue hard, he gave it up and left the way he came.

When Hale snuck into their room, Eleksander was in bed. His covers were pulled up high and his face turned to the wall. He was asleep. Or was he pretending? It wasn't all that late. Either way, he wouldn't want to speak to Hale.

The story of the whisperer would have to wait until morning meal. So would the apology.

Chapter Twenty-Three

THE COUNTESS AND THE WHITENGALE

The sad ending to the evening's adventure stayed with Avelynne, making it hard to sleep. The increasing dread of her secret having repercussions and her frequent nightmares didn't make slumber any more enticing.

When she heard melancholy birdsong and identified it as a whitengale, one of the birds that migrated down from the North, she gave up on sleep and decided to obey her full bladder.

She pulled her blanket around her shoulders and tugged on her boots. It was still far too hot for autumn. So why was she cold? She tiptoed out to not wake Sabina and Kall.

The air was warm and humid in the courtyard, and, as she left the privy, she decided that the cold she felt must come from her restless mind.

Returning to her room, she wished that whitengale would sing again. Everything was overly quiet now, it gave her too much opportunity to think.

When she silently closed the door to their bedchamber she heard Sabina mumble, "Hey. Are you all right?"

"Yes. That water I had before bed kept me awake," Avelynne said, replacing her boots.

"I think it was more than a full bladder keeping you up," Sabina said. "You've been laying there fretting and sighing like a spoiled princess with a bellyache."

"Only because my bedding is covered in coarse tiger fur," Avelynne teased back.

Sabina chuckled. The sound of it was soothing in the far too quiet night, making Avelynne step closer to her.

By the light of the moon, Avelynne saw her stretch in her bed. Her white hair splayed over her pillow and her firm figure looking warm and inviting. The reassuring, sweet scent of her lingered in the air after her stretch, coming off her bed clothes as well as her body. Tiredness finally crept into Avelynne and she had an urge to crawl into Sabina's arms and fall asleep.

Deciding on something more appropriate, she switched out her own blanket for Sabina's. Haughtily repeating that Kall had shed fur all over hers and demanding they switch.

"Fine, little Countess. What's mine is yours," Sabina mumbled and moved the new blanket so it barely covered her legs. Her torso was only covered by her nightdress, which lay taut against her beautiful shape.

Avelynne made a point of not staring anymore and, with an amused hum, went to her own bed. The whitengale sang again, this time its melody sounded less melancholy. Less lonely. She pulled Sabina's blanket over her and enjoyed the other woman's scent on it. Sleep finally came for her and she welcomed it with a long exhale.

The next morning, Avelynne stood by the dressing table and pulled on her last garment while yawning enough to make her jaw click. She had endured bone-chilling night terrors. Some about Sabina and Hale hating her for her secret, others about silver beasts coming into the Centre. They were milling over the ground until there was no more soil or stone slabs to be seen, only beasts, crawling and biting with those vicious fangs. Everywhere. Until they gobbled the whole Centre up, her friends included. She awoke in a cold sweat.

I cannot wait to leave this land and sail somewhere without silver beasts.

During both sets of nightmares there had been a question looming over her: what were the warnings they'd received regarding? Not knowing but constantly having to be vigilant had been a theme as terrible image after terrible image played out in her mind. No wonder she felt like she'd been in stave lessons with Tutor Rogan for the last seven hours.

She adjusted her necklace, noting the dullness of the silver quill. She should have asked Myllie to clean it weeks ago, but she simply hadn't had time. Or prioritised her looks. Which certainly wasn't how she had been raised. Staring at her reflection in the mirror she'd brought, she frowned at the shadows under her eyes until she was distracted by a harsh whooshing noise. It was Sabina raking a brush through her hair. She always went at it with such force. Avelynne guessed she was used to hurrying with her own grooming to then go help others.

She stepped over and took the brush. "May I?"

Sabina stared at her in confusion. "What? Comb my hair?"

"Yes."

Sabina sniggered. "Your fascination with people's hair almost rivals your fascination with eyes."

Avelynne tapped the Northerner's nightdress-clad shoulder with the brush. "Do you want my help or not?"

"Aye. I mean, *yes please.* That would be lovely."

Avelynne began untangling the thick mane of hair, it was hard work, but she managed to be gentler than Sabina had been.

"I wish I could comb my hair out with magic but that never works properly," Sabina grumbled. "I should just sleep with a braid to keep it from tangling, but as I sleep on my back, it gets uncomfortable."

"Yes, I remember that from when I had longer hair. Luckily for me, I sleep on my stomach."

Sabina hummed and Avelynne brushed in silence for a while.

"You know what I miss?"

"No, what?" Sabina answered.

"I miss getting ready for festivities, like banquets or tournament balls. Everyone having their hair styled in the most unique ways. All while dressing in their best garments, Lakelander silks and beautifully embroidered bodices for the women. Elegant doublets, golden rings, and sable-lined cloaks for the men."

"I can't really picture such extravagance. I did use to love getting dressed in my prettiest linen gown for harvest feasts or the Solstice festival, though."

Avelynne could imagine Sabina hurrying to get a

moment to herself while trying to get ready for a festivity in her cold village. They would all go home for the Midwinter Solstice in a few months. Would Sabina get dressed up in her linen gown then?

She caressed the shell of Sabina's exposed ear and said, "I bet you look stunning in that dress."

Avelynne couldn't see Sabina's face but she saw enough of her ear and the start of her cheek to see them bloom into pink.

"T-thank you," Sabina said quietly.

Avelynne carried on brushing, even gentler now. "Why the stutter? Don't Northerners know how to take compliments?"

"Those of us who hear them probably are. I'm lucky if I get complimented on my capability or endurance. Maybe on my strength, on a good day." She let out a hollow little laugh. "I'm not counting those memorable times when my many uncles have pointed out that my curves show I'm 'good breeding stock' and other comments to that effect."

Avelynne stopped the brush. "What? That's absolutely ridiculous! There's so much more to you than your physical aspects and what use you can be to others."

Sabina only scoffed.

"There is! Your intelligence, your big heart, your humour, your confidence, to mention a few. You're one of a kind."

Sabina cleared her throat. "It pleases me a great deal that you think so."

"I *know* so, Sabina. Anyone who gets to be around you is exceedingly lucky."

Avelynne's chest filled with affection for the other

woman. The same way it had last night when she saw Eleksander run into the lake, the water splashing up his body as he laughed like a child. The same way she'd felt when Hale had chased her into the lake, beaming at her as if she was a miracle he had just discovered.

They were all so dear to her. Which was why her nightmares had centred around danger to them. That was her biggest fear now. The fact that her secret could hurt two of them so badly made Avelynne queasy. Bile rose in her throat and she had to breathe deep to recover her equilibrium.

Sabina's raspy voice broke the silence. "Something wrong?"

Avelynne shook the sensations off and returned to brushing. "Only bad dreams lingering from last night. Nothing to worry about."

Sabina reached her hand up and put it on Avelynne's, stopping the brushing. The hand was colder than her own, as always.

Sabina's voice was steady but kind as she said, "Do you want to talk about it?"

Everything became unnaturally quiet to her then. The sounds of Kall washing on the floor vanished. Even the morning song of the whitengale didn't register in Avelynne's mind anymore. This was her chance to tell Sabina the truth.

She watched their hands. Sabina's paler, longer fingers caressing the back of her hand in such a sweet way. Such a trusting way. They had shared a bedchamber for weeks. They had shared so much. How could Avelynne tell her that she'd been keeping something so huge from her. How could she hurt Sabina like that? How could she stand seeing the hurt of betrayal in those cherished two-coloured eyes? Her insides roiled again.

"No," she managed in barely a whisper. "I'm not ready to talk about it yet. I would like to someday, though. I would like to tell you… about my fear and what it stems from."

Sabina's fingers gave one last stroke along Avelynne's own and then the pale hand was retracted, leaving Avelynne's strangely cold.

"Aye, whatever you wish. I'm here and always ready to listen."

"I know," Avelynne murmured, her stomach churning with more stinging bile. "Thank you."

"No need to thank me. Not only do I care about you, I'm also very curious about what you were on about when you mumbled in your sleep last night."

Avelynne's breath hitched. "I did?"

"Aye, but so quietly I couldn't make out any words."

"Good."

Sabina sniggered. "Good? That confirms it, you were having naughty dreams. Please don't tell me you were running your hands through those chest curls of Hale's?"

"What makes you think I was dreaming of *his* chest?" Avelynne said, trying to make her tone light. Panic washed over her at the thought of her sleeping self revealing what her parents had made her do! "What makes you think I wasn't dreaming of yours, hm?"

Sabina made a noise, halfway between a purr and a hum. "Well, were you?"

Avelynne leaned in close to Sabina's ear—so close her

lips almost brushed the creamy skin—and whispered, "I shan't tell you, my sweet."

"Fine," Sabina said with a casual sigh, one that was belied by her blushing and rapid breathing. "Keep your secrets, little Countess, but hurry up with the brushing so I can get dressed for breakfast. I'm famished and Tutor Hathleen threatened us with 'advanced calculations' in our first lesson today, remember? I'll need plenty of food to handle that."

Avelynne aimed for a chuckle but it came out as a croak. "Yes, of course," she said and quickened her brushstrokes. Panic and guilt made her temples throb. Somehow, she had to tell Sabina everything. And soon.

Chapter Twenty-Four

WATER

Being overheated woke Hale. Despite growing up in a hot climate, he never enjoyed sleeping in the heat, certainly not indoors. How could the Centre have a heatwave this far into autumn? Wasn't it meant to have more clement weather?

He rubbed his face. His morning routine of fifty push-ups, sit ups, and leg kicks were awful in this heat. For once, he was dreading his workout.

The door opened, Eleksander came in wearing only a towel around his hips, clearly having had one of his frequent baths. He meticulously dried himself off and put on freshly cleaned clothes.

Hale sensed the moments crawl by and yet no words of apology came from his useless mouth.

Say something, man!

When he saw Eleksander's hands freeze before putting his braids up in a ponytail, the guilt made Hale groan.

"Don't," he begged.

"Don't what?" Eleksander said, sounding like he was aiming for nonchalance.

"Don't hesitate by your hair like that. There's nothing wrong with it or the way you look."

"That's not the impression you've been giving," Eleksander said in deep-throated growl.

Hale winced. "Look. You're rich. You're taller and more broadly built than me. You're better than me in most subjects. And, of course, Avelynne and Sabina like you more. Shitting silver beasts, even the tutors like you better than me! You have no reason to doubt yourself. Or listen to the things I say. Brush them off!"

Eleksander rolled his eyes. "I can't. I'm soft, remember?"

There it was. His chance to help Eleksander and clean up this mess in one easy sweep. He jumped at it. "I can help you with that. We can work on getting you more used to harsh things and you'll slowly build up a harder shell."

Eleksander's mouth twitched. "Back to the idea of us changing and growing thicker skin, are we?" He sighed. "Hale. Have you ever considered water and rock?"

"Have I ever considered them? What do you mean?"

Eleksander gathered his many braids up while saying, "In the Lakelands, we often talk about how water, which is soft and flexible, meets the hard and unyielding rock. Now, one of them wears the other one down. Which one?"

"The water erodes the rock," Hale said.

"Exactly. Water may have to put up with hulking cliffs standing in it or pebbles being thrown into it, but in the end… its softness and flexibility is its strength, not its weakness." He stopped to get his leather hair tie. "Water can get in anywhere and it can change form. Waves can drown a man while currents can drag a massive bear down the river.

And the gently lapping waters over the rock? It will wear the rock down to nothing with enough time."

"I get it. Water is soft but strong at the same time."

"Precisely. And no one tells water to change, right?"

Hale scratched the back of his head. "Why would they?"

"Why would you tell *me* to change?"

"But," Hale groaned. "You're asking me to change too. To pause and analyse everything. To stop saying stuff that offends." He heard mockery creeping into his tone and quickly fixed it. "And I'll do my best with that! I don't want to hurt anyone. I'm just making the point."

"It's not the same thing, Hale," Eleksander said softly. "I'm asking you to change a behaviour. Not how you feel or how you react to things. If I could stop being hurt by things, don't you think I would've tried that?"

"Mm, that sounds like what Avelynne was saying."

Hale puffed out a sigh. This sort of thing didn't just bore him, it set his teeth on edge. Conversation with his friends back home usually didn't go past ten words at a time. Here, they never seemed to stop.

"You're shittingly clever at these things," Hale finally said. "Emotions, communication, patience, stuff like that. Right now, I'm a lot more jealous of that than of your broader build."

Eleksander hesitated. Hale didn't blame him, he had no idea what he would say if the roles were reversed.

"Well," Eleksander said after a while. "I am jealous of you often, so I suppose I could understand that."

"You are?" Hale's head shot up. "Of what? My scars?"

"No, you acorn! Of your confidence, your fitness, and

all your fighting and navigation skills. How you rarely worry. Even your ability to grow body hair! I'm jealous of how you're the man that everyone always wanted me to be and I could never quite achieve. So, I guess we're even."

Hale's head slumped back down. "No, we're not. You think about others and their feelings. You manage to contain your jealousy. That makes you a better man than me."

"Don't say that. You can do so many things I can't. Neither of us is better than the other one. We're different, that's all."

Hale stood and offered a handshake. Eleksander took his hand without hesitation.

"I'm sorry," Hale said. "I truly didn't mean to offend you. Again."

"I know. It's all right. I..." he trailed off and let his thumb rub the back of Hale's hand before continuing. "I apologise if I'm wrong or stepping out of line here, but I think this time the temper flare came from you being some-what possessive of Avelynne?"

Hale retracted his hand and used it to scratch at his beard-scratchy chin while pondering that for a few heart-beats. "Huh. You may have a point. I like her. A lot. Still, that's no excuse to treat you and Sabina badly."

Eleksander shrugged, seeming less tense now. "As I said, it's all right. I only brought it up so you'd be aware of it."

"Mm," Hale said.

"You'll have to do me a favour. To make up for it."

"Sure! Anything."

Eleksander averted his eyes. "Put clothes on. The fact that you sleep naked makes me..." He trailed off.

"Makes you what?" Hale said, scratching his naked hip with a grin.

Eleksander's gaze returned to Hale and slowly roamed from his face down to the hip being scratched. Then he squeezed his eyes closed. "It makes me, hm, uneasy."

Hale sniggered. "Fine." He picked up a pair of trousers from the pile of clean clothes that Ghar had placed by the foot of his bed. "One thing, though. No one tells water to change, but it still does. It turns hard—ice. And even softer than before—steam."

Eleksander gave his lopsided smile. "Yes, but it does it naturally. Not because some cocky Woodlander told it to, so he didn't have to stop to consider others."

Hale winked at him. "Ha! Fair enough, my friend. Fair enough."

He got dressed with a new lightness in his body.

One down and one to go. Apologising to Sabina will be easier. She's more like me.

Then he stopped, halfway through pulling his tunic over his head. Was she really, though? Or did he just assume that? Had he stopped to analyse that?

He laughed under his breath. He'd never have thought about that before he came here. This place, no... these people really had started to change him. Or made him want to change himself. He pulled the tunic on, finding that he liked this new Hale Hawthorn.

***

While walking to their arithmetic lesson, Hale apologised to Sabina. Telling her that her hair was attractive and that letting it grow long was possibly more efficient then constantly having to cut it when they'd be journeying. With a sniff, she'd accepted his apology. He knew it would take more to completely win her back, but she was too efficient to dwell on things for long. In fact, when he told them what he'd heard the mystery female whisper, she was the one who asked the most questions and congratulated him on his attempts to try to find the disembodied voice.

"It's got to be the servant who mouthed that first warning to you, Avelynne," Sabina said.

Avelynne hummed quietly, biting her lower lip.

Eleksander put an arm around her and said, "I'm sure the fact that she mentioned your necklace has nothing to do with all of this. She was merely repeating things that were silver."

"Yes, but why?" Avelynne asked.

"She was clearly describing something," Sabina said. "Something connected with what she's warning us about."

Hale huffed while pulling at his tunic which clung to his back in the heat. "That doesn't get us much further."

"I respectfully disagree," Eleksander said. "It means we have something else to watch out for. Take a closer look at anything silver you come across."

They had arrived and with determined, conspiring nods went in to greet their tutor. Soon they were sucked into yet another day of lessons and forgot everything but their studies and thoughts of when they could scour up a snack. Hale paused. Or perhaps that was just him? Considering others sure wasn't easy.

Chapter Twenty-Five

RISE TO THE CHALLENGE

They were leaving the Great Hall after an unusually light dinner when Sander tapped Avelynne on the shoulder. "Ready for some practise tonight?"

"What? Oh, yes, I suppose so. In what subject?"

"I still think the physical arts is where we need to put most effort in, it's where you lack most confidence and proficiency."

"True," she admitted, embarrassment heating her cheeks. "What about knife throwing or perhaps swordplay? I still need to be able to feint better."

Sander frowned. "I don't believe it's fighting technique you need most right now. I think you need confidence in your body."

Avelynne looked down at herself. "Confidence? How do I get that? I've put some muscle on during my time here. Lost some fat, too, I believe."

"I didn't mean confidence in how your body appears. I mean in how you can use it."

Unease filled Avelynne's chest. "Use it?"

"Yes, I think we need to train your endurance, balance, and flexibility. You need to know you can trust your body to rise to whatever challenge you come across."

"I see." She touched her necklace. "Do you know how I might achieve that?"

"I do have an idea, yes."

Avelynne disregarded her unease. She had made a promise. "All right. I trust you and will gratefully take any help you can give me."

"Splendid. Meet me out in the courtyard when you've had some time to digest supper."

A little later, Avelynne walked into the courtyard, tucking her hair behind her ears and checking that her boots were tied tightly to allow for uninhibited movements.

Through the fading light of early evening, she saw Sander standing by the sundial.

"Here I am. Please tell me we're not going running?" She said, putting on a brave smile.

He shook his head, smiling as well. "Not tonight. We're going to practise a form of exercise popular in the Lakelands. You've probably seen it during your travels there —equilibriating."

Avelynne felt her eyes grow wide. "You mean that peculiar balancing and deep breathing practice Lakelanders do in parks?"

"Yes, to find your equilibrium. Physically and mentally."

Avelynne recalled seeing people bending and moving

into complex positions her mother had called "unnatural for the human body".

"But those people... they stretched like they were made of string and not muscle and bone. I cannot do that!"

"Yes, you can, Ave. It will stretch and strengthen your muscles, but, more importantly, it will strengthen and stretch your *mind*. It'll centre you and help you focus."

She was about to argue further but he touched his finger to her lips and said, "Please try it, my friend. We'll start simple. Mimic me."

He moved back and shook tension out of his shoulders. Then he slowly hinged at the hips and bent forward. "Breathe in as you go down and breathe out as you rise." He touched his toes and then straightened again while exhaling. Then he started the movement over.

With much doubt, she tried it with him. She couldn't quite reach her toes, but she got much closer than she had expected.

He gave her that pretty, crooked smile of his. "Wonderful. You're more limber than I thought. Must be all that dancing at tournament festivities. Now, keep copying me."

He continued moving in and out of simple positions while breathing deeply and steadily. Avelynne followed suit best she could, trying to swallow her giggles when she fouled up or lost balance.

To her surprise, she found her body heating up, despite that the movements were slow and not particularly strenuous. She got even warmer when he showed her a position that he called "focus." This one *was* strenuous. She stood with legs apart and arms over her head, bent into a twist which she'd never be able to repeat without his instruction.

It took more balance and concentration than anything she could recall having done before.

She wobbled, nearly toppling over. "Sander, this one is too hard."

"No, it's not. You're already in the position and I know you can stay there a little longer. Just notice the muscles that niggle due to being in a position they are unused to, without panicking at the discomfort."

She groaned but tried to obey.

"You're doing marvellously, Ave. Inhale deeply and imagine that you're breathing into the straining muscles. This is the final position we're doing before we're done with the equilibriating. Stay the course."

The muscles were beyond straining and into hurting, but she wasn't going to tell him that. He was being so kind by keeping her secret and helping her improve. Besides, by the time she'd told the others how she came to be here, they'd probably hate her. Sander would be the only friend she'd have. Except Myllie but she was paid to be her friend. Avelynne, for the first time, admitted to herself that Myllie didn't count. Neither did the few fawning but jealous acquaintances from Ironhold castle. Before coming here, she hadn't had real friends. Now she had Sander. She couldn't let him down.

Avelynne's muscles shook and she swayed again, gasping before she regained her balance. Could people see her? Was anyone watching? Was that servant with the strange warnings watching?

Why are you thinking about her? Ow, this hurts. How much longer will he make me stand here?

He was circling her, surveying her body. "Ave, you're

holding your breath and tensing. Breathe slow and stop fighting this. You can do this."

"No, I don't think I can!"

"You *are* doing it, though. Look, I know what it's like to feel like you cannot achieve things. That you're not good enough. Those taunting voices that laugh at you. Doubt you. Berate you. Those voices that soon become your own inner voice."

She stopped whingeing for a moment and considered his words. He'd always talked about his loving, supporting family. Surely they had not been those "taunting voices?" Then who had been the ones to shatter this incredible young man's self-esteem?

He placed himself straight in front of her now. "That's why we're doing this. So I can show you that you're able to do much more than you think. You simply have to stop letting your mind ruin it for you. Stop allowing it to wander and sow doubts. I can see you panicking about things that don't matter."

"I'm not," she lied, eyes shutting against the physical discomfort.

"Yes, you are. Stop telling me what you think I want to hear. I saw you looking around before. No one is watching you." She heard him take a step closer. "But even if they were, you shouldn't be thinking about them. Try to close off your mind. Close it to worries. Don't think about your secret. Or Tutor Rogan. Or the servant who warned us about the mystery. Or Hale or Sabina. Think only about your breathing and what your body is doing."

She tried. And failed. Her muscles shook even worse and she lost balance again. Thoughts of Hale hating her came into her mind. Then Sabina being disappointed. Then disappointing Sander right now... She tried again. She attempted his earlier suggestion: pretending to breath into the parts of her body that strained and stung with the pain of staying in the posture.

It took a few attempts, but it almost.... appeared to work? The muscles felt like they grew longer and warmer, no longer tight as coils. She breathed in as much as she could, inflating her lungs and belly.

"Good," he said affectionately. "That frown of yours has smoothed. I think we'll stop it there for tonight."

She released the position and stood normally. Her body was throbbing and her legs wobbled. But she was smiling.

"Welcome back and well done. Now that you can focus your mind a little, you should try hitting that bullseye again."

"Pardon?"

Sander pointed to something Avelynne had missed before. Leaning against the sundial was a bow and a quiver of arrows.

She took a step back. "No."

"I think you should try it. Now that it's only us and you're balanced."

"I-I can't. My arms ache. I'm tired. I can't."

Sander opened his mouth to answer but never got that far as from the other side of the courtyard they heard Hale call, "You two. Come here. I need to talk to you."

Happy to be saved from disappointing Sander, Avelynne stood on her tiptoes to give her instructor a quick peck on the cheek. "Next time. I'll practise my equilibrium every morning before breakfast and next time you and I train, I'll try to hit that bullseye."

Sander sighed. "Mm. All right." He glanced over at Hale with tender reproach. "Let's go see what our good-looking rogue of a Woodlander is up to."

Chapter Twenty-Six

BEST LAID PLANS

All Hale's preparations were complete. The fruit. The wine. Then fetching Sabina from reading in her room and finding Avelynne and Eleksander out in the courtyard. Finally, asking them all to follow him into a quiet corridor for a chat.

Yes, those steps had all gone to plan. Now he could only hope the rest of the night would pan out as well. He stopped, puffed out his chest and said, "It's warm."

Sabina bumped into his back. "Ouf. Yes, Hale. It is. Very perceptive. Did you drag us into this corridor to tell us that?"

"No. Um. No, I didn't."

Why was he suddenly unsure?

He leaned one shoulder against the wall, trying to display confidence he didn't feel. "Actually, I thought I'd suggest that we all sneak away to the lake for a cooling swim tonight."

No one answered right away, and Hale flinched away from the wall. "I've bribed one of the kitchen maids to sneak me some fruits and dipping sauces. A-and this time I absolutely won't say or do anything shitty."

Eleksander hummed and gave him a smirk. Hale bumped him with his shoulder and amended, "Fine, I'll try at least."

"Fair enough," Eleksander said. "We'll *all* make sure this adventure is better than the last one."

"Hear hear," Sabina agreed.

"Well, if the two responsible ones are willing to go, I'm certainly not going to be the one to say no," Avelynne said. "Do we wait until it grows dark, like last time?"

"That'll be best," Hale replied.

Sabina was stretching, her shoulder muscles straining against her tunic in a way that made Hale want to go do push-ups. "Well, twilight is already upon us," she said. "Soon the servants will have finished for the day, while the tutors are getting drunk on cider and complaining about us."

"That reminds me! I got Ghar to sneak me out a quart of wine too," Hale said.

"Great. I'll be both exhausted AND drunk," Eleksander said with an eyeroll. "Someone save me if I drown."

"Don't look at me," Avelynne grumbled. "I struggle enough to keep up with you three while swimming without carrying a big Lakelander."

"I'm not big. I'm broadly built," Eleksander said with a huff, causing the others to have to hide sniggers.

Later on, they headed to the lake in the same way they had the last time. The surroundings were different tonight, though. The air was even warmer but still had the crisp scent of autumn. Hale saw a fragile willow shed a handful of leaves as their footfalls shook it. It was amazing how fast autumn could move.

"This is my favourite season. It's like all of nature gets to relax out of its summer finery and settle in for the long winter sleep," he mumbled.

"Why Hale Hawthorn, you romantic soul," Avelynne teased. Her beautiful smile made it impossible for him to think of a retort, so he stuck to grimacing at her.

When they arrived by the lake, they sat down on the leaf-strewn bank. Hale opened his satchel and took out the fruits and the wine. Everyone ate, watching the waters and the sky shrugging off the last of the light and settling into its nightclothes. By the time Hale offered Sabina the last of the wine, it was dark but for the stars and moon, the latter painting a long line of white across the lake's surface.

"Thanks, but I've had sufficient," Sabina said when the bottle came her way. "I don't want to lose control. You finish it."

It was hard to tell facial expressions by the moonlight, but her voice sounded happy through its normal scratchiness.

Pleased with his efforts so far, Hale petted Kall's head and drained the bottle.

Eleksander stood. "That's it. I can't wait for you snacking little trolls anymore. I'm going for the swim we came here for," he said, his face and tone showing uncertainty at ribbing his friends. With twitchy, unsure motions, he unlaced his boots.

"Ugh, you condescending Lakelanders," Sabina replied with a laugh. She got up and began to undress as well.

Avelynne brushed leaves off her bum and said, "Sander's right, we're here to cool off and swim. I've been trying to convince my anxiety that this is much needed swim practise and not a waste of my precious studying time."

"Sure! Swim practise it is," Hale agreed before starting work on his own boots.

Soon they were all in their long tunics, the white garments standing out against the dark night. So did Sabina's milky skin and hair, the latter currently being taken out of its braid by Avelynne. Did that process have to be so slow and gentle? Why couldn't she leave it in the braid?

Hale kicked a twig out of his way. "You women are obsessed with hair. Come on, Eleksander, let's swim away from them."

The Lakelander was already stepping into the water and called back over his shoulder, "Are you sure that's what you want? You can loosen my braids out of my ponytail if you feel left out?"

"Less talking and more swimming," Hale bellowed, trying not to laugh.

Soon they had all entered the dark currents of the lake and were splashing each other. Everyone but Kall, who laid on the banks and either watched his mistress or chomped his huge jaws at passing moths.

Hale did his headstand to great applause and then Eleksander showed off how long he could hold his breath under water.

"Not bad," Hale admitted when the other lad surfaced.

Eleksander was close enough that Hale could see him shrug. "I grew up around lakes and the sea. It's all second nature to me."

"Still impressive," Sabina said.

She was swimming into the line of moonlight reflected on the water. When she reached it, Avelynne groaned. "That's stunning, Sabina. Stay right there for a moment. Your colours match the moonlight so beautifully. I want to… paint you."

The way she looked at Sabina and how she said "paint" made Hale think that the word could be replaced with "kiss." No, surely that was his jealousy talking. Was Avelynne attracted to women? It wouldn't surprise him, but who could know for sure? Avelynne hadn't claimed a romantic interest in any of them. Sadly, not even in him. Although, when she held his hand after their long talk. Wasn't that how you held and caressed the hand of someone you wanted to kiss?

On the other hand, she had been spending more time with Eleksander than with anyone else. And they always touched and called each other nicknames. They were obviously getting close. Hale's head hurt trying to figure out where, if anywhere, Avelynne's interests lay. Suddenly he wished he'd paid more attention to when his Woodsfolk friends spoke about their lovers.

"The light and the shades of white and blue are very pretty," Eleksander agreed.

"The *colours* are pretty?" Sabina said in a jesting tone. "Thank the stars that Avelynne at least knows how to compliment a person."

Avelynne laughed. "It's easy to compliment someone as beautiful as—"

She was cut off by Kall growling and then making a screeching noise Hale had never heard from him. Their attention turned to the sound. Sabina cleaved through the water in a fast swim to get to her snowtiger and Hale followed.

When they got to the shore, they saw Kall staring at something by the bushes. The snowtiger's ears were back and he was growling with such a rumble that Hale was surprised not to feel it reverberating in the ground. Sabina and Hale got closer, realising that what Kall was staring at was a man in a tattered surcoat.

"Who are you? What are you doing here?" Sabina called to the stranger, one hand on Kall's back and the other glowing with magic ready to be launched.

The man cackled. "I'm the Hall of Explorers groundkeeper. Not that you spoiled little brats would know that. You never see us underlings unless you want something fixed or fetched."

"That's not true," Hale said, thinking of Ghar. "More importantly, you can't speak to my friend like that. Answer her question about what you're doing here, instead."

He heard the sloshing footsteps of Eleksander and Avelynne coming up behind them to form a line of defence.

The groundskeeper sneered. "I'm here to remind you that you're not allowed to venture outside of the academy alone. The Centre may not have silver beasts, but other things lurk here, especially in the swamplands behind the castle. *Things* live down there, ones that may pop into this lake for a bite of some bratty youths."

He sniggered, showing no fear of them or the snowtiger currently baring its teeth at him.

"Will you report us?" Avelynne asked.

The groundskeeper tapped his fingers against his chin. "Hm. No. Not today anyway. You should head back to your snug little chambers and keep safe. You'll be useful to me one day, I reckon."

"Useful? What do you mean? Because we'll find new lands one day?" Hale asked, putting all his menace in his tone and body language.

The groundskeeper put his hand to what must be his sword belt. "Wouldn't you like to know, woodsboy? Run along home, children. Carry on with your learning. Be good little minions and do as you're told."

With that, he vanished back into the high bushes.

Hale went to follow, but Eleksander grabbed his shoulder and whispered, "Let him go. We don't want any trouble."

Through an unspoken agreement, they all dressed and then gathered up the traces of their picnic.

As they walked back, Avelynne broke the silence. "So, what are the odds that he is who we've been warned of?"

"High if we're to go by Kall's instinct for people who cannot be trusted," Sabina said.

"True. But then he didn't like the king either," Hale pointed out. Adding, "He's a smart cat."

"Yes, but that leaves us without definite answers," Eleksander said.

"What else is new?" Sabina snarled.

Chapter Twenty-Seven

SILVER BEASTS AND THE UNDERCROFT

Days passed, bringing about another scorching afternoon which was currently making the back of Avelynne's neck perspire.

They were in the day's final lesson, led by Tutor Santorine. She was drawing star charts on parchments tacked to the walls and showing them how to navigate by those strange lights. Strange to the tutors at least, Avelynne's grandmother had always said they were old gods watching from afar. It was a sweet notion, if somewhat illogical.

I wish I'd never grown logical. It was better being a child and having some marvel in your life.

Avelynne had finished copying the star chart and now let her quill wander. It shaped lines into a silver beast. One with wings and lifeless, big eyes to match its giant mouth. It ended up looking like the first one Avelynne had seen up close. It had been a wasp-like creature that was aiming to take a bite from her grandmother on the morning they found her cold in her bed, having passed away in her sleep.

Avelynne had used magic to lure the beast to her and

then heaved a stone statue on it with such force that its silvery, magic-imbued blood splashed up her velvet boots. Her mother had been furious about the ruined boots. For once, her anger had meant nothing to Avelynne. Grand Countess Helenna Ironhold had been the one person who had loved Avelynne, and this fiend thought it could use her willowy, lifeless body for a morning snack.

Avelynne sketched a mace being smashed down upon the silver beast she'd drawn.

"Good. That's what they deserve," Eleksander mumbled as he sneaked a glance at her drawing. "Now, calm your quill before you get Santorine's attention. I don't think *that* counts as star navigation."

Avelynne put her quill down right as Santorine clapped to get their attention. "That's enough for today, second wave. Go have an early supper! Then I suggest you get some extra sleep, as our packed days seems to be wearing on you."

They all agreed and thanked her in unison before filing out. Halfway down the corridor, they saw Tutor Rogan. He was storming out of the room where the tutors all met and kept their supplies. His face was blotchier than usual and under his breath he hissed, "shit-headed fools. I should've never agreed to work here. They should torch the whole structure and start over with people who can actually help Cavarra."

He noticed them and pointed a finger in their direction. "That includes you! Spoiled, brainless children. Is that who's going to save us all? We'd be better off sending my hounds out on a ship."

Then he marched off while cursing and punching the wall.

"I swear, his temper gets worse by the day," Sabina said. Next to her, Kall growled. Avelynne reached down and scratched behind his big, soft ear. "That's my sweet, brave darling. You could eat him and his stupid hounds for breakfast," she cooed to him.

"No, he couldn't… *darling*," Sabina said, clearly teasing Avelynne for her cooing. "He'd get indigestion."

Avelynne bumped her with her shoulder and got a beaming, apologetic smile in return.

The subject of indigestion came back to Avelynne when they were having supper in the Great Hall. The main course was a peculiar stew. Avelynne could identify carrots and some sort of white meat in a tangy, wine sauce. She had no inkling what the rest of it was, though.

She held up her spoon with a long purplish stick on towards Hale. "Do you know what this is?"

Without answering, he ate it. Then he fixed her with a serious look and replied, "fuel for my superior mind and body."

She tapped the side of his face with the back of her spoon and said, "You're incorrigible."

He wiped sauce from his cheek. "Possibly, but I now have more food in my belly than you will, so I'm winning at life as far as I'm concerned." Without stopping he waggled his eyebrows and added, "Is there anything else tasty you want to offer me?"

He recoiled. Probably due to the flirtatious banter now hanging between them, obvious and unwavering. Then he lowered his gaze but still glanced up at her, like a mouse wondering if the cat will attack.

When she giggled and said, "Anything would be tastier than this mystery mush," he stuck his tongue out as if to lick her spoon.

She moved the spoon but couldn't withdraw her gaze as easily. His cheeky smile made her pulse pick up. His tan was fading a little now that he wasn't out in the sun so much, making his white scars stand out less. He only had two on his face, she realised, one across his left cheekbone and one over his right eyebrow.

I wonder what it would feel like to trace those scars with my fingers. Or my tongue.

"Hang on," Sabina suddenly said from their right. "Is that…?"

Avelynne followed her gaze. Then she dropped her spoon which hit the table with a clatter. The blonde servant! The one who had mouthed that warning and probably sent the note and whispered to Hale.

"Yes," Avelynne breathed. "That's her! Why isn't she avoiding us as usual?"

"Because she didn't know we'd be here. We're early, remember?" Hale said, already getting up to go over to her.

They all followed him, which may not have been the stealthiest approach, since it made the servant drop her tray and take off running.

They wasted no time in giving chase. Out of the Great Hall and down the wide corridor they went, the servant first, closely trailed by Hale, then Sabina with Kall at her heels, then Sander. Avelynne was following them as fast as she could. She had hoped she'd be able to keep up with them but was failing. How fit could this servant be? Surely, she'd have to find a hiding place soon and give up this mad dash?

The woman made a quick turn to the right, a flash of yellow clothes disappearing down a narrow corridor Avelynne had never explored.

"Hunt," Sabina growled to Kall. The feline picked up the pace, as if he'd merely been jogging before, and chased after the servant. Shortly, he was next to Hale and overtaking him. They turned down another corridor and then Avelynne couldn't see their quarry anymore, she had to settle with following Sander, who's long legs were bringing him closer to Sabina. Soon Avelynne would be left behind.

She closed her eyes and tried to summon up more energy and speed. It would be shameful to lose the others. Every desperate breath stung her lungs and she was developing a stitch. Why did this have to happen right after they'd eaten?

She worried about tripping on the stone tiles, which became rougher the further into the bowels of the building they went. To make things worse, they were headed down a spiral staircase. There was a basement here? Avelynne knew the servant quarters had one but she'd never considered that the building holding the Great Hall might too.

Obviously, you dimwit. They're connected by the kitchens which are underground.

Clearly, she wasn't getting enough blood to her brain. They ran past open rooms and despite her laboured dash, Avelynne saw a larder with skinned animals hanging on hooks and a pantry in which a boy was stocking jars on a shelf.

She saw him two of him as her vision swam. The stitch in her side was getting worse. She'd have to give up. She'd have to stop here and fall into a heap on the floor. Possibly vomit, to make her humiliation worse.

Then there was a reverberating growl and a human scream as they ended up in the final room of the basement: a vaulted undercroft. There were stacks of barrels and bottles along the walls, otherwise the area was empty. In the middle lay the servant on her back and on top of her was Kall, his front paws firmly on her chest and his teeth bared.

"Good boy," Sabina panted. "Now, stay still."

Next to her was Hale. His nostrils were flaring, and his night-black eyes had a wild look to them. He was the only one not seeming tired after their run.

Avelynne wretched but managed to keep her stomach contents down.

"Are you all right?" Sander whispered to her.

"I'm… fine," she croaked.

"Get this monster off me!" screeched the servant while panting.

"Not likely, Miss. Not until you answer some questions," Sabina said, wiping her forehead.

The pinned woman sucked in a breath and snarled. "I'll lose my job if I do. Maybe even my life. Look at Thomey!"

Sander stopped adjusting his clothes. "Thomey? Was he… killed, then?"

"Yes," the servant panted through clenched teeth.

Hale took a step forward. "Tell us more."

"You've asked me that once before. That night when you were outside my window," she said, a mocking tone breaking through her desperation.

"Then answer it this time," he snapped.

"Because we're both Woodlanders?" She cooed sarcastically.

He grimaced. "No, because my friend's snowtiger will rip your throat out if you don't."

Avelynne was still trying to get her breath back but her gaze went to Kall. He wouldn't actually hurt the woman, would he?

I bet he would if Sabina told him to.

The servant surveyed Kall's fierce face and grunted. "Fine. I'll talk. I want to leave this place anyway. I shan't try to do the right thing and inform the officials, like Thomey did. Doing the right thing gets you poisoned. I'm getting out of here."

"Who poisoned him?" Sabina asked.

Sander tilted his head. "And how did they poison him? Heartsbane tastes vile."

"*He* did it," She growled. "He gave Thomey glass after glass of wine while pretending to persuade him not to inform the Centre officials. When Thomey was senseless with drink, he said there was a new strongwine from the Peaks they should try." She scoffed. "It was Heartsbane mixed with honey. Thomey said it was vile and they shouldn't drink anymore. But one big gulp was enough. The poison was slowing his heart with every beat it took. That shithole admitted it straight to my face! Probably meant it as a warning."

"Who is this *he*?" Avelynne asked.

The servant cackled mirthlessly. "He's silver beast in man-form! He hired some of us servants to spy on all students and keep certain information from reaching you.

To keep you docile and obeying orders."

There was a sound by the entrance to the undercroft, they turned and saw the young boy who had been stacking jars.

"We cannot speak here," the servant said, pushing against Kall's hold. "I promise to tell you all before I escape tonight. Let me go and I swear that I'll meet you in the stables tonight."

Sabina crossed her arms over her chest. "Perhaps. If so, when?"

"When the bell rings out for the locking of the gates. It won't take me long to pack up my few belongings and say my goodbyes."

"What's your name?" Hale said in a low voice.

"Karlinne."

"Your *full* name," He amended, his face stern as stone.

"Karlinne Ash," she said.

Hale planted his feet. "Then do you swear by the ash tree you were named under that you will meet us by the stables when the gate bell tolls? That you will tell us all, then and there?"

Karlinne nodded as much as she could without hitting her head on the flagstones. "I swear it. By the ash tree my parents chose for me. Shitting silver beasts, I'll swear it on the heads of my parents themselves. Just let me go before anyone else finds us here!"

Hale stood back. "It's all right. Few Woodlanders would betray that oath."

"Everyone in agreement?" Sabina asked.

"Yes," Avelynne said, trying to ignore the stitch that refused to subside.

"Well, I," Sander cast a glance after the boy who was scampering back towards the pantry, "suppose so."

"To me," Sabina said to Kall. He lifted his large paws off Karlinne's chest and stalked back to his mistress.

Karlinne got up and brushed down her clothes. Then she gave them a solemn nod and walked out. Avelynne had a sensation of helplessness as she watched the woman go. If she hadn't been so preoccupied with her stitch and lack of breath, she would have asked the servant to at least whisper the miscreants name before she left. But here they were. Four young, inexperienced, *normal* people suddenly embroiled in some sort of conspiracy involving threats and death.

And to think she had worried more about her secret than all of this.

"Let's go get something to drink and calm our nerves. Then we'll head out to the stables and wait for Karlinne," Sabina said.

She strode out and they all fell in line, like ducklings after their mother.

Avelynne kept her eyes on Kall, who appeared to vibrate with the rush of the hunt. Was this the same, cute animal she burrowed her face into and gave belly tickles?

I suppose none of us are only what we seem at first glance, she thought as she held her aching side.

Chapter Twenty-Eight

KARLINNE

Hale marched out into the courtyard, cursing that he'd drunk so much water in the Great Hall. If they had to give chase again, his belly would probably slosh about, and he'd get the same sort of stitch that Avelynne was still complaining about.

Or rather, clearly trying not to complain about. Although that was hard when Sabina and Eleksander kept babying her.

"Try to take deep but calm breaths. That should help," Sabina said, linking her arm with Avelynne's.

Hale rolled his eyes. The stitch would pass quicker if they let her be distracted. Honestly, their soft hearts would be the end of him one day. At least the end of his patience.

"Has anyone heard the bell?" he called back to the others.

"No," Eleksander said. "I think we have a while to wait."

"Let's get to the stables anyway. It must be cooler than

the muggy air out here," Hale said, wiping the back of his neck.

Avelynne, who had borrowed one of the lanterns that flanked all the doorways, went first. Entering the stable, Hale found that the humid weather brought out the smell of horses and hay even more than normal. There was another scent just beneath it, something sharp that seemed out of place in the cosy stables. Kall sniffed the air and his ears went back.

I'm not the only one who doesn't like that smell.

The little hairs on the back of Hale's neck stood up. The horses were nickering and stamping their hooves. They didn't seem frightened to Hale, who'd been around horses since childhood, more like they were recovering from a shock.

Wondering if he was imagining things, Hale followed the others further into the dark stable. That sharp smell grew stronger. Was it metal? No. Blood. Lots of it to reek like this. Hale squinted into the stalls they passed, scouring them for the source.

The stall furthest in had what he was dreading. Karlinne. Or at least what had been Karlinne. Now it was a dead body hanging by the neck from a rafter. Despite the horror, he refused to look away. He owed her that much. The hanging was obviously not the cause of the bleeding. Where was this blood coming from?

There was a loud gasp, and someone cried out. Hale didn't check who. He wouldn't take his eyes off Karlinne.

"Avelynne," he croaked. "Lift the lantern so I can see where the blood is coming from."

There was no reply and Hale didn't have time to make

sure Avelynne was all right. Instead he grabbed for the lantern and held it up himself. The blood trickled from wounds on her hands, probably defensive wounds, but it *streamed* from her neck and mouth.

Apparently, Sabina had spotted that too since she said, "Silver beasts, was her throat cut while she was hanging there?"

"It was cut, all right. Must've been before she died, though," Hale said, suddenly cold to the bone. "I'd wager it was to shut her up when the gurgling and thrashing scared the horses and threatened to alert someone to the murder."

"Oh," Avelynne said in a small voice. "Then why is there blood from her mouth?"

"Could she have bitten her tongue or cheek or something?" Eleksander asked quietly.

Hale held up the lantern to the dead lass' open mouth. Bile rose to his throat, and he worried that he might see the return of all that water he'd drunk. "No. Too much blood and something is... missing in her mouth. I think her tongue's been cut out."

"Well, I guess someone kept her from talking after all," Sabina said shakily. "We need to alert someone. Now."

"Yes," Eleksander said. "But who? Anyone we tell might be the 'he' that she wanted to warn us about. The 'he' that killed her."

"I know that! We still need to trust someone!" Sabina shouted.

"I'll go find Tutor Santorine or Tutor Hathleen," Hale said. "A woman seems our safest bet here." He handed the lantern to Sabina and took off running.

His lungs burned as he ran as fast as his feet would carry

him. It was a relief to have something to do. He couldn't help Karlinne. In fact, his permitting her to leave and then be on her own had pretty much caused her death, but at least he could do this.

He found Atha Santorine outside the servant quarters, laughing with one of the cooks.

He skidded to a halt in front of them. "C-come with me. We found her. She's dead. Hung and knifed. I mean cut. I mean—"

Tutor Santorine's face fell. "Hale. Calm down. What are you talking about?"

"Come with me. Please."

She didn't hesitate. "Lead the way."

He did and, when they got to the stable, Santorine observed the body with a whispered, "By the waters, what happened here?" and leaned against the wall for support.

"Murder," Eleksander croaked. Then he told Santorine everything, with the other three adding details when needed. They covered from the night when Karlinne had mouthed the first warning up until this moment.

By the end of the tale, Santorine had gone ashen-faced and said, "I see. You should have informed us about this earlier."

Hale shrugged. "We didn't know who to trust."

She seemed about to argue but then her shoulders slumped. "I can understand that. I shall personally liaise with the Centre's officials. They will alert the academy's guards and the king's army. No matter who is to blame here, even if it's the king himself, I will make sure justice is done."

Hale nodded, unsure of what else to say. Everything was surreal. He was still cold and grateful when Sabina leaned into him. It wasn't warming him, but it was somehow… steadying. He took her hand and squeezed it. He noted that Avelynne had a grip on her necklace so tight that her knuckles whitened, then she began sobbing against Eleksander's chest. The Lakelander held her close but stared straight ahead with glassy eyes.

"Go to bed," Santorine said. "After today, you all need the rest. If you cannot sleep, I shall have the physician mix up a sleeping draught for you."

They stumbled off to bed without more than a few shuddering words of parting.

When Eleksander had blown out the candle in their room, Hale stared into the dark and asked, "What do we do now?"

"You mean tonight?"

"No, in general. Do we keep investigating? Should we leave this academy for our own safety? Do we alert the leaders of our counties or something?" He could hear his own voice turn strangely shrill and wondered if this was what anxious people felt all the time.

Eleksander was quiet for a moment. "Hm. I suppose we can write home about it. Other than that, I think it's out of our hands. We have to carry on with our training."

Hale writhed in his too soft bed. "Although, we'll keep vigilant, of course."

"Yes, we shall have to," Eleksander murmured.

Hale nodded even though the other lad couldn't see him. "Yes, we'll keep vigilant. That's what we'll do. Focus on our studies but stay alert for any threats."

"Mm-hm."

"Well. Goodnight then."

"Goodnight, Hale."

Then they laid there. He could deduce from Eleksander's breathing that he was awake too. As awake as the whitengale singing mournfully outside. It was a suitable farewell song for a lass who shouldn't have had to die.

In Hale's head, Karlinne's whisper played like a repeating melody, haunting and bewildering him.

"Silver like magic. Silver like the young countess' necklace. Silver like the beasts."

Chapter Twenty-Nine

INTIMACY

Four weeks passed without anything of import, except for Karlinne's funeral, at which Santorine told the second wave that the Centre officials were still looking into Karlinne's and Thomey's deaths. Otherwise it was lessons and library sessions as usual. With the difference being the unnatural silence that came from people in shock and confusion.

The passing of the weeks calmed Avelynne's frayed nerves a little. By the time autumn had ended and the first days of winter—such as it was in the mild Centre—had arrived, Avelynne's nightmares no longer centred around a poisoned man, a hanged woman, and the guilt stemming from a sense that she could've prevented their deaths.

This night, it was another sort of nightmare that plagued Avelynne. The guilt was there, but it came from scenarios in which her secret spilled out and made the other three hate her.

The mystery of the murders had overshadowed her guilt over her false admittance to the Hall of Explorers and that she was keeping that secret from Sabina and Hale. Apparently, that was over now as her secret haunted her night-mares once more.

Like right now when she dreamed that her inability to keep up with the team was getting them all killed, one by one. She woke to Sabina shaking her shoulder. "Avelynne. You need to wake up!"

Avelynne started and sobbed at the same time, making herself choke on her own rapid breaths.

It was pitch-black in the room. Even though the mornings were growing darker, this was too dark to be anything but the middle of the night.

"I-I'm awake. I think. I…" She sat up in her sweat soaked bed and rubbed her face. "I don't know. Those dreams were so vivid."

Sabina let go of her shoulder. Instead, she picked up the tinderbox to light the candle. It sounded as if she trembled too much to manage it.

Strange. I'm the one with nightmares, why is she trembling?

In the end, Sabina had to strike the flint and steel with the aid of magic. When a flame finally caught, she lit the candle on Avelynne's bedside table.

Avelynne blinked, first at the clear silvery light of Sabina's magic and then at the warm glow of the candle.

Down on the floor, she saw Kall stare at her. He wasn't greeting her in his usual way. Neither was Sabina, come to think of it. Both she and her snowtiger seemed grave.

The dread of Avelynne's nightmares now seeped into the real world. It lined her heart, making it pound desperately.

"Sabina, is everything all right?"

"You were talking in your sleep again. Tonight, however… I could make out the words."

Avelynne's heart beat so hard and fast that she worried about passing out. Everything was cold and hot at the same time. She managed to wheeze out, "What, um, what did I say?"

Sabina was quiet, her hands clasped in her lap. The candle light illuminated those beautiful eyes but Avelynne didn't care about their appearance now, only the feelings in them. The disappointment. Or was it suspicion?

Sabina's mouth curled down before she said, "You spoke of secrets. You said my name. Said that I could never know. That I wouldn't understand."

"Mutilating silver beasts," Avelynne swore under her breath. She put her hand in front of her eyes, she couldn't look at Sabina.

She still heard the other woman sniff disapprovingly. "I hope it was a silly dream and there's no truth to the notion that you're keeping secrets from me. Or to that you think I am too dull-witted to understand things, but your behaviour belies that."

Avelynne removed her hand. "Not dull-witted, Sabina! Never that. I... think you might be too good and too honest to understand what I did and why I did it."

"Perhaps now would be a good time to find out?"

Avelynne reached out. She wanted to touch her, for reassurance and to show her affection. But Sabina sat still as a statue, a crinkle between her white brows. Avelynne retracted her hand, sighed, and then told Sabina the story of how she came to be the Peaks' chosen one. She hoped with every fibre of her being that Sabina would take it as well as Sander had.

Sabina gave nothing away as the truth poured out of

Avelynne. She sat there, straight-backed and tight-lipped, as the candle light projected dancing shadows on her face.

When Avelynne wrapped the tale up with, "I should've told you all the truth when I realised you were trustworthy and how much you already meant to me. But I couldn't." She stared down at her hands. "I was as ashamed as I was terrified that you'd tell the tutors the truth and that one of the Peaks' warring families would send their child here, starting a conflict which would tear the Peaks apart. More than that, I was selfish enough to worry that you'd hate me, because I need you to… like me."

Sabina stood up so fast that she nearly stepped on Kall. "You haven't earned your place here."

"No. However, I'm trying to do so now. I study and train every moment I get." Avelynne was babbling, speaking too fast for her own brain to catch up." Sander has been training and tutoring me, actually. I worried I might not be able to keep up, but, so far, it's going well. He knows how to teach me things without making me panic and lose focus."

Sabina gasped. "Eleksander knew?!"

Avelynne winced at her injured tone. "Yes. I'm so sorry. I accidentally told him after I failed in the archery lesson. He only kept my secret from you because I begged him."

"You lied to us."

"Not exactly, I never—"

"By omission, Avelynne!" Sabina barked.

Avelynne deflated. "True," she replied. "I fear I have no defence and no better excuse than what I have already provided."

Sabina slumped back onto the bed. Her husky voice

turning all the way to gravelly as she groaned. "I don't want to be angry with you. I *need* you. I need your company," she lamented.

Her sudden sadness was even worse than her rage.

Avelynne couldn't stop herself this time. She reached out and took Sabina's hand.

"I'm sorrier than I can ever put into words. I need you too. I'll make it up to you, I promise. I'll do whatever it takes."

Sabina yanked her hand back. Then she cursed long and low before looking away, as if she couldn't stand the sight of Avelynne. Agonising moments passed before Sabina cursed again, louder this time, making Kall come to her side as if to check up on her.

Avelynne swallowed and told herself, *Don't cry. Don't beg. Let her decide whether or not she'll forgive you. You owe her that and so much more.*

She started to withdraw her still outstretched hand, but Sabina caught it. Avelynne worried she was taking a grip of it to get Avelynne's attention so she could reproach her more thoroughly.

Instead, Sabina interlaced their fingers, wound them tight together. "I believe you will make it up to us," she said hoarsely. "You already do a lot for us. You brought us together so fast and firmly that we became a family after the first few weeks. You instil confidence in Eleksander and you're the only one who can make Hale bearable. In fact, that's probably more use to us than if you'd been the top student."

Avelynne twitched her lips into something like a small smile.

Sabina sought her gaze. "I'm not joking. I mean it. Thinking about it..." She tilted her head. "Your social skills and how you keep us working together will be vital when we set off exploring. In fact, it's vital now, when we face the mystery of these threats and deaths."

"I," Avelynne blinked a few times, "hadn't thought of that."

"Neither had I until now." Sabina blew out a shaky breath. "Look, I'm angry about the cheating and the lying. However, as someone who's felt responsible for others my entire life, I understand making uncomfortable decisions because you think it is the best for your people. Be it family or everyone who lives in your county."

Avelynne leaned in, so eager to explain. "I can't promise that my parents' motives were only to keep the peace, but I can promise you that mine were. I never had ambitions to be a mapmaker or to be unique in any way. I wanted to do what was right, what helped others, and, I suppose, make people—"

"*Like* you. I know," Sabina interrupted, tightening the grip of their interlaced fingers. "You needn't be so ashamed of that. However, you must learn that your worth doesn't hang on the approval of others."

"Tell that to my parents," Avelynne said.

"I'll tell it to you. Because they don't matter to me. You do. That, and my belief in your actions coming from good intent, means... I'll forgive you."

Avelynne flinched, barely breathing. "You will?"

"As long as there are no more secrets between you and me."

"Of course, hang on. What are my secrets?" Avelynne

thought hard, so desperate to make this work. To make this right. "When I was six, I used to steal honey from the kitchen. When I was ten, I pushed my cousin into a creek. The only member of my family I could ever stand to be around was my grandmother. What else?" She chewed her lip. "I enjoy making Hale flustered when I flirt with him. I abhor Tutor Rogan. Also, both times we went swimming at night, I snuck glances at your body when your tunic became see-through."

She paused when she was out of breath. Had she really said those intimate, embarrassing things out loud? "You now know more about me than anyone ever has. I have no secrets from you," she finished.

She was still reeling and bewildered from the fact that Sabina had forgiven her. How could she be that lucky?

Sabina laughed, and it filled the room, making it warmer with its cosy, raspy melody. Avelynne wanted to wrap herself up in that laugh and fall asleep in it.

"Those are quite the juicy revelations," Sabina said. "I'll take that as part of your repentance and as a sign of good-will. One day, I'll tell you all my secrets too."

"Not today?" Avelynne said, her giddy relief making her unable to know when to shush.

"My, you are an impatient little thing at times. Well, you're apologising to me, so I call the shots. I will tell you one secret, though. I noticed you admiring my body when we went swimming. Both times. I caught all three of you looking, in fact."

"Ooh. Are you boasting, Northerner?" Avelynne teased.

"No. I believe you all had different motives for looking, you probably being the only one who did so out of sexual interest. Consequently, I was not boasting but only telling the truth, little Countess."

"Hm. 'Little Countess.' 'Impatient little thing.' Stop calling me little. I'm not *that* much smaller than you."

Sabina quirked an eyebrow in response.

"All right, fine." Avelynne rolled her eyes. "I'm a lot shorter, slimmer, and reedier."

"You're getting there with the muscles, but you'll always be smaller than me. Nothing wrong with that. I'm sure Hale appreciates your ladylike stature."

"Stop teasing me about him!"

Sabina chuckled. "I will when it stops making you blush."

"You, my wonderful and most beautiful Sabina, make me blush in your own right. No need to involve Hale."

Sabina's chuckle perished on her lips. "As you say," she whispered.

There it was again. Sabina was happy to tease and flirt but whenever it became obvious that Avelynne was taken by her, Sabina became... what? Serious? Shy? Uncertain?

Avelynne moved her fingers, brushing Sabina's slight calluses and the soft skin around them.

They sat in the sort of silence that follows after an emotional outpouring. The candlelight bathed them and the area around the bed in warm light. The rest of the room was shrouded in darkness, making their space seem so much smaller. So much more intimate. Even Kall had skulked away to a dark corner of the room. Now, it could as well be only the two of them left in the entire world. A silly thought, the boys were just across the hall and the building was full of people. Nevertheless, they weren't in this room.

In the pool of light. In the soft bed. In this private bedchamber, which carried the unique scent of Avelynne's and Sabina's sleep-warmed bodies mingled together. In the connection of what the two of them had just shared.

"You said what my 'social skills' do for the boys," Avelynne said softly. "Not what I do for you. Tell me, so I can make sure to do more of it. Please?"

Sabina's mouth opened to say something, but she closed it again. Avelynne dared to move nearer, breathing in that wonderful scent of her, wanting to be as close as she could. She wanted to do anything and everything for this woman.

Sabina fixed her gaze on their hands and eventually said, "Continue keeping me relaxed. You calm me and remind me that I'm allowed to simply have fun. To think only of myself and to allow myself to make mistakes or be silly. I need that right now. I'm… fretful."

"About?"

She saw the column of Sabina's beautiful throat move as she swallowed hard. "The warnings. The deaths. The *king*. I think he is the 'he' we were warned about."

"The king?" Avelynne whispered, as much due to surprise and knowing the repercussions of speaking ill of their sovereign as that she didn't want to break the intimate mood in the room.

"Yes! Think about it, as the monarch, he's in control of all magic and of ridding us of the silver beasts. That gives us the connection to silver that the whisperer mentioned."

"That is quite a forced connection, isn't it?" Avelynne asked, making sure to not sound dismissive.

"Not necessarily. He's the one in power, he is in charge of our mission. Remember what the note said about not trusting what they're teaching us? And what Karlinne said about getting servants to spy on us and keep secrets from us —that's all within his purview."

"Mm, I suppose."

Sabina tightened her grip on Avelynne's hand. "Also, when we met him, he was awful! Arrogant and controlling, not trustworthy at all. Besides, you may think this is silly, but Kall hates him and that always means something."

Avelynne was quite sure Kall usually mirrored his owner's feelings, rather than being an astute judge of character. She wouldn't mention that. She was meant to help Sabina, and to regain her trust and affection, not bat away her worries as simple paranoia.

"We shall keep an eye on the king," Avelynne settled on. "Furthermore, perhaps we should sit down with Hale and Sander and decide how to get to the bottom of all of this?"

"That's a great idea."

She caressed Sabina's fingers for comfort, shivering at the pleasure of their sensitive fingertips meeting, but pushing that aside to concentrate. "Consider it done. In fact, why haven't we done that in the last couple of weeks? After Karlinne's funeral would've been a perfect moment."

"Perhaps you've been too preoccupied with keeping your secret and all the extra lessons?" Sabina said with a shrug. "For the rest of us, I suppose shock has muddled us all. Not to mention that we were told to leave it in the hands of Tutor Santorine and those in charge."

"Still, I feel terrible that I haven't tried to do something more, since it has weighed so on your mind."

Sabina clicked her tongue, gaze again on their interlacing fingers on the bed. "That's what happens when you're the serious one. The responsible one. Trust me, I know that pain."

Avelynne used her free hand to tilt Sabina's chin up and when they were eye to eye again, she leaned in to brush the tip of her nose against Sabina's. "Then let me take some of that responsibility from you this time. Let me shoulder some of the burden by arranging for us to discuss this matter with the boys and lead the enquiry into who this 'he' is."

"Yes please," Sabina said quietly. Avelynne felt her warm breath against her face, it smelled faintly of the herbal tonic they both used before bed. Then Sabina tilted her head and leaned yet closer. Almost as if to kiss Avelynne. At the last moment, just as their lips might've touched, her face turned from seriousness to impishness and she blew a raspberry on Avelynne's neck instead.

"That tickles!" Avelynne squealed, before laughing and pushing Sabina away.

With a grin, Sabina stood, putting her hands on those generous Northern hips of hers. "Fine, I'm going back to my own bed! But you had that coming."

"I certainly did," Avelynne agreed. "Thank you for being so forgiving and sweet."

"No need to mention it. Unless you make me regret it, then I shan't be so understanding." She strode toward her bed but then stopped to add, "Oh, and if you need extra lessons in something that Eleksander is unsure of—not that I think such a subject exists—then ask me."

"I will. If nothing else, Sander might need a break."

Sabina whistled low, making Kall follow her. "I'm sure he will at some point. You're trouble."

"Yes, but I'm *your* trouble."

"Great," Sabina groaned while getting into bed.

When she was tucked in, with her covers pulled over her and her snowtiger laying right next to the bed, Avelynne blew out the candle.

For a tummy-tingling moment she thought about Sabina leaning in like that before. Surely, she hadn't been about to actually kiss her? No, all the banter and play-flirting that the second wave did was going to Avelynne's head, making her believe they all had some hidden romantic interest in her.

Avelynne grimaced at herself. *A little bit of attention and I grow an enormous ego, how vile. Not to mention embarrassing.*

Sabina probably had a ladylove back home. In fact, she'd have to ask her about that. Was Sabina a virgin? The fact that Avelynne wasn't should have been on the list of her secrets. She'd have to tell Sabina about that soon.

Now, she needed sleep. Moments ago, agitation and fear would have made her think she'd never sleep again. However, the shelter of Sabina's complete forgiveness and affection promised rest. Despite not having told Hale yet. Despite any threats, warnings, or even murders. For some reason, having Sabina on her side gave a deep but overstated sensation of protection.

Avelynne burrowed into her downy pillow while thinking of a sweet-smelling, strong but lithe body with gentle hands and a pair of steadfast blue eyes with purple around the irises. Safe and a little tingly, she fell asleep and dreamt of kissing Sabina.

Chapter Thirty

HALE IN PAIN

Hale's ankle throbbed, making it hard to sit comfortably at his desk. That's what he got for showing off while catching the bat that had flown into their room this morning. If he'd only climbed up on the dresser in the normal way and caught the bat, then he could've shown it to Eleksander and let him draw it like he wanted to. But no, child that he was, Hale had to show that he could do it with his eyes closed, following the sound of the bat's wings.

He scoffed at his own stupidity. That sort of thing was all very fine outside, but in a small, furnished room with lots of things to smash your ankle on if you fell, not so fine. He ignored the throbbing and focused back on the parchment of text explaining how to navigate by the stars. Or at least he tried to.

The room was stuffy and, since there was no tutor present—Santorine had stepped out to talk to one of the Centre officials about the ongoing investigation—it was easy to drift off. It was equally easy to focus on his ankle or on Avelynne wrinkling her perfect forehead while reading something complex. Where was his usual discipline? He forced his focus back down at the parchment.

Then he heard whispering and turned his head towards the sound. Eleksander and Sabina had been standing by the map of the Lakelands that took a up a large part of the left wall. Avelynne had joined them now and it was her voice he'd heard.

She blew a breath out through her nose and murmured, "Of course I'm going to tell him. Later. Now shush before he hears us."

Hale slammed a hand on his desk. "Really? I told you this morning, Eleksander, I have brilliant hearing. If I can hear that bat's wings, I can sure as shit hear you whispering about me. Fancy sharing?"

They went dead silent. Standing there unmoving like three embarrassed rocks.

"Come on, tell him," Eleksander said.

Avelynne paced over to Hale's desk. Taking her time and biting her lower lip. When she was right in front of him, filling his entire vision, which she always did in his mind anyway, she said, "I must speak to you after the lesson. I wanted to wait until we broke for the midday meal, but I'll have to fit it in while we go outside for the polearm training."

Hale shifted in his seat. "Why not now?"

"Because you're likely to be upset and I need time to explain. Tutor Santorine could be back any moment," Avelynne said, her voice breaking a little. What had her this upset?

"Great, now I'm going to sit here in torment until the end of the lesson."

"I know, that's why I didn't want you to overhear us. I'm terribly sorry."

There were footsteps outside the door.

Avelynne cupped Hale's face in her hands and quickly said, "I'll tell you soon. Neither of us are in danger. What I need to tell you will keep. Don't worry."

He nuzzled into one of her cupped palms. "All right. I'll wait."

"Thank you." Avelynne planted a quick kiss on the crown of his head and hurried back to her seat right as Santorine came back into the room.

They all returned to their parchments and books. Hale was no longer concerned with his ankle. Pain he could handle. Whatever it was Avelynne was going to tell him, though, he wasn't so sure how he'd fare with that.

The navigation lesson finally ended, and they headed for the courtyard. Sabina and Eleksander had hurried ahead to keep Rogan busy if needed. Hale walked alongside Avelynne, as she told him how she was not the best of her age in the Peaks. How her parents had cheated to get her here and why they had done it. How she felt compelled to go along with the ruse. Her guilt and grief for having kept a secret from them all.

That was where he stopped her. He threw his rolled-up parchment against the wall and shouted, "But you didn't keep the secret from us all! You told the others!"

She shot backwards and held her hands up. "I know.

Not intentionally, though! Sabina only found out last night when I talked in my sleep."

"All right. What about Eleksander then? What about the pretty coin-hoarder you've been spending so much time with? When did he know? Did he hear you talking in your sleep one night too?"

Avelynne's forehead furrowed. "What do you mean? Sander isn't there when I sleep. He's in a bedchamber with you."

"Unless he sneaks out and into your bed."

"What? That is not only preposterous because he wouldn't want to do that, but also because you hear everything. Besides, Sabina is in my chambers, remember?" Avelynne gave an exasperated sigh. "Is this really what you're angry about?"

"Answer my question, Avelynne!"

"Fine! He's known for a few weeks. Since that archery lesson when Tutor Rogan said he knew that there were Peakdwellers my age who were superior to me. The shock of Rogan maybe guessing my secret made me unable to keep quiet."

That day. Eleksander had gone after her instead of him. All because Rogan had already seen Eleksander fire a bow. All because Eleksander sucked up to the tutors.

"Hale, don't let jealously and *cursedly ever-present romance* or whatever this is, get in the way of what is important here. I have lied and cheated and I'm trying to explain it to you and, if I'm lucky, seek your forgiveness."

He banged a fist into the wall as a reply.

Avelynne carefully put her hand on his arm. "The reason I've spent so much time with Sander isn't that I like him better than you. He's been tutoring me to catch up with the skillset of you three. He didn't know my secret before you because I like him better either. He was simply there when I needed to tell someone."

To have something to do with his prickling body, Hale kicked his bunched-up parchments that had landed next to his feet. "So, you've robbed someone else of their rightful place here."

"Yes. I've taken someone else's place and that is an immoral thing to do, even if I had a moral reason for it." She closed her eyes as if steeling herself. "You're perfectly within your right to tell the tutors or the Hall of Explorers officials. We know they're here today since they spoke to Tutor Santorine."

"I don't snitch," he growled. "Especially not on my friends. Even if they have done something shitty."

"All right," Avelynne said on an exhale. "Then, please, let me earn my place here. Let me carry on working to be as good as the three of you. You've said yourself that I'm improving. Sabina says my social skills help the team and Sander says I work remarkably hard. If you don't trust me when I say that I'll be the best part of the second wave I can be, trust them."

Hale said nothing, he stood there clenching and unclenching his fists.

Avelynne retracted her hand from his arm and bent to pick up his parchments. "If you find me lacking or not up to the task by the end of the year, inform the tutors. I'll make sure no one sees it as snitching."

She held out the mangled papers to him. What was that in her gaze now? Defeat? Remorse? Pity? All three?

He ignored the parchment. "Is that it?"

"What do you mean?"

"Didn't you want to 'seek my forgiveness'?"

"I... dare not ask that of you yet."

"Fine. You know what, I don't want you to ask anything of me right now." With that, he took off running. He sprinted as fast as he could, putting all his confusion, jealousy, and hurt feelings into his running muscles.

Soon he found himself by the servant quarters. There was no one around. He couldn't stay here. He scaled the wall and over the roof until he could jump down on the other side. He wanted to run towards the lake.

Until his lungs ached and his legs burned.

Until he couldn't think, only continue running to keep from falling.

Until he could jump into the lake and hide under the cool surface for a while.

Except, he never got that far, two steps into running, his ankle stopped him. Pain spiked through it and made him gasp. He dropped down next to a large oak. He had forgotten about his ankle until now. He wished he could focus completely on it instead of having to try to make sense of what had just happened. Of what he was feeling. Why hadn't she confided in him? He would've loved to help her. To keep her secret. To protect her. To be of some sort of use to her. But no, he was the clueless forest lad who didn't know how to behave around people. Why should she tell him anything important?

He rubbed his ankle and stood to test it out, resting against the oak.

No one had ever turned to him in time of need. What

could he do? He was an orphan. No power, no connections, no idea of how to influence people, or what to do in a crisis. When one of his best friends had accidentally gotten pregnant, she had asked everyone else for advice. Even though he'd been the one who did best in all their lessons and therefore surely had been the smartest? It had never occurred to her to run to him. Nor had it occurred to Avelynne. His only use was his muscles and his work ethic. Did Avelynne need either of those? No.

He banged a fist into the tree. Then another. Soon he was pounding out his frustration into the trunk of the innocent oak, probably making his knuckles bleed.

"Stop that racket! If you think you'll make a dent in that tree, you'll be wrong, brat. It was here long before you and it'll be here on the glorious day when you're dead and all eaten by worms."

Hale twisted to see who had spoken, a mistake as pain lanced from his ankle up his leg.

The groundskeeper loomed over him. He was grinning, his rotting teeth and the gleeful malice in his eyes making Hale nauseous.

"Ah, leave off," Hale panted.

"Like silver beasts, I will. Once again, you are where you're not permitted. You're lucky I don't take a belt to you and teach you a lesson; I bet you'd squeal like a pig. Back into your little academy pen you go, wayward piglet."

Hale reeled. What was this man's problem? "I'm going. I only needed a moment alone. And don't call me piglet!"

The groundskeeper stepped even closer, prodding a finger into Hale's chest. "I'll call you whatever I please. I'm a grown-up performing an essential job. You're a spoiled, bookish piece of filth wasting my time and the king's patience."

"Get that finger off me or I'll break it off, you shit-stained maggot!"

"There's that nasty temper again. I'd get that under control before I go out to sea if I were you. Can't have some moss-stinking Woodlander losing his head with his fellow recruits and bashing their teeth out."

"I'd never hurt them. You on the other hand…" Hale said, trailing off while baring his teeth. Strangely, his heart beat calmer now.

The groundskeeper retracted his finger and jutted his chin out. "Careful, little woodworm. Or I'll let silver beasts into your room at night. The last thing you'll see is a silver grin before they gobble up your eyes."

With that, he left, hand on his sword hilt. Hale wanted to punch the violent bastard, like he had the oak tree. He tried to smother the fight in his blood and regain control. He had a lesson he was late for. An important future mission to prepare for. What held him back in the end, though, was the thought of Avelynne's disappointment if he couldn't master his temper.

Shoulders slumped, he dragged himself and his infuriating ankle back towards the servant quarters. How in the name of the silver beasts had he managed to jump down that roof without feeling the pain in his ankle? And how he would get back up there now?

In one of the windows a lass was airing sheets. He knew her. Where had he seen her before? Spotting her familiar body language, poised and precise, made him remember. This was Eleksander's sister!

"Woodlander, what are you doing on that side? You should be inside or out in the courtyard."

"I know," he grumbled.

She pursed her lips. "Then why are you out there?"

"Maybe they kicked me out of the Hall of Explorers."

"No, they didn't," she said curtly. "Sander would have told me. Furthermore, the rumour mill would spread such a rumour like a plague."

He bent to massage his ankle. "It's only a matter of time. I keep ruining everything."

She folded the sheet neatly. "Sander told me that you've been struggling with upsetting the others." She shook her head. "He believed it to be his fault at first, as usual. He's very sensitive, has been ever since my father brought him home one thundery night. He was drenched and petrified but still so fretful of getting mud on my mother's floor."

"He wasn't a baby?"

She stared at him with raised eyebrows. "With my skin being this snow white and his so dark brown? It never occurred to you that our parents might have adopted children?"

Hale blew out a breath. "Uh. I never really thought about that. I suppose that makes sense."

She stared at him as if he was as witless as a dead sloth. "Anyway, Sander was a foundling that our father came upon outside the city. He was completely naked but had neatly trimmed hair and fingernails. He was perfectly cared for but was found walking next to the road, heading for the city gates."

"Where were his kin?"

She picked up another sheet. "He didn't know. He

couldn't remember anything, due to some form of shock the physicians claimed. Also, they gauged his age at a mere five years old." She shook the sheet out the window before continuing. "Our parents spent a decade looking for his biological parents or someone who knew what had happened to him. Nothing. When Sander turned eighteen, he told them to stop looking. He said that whatever blood relatives he might have had abandoned him and were no family of his."

Hale rubbed the back of his neck. "I never knew. He's an orphan like me?"

"Sander *was* an orphan. As was I when our parents adopted me as a baby. After that, both he and I had a loving family, including excellent parents." With efficient movements she folded the sheet. "When Sander was accepted to the Hall of Explorers, my mother wanted to send a servant with him. I said no, I'd go instead. He needs support from someone he trusts."

"That's very good of you."

"No," she corrected with some impatience. "It was the right thing to do. He needed me and I had to get out of our quiet house. As soon as he's out to sea, I'll try to get a job as a tutor here. My arithmetic skills are even better than Sander's. Speaking of doing what's right, what did you do that was so bad that you worried about being expelled?"

He rubbed his ankle again. "I, um, I lost my temper and took off. I'm meant to be in a lesson now. Polearm training. There was this big, infected secret and I wasn't told. Or, rather, no one wanted to confide in me. Back then. Avelynne told Eleksander instead and—"

She held up a hand. "Stop. You're babbling."

"Sorry. I suppose I could sum it up with…" he paused to think. To analyse. "That I feel shitty because the others don't need me."

"That's ridiculous. Sander needs you."

Hale jerked back. "He does?"

"Obviously." She aired another sheet. "Sander struggled to make childhood friends. He was too quiet, too unsure of who to talk to. The others mocked him for his unknown origin or for his sensitive nature. By the time he grew up to be bigger and smarter than them all, they hated him even more for being superior. Then they made his life a nightmare." She folded the sheet while sighing. "He's always wanted a close friend, perhaps even a lover, who accepted him. A person he didn't have to be somebody else with. Someone to help him be more confident."

Hale tucked his hands in his pockets. "And… I do that?"

"Yes. At least when you're not complaining about his looks or telling him to stop being sensitive."

He winced. "I've apologised for that."

"I know, and he has forgiven you. That doesn't mean I have. Until his education is finished, he's my responsibility and I expect you to be a positive thing in his life, not another negative. If you upset him, you'll be dealing with me."

"Fair enough." He hesitated. "I want to be something good in his life."

"Good. Now, if you will excuse me. I have to finish this and then get ready for the servants' feast tonight."

"The what?"

"Our feast," she said, slower this time. "We have one every week."

"You do?"

She gave him a look. "We work as hard as you, but unlike you, we can do our jobs without a clear head. Also, we're not as tightly supervised as you students. In short, we can get drunk on a frequent basis." She put her hand on the latch of the window. "We can even eat ourselves chubby without worrying about being in shape to escape dragons on some foreign shore. Not that I would let myself go in either of those ways."

Hale gaped at her. It had never occurred to him that the servants and workers could be having more fun than the students did.

Her lips twisted, making her look older than she was. "Don't stand there with your mouth open, boy! Get inside before they catch you out there. People are dying around here, this is no time to be running around where you're not allowed."

With that she pulled the latch until the window slammed shut and was gone.

Hale took his hands out of his pockets with heavy movements. Now there was nothing to do but groan with pain as he climbed the wall. When he finally made it to the roof, he decided to climb down on the other side instead of jumping. It didn't demonstrate his agility and pain threshold as leaping down would, but it was the smart thing to do. It was what Eleksander would do. It was what someone Avelynne could confide in would do.

Chapter Thirty-One

POLEARMS, TATTOOS, AND BOATS

Avelynne rested her war scythe, the polearm she'd picked, against the wall and hugged her arms around herself. Not because of the cold, although it was certainly winter now with cold winds creeping along the stone walls, but because of her emotional state.

Sander leaned in to whisper, "Don't worry, Hale will be back. He merely needs a moment to digest."

She gave him a tight-lipped smile and a nod. Neither was heartfelt.

Sabina was currently sparring with Tutor Rogan, and he was shouting at her. First for having the wrong grip on her glaive. Then for choosing a glaive when her fighting style would be better suited to a heavier pole weapon, like a halberd. Thirdly, for grunting "like someone raised in a barn" every time she thrusted her weapon.

He must despise us all, Avelynne concluded.

Sabina scowled but dutifully quieted and changed her grip. At the start of the lesson, she had stepped up and told

Rogan that Hale was ill and that he'd gone to throw up. Sadly, the one who's stomach was rising to her throat was Avelynne. Hurting any of her friends was horrible. But Hale. He was harder to talk to than the others, harder to get to open up about his feelings. She hadn't even been able to ask for his forgiveness. If he wouldn't talk to her, wouldn't let her explain… she didn't know how she'd move on. It pained her that he had run away like that.

A few moments later, Hale slunk back in. He was limping, something that drove Avelynne towards even more worry. He stood next to Sander and watched Sabina spar.

Rogan attacked with a lunge and managed to knock the glaive out of her hands.

"See," he sniped. "If it had been a heavier polearm, you would've held it differently, making it harder to disarm you."

Sabina tossed her head, bouncing her thick braid onto her back. "Isn't the point of these lessons that we're able to fight with whatever weapon is available to us when we're in danger? If not, let me know and I'll stick to my axes."

"Insolent girl!" Rogan bellowed, circling her as if sizing up for an attack. "I am here to teach you how to fight with a range of weapons. I say that includes teaching you to pick the weapon that suits your frame. If you disagree, take it up with the officials. Or the king himself!"

Sabina's features grew grim as she circled as well. Rogan using the king to impress and subdue her had been the wrong choice. Her weapon-less hands clenched into fists and those whitish eyebrows lowered. For a moment, Avelynne wished Sabina would punch Rogan right in his huge face.

Torn between watching Sabina and worrying about Hale, Avelynne noticed Hale moving behind her. She ached for him to say something. To indicate what level of anger he felt.

Instead, he leaned in and kissed her cheek, so gently that she only felt the warmth of his lips for an instant. Then he grabbed her abandoned war scythe and limped over to the two fighters. He threw the scythe to Sabina.

It gleamed as it flew through the intense winter light before Sabina caught it with both hands. She smiled at Hale and nodded. He returned both smile and nod and then stepped back.

Rogan scowled but said nothing, he merely returned to fighting stance and attacked. She parried the blow, hefting her new weapon in her hands with a hint of a smirk.

When Hale was back between Sander and Avelynne, he stood tall and said, "Right, this is how I see it. We're a team. Maybe even a family. We'll provide what the others need, be it a weapon or our loyalty. There'll be no more secrets between us and we'll aim to forgive each other's mistakes. Always."

After a surprised look at Hale, Sander echoed, "Always."

The weight that had stuck in Avelynne's chest melted and poured through her into the ground.

"Agreed," she whispered. "And I'll make it up to you, Hale, to all of you."

Hale kept his eyes on the sparring match as he replied, "All you have to do is keep catching up on all the subjects. And continue helping the three of us to be sane and happy. None of us are perfect, but together the four of us might get pretty close to it."

"Yes," she breathed. She was pushing down the urge to embrace Hale so tightly it knocked the wind out of him. The only thing keeping her from showering his scarred, beloved face with kisses was what Rogan would say.

The harsh tutor now disarmed Sabina, who was busy sneaking a glance at the three of them, again and shoved her to the ground to prove her defeat. When she fell with a grunt of pain, he smiled to the other three. "One down. Which one of you spoiled children want to learn their place next?"

"He sounds like the groundskeeper," Sander said through partly closed lips.

Avelynne watched Sabina brush dirt off her back. She'd be bruised after that landing. *He certainly dislikes us as much as the groundskeeper does.*

Eager for a chance to aim for Rogan's big, puffed out chest, she stepped forward. Just like when she'd promised to shoulder some of Sabina's burden, affection made her braver. She swallowed the lump of trepidation in her throat and tried to make her voice clear and confident. "I'll go next."

He looked at her with disdain. "Then pick up the Northerner's abandoned glaive, Ironhold. You need a lighter weapon with those puny arms."

Avelynne didn't care what he said or did to her. Her secret was out to the only three people who mattered and… they didn't hate her. Instead they stood by her side and would help her. More importantly, they would let her help them. Sander handed her the glaive.

With her head held higher than it had been for months,

maybe for all of her life, Avelynne strode into her sparring match.

The sun shone with that desperate light which spoke of early afternoon at winter's start. Avelynne gazed out the window. Did it ever snow here at the Centre? She hoped it would stay like this, sunny and only a touch chilly. She returned to her parchment.

She was so much more relaxed in this class than others. At least drawing was one subject she didn't have to study extra. Tutor Myle had complimented her technique and eye for detail in nearly every lesson.

Currently, she was drawing the water bodies, tree copses, and fields surrounding the Hall of Explorers. They had walked this area so many times with compass in hand, learning to find their way but also to make quick sketches and notes which could later be drawn into detailed maps.

One of those outings had been in Tutor Rete's lesson only an hour ago. Now, she was using those rough sketches to draw out full maps. Marking distances with the mathematical formulas they learned in their arithmetic lessons. After all these past months, the lessons were all starting to come together to show how they would be useful in their future endeavours.

As she carried on marking out the big lake they had their swimming lessons in, she heard whispers from the other desks. She picked up the words "I still can't believe that one day we'll make maps of new lands" and sharpened her ears.

She heard Sabina asking Sander, "Do you think there are people out there?"

He whispered back, "On any foreign lands we or the first wave might find? If so wouldn't they have come here to trade?"

"I don't know," Sabina said. "Maybe they're not that advanced? Perhaps like us, they've been fearful of venturing too far?"

Any answer Sander was about to give was interrupted by a knock on the door. They all watched as Myle went to answer it. It was Tutor Rete. He was wringing his hands and staring wide-eyed at Myle. Avelynne gaped. Rete was usually so calm and collected.

"You tutor the king in drawing, do you not?" Rete asked.

The younger man nodded. "Yes, his majesty and I have a lesson every fortnight. Why?"

Avelynne frowned. Why would someone as brutish as the king want to learn the art of drawing?

"That scoundrel! I need your help. Tell me you'll assist me, Myle!" Rete said in such a shriek that they all jumped in their seats.

He made his usual gesture of adjusting his high collar, but this time he tugged harder on it and it opened, revealing something bright.

Avelynne squinted to get a better look and saw what looked like silver patterns running up his neck.

What is that? Streams of magic? No, it's not vivid enough for that. Those are drawings or tattoos.

Myle glanced over at the students and then pushed Rete towards the door, saying, "I don't know what trouble is afoot. Or how I can help, but perhaps we should speak of this privately?"

Rete unsteadily backed out while rasping, "Yes."

"I'll return presently," Myle called to the four of them. "Carry on with your maps."

The second the door closed behind them, Sander burst out, "Did you see his neck?"

Hale was tugging at his ear. "Mm. Hard to miss. Were those tattoos?"

"Silver tattoos," Sander said with wide eyes. "Remember the whisper you heard 'Silver like magic. Silver like the young countess' necklace. Silver like the beasts.' Maybe it was about Rete and his tattoos!"

Sabina gave him a stern look. "You're grasping at straws. It's only some grey tattoos and—"

"Shh," Avelynne said. "Tutor Myle's coming back, we'll discuss it later."

The afternoon progressed with little time for conversation. Before Avelynne knew it, they had reached the final lesson of the day. For which, tutor Santorine had told them to prepare for a swim. Thus, they were all dressed for a swimming lesson in colder water, meaning that under their normal clothes they wore a short, fitted waxed canvas tunic and matching tight trousers, which they'd been given for this particular reason. It had amused Hale to no end that they had the Hall of Explorers insignia in bright emerald green on the rump.

Santorine led them to the lake. Avelynne rolled her

shoulders in preparation. Her stamina was almost up to the level of that of the others and she was starting to enjoy swimming. She liked Tutor Santorine too. She was knowledgeable, fair, and had a clever, dry wit. Moreover, she'd been very supportive and open with them, sharing whatever developments occurred in the case of the deaths. She was Avelynne's favourite, something which made her itch with guilt as Rete was their head tutor and he had been extra kind throughout the weeks since Karlinne's death.

Thinking about Rete reminded her of something. She turned to the others to whisper, "Can we gather in the library tonight to address Rete's strange behaviour? And also, the deaths and Karlinne's warnings. I promised Sabina I'd arrange a meeting for us to try to find answers."

"Great idea," Hale replied. "I'm tired of sitting around waiting for updates."

"Well, we haven't exactly been sitting around," Sander said. "We've had other things to attend to. Making this place our home, getting to know each other, and Ave's secret, of course. Not to mention lessons all day, every day."

Hale kicked a pebble. "Nonetheless, I want to take action. Find answers."

"No chatting back there," Tutor Santorine called to them in a reproaching sing-song.

"Sorry," they all replied in unison.

"Library after supper tonight," Avelynne muttered through the corner of her mouth.

They arrived and Avelynne took in the serene surroundings. The tree branches were bare and looming over the placid surface of the vast lake. There was something at the bank closest to them.

"Boats?" Sander said.

Tutor Santorine put her hands on her hips. "Astute observation, Eleksander." She smiled as she used his name, she'd become so much more informal than the other tutors. She didn't, however, allow them to call her Atha. "We shan't be swimming today, second wave. Instead, we are going to practise rowing."

"Why?" Hale blurted out. "We won't be rowing on our longships. We'll have sails and sailors under our command."

"Yes, but you cannot ask your sailors to do anything which you yourselves have not mastered. You are to be trained to be the best explorers and captains possible. That includes being able to handle the two row boats attached to your longship."

Sabina stopped scratching Kall's chin. "It'll have little boats on it?"

"Of course. In case of your longship taking damage or being shipwrecked."

"I see. Well, what if we use magic to—"

Santorine held up a hand. "I'll stop you right there, Sabina. Using magic to achieve things will only get you so far until you are exhausted. You need to be able to do things the manual way. Your life may depend on it, and, equally importantly, so may your mission."

No one argued.

"Right," Santorine said, her tone mellowing. "As a fellow Lakelander, I know you'll have experience with this, Eleksander. So why don't you and Hale take one boat. I and the ladies will take the other. You will all take turns rowing."

Hale scrunched up his nose. "Fine. How hard can it be?

You simply put your back into it and cleave the water with your oars."

"No, there's a technique," Sander said. "Especially if you want to preserve your strength to be able to do it for a long time."

"Exactly," Santorine agreed.

They got in the boats and Avelynne listened closely to Santorine's instructions on how to sit, how to hold the oars, and, of course, how to row.

Then they took to the water. At first, it was funny to note her own uselessness at this, and to watch Hale ignore the directions and try to muscle his way through it and soon exhaust himself.

Avelynne stopped giggling when she saw Sander row. With long even pulls, he easily transported the vessel wide distances. He gave a deep, rough grunt every time he heaved the oars to him. One that made Avelynne's cheeks heat up. Actually, it made all of her heat up. His movements were so efficient and natural, like he was built for this. The rest of them looked like children splashing about compared to him.

He spotted her staring and seemed to mistake her admiration for a cry for help. He lowered himself into the water, waded over to her boat and asked Santorine if they could switch.

The tutor agreed and, while getting into the other vessel, began scolding Hale for losing his temper and throwing the oars overboard earlier.

Sander heaved himself into their boat, making it rock a little but not go off kilter.

"Easy there, big fellow" Sabina said. "Don't drown yourself. Or worse, the little Countess. Her parents will flay you if you do."

He merely gave her that sweet, crooked smile and crouched down in front of Avelynne. He took her hands and adjusted them on the oars. "You have to make allowances for your lesser muscle mass with how you hold the oars and how you move. Your stomach and back are quite strong, use them more than your arms and legs."

He touched her muscles as he mentioned them and Avelynne lost any remaining trace of the calm she normally felt around him. His tunic and trousers clung to him like a second skin and water dripped down his cheeks and off his square jaw. The cold water had given his luscious skin goose bumps. She wanted to trace them with her fingers. Why was she so weak for beautiful bodies and sexual pleasure? In someone wanting to avoid romance, it caused such strife.

As he placed a firm hand on her stomach and said, "Bend from your core when you pull the oars, Ave," she shivered. Like she did whenever Sabina or Hale flirted with her.

What's wrong with you? This is Sander. He sees you like a sister!

She made herself focus. This wasn't different than when he helped her train or tutored her in arithmetic. She bit her lip. No, it was different. He was so confident now. Not in a cocky way, but in a comfortable and almost adult manner. This was his element and, by all the silver beasts, how it suited him!

She followed his recommendations and then began to row. It was easier now and she told him so.

"Splendid," he said. "I'm going to go suggest that Hale

try the same. He relies too much on those beefy arms of his."

He stood, barely rocking the boat, and dove into the water, moving like a knife slicing through a soft pear.

Avelynne watched him go, oars limp in her hands.

Sabina groaned. "Do stop drooling, Avelynne. It's only Eleksander, you've seen him before."

Avelynne jumped, having nearly forgotten that Sabina was in the boat with her.

"Yes. Sorry. I don't know what happened there."

"I do," Sabina muttered. "You stopped seeing your friend and began seeing a possible suitor."

"No! Not a suitor. You know how I feel about romance. I only noticed how attractive he is when he's comfortable and too busy to remember to hide himself away."

"Mm-hm."

"Stop it, or I shall think you jealous," Avelynne said with a laugh.

Sabina wasn't laughing. Or joking back. She kept her eyes on the setting sun.

Avelynne reached out and stroked away a strand of white hair that had escaped the braid, making the North-erner face her again. "Hey. I… don't like him more than I do you, Sabina."

"You don't?"

Avelynne's heart twinged. "No, my sweet snowdrop. The three of you have become my dearest friends. Family almost."

"I don't look at family like you just did at Eleksander."

"No. Fair enough. That's me being…" Avelynne shook her head. "Never mind. The point is that you all mean as much to me as if you were my blood. When we travel together, I'll happily lay down my life for any of you."

"I would do the same," Sabina said with a solemn, stoic expression.

Avelynne leaned her forehead against Sabina's, making the boat rock. She didn't care. This had to be cleared up once and for all.

"Then let's not allow attraction to muddle things," Avelynne said gently. "I love you all and I will learn with you, laugh with you, fight with you, and try to save the people of Cavarra with you. That's all I should be doing."

"Fine. Agreed. Well, for now at least. We won't be mapmakers forever. One day I plan to settle and take a wife."

Avelynne moved away to let Sabina see her tension-breaking smirk. "Don't tell me that when that day comes, you'd settle for loving a frail little Countess like me?"

"Picking you would not be settling. I'd be fighting for the honour to be the wife of a most extraordinary woman," Sabina stated, calm and clear. She wasn't going to allow Avelynne to break this tension. Her eyes shone serious in the wintery twilight.

Lost for words, Avelynne simply took her hands and held them tight.

That sensation of it only being the two of them in the world came back to Avelynne.

It was shattered when Hale flipped the other boat over by standing up, gesticulating, and shouting happily to Sander that he did too have "sea legs".

Surfacing after her involuntary dunking, Santorine threw out her arms and said, "That's it. I'm not teaching you lot anything while soaked. We're going back to the Hall. We'll return to this at our next lesson." There was a gulp from beside her. "Hopefully, by then our Woodlander will have gotten the water out of his lungs," she added with a sigh.

Chapter Thirty-Two

MYSTERY AND MOTIVE

Hale glared at his embarrassing goose bumps. He wasn't used to his body not adjusting to his surroundings. Curse this cold. It was chilly outside tonight, but it seemed twice as bad in the library. It made his healing ankle hurt more. He checked the ceiling, wondering if it had cracks which let in the wind. Eleksander followed his gaze while Sabina was fussing over Kall who wanted to leave the library.

Avelynne cleared her throat to get their attention. There were crumbs on her tunic's neckline, clearly from the rare slice of bread they had each been treated to at supper.

Hang on, I should reach out and brush it away!

Right as Hale thought that, Eleksander sent a gentle gush of magic which blew away the crumbs.

"Thank you," Avelynne said. "All right, everyone. Let's focus."

Hale bit back a growl. He had to become better at flirting with her. He needed to muster some of his usual confidence. He sat back in his seat in a casual, roguish way and returned to listening to her.

"We're here to discuss the deaths, the warnings, and the apparent danger we're all in. To try to take action if we can and not simply leave it to our elders. Like I promised a certain someone we would," Avelynne said with a smile towards Sabina, who leaned in and kissed her cheek.

Hale's jaw tightened. Why were those two getting so close? He banged his fist against his thigh. *Stop! She doesn't belong to you and you have no right to be jealous. Stop being an entitled beast and listen.*

Avelynne placed her palms flat on the table. "I suppose it all starts with one question. Who is this 'he' that Karlinne warned us about?"

"Tutor Rete," Eleksander said without hesitation.

With a sceptical frown, Sabina sat back in her chair. "Why? Because of his tattoos relating to that strange verse about silver that Karlinne kept repeating?"

"Yes," Eleksander retorted in the same accusatory tone. "And because we saw him rip up a decree that clearly came from the king. Thereby keeping information from us like Karlinne said that the mystery man did." When no one replied, he added, "Besides, if there's someone spying on students, our head tutor would be a good choice, right?"

Sabina raised her eyebrows. "If he were only spying on us, sure. But if he's interfering with all students, being the tutor of only our group means he gets to spend very little time with the other one. When did he even last see the first wave?" Her brows lowered into a scowl. "Now, the king—who we know has ordered people to spy and kill in the past—can use all staff and servants to spy on anyone and everyone. He has much more power than some lowly tutor."

"The king? You said he was too useless to be a threat before," Hale said.

"Aye, but since then I've heard more about him. Tutor Santorine admitted to me that he likes to scheme and prove his power by interfering. And I've had time to think about it," she tapped the table with a finger. "I think this is all organised by someone with power. Someone who doesn't mind spilling blood for what he wants. I can't imagine Rete doing that. He's a fair, kind man. Also, as I said, Rete couldn't spy on the first wave."

"Do we know for certain that the mystery 'he' is spying on the first wave as well?" Avelynne asked.

"No," Sabina admitted. "However, Karlinne said 'students', not only the second wave."

Eleksander rubbed his face. "Why is anyone spying on two groups of students in the first place? What information or secrets could we have? What use could we be?"

"We need to ask why someone would want to spy on us AND keep information from us. The only answer I can think of is that they want to control us. My prime suspect has admitted as much," Hale said.

Sabina sat forward. "Aye, the king talked about us obeying his orders. And if the motive is to control us when we leave for our mission, it makes sense to spy on the first wave as they sail next year." She slapped her palm against her thigh. "King Lothiam was there when they were chosen! If I'm right and he's Karlinne's 'he', then it makes sense that he would spy on them first and foremost."

"He's not who I was referring to," Hale said. "I have no love for the king nor do I think he's too innocent for this. Anyone who has his queen beheaded for flirting with a knight is clearly unstable. But…" He tried to think of the right words to make them understand why his gut was telling him that it wasn't their useless monarch at the heart of this. "Look, the king orders people dead in unimaginative ways and does none of it himself, right?"

"Right," Avelynne agreed with some hesitation.

Hale nodded to her. "To poison someone's heart into stopping, while sitting in front of them? And to hang, maim, and slit the throat of someone? That doesn't sound like him. It sounds like the only one who appears more violent and cruel than the king—the groundskeeper."

Avelynne's brow furrowed. "The groundskeeper?"

"Yes," Hale said. "He's threatened us several times. Also, Karlinne mentioned that this villain did what he did 'to keep you happy and obeying orders,' right? That sounds a lot like what the groundskeeper said to us when we met him that night by the lake."

Sabina groaned with exasperation. "Aye, but the groundskeeper has no stealth or real power. How could he withhold information from us, for example? It can't be him. The king however, he has power, cunning, and the means!"

"So does Rete," mumbled Eleksander.

Avelynne quietly said, "And Rogan."

Hale took in Avelynne's shrinking form. "Tutor Rogan? He's just a brainless tyrant, isn't he? What does he have to do with any of this?"

She shrugged. "He hates us. He has power. He seems like the sort of man who wants to… burn everything down because he's angry."

Sabina bit her lower lip. "I agree that he's constantly furious and dislikes us. That may give him motive to want to punch us or get us thrown out. But withhold information? Spying? Slaying two innocent people? All to influence or control us? I can't see it."

Eleksander turned to Sabina. "If that even is the motive? Perhaps this has nothing to do with influencing us. Hey, maybe this 'he' is someone we haven't even met?" He closed his eyes. "Let's start over and focus less on suspects and more on motive. Why is someone killing servants, spying on us, and withholding information? What can they possibly gain from that? When we know that, we'll know who the killer is!"

Avelynne hugged her arms around herself. "I think Rogan wants to take our place on the mission. For that to happen, he'd need to get rid of us. Or make us fail so that the king and the Centre officials would want us replaced with older, more experienced people."

"How is spying on us going to get rid of us?" Sabina asked gently.

Avelynne whined. "I don't know! I've been trying to figure out possible motives all day. Before I was so focused on who was behind all of this, that I forgot the why. Maybe it was because I was distracted by my stupid secret."

"No, I think we all focused more on the *who* than the *why* actually," Hale said. "Probably because Karlinne started this off by warning us about a 'he' every chance she got. She should've been warning us about what the greater plot was."

"Perhaps she didn't know," Eleksander said. "If you were a manipulating, murdering maniac, would you expose all of your plans and motives to the underlings you threatened into helping you?"

"No, I suppose not." Hale scratched his chin. "Underlings… huh. Do you think the groundskeeper could be the killer but he's working for one of the others? Maybe the 'he' was actually referring to two different men? Or three?"

Sabina was the first to answer. "You mean Karlinne could've been warning us to keep away from the groundskeeper when she first spoke of a 'he' but been talking about the king when she later said that 'he' was in charge."

"I think it's possible," he replied.

In the ensuing silence, Hale watched Kall. He was pacing around them in a tight circle. Was he protecting them? Or was he picking up on the tension and needing to move? Either way, Hale sympathised.

Avelynne ran a hand down her face. "We should've pressed Karlinne for a name before we let her go."

"We shouldn't have let her go at all," Hale replied in a broken voice. "Not alone."

Eleksander sighed. "There is a lot we should or should not have done, but here we are. The question is what we do now. We can either leave it all to Santorine and the Centre officials or…"

Sabina finished his sentence with, "Or we start talking to people and try to gather evidence and eliminate the suspects until we have the beast-shagger who did this."

"Exactly," Eleksander replied.

Avelynne looked to Hale. "What do you think?"

He smiled at her. "You know what I would choose if the options are do nothing or take action."

She returned the smile. "Of course. Then the only question is who we start with." She turned to Sabina. "I'm sorry but I don't think we can storm into the royal castle and start asking the king questions."

Sabina held up her hands. "Agreed. We have to start with someone else. Honestly, I think Rete or the groundskeeper—whatever his name is—are more likely suspects than Rogan. Sorry Avelynne."

"That's fine," she replied. "I'm glad you're being honest."

Hale pondered the two suspects and, even though it pained him, said, "we should start with Rete. We know he's friendly, he listens to us, and he'll want to help us find whoever is at fault. Unless he's the killer, of course."

"Also, we know where he is'" Eleksander said. "The groundskeeper could be anywhere."

Avelynne pointed to him. "True. Let's start with the one we know the location of and who won't bite our head off, like Rogan. Or cut it off if we're talking about the king."

Hale stood up. "I need to fetch something to wear from my room first. It's cold."

"Sure," Sabina said, calling Kall over to her. "We'll all go get something to ward off this sudden chill. Avelynne and I will meet you in your bedchamber when we're done."

Sabina, Kall, and Avelynne walked off towards their room.

Yes. I'll get something to warm me, but it'll be my cloak instead of the jerkin. That'll hide the thing I actually want to wear.

He strode off, wondering how he was going to put his knife belt on without Eleksander questioning him.

Chapter Thirty-Three

QUESTIONS

Avelynne had to take the lead as they headed for the tutors' room. She'd promised Sabina she would shoulder some of the burden of responsibility. That meant she was in charge. No matter if everything in her shouted that the others were better qualified for it.

She wrapped her cloak tighter and pulled the hood up, even though they were inside. It was a peculiar sort of armour for a peculiar sort of venture.

Outside the door of the room stood Rogan. He was watching something on his arm, right below where his tunic was rolled up. When they got closer Avelynne saw that it was a trickle of blood.

"Tutor Rogan? Are you all right?" Sander asked.

He didn't look up. "Yes. Must've let one of the sodding silver beasts nick me when I was moving them into sturdier cages. Only noticed now because it was dripping onto my boots." He dabbed at it with the surcoat held in his other hand, looking embarrassed that they caught him displaying vulnerability.

Avelynne couldn't help but wonder why he was moving silver beasts around. Sturdier cages? The cages she had seen were fine.

"Never mind my injury," he snapped. "What are you all doing here? Should you bookworms not be engaged in something useful, like studying or practising?"

"We… had some questions for Tutor Rete," Sabina said.

Avelynne's heart skipped a beat. *Why did she say that? She could have merely said they wanted to see Rete.*

She made herself calm down. It was fully natural for students to ask their head tutor things.

Rogan rubbed at the blood welling on his arm again, only making it drip more. "Questions?" He barked out a cynical laugh. "You're supposed to be so clever and perfect, you should have answers, not questions."

"Actually, you're meant to teach us the answers," Avelynne replied, suddenly unable to hold her tongue.

He thrust out his meaty, blood-flecked hand and Avelynne didn't have time to duck. She was certain he was going to strike her but instead he pushed her hood down and then growled, "I figured it was you under there. Only an inbred coward would walk around with her hood up indoors. That's enough of your insolent tongue, Ironhold!"

"Get away from me," she screeched.

Then he let go of her hood, pushed her against the wall, and said, "Oh, stop whinging for once. I have trained the first wave and now you silver beast-loving second wavers, and I grow so weary of all of Cavarra thinking that it will be rescued by a gang of bookish toddlers."

"We're eighteen," Sabina said. "Old enough to marry, to join the king's army, or to own land. Hardly toddlers. And we're not your dogs, you can't push us around and shout commands at us."

She placed herself between Rogan and Avelynne and added in low tones, "Unless you'd like to shove me too. Because I can promise you that I will not be as even-tempered about it as Avelynne has been."

"He won't be pushing any of us again," Sander said. He stood to his full height, looking Rogan straight in the eye. "To think I used to be impressed by you. You're a bully. And for what? Because you want to be the one commandeering that longship?"

Rogan roared, "Why not? I was a major in the army. My family were fishermen who lived by and from the sea. I've hunted and bested swarms of silver beasts in every part of our nation." He stomped his foot. "And yet, because I am not some youngling who can add up numbers and draw pretty maps, the king would never consider sending me. Yet, ask yourselves this, why is he so sodding determined to send inexperienced children? Huh!?"

With that, Rogan stormed away down the corridor.

Glaring after him, Sabina planted her feet. "I believe I'm seeing Avelynne's point now. Rogan could be the culprit. Or at least be in on it somehow."

"We don't know that," Sander said with hesitation. "He might only be bitter and hot-headed. To me, he still appears more likely to want the king to scrap the whole academy than to start spying on us. We need to talk to Rete."

Avelynne coughed to clear the lump in her throat. She couldn't take her eyes off the blood stains on the floor. This was a bad start to their venture and made her anxiety grow tenfold. But Sander was right, they needed answers.

"Let's go talk to him then," she said as loudly as she could muster.

Hale walked ahead and knocked on the door. It only took a few heartbeats until Rete opened.

"Um. Hello, may we come in and ask some questions?" Avelynne forced out.

"Certainly", he said, standing aside. "I have just lit the fire, so it should be nice and warm here soon."

They filtered in and Avelynne considered how to lead up to their questions. Perhaps some small talk? To make him comfortable and set a friendly tone. She could start by mentioning today's lessons.

While she was deciding, Hale said, "Tutor Rete. Is there anything you'd like to tell us about the accusations that Karlinne Ash made? Or about her and Thomey's deaths?"

In shock, Avelynne saw Sabina close her eyes and Sander shift his weight from foot to foot. Hale was being Hale. Well, at least now she didn't have to consider how to bring up the subject anymore.

Rete's thin eyebrows shot up his forehead. "Do I know anything about it and who was involved? Dearest boy, don't you think I would have mentioned that to the officials if I did?"

"Well, yes. Unless…" Hale trailed off.

Rete stood to his full height, towering even over Eleksander. "Unless I had something to do with it? Unless I spied on you? Kept things from you, and, of course, murdered this Karlinne and our dear Thomey."

Avelynne tensed, expecting Hale to get a scolding or maybe even a shove, like Rogan had given her. Instead, Rete sighed.

"I cared for Thomey. As I believe I mentioned, he started here the same day I did; the academy's opening day. The stones were still settling into place and none of the tapestries or decorations were hung." Rete stared into nothing, eyes glazed. "He, I, and a handful of others shared a meal and discussed how this place would help Cavarra. How we would finally dare to leave our lands. Not only to get away from the silver beasts and the famine, but to *explore*. We would be part of that by helping you all be prepared."

"I see," Hale said, hanging his head in shame, or perhaps guilt.

Rete carried on as if he hadn't spoken. "Thomey, as I, looked forward to helping you students in any possible way and to watch you learn from the best and get the best service. Unlike people like Coth Rogan or Groundskeeper Adelard who both have..." he swirled his hand in the air, "*concerns* about your age and inexperience with being in charge."

"Adelard, so that's his name," Hale mumbled.

Avelynne decided that it was time for her to take the reins, she stepped in front of Hale and sought their head tutor's gaze, smiling as compassionately as she could.

"I hope you shan't think our questions too impertinent, Tutor Rete. We will be asking others the same ones. We, well, we simply need some answers to settle our minds, then we can focus fully on our lessons again."

Rete clasped his hands behind his back. "I understand. Like you, I wish to return to a serene environment conducive to learning. Ask away."

Avelynne hesitated. "In one of our lessons, we saw you

get a decree from the king. You tore it up with some vehe-
mence. We also saw you storm into our lesson in an agitated
state to talk to Tutor Myle about the king. I'm sure there are
harmless explanations for both those incidents..." she
trailed off, waiting for him to fill in the rest.

Rete smiled. "Yes. I tore up that decree from the king
because he was once again ordering us to teach you as
meticulously as we could. As if we weren't already doing
that." He shook his head. "My agitation over the king when
I spoke to Tutor Myle stemmed from the same... difficult
behaviour of our monarch. He is not an easy superior to
have. Sometimes you need to speak your frustrations out
loud to get them out of your system."

"I see," Avelynne said.

"Let us clear this up. I was not involved in this horrible
affair," Rete said, his brow furrowing. "I understand that
you want to find who did this. I do too. Those deaths still
haunt me. Thomey was dear to me and, by all accounts,
Karlinne was a hard-working, good person. I wish Thomey
was still here and that Karlinne had been able to leave that
night, as she had planned."

"So do we," Sabina said.

Rete stood, still solemn but now also appearing quite
drained. "Did you have other questions? If not, I think I
need a strong drink and a moment of quiet."

"Of course," Avelynne said.

They had to head back into the cold corridor. Avelynne
didn't want to see the ominous blood on the floor out there.
She didn't want to face the fact that they now had to go ask
these questions to the less reasonable suspects. She wished

they could go back to when the biggest worry was her secret.

"Wait," Sander stopped with his hand on the door handle and whispered, "I never told Santorine that Karlinne had been planning to leave that night. It didn't seem important. Did any of you?"

One after the other, they all said no. Every response making the air feel thicker and harder to breathe.

Sander let go of the door handle. "Excuse me, Tutor Rete?

He turned from where he had stood, watching the fire. "Hm?"

She saw Sander's throat bob as he swallowed hard and then said, "How did you know Karlinne was planning to escape the night she died?"

For a few heartbeats they all stood there, like they'd been petrified by some spell.

Then Rete's face changed. Every semblance of the solemn, reasonable, innocent tutor vanishing like dust being blown off a surface, revealing what was truly underneath.

Chapter Thirty-Four

THE TWELVE

Hale automatically took a fighting stance. Eleksander had pulled it off! He'd found the thread that unravelled Rete's lies. Could it actually be him at the root of this? Their patient, sensible head tutor?

What was revealed now that Rete's mask of innocence was gone was a peculiar blend. His body language was serene, and his tiny smile was that of a charming trickster being caught mid-trick. But, there was something stranger and darker flashing in his eyes. Was that what had made the other three retreat from him?

"Yes," Rete said, holding his hands up in surrender. "I knew what Karlinne planned to do that night. She told me. Do you know why she told me? She understood that I care. Unlike our king. Which is why we are in this mess. Our king is why I, and those I work with, have taken these actions."

His smile grew but turned sad. "Did I order some of the servants to keep an eye on you? Yes. To keep you safe. Did I withhold the king's decrees from you? Yes, because of what was *in them*."

"That's all very well and good," Sabina spat. "But what I want to know is, did Karlinne tell you her plans right before you *murdered* her? Did Thomey have to die because he wanted to inform the officials?"

Rete squeezed his eyes shut and grimaced. It was the grimace of a man trying to tell a bunch of children that the room was on fire and only getting questions about treacle tarts and playtime in return. "That is not what you should be focusing on! The important question here is what was in those decrees!"

Hale stepped forward. "Maybe to you. But not to Karlinne. Nor Thomey."

Rete made a move. Was he heading for the door?

"Wait," Avelynne cried. "Fine. Tell us what was in the decrees. We'll start there."

Rete stopped but wasn't still. Was he shaking? Trembling maybe?

"The king ordered your education to take a different turn. He wanted you to be indoctrinated to be more predatory. More likely to break our motto of 'To Explore. Never Exploit.' He wanted us tutors to unofficially lead you towards conquering the lands you would find." Rete's expression soured. "He started asking the first wave to come up to the castle, filling their minds with thoughts of Cavarra's superiority to any other hypothetical people and our greater need for whatever natural resources were out there. Luckily, Tutor Hathleen took them to their new ship for on-site training, out of his reach. You, however, were still within his grasp."

"Is Tutor Hathleen working with you?" Avelynne asked carefully.

Rete shook his head violently. "No. She and Myle... they have little backbone. They try to keep the peace and walk the line between doing what's right and following the king's orders. They won't do what's *needed*." Rete rubbed his face hard enough to make it red. "And Rogan! He is impossible to get to work with anyone. No, it was left to me and Atha. We recruited some servants to keep an eye on you. To see if you had any leanings towards the king's views. If not, the mission of exploration would be safe in your hands." He stared wide-eyed into the air above their heads now, as if talking to himself. "And you'd be viable candidates to join The Twelve."

Eleksander looked about to explode. "Wait. Atha? Tutor Santorine? She's in on this too? And what in the name of all the waters is The Twelve?"

Rete didn't seem to hear him. He was still staring into space.

"The Twelve," he intoned. "They provide you with the silver tattoos to mark you as one of them, so we can find each other without having to say a word. Then they ask you to serve. And you do so. Proudly. It's what's right. The king has to be stopped. He has to be..." his mouth was working wordlessly.

Sabina stomped her foot. "What are you talking about, madman? What is the Twelve?!"

A clearer voice rang out from their side. "The Twelve is an underground group that works to undermine the king. It was founded many years ago by the queen. That was why our *beloved monarch* had her beheaded, not for any dalliance with some knight."

Standing in the doorway, speaking as if she was lecturing, was Tutor Santorine. She came in and closed the door with a low and strangely unnerving click.

She cleared her throat. "The Twelve was originally twelve of the queen's confidants. Ones who saw what she saw: King Lothiam being an unsuitable ruler who grew more and more maniacal by the day." She lifted her chin. "He wants three things: riches, absolute power, and to be remembered as Cavarra's greatest ruler. He doesn't care if people have to die for it or if any moral rules are broken."

"Sounds like most rulers to me," Hale muttered.

Santorine gave him a disappointed look. "Lothiam is worse than you grasp. Only careful guiding from his counsellors, some belonging to The Twelve, keep him from opening more labour camps for anyone who speaks against him. Anyone who reports about the torture, assaults, and humiliation that happens in those camps—he brands as a liar." When Hale only huffed, she carried on. "He wants greater tithes from the counties and has spoken about making new laws that state that the king does not have to follow the rules and laws of our nation."

Sabina had been busy trying to calm Kall, who was growling at the tension in the room, now she stood and said, "If he's that bad, why aren't there more rebellions against him?"

"Because he quashes rebellions by misdirecting people's anger!" Santorine grew more agitated. "He says he needs bigger tithes to keep the silver beasts under control, even though he spends it on his army and his own whims. He ensures each county think that the other three are the drain on resources."

Hale realised that he had seen that in action. The Warden had often complained of their tithes going to keep the Northerners in food and firewood.

Santorine shook her head sadly. "Lothiam makes Cavarrians dream of new lands where everything will be safe and fine, so that they will not fight to improve things here. Yet, even with all of this going his way, Cavarra is not enough for him. He wants more land. More subjects to rule. More undeserved praise. More riches."

Avelynne fidgeted with her necklace. "And what does your organisation want?"

"To open people's eyes and to overthrow him. Something we cannot do from here, where anyone who speaks against him disappears. We need to build our rebellion on a faraway base where we can be left alone to plan and to raise funds. A new land with natural resources that can sustain us and help us fund our revolution."

Eleksander frowned. "You want new land? How does that make you different from the king?"

"In many ways, dear Eleksander. Most importantly, we would ask you to travel far enough to ensure we found somewhere *uninhabited*. Then, together, we can free Cavarra of that tyrant. After he's gone, we can put all resources into fighting the silver beasts here and start a colony in the new land, peacefully and for the good of the people. All people."

"The tattoos. The servant girl saw the tattoos," Rete mumbled from behind them.

"Is he all right?" Avelynne asked.

Santorine's proud bearing slumped. "No. He's sick to heart and soul. It started with Thomey's death."

"What happened to Thomey?" Hale inquired. He wanted less monologuing and more answers about the deaths.

"We found out that the heartless boy was planning to sell our identities to the king," Santorine said. "He said he didn't believe in our cause and that the king was right in that we must take what we want by force. That the strong must conquer the weak." She frowned. "He wouldn't see sense. He wouldn't take our bribes to keep quiet either. We had to get rid of him. Since they had an intimate relationship, Hason…" she glanced over at Rete who was frantically pulling at his open collar, as if there was a point in hiding his tattoos now. She looked back to her students. "Hason volunteered to give Thomey one last chance to reconsider and if he didn't, he'd slip him Heartsbane."

Sabina cursed under her breath. Hale echoed the sentiment.

Tutor Santorine ignored the interruption. "Hason was always the most dedicated of us. The more involved in the Twelve you are, the more silver tattoos you have. As you can see, his cover most of his body."

"So that was why Karlinne kept repeating things that were silver. To give us something to look out for without having to break her vow to keep your secrets," Avelynne said.

"I suppose so," Santorine said. "Karlinne was unhappy in our employ but grew fearful of Hason. No wonder since she knew what he did to Thomey. I have been trying to help Hason ever since. But he seems to become more—"

She was interrupted by the sound of Rete's elbow hitting the wall. He was twitching, like something deep inside him wanted to escape his body.

"More disturbed by the day." Santorine's shoulders slumped. "He killed poor Karlinne without consulting any of the Twelve. It was as you surmised, when she struggled and made noise, he cut her throat and then … as some sort of misinterpreted, dreadful way of keeping her quiet forever, he cut out her tongue." Santorine squeezed her eyes shut and shook her head. "I have been trying to convince him to travel somewhere quiet, perhaps speak to a physician."

Hale scrutinised Rete, who still mouthed words soundlessly and stared into the empty air as if there was something, or someone, there. How had he not seen how near this man was to stepping outside of sanity and decency?

"Obviously that hasn't worked," Hale muttered, watching the twitching man.

Santorine was watching her friend and colleague too. "No. He refuses to go, saying that he has to be here to steer you in the right direction. To make sure you are good, unselfish, and ready to do the right thing for Cavarra."

"The right thing!" Sabina shouted. "He murdered and maimed a girl not much older than us and then wants to stay to keep us 'good'! Really?"

Santorine's face was a mask of shame. "As I said, he has become disturbed. His actions are no longer directed by the Twelve."

"But the murder of Thomey was," Avelynne said quietly.

"Regrettably, yes. There was no other way to stop him from revealing our cause and having us tortured and killed. Still, we didn't make that decision lightly." She looked at them, eyes brimming with tears. "We wanted Karlinne to live, to walk out of here as soon as she promised to keep our secret. Her death was the action of a man driven insane by the guilt over having to murder a lover."

Hale's stomach turned. If Rete was a mad murderer, why didn't these people forcibly remove him?

Santorine walked over and gently pushed Rete's chin up until his mouth closed. For a moment he stood there, trembling, then he muttered, "Cavarra needs leaders. Needs leaders. *Leaders.* Ones who care about the people, yes the people, and the ideals we hold dear." His eyes refocused on them and cleared a little. "But don't you see! Everyone in power is blinded by the king's rousing speeches! All those promises to find them someone they can be superior to, someone to blame, to look down on, and to exploit." He frowned so deep it looked like his face would never recover. "As the accords forbid that we turn on each other, the beast on our throne will send you children out to find them a new enemy."

Hale was as impatient with all these explanations as he was with the fact that he couldn't think of what to do. "Here we are with the children thing again," he grumbled.

Santorine put a hand on his arm. "You're not children, Hale. However, the king did order the new mapmakers to be young. He has all but admitted that he did that because you'd be easy to lead."

"What?" Eleksander said.

She nodded. "I'm afraid so. He believes that young people are more impulsive and stormier. That you'll have less empathy. That you'll want glory and won't remember the atrocities of our past with the colonisation and slavery we subjected each other to."

Sabina snarled, "What a load of silver beast dung."

Santorine laughed mirthlessly. "Yes. A lot of what the king says is just that. However, he knows what to say to make people listen."

Rete wrung his hands, rubbing them together faster and faster. "And anyone who disagrees, he mocks and undermines. Or kills! Or throws in labour camps. He wants us hating everyone but him, wants us giving him all our coin and reverence." His voice rose to a scream. "And Lothiam won't stop! Not at anything. He'll have the four counties in war. We are running out of time!"

"Aren't the silver beasts enough of an enemy for him?" Eleksander asked.

"No, because winning that fight would take more time and riches than he's willing to spend. He doesn't care," Santorine said, voice dripping with disdain as thick as sap. "Even here at the Centre, the silver beasts sneak in over the borders and are only killed when they get too close to the castle. That is why you are not allowed out alone."

From the corner of Hale's eye, he saw Rete bounce on the balls of his feet and continue to twitch and rub his hands raw. Hale didn't like this. The man was dangerous and about to ignite and scorch his surroundings like a forest fire. Still, they needed answers and they were finally getting them. They had to stay. He rested his hand on the reassuringly hard metal hidden under his cloak.

Avelynne on the other hand, was clearly still focused on Santorine as she asked her, "What exactly do you mean about King Lothiam not caring?"

"He's stopped caring about ridding his kingdom of the silver beasts. As long as they don't threaten him personally, at least. He has retracted the great minds of our nation from working on the silver beast problem, making them focus on this academy and your mission," Santorine said with a sombre nod to them. "On figuring out what we would need to teach classes of young geniuses sent out to conquer new lands. *His* new lands. Where he and his favourites will live. Leaving the rest of us here to fight off the beasts best we can."

Meanwhile, that vein in Rete's forehead appeared to be ready to pop. He wrung his hands even faster and garbled, "The king... he is the true silver beast. And the callousness of Cavarra's people was the magic that fed him." His face was getting redder by the moment and spittle flew from his lips as he spoke on. "Changed him from a harmless, ordinary garden moth to a huge, magical silvery plague that bites your fingers off when you sleep. Monster. Monster, I say! It cannot continue!"

Rete seemed to vibrate with a strange energy, unable to be still. Hale might not be as good at reading people as the others, but even he saw that something had broken in this man's mind, and it was breaking further with every passing moment... piece by jagged piece. Their head tutor was far out of reach from common sense.

Hale was just thinking that he had enough, that they needed to subdue Rete before he hurt himself, when the tutor's bulging eyes found Avelynne and he screamed, "You! You weren't chosen to come here because you were the best in the Peaks. We found out! Yes. The Twelve have members everywhere. Your parents sent you here! To spy, yes, to SPY.

Sent by your father, the Grand Count—who serves the king!"

"Only in name," Avelynne said. "All ruling classes must answer to the monarch. In truth my parents dislike the ki—"

She was cut off by Rete throwing himself at her. With a sound like an animal being skinned alive, he grabbed her slender neck in his raw hands.

Hale saw those reddened hands whiten at the knuckles as the madman began to squeeze with all of his might.

Chapter Thirty-Five

THE DAGGER AND THE NECKLACE

Avelynne couldn't breathe. The hands around her neck were not only unbelievably strong, they were feverishly hot. This man was mad, and he had killed before.

This wasn't how she had imagined her death.

She banged his wiry, muscular wrists with her fists, trying to bat his grip away, but to no avail. Lights danced before her eyes and her lungs were aching almost as much as her throat. She was backing up, instinctively trying to get away from him but he followed, the two of them attached as in a macabre dance.

Through her blurring vision, she saw Sander, who had been closest, rush them. He managed to punch Rete on the ear hard enough that he let go and staggered back.

Avelynne's throat was free and she instinctively sucked in the largest breath of her life. Her necklace had ripped, the broken chain still in Rete's hand and the little silver quill flying across the room. She only barely noticed it, more focused on the pain in her throat and the commotion around her.

Santorine cried, "Leave them be, Hason. They're not the enemy. We can still convince them to help us!"

"We cannot trust them, they're the king's puppets. Thomey persuaded them to join the king. Like he did before them," Rete screeched back before kicking Sander's midsection.

All the screaming became background noise when Avelynne saw Hale draw a dagger from underneath his cloak.

Santorine stepped towards them, reaching for the blade with a snarl on her face. Avelynne wasn't sure if she wanted to attack them as well or simply remove any weapons from the frenzy.

Clearly, Sabina wasn't taking any chances. She shouted "subdue" to Kall and the snowtiger launched for Santorine. His big jaws ripped her clothes but didn't pierce her skin. Still, Santorine cried out and made a run for it.

Kall turned to Sabina for further instructions. Unwavering in both expression and voice, the Northerner roared, "Hunt!"

The snowtiger obeyed, chasing after Santorine with his mistress close on their heels.

Avelynne's focus went back to Rete. He was on the floor now, rolling around with Sander, who was punching and smacking Rete against the ground whenever possible. He was much bigger than the tutor. Madness and not having anything to lose gave people strength, though, and Rete was obviously using all of that to his advantage now.

"Keep him still," Hale bellowed, blade raised to stab whenever he got a chance.

Rete extended a hand and fired a great mass of magic

towards Hale, knocking him into the wall. His head hit a sconce and he sagged down with a horrible moan. He was definitely conscious, but his eyes were unfocused. The candle of the sconce fell with him, lighting the edge of his cloak on fire.

Avelynne shrieked his name and ran to him. There was so much blood on the back of his head and his pained groans were growing alarmingly weak.

Avelynne pulled off her cloak and extinguished the flames with it, but not until the fire had managed to burn through parts of Hale's trousers and her own tunic. Not that she cared about her clothing or any burns to herself, her worries right now were for Hale's possibly fatal injuries and Sander still fighting a mad murderer. She held the cloak against Hale's gushing head. "We must keep this tight against the wound, to stop the bleeding."

"I can—" Hale drew in a ragged breath. "I can do that. T-take the dagger and help Eleksander. Stab—" Another quivering, sharp intake of air. "Stab Rete. Pin him that bag of bones in place." He held the cloak still and blinked sluggishly at her.

Avelynne's gaze went to the dagger and then to the two combatants on the floor. They weren't stationary long enough for her to hit Rete with magic, how could she possibly manage it with a weapon that she was not skilled with?

You aren't half the fighter or magic wielder that Sander is. If he can't best Rete, neither can you.

"Avelynne," Hale mumbled. "Help him."

Her pulse picked up further, her heart battering against her ribcage like an animal desperate to get out. Her fingers tingled and her mind raced. Could she do this? The realisation hit her like a bucket of cold water over the head. She had to. Sander needed her. He could die. She'd have to be able to do this.

The dagger was right there. It was made in the typical Woodlander style, an incredibly sharp blade with an unadorned, rounded hilt. Avelynne picked it up.

Her heartbeat's speed made the blood rush in her ears, sounding like the rhythm of a drum. She walked to the beat of it, hypnotized, keeping her eyes on the figures on the floor. There had to be a way in, a moment where the tangle of limbs was still enough for her to be certain of who she was stabbing.

When she found that, she had a decision to make. If she was to stab Rete, would she do so to kill, to distract, or to incapacitate? The crippling self-doubt crept in and she recalled the silver beast attacking her and Myllie the day they packed to leave the Peaks. She remembered that, and all other times, she had been unable to pick the correct course of action. Remembered her parents telling her that she would always get things wrong.

Sander rolled them again, getting himself on top. He was about to punch Rete in the face right as the wiry man kicked up and made impact with Sander's groin.

There was a shrill scream but Avelynne was busy watching Rete's leg. After it had kneed Sander, it had fallen to the side. Avelynne made her decision. She sucked in a breath, held it, and then struck with all of her might. The dagger buried itself into his thigh with surprising ease. Or perhaps it had been the desperation in her stab that made the blade sink into his flesh as if it was softer than a plum.

She yanked the dagger back out, making droplets of blood hit her cheek.

Rete wailed and began cursing, his words making no sense. Sander had recuperated enough to aim a blow now, but Rete managed to send a push of magic at him, knocking him over. How did Rete still have that in him? He must be killing himself with all this manic energy. He was able to get away from Sander for a moment and lunged at Avelynne, staring at the dagger.

She froze and time appeared to do the same, or at least slow so that every action became a clear image, like a row of paintings depicting a battle.

Rete got nearer with every frantic beat of her heart. His face was so close to her now, she could see his eyes growing even wider than before and spittle dripping from his lower lip as he bared his teeth. Something in her shouted that she should stab. Or run. But she did neither, the idea of stabbing him in the face or neck seemed abhorrent to her. She couldn't!

Then there was a hand on her own, gripping the dagger and pushing it forward. It met with the pouncing Rete and thrust into his throat with a squelching and tearing sound that Avelynne would never forget. This time, the thrust wasn't smooth and easy. The dagger met with layers of resistance—veins, tendons, bone—and greater force was required.

Rete stared at her throughout all of it, his eyes now bulging and his mouth gaping wide open.

She wasn't breathing. Her breaths had halted, like everything else in her body, in unyielding horror.

Then, the hand that had pushed hers to thrust the

dagger, let go. Avelynne retracted her hand too, as if the dagger would burn her otherwise.

Sander caught Rete's falling body and laid him down on the ground. Far enough away that he couldn't reach them. Rete was making gurgling, desperate noises. Blood was surfacing from around the blade now.

"Don't pull the dagger out," Avelynne heard herself whisper. "The blood will spurt. I cannot stand more blood."

Sander gaped at her, as much in shock as she was. Avelynne turned to see who had helped her thrust the dagger, but deep down she knew. She recognised the feel of that hand. Soft, strong, and a little cold.

Sabina was behind her. Her face was even paler than usual, an unnatural, chalky white. Her lips quivered but she didn't speak. Instead, she was staring at her hand. It was lily-white and pristine. It trembled as much as her lips did, but it was spotlessly clean.

Unlike Avelynne's sooty and blooded hands and clothes. Unlike the floor, where from one direction soot and a trickle of blood came from Hale, while in the other direction blood rushed from Rete's leg and dribbled from where the dagger was still shafted into his neck.

Rivulets of scarlet chasing Avelynne from two directions, barricading her and Sabina in the middle of the room.

The sound of pounding footfalls rang out. Someone was coming. A moment to breathe, then the room filled with guards. "What happened here?" one of them barked.

They had Santorine with them. Kall was walking next to her, growling at the guards who had taken his prey. Santorine must have headed for the gate and been stopped by the guards there. Or herded to the guards by Kall and Sabina.

And then… Sabina had come back to help them. Help *her*.

Avelynne heard a rattle from Rete's lips and then his noises ceased. So did his breathing. One of the guards rushed over to him and quickly stated, "He's dead."

Sabina whimpered achingly before collapsing to her knees. Avelynne crouched down next to her and pulled her close.

"Good," Hale grunted from behind them. He was sitting up now, still holding Avelynne's blood-soaked cloak to the back of his head. His tanned skin was almost as pallid as Sabina's.

Sander grabbed the sleeve of the guard next to him. "My friend is seriously injured. Please help him!"

Two of the guards checked on Hale. One of them, a Northerner by the look of her, said, "You should all see a physician. Can you stand, or should we call him here?"

"I can stand," Hale said through gritted teeth.

"Call the physician to come here," the other three students said as one.

The guard nodded to them and left.

Avelynne got more comfortable on the floor, still cradling the quivering Sabina. Sander stood a few steps away, tears trickling down his cheeks. She wasn't sure if they were from pain, shock, or fear.

Kall stalked by him, giving him a gentle nudge before striding over to Sabina and laying down with his big head on his mistress' leg.

Distractedly, she stroked his fur with one hand and

grabbed onto Avelynne with the other. Avelynne held her as tight as she could, squeezing the shaking young woman to her as if that could make it better.

Hale dragged himself over. He smelled of blood and smoke. Clumsily, he put his forehead against Sabina's hair and croaked, "Well done. You protected your family. I wish it could've been me, but I'm grateful that you were there to do what had to be done."

Sander wiped his cheeks and came over. He was limping a little and his eye was swelling up, otherwise he looked unharmed. He crumpled into a seating position next to Avelynne. He brushed Hale's arm with a tentative hand and then leant in to kiss Sabina's hair.

"I always knew we would have to do dangerous things," Avelynne heard herself say. "Fight for our lives. Do battle on sea and land. I never thought it would be like this, though. Not here. N-not him. Not like that."

She remembered how it felt when a dagger was forced into a body. "Not like that," she repeated in a whisper.

They sat there, the four of them, huddled together in unnatural stillness. Watched by the guards and waiting for the physician. Waiting to see what would happen next.

Chapter Thirty-Six

SCARS

Hale and the physician were alone in a corner of a small room. Hale was so tired he didn't even have the energy to yawn. He ran a finger over an old scar on his hand. A moment ago, the physician, a jovial old Woodlander, had made a joke about him adding a head scar to his collection. Hale hadn't laughed. Social niceties could go take a leap off a cliff.

"Anyway, you'll have the pain and stitches for a while, lad," the physician said cheerfully. "But as your sight, hearing, and clarity of thought are intact, I don't think it's more serious than a few weeks of discomfort. Oh, and you might feel a bit weak from blood loss, so scoff down plenty of red meat and iron-filled vegetables until that replenishes. Otherwise..." He moved Hale's head a little to take another look. "While the soot from the garment held against the wound was a beast to get out, at least the scorching fabric meant that there shouldn't be any infection."

Hale tried to sound interested. "Really?"

"Mm. We're not sure why, but fire-hot heat on an open wound diminishes the risks of fever and other follow-up symptoms… like death. Ha!" He let go of Hale's head. "And as I said earlier, you'll now have another scar to impress your lovers," the physician finished, chuckling again.

Hale clenched his jaw. The idea of trying to impress anyone with scars and wounds seemed silly now. Childish, even. The throbbing ache at the back of his head reminded him of death, blood, and not being able to protect those he cared about. It wasn't something you used to impress people.

"Can I go now?" Hale asked.

"You may. Come see me or my colleagues if you feel peculiar or lightheaded. Do you need something for your pain?"

Hale reached back to feel the sewn-up hole he owed to that sodding wall sconce. "No."

"Then off you go. Your friends are waiting for you outside. The Lakelander needed stitches on his eyebrow and he'll have loads of interesting bruises all over. The Peakdweller had some slight burns on her side but that should heal nicely. Other than that, they're all fine. Physically, at least."

"Thanks," Hale grumbled and left.

When he joined the others, he gave them a damage report and promised he'd be fine.

"Splendid," Tutor Myle said, licking his lips nervously.

Hale had no idea when their least useful tutor had shown up. He supposed it made sense, though. With Rete dead, Santorine being questioned by the guards, and Elya Hathleen still on the coast with the first wave, Myle and

Rogan were the only tutors left. Great. Myle was a mediocre tutor and about as supportive as a wall made of mashed beets, while Rogan was a great fighter but an equally great arsehole.

Myle's pristine hands toyed with the sleeve of his surcoat. "Attention, second wave. The king ordered me to escort you to a lesson room where you'll be safe until he can speak with you. The court received the report from the guards, but his Highness will still want to check up on you."

Eleksander groaned and Avelynne pursed her lips. Hale assumed Sabina was trying as hard as he was not to curse and scream.

Myle scanned their surroundings for anyone over-hearing before adding, "King Lothiam can be abrupt and, well, some of the complaints Rete and Santorine had against him might have... merit. Don't tell anyone I said that, or I might end up dead! Just don't put your full trust in the king. Take his words with a modicum of scepticism."

"Oh, don't worry. We will," Eleksander muttered before exchanging glances with Hale.

Myle relaxed. "Good. Then follow me."

Hale took the lead, the others mere steps behind him and on both sides. It would probably be a while before they stopped moving as a single unit, trying to protect each other.

As they walked, Avelynne asked Sabina, "What happened when you and Kall left us to chase after Santorine?"

"Not much," Sabina said, her voice hollow. "She ran for the gates. I thought she was going to be sly and tell the guards that I and Kall were attacking her without provocation, but she was so panicked that she tried to fight her way through and run out. She didn't even answer the guards when they greeted her and asked what she was doing."

"Which they found suspicious?" Eleksander asked.

"I suppose so," Sabina droned. "They stopped her and when she began ranting about death and going into hiding, they grabbed her. When her sleeve was bunched up under their grip, I saw a bit of a silver tattoo. I told Kall to stay and watch her. Then I ran back to you. To help."

Cold shame bloomed in Hale's chest and sent icy roots down to his stomach. How could he have failed them all so? How could he have let Eleksander and Avelynne have to do all the fighting? And Sabina do all the killing.

Somehow, he knew that taking a life would weigh less on him than it did on any of the others. It should have been him! He shouldn't have been immobilised right away, like one of those shitting silver beasts they'd fought in the courtyard.

Myle opened a door for them and they stepped into the quiet room. The tutor hesitated before closing them in. "I... wanted to say that you've all been braver than I could ever be. You'll make good mapmakers. No matter what Rogan says."

He closed the door without waiting for a reply.

The soft click of it shutting grated on Hale's nerves. He wanted crashes and bangs. He wanted to shout. He wanted to throw things, break things.

He stopped to consider his teammates. They were in shock and finally calming down after all that fear and adrenaline. They needed quiet and peace, didn't they? They were his family and he loved them, now more than ever. Hale closed his hands into tight fists and forced himself to slow his breaths. He could release his frustration later, when it wouldn't startle them.

He shoved his fists into his trouser pockets and began pacing.

Chapter Thirty-Seven

GUILT AND CONSEQUENCES

Avelynne couldn't believe what had happened. No matter how many times she played the events over in her mind, they were as unlikely to her as growing a second head.

They sat in front of the fireplace in the quiet lesson room, watching the small fire struggle to heat the room. Or rather, she and Sander sat. Hale was pacing along the room and Sabina was bent over Kall, burying her face in his fur.

"How long have we been in here? Feels like a lifetime," Hale snapped.

"Mm. I suppose they have to clear up a lot and, well, they must decide what to do with us," Avelynne said, folding and unfolding the sleeve of her tunic.

"I wish they'd have given us something to eat," Hale said, banging his fist against his thigh. "Or a task to perform. Leaving us in a bare room with nothing but our thoughts is cruel!"

"Maybe it's what we deserve," Sabina whispered.

Avelynne went to her. She sat down and placed an arm

around her crouching friend. "Of course not. What happened… couldn't be helped, Sabina. It was self-defence."

"I know. That's what I've been telling myself. Yet, I keep seeing his face as I pushed the knife in! And wondering if he," her voice broke and she had to clear her throat, "if he had a family. Parents. Siblings. Friends who loved and needed him. It wasn't only that I ended his life, I might have torn theirs apart too."

Avelynne hesitated. What did you say to that? She squeezed Sabina close as she scrambled for a reply. "I know you're filled with guilt and that guilt doesn't follow logic. You know you had to kill him, or he would've killed me and possibly everyone else in that room."

"Yes," Sabina said softly.

"Guilt doesn't care about that sort of thing, though, does it?"

"No," Sabina whispered, barely audible.

Avelynne still searched for the right words but had to settle for ones that were at least true. "It's certainly not comparable in any way, but when I carried my secret, I knew that the guilt would alleviate if I told someone. Except, the guiltiness made me unable to do that. Guilt is like a trap that closes tighter if you struggle. You have to accept it. Look it right in the eye and *then* you can logic yourself out of it."

Sabina kept her gaze down on Kall, stroking one of his ears. "Do you think that's what it'll take? Me confronting what I did and its consequences?"

Avelynne brushed white strands away from Sabina's forehead. She remembered killing that silver beast who had tried to eat of her grandmother's body. She had felt no remorse when she smashed it. No guilt. What did that mean? Was she a bad person for that? When did you feel guilty? Did that depend on who you were or the situation you were in?

Avelynne swallowed. "I'm not sure. I… don't know if I'm the person to speak to about this. Perhaps you need someone with more experience?"

Sabina wrapped her cloak tighter. "When I go home for Solstice, I'll speak to my parents."

"That could work. However, my sweetest snowdrop," Avelynne said, lifting Sabina's chin so they locked eyes. "If they don't understand or they say something that upsets you… please find someone else to speak to. Perhaps some sort of village elder or a physician? You need help, not someone expecting you to be strong and capable all the time."

Sabina gave a faint smile. "Sounds like you've met my parents."

The rush of affection almost made Avelynne dizzy. She wanted to take away Sabina's every worry, smooth down every jagged edge her heart might snag on.

She cupped Sabina's cheek. "No, but I've met you. We are all products of our environment and soon we return home to the people who shaped us. When we do return there, though, we'll be a different than when we set off. These six months, and especially the events tonight, they changed us."

"I'll say. I feel five years older," Sander mumbled.

Outside, storm winds assaulted the window, taking Avelynne's attention. Was that hoarfrost lining the edges of the windowpane? It looked like menacing lace was forming, threatening to cover the window and increase Avelynne's sense of being closed in.

Hale walked over to it, clearly having other concerns. "Is this thing properly shut? I swear I can feel those shitty, icy winds like they're in the room!"

No one told him to mind his language. His emotions needed to escape somehow, and cursing was a safe option.

"I don't know. Can you feel a draft?" Sander asked, joining him.

Hale shook his head but neither of them left the window. They stood there, shoulder to shoulder, both looking like they were searching for answers in the ink-black night outside.

Kall was glaring at the window too. Sabina brushed a hand over him, making him calm. "It's all right, my love. It's only a storm."

She looked back up to Avelynne. "Isn't it peculiar that Kall didn't react to Rete? He always senses evil."

"Oh." Avelynne hoped her pity didn't show on her face. "Have you considered that Kall only reacts to more clear threats, like someone actually assaulting you? Or perhaps... merely mirrors your emotions?"

Sabina's brows knitted, and her gaze flitted away.

"Or," Avelynne hastened to add. "Perhaps Kall only picks up on evil that has truly malicious intent? Both Santorine and Rete believed they were acting in everyone's best interests. That they were saving Cavarra and protecting us from King Lothiam."

Sabina's eyebrows relaxed back, showing some sense of mollification in the proud young woman.

"Do you think we need protecting from the king?" Eleksander asked.

"Yes," Hale muttered. He was leaning against the window, his forceful frame still tensed in frustration, muscles moving in his arms and shoulders. Avelynne watched his reflection in the glass. The rage was intensifying his black eyes and the scowl on his scarred face. For a moment, the raw power of him took her breath away.

What a shameful time to be attracted to someone, Avelynne thought, clamping her thighs together tightly.

"I don't know who was worse," Sander groused as he left the window. "Rete with his murdering madness or the king wanting to make us conquerors. Can you believe he actually thought he could make us violent, obedient tools for his planned colonisation and slaughter?"

"If Rete was telling the truth about that," Avelynne interjected.

"I bet he was," Sabina said quietly. "In hindsight, it tracks with the king's behaviour."

The wind howled as a reply.

"I'm exhausted. I want a square meal and some sleep," Sander said, rubbing his face. Despite his size, he seemed so small right now. Avelynne's heart ached for him, almost as much as it ached for herself and Hale, trapped in their own traumas. Not quite as much as it throbbed whenever she saw Sabina's broken expression, though. All her calm strength was now frayed by fear and pain. Avelynne keened inwardly. She would do anything to make Sabina heal but could think of nothing. Nothing at all.

Hale turned from the window. "I... wasn't going to say anything but," he stared at the wall behind them, his muscles still moving as if in flight or fight mode, "You've taught me that I need to explain what I'm thinking and feeling so I'll just say it: I might've failed you tonight but from now on, I'll protect you all. With my life if necessary."

"Silly," Sander said with a smile. "That's what you did. You took the worst damage of all of us while protecting us."

"Aye, and between you vowing to safeguard us all in the future and Avelynne promising to make her secret-keeping up to us, I and Eleksander should be set for life," Sabina said, the mirth in her words not mirrored in her tone or expression.

Hale didn't completely relax, but some of the tension in his frame seeped out. "You were the one who protected us, Sabina. As far as I'm concurred, that means we should honour you for the rest of your days. I know I will."

Sander sat next to Sabina and clasped her shoulder. "Hey! Take the opportunity to ask for half of his food. You know he always grabs the best cuts of meat!"

They chuckled, some with more conviction that others, then they all fell quiet once more. The only sounds being the crackle of the fireplace, the wailing winds, and the eerie creaking of the stone building against the storm.

Time passed, Avelynne couldn't tell how much, until the door was thrust open. The doorframe was filled by Tutor Rogan. "Ah, there you are. Why did you stick them in here, Myle?"

Myle followed him in. "I thought they needed some-where quiet to collect their thoughts."

"Don't be daft. What they need after something like that is large amounts of booze. Perhaps with some meat to replenish their energy."

As if answering that comment, Avelynne's stomach gurgled. She hoped no one had heard it.

"I didn't think that appropriate," Myle murmured. "Considering King Lothiam will be here any moment."

Hale straightened up. "Speaking of, when is that shit bucket finally coming?"

Myle's fine features fell. "Do not speak like that of your sovereign. Show some deference. Or at least be discreet." The last words were said in a whispered hiss.

As if knowing he was being spoken of, there were the unmistakable sounds of a monarch with far too large an entourage clomping down the corridor. When they all entered the room, the fire in the sconces on the walls flickered with the draft of their haste.

"Great. Crowd the place," Hale said. "Who needs air left in the room?"

The king guffawed as if Hale had been joking. They all bowed, only Myle being as enthusiastic as they were all meant to be.

"I don't have much time," King Lothiam said in the way of greeting. "I am entertaining the Baron and Baroness of the North up at the castle. Nevertheless, I wanted to stop by. Not bad work, younglings! I have long suspected that this academy held corrupt forces. Haven't I?" He turned to a nearby advisor.

"Yes, your Majesty," the pock-marked courtier replied. "You said it was strange that you never got updates on how your decrees were being incorporated. Nor got invitations to come watch the lessons."

"Exactly," the king boomed. "I only ever got invited to attend drawing and arithmetic lessons and who would want to watch children doodle mountains or calculate tedious distances?"

The royal following and Rogan laughed. Myle only squirmed in silence.

"Now, however, you shall be doing more fighting than counting and drawing," The king said. "Those subjects will probably be the ones you do most since Myle, Rogan, and what's that frizzy-haired, scholarly spinster of a tutor called…"

"I suppose you mean Elya Hathleen?" Myle suggested.

The king pointed to him. "Yes, her! They will pick up your lessons for these last weeks before you go home for the Solstice." He smirked at the second wave. "Although, I'm sure they can also help you a little with magic, orientation, swimming, and whatever the subjects those traitors taught. How hard can it be?"

Rogan looked uncomfortable but said nothing.

"We will see what we can do. When Tutor Hathleen returns from the coast, of course," Myle said. "The craftsmen who built the ship, and have been training the sailors, are still tutoring the first wave at an intensified pace. As you ordered."

King Lothiam eyed the squirming Myle for a long time. Avelynne couldn't tell what that look on the king's broad face was, but it hinted at some deeper meaning. There was a flash of cunning which she'd never seen on his face before. Was it in regard to the first wave having their education intensified? Or Myle apparently buying time until Tutor Hathleen returned?

There it was, the throbbing at Avelynne's temples that signalled one of her headaches coming. No matter how many questions they got answered, new ones constantly popped up.

The king returned his focus to the second wave. "Anyway, now you know what the future holds. Your remaining tutors will teach you, while the surviving traitor rots in a dungeon and the dead one gets left to rot in one of my fields. He is sure to make good manure." He paused to spit on the floor. "He—no one speak his name—was meant to teach you leadership skills in your second year. I will move that training forward to when you return from the Solstice holiday and put Tutor Rogan in charge of it."

Then he slapped Rogan's back. "Teach them to be fierce and to take what they want. Or rather what I want. No more treating them like gentle flowers or future diplomats. Make our pliable younglings predators who can take an order."

Rogan bowed, his huge back popping with the unusual movement.

King Lothiam turned back to the students. "Oh, and I am looking into moving your sail date forward. With traitors in our midst and this rot of discontent spreading, I desire swift action. Your education may be cut by half a year or even a full year. That will get you out on those waves and on your way to my new lands faster."

So that's why the first wave's tutoring was sped up, Avelynne realised.

The king finished with, "I'm certain you shall get by with what skills you have managed to pick up by then." After a wave of one of his jewel-ringed hands, he marched out with his entourage at his heels.

Myle followed, trying to get the king's attention. "Your

Majesty, I would never question your wisdom… but if they sail so soon, they shan't have been tested! They will only have received half of the instructions needed to steer a ship, make maps, survive in all possible environments, and so on."

There was no reply and they heard Myle give up the line of questioning.

Rogan gave them a wolfish grin. "There you have it. I'm in charge. We shall see if I can make you worthy of the honour you've been given and program you with the colonising spirit. If I manage it, it'll be easy to convince King Lothiam that I should come with you on your trips. If I don't, well, I'll simply have to go in your stead."

Hale was about to speak, but Avelynne quieted him with a stare. They had been through enough strife tonight without picking a fight.

"Now," Rogan said. "Stop moping and head to the Great Hall. I'll make the servants put out meat and enough ale for you to drown yourselves in."

Then he left the room as well, chortling to himself.

The four students of the second wave lingered, motion-less and forlorn.

"Am I the only one who feels…" Sabina trailed off.

"That there are worse monsters on Cavarra than the silver beasts?" Sander suggested through clenched teeth.

"That too. I was going to say that 'we can only trust each other from now on?', however," Sabina grumbled with a face like thunder.

Avelynne thought about Myle bending to the king. Rogan being… well, Rogan. And Hathleen being far away and an unknown quantity when she was here.

"For now, I think so, yes," she whispered.

"We can clearly only trust each other to fight against having to journey out before we know a sail from our own arse," Hale said, his jaw set in defiance against the idea of departing before their training was finished.

Avelynne nodded. "Mm, and *we* will have to ensure our mission doesn't escalate to something horrible whenever we do sail."

Hale's jaw was still tight like a sprung bear trap, the muscles spasming with the strain. He parted his lips enough to ask, "Something horrible? As in giving the king what he wants?"

She gave him another nod. "As in violating the rights of others. Or behaving in ways that go against our moral codes in any other way. We cannot let Rogan, what were his words… 'program' us."

Sander stood. "Then we'll rise to that occasion and take whatever fight we must, come what may!" He scrubbed his face with his hands. "For now, let's go get something to eat, have a bath, and then get some sleep. It's been the longest night of my life."

None of them would argue with that.

Chapter Thirty-Eight

END OF TERM

The bitter wind blowing through the courtyard made Hale shiver, he could only hope no one had noticed the cold besting him. The temperature had dropped fast now that they were days away from the Midwinter Solstice. Sure, the morning frost covering the tree branches and lining the buildings had been gorgeous when he convinced the others to do laps around the courtyard with him. And, he admitted to himself, the cold making the colour high on Avelynne's cheeks was something to behold. However, all that prettiness couldn't be worth this goose bumping and shivering that his body was doing without his permission. He could fight against the heat and humidity of the rainforests in the Woodlands but this... How did the Northerners and Peakdwellers put up with temperatures much worse than this? It was ridiculous!

The clang of colliding steel brought him back to the swordplay happening out in the middle of the courtyard. Dressed in their usual student attire, plus goatskin gloves and fur-lined cloaks with hoods up, they were sparring today.

Rogan had picked Avelynne to go first. Pride thrummed in Hale as he saw her almost hold her own. The lessons he'd given her since the fight with Rete—after which she decided that she needed a more ruthless sparring partner than Eleksander—must've helped. Despite that they had needed to be held in Ghar's servant chamber to keep away from Rogan's ever-vigilant eyes. Rogan found ways to stop them from doing pretty much anything they wanted since he became their new head tutor.

Hale heard the rustling noise of Sabina and Eleksander whispering behind him. He hadn't cared to join them as the conversation had been about swords from their respective counties. Who cared about quality of blades or what hilts were decorated with? What even was an 'emerald'? What mattered was that your weapon was sharp enough to cleave a poisonous snake in half with one blow. The rest was up to the wielder.

Now, however, the topic must've shifted as he picked up the words, "Strange to have lessons without Rete and Santorine."

Eleksander sniffled, probably suffering from the cold as much as Hale. "Yes. Do you know what's even stranger? My sister told me that the Centre officials have told the nation that Rete and Santorine were acting *alone.*"

"What?" Sabina hissed. "No mention of the Twelve?"

"No. They claim that Rete and Santorine did what they did to overthrow the king. Furthermore, they're denying any complaints about King Lothiam. They say that our former tutors had nothing against the king, they only wanted the throne for the power and the coin."

"I suppose that makes sense," Sabina said. "They don't want more people questioning the sovereign. Or gathering behind the Twelve."

In front of them, Rogan disarmed Avelynne. As she gasped and stepped backwards, Kall growled from where he lay on the ground.

Hale gave Sabina a querying look.

"Kall's been very protective of us all ever since the incident," she said with a shrug. "Besides, he has a soft spot for Avelynne. She spoils him with food and cuddles."

"Lucky cat," Hale said with a snort.

"You can say that again," Sabina replied with a half-smile.

Subdued as she still was, it was a relief to see her getting on with her life. Even though Avelynne said Sabina struggled to sleep at night and when she did sleep, she awoke screaming. There were wounds in her mind that hadn't healed. Even Hale could see that. He wished he could help.

Rogan returned Avelynne's sword with a taunting grin, then he attacked whip-fast again without warning, aiming for her face. Luckily, she parried and bounced back.

Hale snarled. "That *shitting silver beast shagger*, he could've taken her eye out."

"Unfair as always," Eleksander hissed, his broad chest heaving with angry huffing. "I cannot believe he's allowed to tutor us."

It was nice to see that some things didn't change. Their meek Lakelander was still as furious about injustices as always. It made Hale want to... what? Hug him? Clap him on the back? He decided not to analyse it or act on it.

"I can't either," Sabina said low. "Thankfully, we won't be around him forever. I doubt the king will send Rogan with us to sea. He cannot be trusted or controlled."

"It's bizarre. Another year and a half. Or less if King Lothiam expediates our plans," Eleksander said. "Then we leave this place, not only the Hall of Explorers but *all of Cavarra.*"

"Mm, with the king's orders in tow. Are we still assuming he actually wants us to break the academy's motto? That he expects us to conquer and enslave?" Sabina said.

Eleksander scowled and stood tall. "All I know is that I refuse to go against my morals. If we are ordered to do anything but peacefully explore, I will disobey."

"We all will," Hale growled, certain he could speak for them all.

Sabina hummed her agreement. "If he does give us that order... Rete and Santorine were right. The Twelve are *still* right, I suppose. Do you think they're out there still?"

"Yes," Eleksander replied. "I don't see why they would've disbanded simply because the king knows about them now. I'm sure he was aware of them and their cause before."

Hale crossed his arms over his chest. "Probably."

"My question is if we'll hear from them again?" Eleksander said.

Sabina bent to pet Kall who was still growling at Rogan every time he launched an assault. "Aye, I bet they'll be in touch before we set sail. We'll have to keep an eye out for people with silver tattoos and odd behaviour." She sighed.

"There's so much going on behind the curtains that we normal Cavarrians don't know about."

"We're not normal Cavarrians anymore," Hale said.

There was nothing more to be said. They watched Avelynne finally manage to get a few good attacks in. Somehow it felt like they should be more cheered by that. Like they should be able to shrug off all this weight on their shoulders.

Hale lifted his chin, he would at least pretend for Avelynne's sake. He clapped and shouted, "You show him, Peakdweller. Aim high!"

Hopefully his tone sounded as carefree as he wanted it to.

The last lesson of the day was on the subject of magic and was currently nearing its end. It was being taught by Myle, who made them read from dusty old tomes instead of practical practise. Hale liked reading, and he really liked being out of the cursed cold, but he wished that his last lesson for the day had given him less time to think. Now, he was overthinking his little plan and that drove him to distraction.

Finally, Myle let them go and Hale caught Avelynne before she had time to follow the others to the Great Hall for supper.

Time for the finale of the plan. Now or never.

"Wait. I have something for you."

She turned fast, wafting the sweet scent of her hair towards him. "Really? What?"

He fished in his pocket and brought up the gift in his

closed fist. When he opened it and noticed the delicate silver chain and dainty quill shimmering against his scarred and calloused hand, he was suddenly embarrassed by how his hand looked. What the shitting silver beasts was that about? His hands showed that he was a warrior and a survivor. They were practical. Why did he wish them to be soft and smooth like Eleksander's, just to be a velvety cushion for a lass' necklace? Internally, he snarled at himself.

Out loud he said, "I, um, I went back to the tutors' room and managed to find both your chain and the quill."

She gasped but he didn't stop. "I know your grandmother gave it to you and how much it means to you. I even mended the clasp. It's not pretty work, but it'll hold until you can get it to a silversmith back in the Peaks."

The big smile, which gave him a highly anticipated look at her dimples, made his heart soar.

"Thank you," she breathed out, taking the necklace. Then she gave him a one-armed hug and said, "That's so extraordinarily sweet of you! You know, it's funny. Sander told me this morning that he'd gone back to look for it but not found it. He was so upset, worrying it might've been buried with Rete. I truly do have the kindest friends."

Hale's heart dipped in its soaring.

Eleksander.

Friends.

This wasn't how he'd seen this playing out in his mind. He knew he had no right to expect her to show signs of romance, but he had still hoped.

Avelynne put the necklace on, not even needing his help with the clasp. Something she always had in his daydreams about this moment.

She smiled again and then squeezed his shoulder. "Come, let's go get some food in that ever-starving stomach of yours. Sander and Sabina will be thrilled to hear you recovered the necklace."

She walked towards the Great Hall and he followed, aware that he would always want to follow her. No matter if he did so as a suitor or a friend. No matter what his pride or jealousy had to say about it.

Chapter Thirty-Nine

EQUILIBRIUM AND ARCHERY

Avelynne smiled at the memory of their delicious supper. The slices of spuds and beets had been richly buttered and salted, the creek salmon smoked to perfection, and the dessert pots of candied ginger had offered a tongue-tingling mix of sweet and spice. While the cooks had outdone themselves with their limited supplies, the portions had been reduced. Probably due to provisions dwindling. Another thing to fret about.

She stored it away with the other worries, like Hale's silence tonight. He had been quiet as he ate every morsel he could get his hands on. She had wondered if something was wrong, but as he perked up as he ate, hopefully his behaviour was down to hunger. Still, she'd keep an eye on him.

As they left the Great Hall, Sander suggested she join him for some training in the courtyard. Not sparring—that was kept for Hale or Sabina these days—all other training however, worked best with Sander and his endless patience and calm.

"Why not," Avelynne said. She turned to Sabina and Hale. "Care to join us?"

Hale claimed he was too full while Sabina said, "No, I need to go for a run. I swear the bones in my legs are welded together like metal hinges. Besides, Kall needs to expend his energy. This colder weather has him excited like a kitten."

"I shall see you later, then" Avelynne said.

When Sabina and Hale had left, Sander smiled at her. "Same procedure as always? See you in the courtyard when we've digested?"

"Absolutely."

"Make sure to wear more layers, though. The night is unforgivingly cold."

She gave him a look. "It's not *that* bad. That's your thin Lakelander blood speaking."

His curved eyebrows rose. "Ave."

"Yes, yes. Obviously, I'm going to wear enough clothes. See you soon, mother hen."

He ambled off and her smile faltered and fell. No matter how good her friendships and her food were, there was still that shadow lingering. A sense of that ominous events took place around her, deaths and schemes, and that she didn't know for how long they'd be safe. She shook it off best she could. They had made it through this far. *She* had made it through this far, which was more than she thought herself capable before coming here.

Now, she only had to focus on digesting that food and then meeting Sander back here. Taking it one day at a time, as she had ever since that night in the tutors' room.

Their training session had started with equilibrating again. The practice Avelynne had put in was showing, her body moved into the positions with unexpected ease. Her heartbeat kept calm and her breathing steady. For a few moments at a time, her mind peeled away all the things she need not concern herself with right now. When it had grown dark, they finished with the dreaded focus position. Avelynne barely wobbled.

Sander did wobble, but that was because he performed the positions while occasionally helping Avelynne adjust her arms or twist without moving her hips. The strain of keeping control of his own muscles while coaxing hers into place too, clearly took serious effort. The lantern light made a bead of sweat glisten against his dark skin. Like a shooting star across the night sky, it trickled down his forehead and into his curved eyebrow. It was mesmerising. Avelynne focused on it to take her mind off what would come after this. Archery. She must face that cursed target and its taunting bullseye again.

Still. This time it would be only her and Sander here. He would never judge her or snigger at her. The dim lantern light would also give her an excuse if she missed.

So, it won't be that bad this time. It can't be. Can it?

"Great. That's enough," Sander said. "Take one last centring breath and then come out of the position."

She acquiesced, stretching and enjoying the limbering of her body.

Sander turned away to wipe his brow with his usual

refinement. How could someone make a gesture like that look graceful?

"Well done, Ave. Now, are we ready for some archery?"

"I…" She clenched her fists. "I think so."

"You should know so."

She moaned. "You *cannot* expect me to be excited about it. Or to believe that it'll go well."

"I do expect that. Your fears and low self-esteem lie to you when they say it won't go well."

"Mm-hm," she said, sounding as unconvinced as she was.

"No, really. You thought you couldn't do the 'focus' position. Now you're splendid at it. You thought you couldn't keep up with the rest of us in lessons. Now you have half a year that proves otherwise."

She looked down. "I suppose."

"Ave, that night in the tutor's room with Rete… It was a confusing and shocking situation and you mastered it. With composure and purpose, you incapacitated an enemy superior to you in skill, experience, and full of madness-driven power."

She stopped between two breaths. That was true, wasn't it? She hadn't thought of it that way, only focusing on that she hadn't been the one to end it all, that she had needed Sabina to help her thrust the knife in the final time. But maybe that wasn't what was important here. Nor was it the point that Sander was making, that she could achieve more than she thought. The significant point, Avelynne realised, was that she'd finally taken action when danger confronted her. She had dared trust in her decision and followed through. Avelynne Ironhold had faced her fears and acted in the correct way. She hadn't messed it up!

Unaware of Avelynne's thoughts, he continued. "You risked your life to stand up for what was right that evening. You protected those you love, and who love you. If you can do that, you can certainly shoot an arrow into the centre of a bunch of rings, trust me."

She rolled her shoulders. "Only one way to find out."

He fetched a quiver and a bow. When he handed it to her, she saw that the bow was the same one she'd failed with that day with Tutor Rogan. It was warm where Sander had held it and she clung to that, the warmth of him equating safety.

Her precious friend pointed to the target board while wearing that sweet, lopsided smile of his. She was so grateful that he was here with her, helping her. She knew on a cold night like this, he'd prefer studying in his bed, cosied up with a cup of leaf tea.

No, if he could choose what to do tonight, he'd want to be with Hale. Possibly still cosying up in bed, probably doing something quite different from studying, though.

Although, she could be misreading that.

Either way, she wouldn't waste anymore of his time. She took the sideways stance, feet shoulder length apart and pointed correctly. She nocked an arrow. Then drew the bowstring to the anchor point by her face. She breathed as she had during the equilibrating, deeply and through her nose, noting the cold air carrying the scent of the lantern flames and the nearby stable. Her heart slowed and her arm tensed, holding the bowstring taut.

"See the arrow hit the target in your mind," Sander said quietly.

She aimed, and, on an exhale, released the string. The arrow made that clean, swift sound as it shot through the air and landed with a pleasing thump in the board.

Not the bullseye. Two rings out.

She knew she could shoot that well, she'd done so while practising alone back at Ironhold castle. However, she *should* be able to do better at this point. The old Avelynne would've given up, accepted that it was all she could do and slunk away with her tail between her legs. Now, she knew herself better.

She squared her shoulders. "I'm going to try again. This time I'll do better. I won't let you down."

"Ave, please stop that."

"What?"

"Stop doing this for me. Do it for you."

She lowered her bow and stared wordlessly at him.

"I mean it, Ave. Do it to prove to yourself that you can. To quiet that voice inside you that always doubts you. I already believe in you and think you're incredible, you have nothing to prove to me. This is about you."

He stood behind her and grabbed her shoulders and, exactly like when they were equilibrating, he coaxed her body into the right stance. He put his big, gentle hand over hers and drew the bowstring to the side of her face. Then he said in her ear, "Now, *you* aim. You fire when you are ready. You do this. All by yourself and only for yourself."

With that, she heard his steps disappear behind her. Her hands faltered on the bow, loosening the string a little. He'd left? Then, who would be here? Who would watch her if she managed it? And console her if she failed? Who would be here for her to focus on?

She stared at the target for a while, making sense of things. She faintly heard the guards chatter in the distance and an owl hooting far away. The sounds slowly faded until all she heard was her own steady breathing and the comforting thud of her own pulse.

Then she hummed a little laugh. "Right. I guess it's just me then," she said.

She drew the string taut again, tensing her muscles to hold the grip. There was a flutter in the pit of her stomach and she couldn't tell if it was fear or excitement. She aimed, staring at that bullseye while convincing herself that the arrow was about to penetrate it perfectly, and then released the arrow.

It flew with impressive speed and clarity and landed... mostly in the bullseye! It wasn't perfect, but it was close. And it was the best shot she'd ever taken.

She squealed and looked around. Maybe the guards at the gate had seen it? No, they were too far away. Never mind, she only had to prove something to herself.

Right. Yes. That was it. She placed the bow against the sundial, breathing in the crisp evening air and smiling up at the twinkling stars. Yes, the only one who needed to know she'd achieved it was her.

Then, a very unladylike sentence formed in her mind and soon escaped her lips: "Sod that!"

Yes, she was enough. However, she still wanted to celebrate with someone!

She took off running in the direction Sander had gone. When she saw a tall, broad figure further down the corridor, she didn't even stop to make sure it was him. She shouted, "I did it. I hit the bullseye! Not square into it, but it was absolutely in that centre circle!"

He turned and gave a victory yell. "I knew it! I knew you could do it."

She ran to him and he picked her up and spun her around as she giggled.

"Those sea monsters better watch out, Countess Avelynne Ironhold has arrows for them all," he bellowed.

Still held in the air and his arms, she put her hands around her friend's solid neck and touched her forehead to his. "Yes! Well, as long as the monsters are stationary targets. Or as long as Rogan doesn't pop out of the waves to tell me I'm useless."

He chuckled. "One thing at a time. You'll have the rest of your education to deal with moving targets and Rogan."

"And maybe combine them! I might accidentally shoot Rogan in the leg when he's running over to scold the horses for being too tall or the leaves for being too green."

Sander put her down with another chuckle. "Perhaps. Either way. I'm proud of you."

She bit her lip. "You know what? I think for the first time in my life, I might be proud of me too."

Chapter Forty

MORE THAN FAMILY

Hale reached his arms up, trying to stretch the restlessness out, but stopped mid-stretch. What was the point?

Avelynne and Eleksander were still training out in the courtyard, probably doing that odd balancing stuff, while Sabina and Kall stalked the corridors.

Not in the mood for his usually beloved physical endeavours, Hale had returned to his room. Relaxing and reading hadn't worked, though. His stomach, trying to digest after his extreme comfort-eating, had distracted him. His book lay abandoned on the bed and his stomach was bloated.

He ran his hand over his head but stopped when he touched the stitches. They taunted him, reminded him of that night and his own uselessness. He huffed and. The cursed things would be removed in two days, right before they all went home for the Solstice.

Did he want to go home? His old friends would be there, waiting for him to tell his tales and to show off. Perhaps even a lass or two wanting a kiss from their chosen second waver. The surroundings would certainly be warmer and freer than here. Not to mention the lack of long lessons every shitting day. But there would be no Eleksander. No Sabina. No… Avelynne.

The door opened to reveal a panting Eleksander.

"She did it, Ave finally hit the bullseye!"

"Huh? Oh. Good."

"Yes, she's gone to tell Sabina and—" The Lakelander stopped halfway into the room. "What's wrong?"

Hale merely grunted.

Eleksander creased his brow theatrically. "Oh dear, that's vague and low on words even for you. Must be some sort of record."

When Hale didn't respond, Eleksander's expression grew serious.

"You're actually upset. I'm sorry, Hale. Is it due to… you know, the king, the Twelve, and our future mission?"

"For once, no."

Eleksander's frown deepened. "All right. Is it Rete's death and your guilt for not being the one to defeat him?"

"No, not that either. Well, not more than usual."

His brow smoothed. "Ah, I've got it. It's our fair Countess, isn't it?"

Hale's mood lifted as he spotted a kindred spirit and he moved to close the gap between them. "Ah, she is so very fair, isn't she? Curse her dimples and sweet laugh, she's cast a spell on us all."

"Oh, I'm not under her spell." Eleksander said as he took his tunic off. "I love her, but not in a spellbound way."

Hale halted. "Why the shitting silver beasts not? She's *perfect*."

Eleksander hummed as he poured water on a towel and began wiping his torso. "No one is perfect. She's kind, smart, funny, and sweet. However, she's also fragile, sometimes a little self-centred, and overthinks everything. She came here under false pretences and lied to us all about it."

"That wasn't her fault! Her parents—"

Eleksander held up a hand to stop him. "I know, I know. As I said, I love her, and I think the world of her. I'm only making the point that, like the rest of us, she isn't perfect." He returned to towelling himself down. "Waters know, I'm riddled with faults, Ave has nothing on me." He sighed. "Nevertheless, I've learned that I have good qualities too. So do you, you're brave, driven, caring, and strong. Those are things that I, well, that I value very highly."

"I value you and, um, your things too," Hale forced out.

Why was talking like this with Eleksander so hard? So uncomfortable? So unlike when he spoke to his friends back home? It reminded him of something he had been holding off on because mentioning it would make him feel... like this.

"When I spoke to your sister, after I ran off when Avelynne's secret came out, she mentioned that you were— sorry—*used to be*, an orphan. Like me."

Eleksander's movements slowed. "Some might say 'orphan'. I see it as that I was waiting for my real family to find me. Which they did, giving me brilliant siblings and parents. Speaking of siblings, Ellenaria would of course prattle on about my personal history. She has no discretion."

"Don't change the subject. I... want to know. About where you came from."

Eleksander put the towel down and faced him. "There is nothing to tell. I only have the vaguest memories. The rest, my mind has blanked out, probably to protect me from something horrible."

Hale shifted his footing. *Do I push him further? Or shut up?*

His first thought was to do the easy thing, drop the subject and start talking about food. So that was what he should *not* do. It was time to keep pushing. Gently.

"What are those 'vaguest memories', then?"

"I. Don't. Know!" Eleksander suddenly roared. "They're only glimpses. Music, traveling, bright fabrics. Could be my parents were tumblers. Or jugglers. Musicians perhaps. Entertaining for a few coins in every village and town before moving on." He put his arms around himself, as if his shirtlessness wasn't the only way he was exposed now. "I've always assumed I was found alone and naked because they ran out of coin and sold my clothes to buy food or booze. Maybe they would've sold me next, but I escaped. Or perhaps they didn't even bother to sell me but simply rode on without me, happy to have one less mouth to feed."

"I don't know, you might be wronging them. Maybe you got lost or taken? Or someone killed your folks?"

Eleksander's grip around himself flew open. "How is that any better!?"

"I don't know," Hale spluttered. "I suppose it's better because then they... wanted you. Loved you."

Eleksander's furious stance slumped and Hale took it as permission to carry on, hoping with all his might that he wasn't majorly messing this up. "I lost my parents to a foolish, unnecessary death. But at least I know they loved me up until their final breath. Maybe yours did too?"

"My family loves me up until this day, Hale. They took me in, fed me, and raised me. They taught me everything they knew and pushed me to learn even more. Their love and support brought me here. I don't need any other parents than the Aetholos."

The way he spoke made it clear, even to Hale, that the subject was exhausted.

Hale moved closer, wondering if the other lad was going to back away from him. He didn't, so Hale put his hands on his shoulders. "Fair enough. I won't prod anymore. This sharing and babbling is dull anyway."

Eleksander smiled and shook his head. "You're hopeless."

"Probably. Whatever else I am, though, I'm first and foremost your friend. Maybe even a sort of brother? Which means I want to help you any way I can." He squeezed Eleksander's shoulders, not as hard with muscle as his own, but certainly wider. "But until I find a way to do that... why don't you count out how many handstand push-ups I can do? I can't count when I'm upside down."

Eleksander's smile grew into a laugh. "Fine. I'll keep count. I shan't call you brother, though. Not only because everything being so masculine, when I'm not sure I fit into the role of a 'man', feels odd but because... you mean even more than family to me."

There was a twitch of Eleksander's lips and a significant look in his expressive brown eyes that made Hale tingle. What was that look? Adoration? Affection? It wasn't arousal, was it?

More confused than normal, Hale didn't know what to do or think about the comment, or the way Eleksander was looking at him. Or that tingle sneaking through his body. He did, however, know that his need to brood had vanished. The time for chatter, analysing, and fretting was finally over.

"Fine then. Call me what you want. Just count!" He said while placing his hands on the ground by the nearest wall.

Hale worked his muscles hard. Because it felt good, not because he needed to in order to impress Eleksander or earn his affection or respect. That worry had long gone, leaving a comfortable relationship with this other lad. One with a sense of belonging. A sense of being accepted for who he was.

Chapter Forty-One

THE NIGHT BEFORE SOLSTICE

It was the night before they all left for the Midwinter Solstice. Everyone was packing, except for Avelynne who due to her anxiety had done so days ago, to Myllie's great relief.

Now, Avelynne sat here in a quiet corner of the library, contemplating what she'd say to her parents when she returned to Ironhold castle. The thought of seeing them again unnerved her even more than she had thought it would.

She moved her chair closer to the fire, crossed her twitching legs, and placed her steaming cup of leaf tea on the table. A book landed with a thud next to it, making the liquid spill a little. The book was thick and bound in maroon leather.

Sabina bent to face her. "There you go. Have some reading material for the Solstice."

Avelynne wiped tea off the book and hefted it. "Rather heavy to travel with." She sighed. "Still, I suppose I do need something long and diverting for the journey back to my gilded cage. Thank you. What is it?"

"A compilation of fairy tales, all from the part of the North where I grew up."

Avelynne pretended to examine the book but was actually surveying Sabina. There were still grey circles around her eyes, showing the lack of sleep, but Sabina was soldiering on. Avelynne had promised her that they would keep things as normal and carefree as possible for the last few days here and she had stayed true to her word. Even though her heart shattered every time she caught Sabina hiding a frown or even a sob.

Avelynne opened the book and perused the table of contents. "Oh, I know most of these!"

"I should think so, my sweet. All the best fairy tales come from the deep, dark forests of the North."

Why was Sabina's voice so low? And were her lips, locked in a wicked smile, more dusky pink and wetted than normal?

Oh, of course! She's flirting again! Well, that's a good sign.

"A lot of things emerging from the deep, dark forests of the North seem to be the best," Avelynne countered, allowing her hungry eyes to linger on those lips. Sabina was sure to enjoy the proof of her desirability and her effect on Avelynne.

Sabina leaned closer, once more looking like she was moving in for a kiss. Instead, she whispered, "If you grow weary of your heartless parents and the sedate Peaks, send me a letter."

Avelynne smiled. She had planned to correspond with them all anyway, but she doubted a friendly update report was what Sabina was referring to. "Oh? What would happen if I did?"

Sabina's eyes gleamed, their circle of purple darkening by the fire light. "I shall come fetch you, beautiful," she said, deepening her voice. "Then we can explore every hidden part of those deep, dark forests together."

"Sounds like quite a dangerous and daring adventure," Avelynne purred. She pretended to brush lint off her trouser leg, slowly enough to ensure Sabina was watching, and then left her hand resting on the top of her thigh. A harmless gesture, she figured. Both she and Sabina knew this was just for fun.

"Oh, you just stay close to me and I'll keep you safe." Sabina's gaze moved from her thigh up to her eyes. "We can go dog sledding or visit the Solstice markets in the towns. And if you miss the mountains, we can go skiing among our snowy peaks."

Avelynne's stomach fluttered at the familiar fun of flirting. "Mm. Sounds cold. How would you ensure I don't get frostbite?"

Sabina picked up the book. "We can sit by huge roaring fires and read these tales to each other. Or we can travel to the warm springs of the northeast and bathe. Or… we can find other ways to keep each other warm."

With a tinkling laugh, Avelynne tapped Sabina's nose. "Bad girl. We said that we wouldn't let attraction muddle our friendships, remember?"

"I don't feel muddled." Sabina smirked, then added, "my pretty little Countess."

Avelynne pursed her lips. "I expect that sort of answer from Hale. *You* know better."

Sabina stood with a bashful expression. "Fine. No flirting, even if you did start it."

"I did not!"

"Fine, maybe you didn't." She held up her hands. "I mean it though, if you get lonely or sad, send me a letter and I'll come fetch you. We'll spend the weeks together as friends."

"The same goes for you. If talking to your parents, or trying to sleep, doesn't work… send for me. I'll cross my snow-dusted mountains to your drift-covered ones. Anything for you."

Sabina caressed Avelynne's cheek and whispered, "My Countess."

Avelynne leaned in to the touch. "What? No prefix of 'little' this time?"

"No." Sabina took a shaky breath. "I want you to know that I—"

She was interrupted by Hale and Sander running in with bottles under their arms and mischievous grins.

Sander nearly collided with Avelynne's chair and exclaimed, "Ave, Sabina! Look! Look at what we found. We went down to that undercroft where we found Karlinne because Hale thought the bottles along the walls might not only be wine but that a few of them were brandy and guess what…"

"They were?" Avelynne ventured.

"Exactly, Ave! Wait, how did you know?"

Hale pouted. "Argh. It annoys me that you get to call her Ave. And Sabina calls her 'puny countess' or something silly like that. Why can't I get a nickname for her?"

Avelynne took in the animated and rambling young men. "Have you been sampling that brandy?"

Sander's eyes widened. "Maybe? Sorry."

"The only thing you need to apologise for is not waiting for us," Sabina said. She went to close the door while saying, "Let's be trying some of that swanky swill. It's bound to be inferior to Northern akvavit."

Sander put his bottles down on the table and pulled up chairs for him and Hale.

Hale's eyebrows were drawn low and his lips pursed. "Hey. You didn't answer my questions about nicknames."

"Put those bottles down before you drop them, you darling drunk fool," Avelynne said, trying to hide her amusement.

"Avelynne!" he wailed like a wounded bear.

"Shh," Sabina said, slapping his shoulder.

He plonked the brandy on the table and sat down, his brows still drawn.

"Oh, make him feel better before he grumbles our last night together away," Sabina said, making Sander snigger.

Avelynne tucked the book Sabina had given her into her lap. "Fine. Hale, why don't you call me Ave too?"

"But that's Eleksander's nickname," Hale said. He started fiddling with the cork on one of the bottles, not making eye contact.

"It's only a name," Sander said. "We're all friends here, who cares what nickname *belongs* to whom?"

"I still want my own nickname for her," Hale slurred. "One that's mine. The name I mean. Although, I'd quite like you to be mine too, Avelynne."

Avelynne sat up straight. "That's it! Let's nip this in the

bud. First of all, I will have none of this jealousy or possessiveness, it is surely beneath us?"

Soft mumbles of agreement came from Hale and Sabina while Sander nodded. "Secondly, I'm sorry if I have led one or two of you on. You've all heard me whinge about how often my books with romance have a love triangle in them, I won't have my own life turn into that."

"Not sure you have much of a choice," Sander said, stifling another snigger.

Avelynne fixed him with a frustrated glare. "I do. I refuse to be in some love triangle, or love square, or whatever this is. I don't like relationships and I certainly don't think this is the time or place for them." She paused to let that sink in. "What you do with each other is your business, personally I enjoy flirting, but that's it. You are all my friends and that's how I'd like to keep you."

Hale clicked his tongue. "Ah, but it's hard to keep friends if you continuously charm them like you do."

Avelynne placed a hand over her eyes. "Look. Brilliant people like you shouldn't even like me! I'm mediocre, spoiled, anxious, and weak. Furthermore, I kept an awful secret from you. I let my parents control me and lead me into something ethically questionable, correct motives or not."

The others were objecting but Avelynne wasn't quite listening. Talking about her parents controlling her brought back the thoughts from earlier: what was she going to say to them? She knew she must stop being frightened of her parents. Stop obeying them without question. She had evolved, in fact her grandmother surely would've said she was now that 'full-grown woman' she had spoken of. It was time to take a stand.

She grabbed her silver quill firmly. "I need to confront my parents about the deception that got me here."

The others quieted their conversation about her flaws and strengths and stared at her. Under the scrutiny, Avelynne dropped her grip on the necklace, instead clasping her hands in her lap.

"Sure," Sabina said, giving Avelynne a stern look. "As long as you don't demand that they inform the officials. Or the king."

"Or anyone else," Hale agreed, slurring a little.

"I… suppose the truth coming out now wouldn't be a good idea," Avelynne said, focusing on her hands in her lap.

"No, it wouldn't," Sabina stated firmly. "Think of the consequences. Your family would be punished. Any Peaks student who'd replace you would have to try to catch up on six months of training and lessons."

Sander held up a finger. "Also, there might be a war or severe conflict in the Peaks."

"Very likely," Sabina agreed. "Most importantly, however, you'd tear our group apart, Avelynne. And we need each other. We need *you*."

"We really do," Hale said. "You make us a team."

Sabina took her hand. "Confront your parents about their manipulation and how you don't want to be controlled by them anymore. Other than that, the way you got your place here… that is best buried deep and forgotten about. You deserve to be here."

"I don't know about that last part," Avelynne said with a sigh. "Nevertheless, you make a good point."

Hale tried to hide a burp. "How did we get from talking about avoiding romance onto your shitty parents?"

"Welcome to the winding maze of my mind," Avelynne said.

"I guess the topic of romances between us is yet another thing we'll have to handle *after* the Midwinter Solstice," Sander said, opening a bottle with a grim expression. "That and our future mission, the king's motives, the Twelve, and everything else. For now, let's focus on having a nice night and then eight weeks of trying to put up with everyone back home."

"Agreed," Avelynne chirped. "How about we play Bottletop?"

Sander tilted his head. "What?"

"It's a drinking game Myllie taught me. Apparently, everyone but the stuffy nobility plays it in the Peaks, especially in all the taverns."

"Great, I love a good drinking game," Sabina said. "How does it work?"

Avelynne got up. "First we all stand."

While the others moved the chairs away and stood. Avelynne removed her cooling tea and all the brandy but one from the table. Then, she fished out a bronze coin from her pocket. "You turn your back to the table and then, using magic, try to land a coin on the mouth of the bottle," she pointed to the opening of the remaining brandy. "Making the coin into a sort of bottle top, hence the name. When everyone has had a go, the furthest away from the opening of the bottle loses and has to drink as big a mouthful as they can."

Hale scowled. "That's stupid. Getting drunk and having

tasty brandy is what you want, so that's what the winner should get. Ha! I'm in, if nothing else then because it gives me a chance to lose."

Sander took the coin from her hand, brushing her palm with his fingertips. "I'm in too. I'll start shall I, Ave?"

They smiled at each other while she nodded. He turned his back and said, "Ready?"

"Yes," they all replied.

Strands of magic carried the bronze coin through the air and then it was dropped. About a hands-length away from the bottle. Hale chortled.

"Huh," Sander said when he'd seen his result. "Well, perhaps I meant to lose, like you, you drunkard of a Woodlander!"

He made a grimace at Hale before they all started laughing.

Avelynne put a hand to Sander's elbow. "That was quite good, actually. The first time I played this I nearly missed the table, never mind the bottle. I'll go next."

She took the coin, turned and then focused on the little bronze disc. Imagining it being levitated behind her back and onto the bottle. When she stopped her magic and turned, she saw that it was right next to the bottle. She bit her lip to keep from crying out in celebration.

"Brilliant," Hale said. "My turn!"

They were interrupted by a strange sound, turning out to be Kall whimpering by the door.

"Ah, I think the *wittle kittycwat* needs to go out and tinkle," Sabina mocked the giant feline, making Hale chortle again.

"I'll be right back. No one take their turn while I'm

gone," Sabina said as she left with the eager Kall leading the way.

When she'd gone, Hale shivered visibly. "Shitting silver beasts. It's colder than a snowman's arse in here."

Avelynne put her hands on her hips. "Then put more clothes on. For someone who loves being outdoors, you really do spend a lot of time complaining about the weather, you ill-tempered child."

After a sobering shake of the head, Hale appeared uncharacteristically hesitant. She could almost see replies playing out and being discarded behind those jet-black eyes. These past weeks, perhaps even months, had robbed him of his ease of flirting. Was it because he was trying to be more considerate and careful with his words? Or the awful events unfolding around them?

Her heart sank as a third option came to her. *Or, perhaps he's skirting around the edges of romantic feelings? If so, I hope he heeded my earlier words on the matter.*

Perhaps she should've spoken to him about that earlier but unlike Sabina, he came off as someone accustomed to flirting or bedding women only for fun.

Hale sucked in a fortifying breath and said, "Maybe that's because you're doing a terrible job at keeping me hot with your embraces or cooling me with sweet breaths against my neck?"

Avelynne quirked an eyebrow. "Really? That's what you're going with, Woodlander?"

"Or maybe you're jealous because I'll be going home to somewhere warm," he mumbled, suddenly avoiding eye contact.

Avelynne's mirth faded. "I'm jealous because you're

going somewhere where you don't have to have a confrontation."

Sander put a hand on her shoulder. "You really don't want to see your parents, do you?"

"No." Her hand went to her necklace as she made a decision. "In fact, when I've confronted them about how they've treated me and told them I won't be manipulated by them anymore, I'll tell them that I shan't be coming back there for any future holidays. I'll remain here."

"Are you sure?" Sander asked.

Avelynne stood taller. "Positive. Moreover, who knows, not being allowed to see me might make them think twice about how they treat me. Or at least make them fret that the heir to the Ironhold castle and name might be lost to them."

Hale planted his feet. "All right. If you'll stay here for all the holidays, so will I."

She blinked. "You don't have to do that, Hale."

"I want to. I mean, it's not like I have family to see," he said with a shrug. "I don't miss my Woodlands friends that much. The only one I need is Ghar and he'll probably stay with me. He enjoys the chillier air here. And the pie served in the Great Hall. And the flirty cook who makes it."

Sabina had somehow returned without Avelynne spotting her and now spoke. "I'll stay too. For most of the holidays, anyway. My family needs to get used to managing without me."

Avelynne swallowed a lump in her throat. "B-but they'll be expecting you?"

Sabina lifted her chin, as if deciding something. "It's my life. If I want to stay, I'll stay."

"Well, one thing is certain," Sander said. "I'm not leaving you three here. By the time I return, the Hall of Explorers will be burned to the ground. I'll remain as well."

"I cannot ask you all to do that." She heard her own voice breaking with emotion.

"When will you realise that not everything is about you, little Countess," Sabina said with a cheeky smile and a wink. "We want to be here. The four of us together."

Hale tapped the table with his fist. "It's decided. Unless Sabina's or Eleksander's families need them, we'll stay here for all future holidays. It'll be practise for our future together on the ship."

"The four of us against the world," Sander said, wrapping his arm around Sabina who was closest.

"Unless we're playing Bottletop," Sabina said before patting Eleksander's stomach. "In which case it's every second waver for themselves. Give me that coin!"

With a laugh, Avelynne handed over the coin. Affection and joy rushed through her veins, heating her up and making her dizzy, without even a drop of brandy in her system.

The library, and the world in general, could be as cold as it liked. These three would keep her warm from the heart out.

Chapter Forty-Two

PARTING

Hale watched their little group. He, Ave, Sabina, Eleksander —and Kall, who was having his morning wash—waited out by the gate. There were noises from the workers who were storing away the weaponry and target boards for the Solstice break, but otherwise all was quiet. Hale refused to break that quietness by clattering his teeth.

Curse this cold. Curse this cold. Curse this cold. Arrrgghh!

No wonder he was chilly, the sun hadn't even melted away the morning frost glittering on the roofs. He wouldn't have to be cold for long, though. Soon their carriages would come to fetch them all. Myllie was already on the other side of the gate, eager to get back to the Peaks. Eleksander's sister, Ellenaria, was surely out there too, keeping a keen eye out. Ghar, on the other hand, was still inside. Busying himself with the search for his training mat which he claimed someone had stolen. Hale was pretty sure his mentor had left it somewhere, forgetful at his advancing age.

Hale wrapped his arms around himself. He was wearing

the linen Woodlander garb Ghar had brought for him. While they were too cold for here and now, he'd be glad of them when he was back in the humid Woodlands. Ghar had been right about that. He might be getting forgetful, but he still knew what was best for his charge. Not that Hale would tell the old grouch that.

The others were dressed in the garments of their counties too, preparing for the climates they'd be returning to. Eleksander in his blue Lakelander silks and a flimsy white traveling cloak, Sabina in a huge sable-trimmed surcoat of leather and long matching boots, and Avelynne, *Ave*, he corrected himself, wore a long-sleeved gown of thick, purple velvet. On top of the dress she was currently fastening a big, ermine-lined cloak. It was grey like iron. Grey like the shield of the Ironhold crest. It matched her eyes and stoic expression perfectly. Hale couldn't say why, but she looked regal.

Much more so than that shitty king of ours.

None of them appeared to know what words to part with.

Hale cleared his throat and breathed in the Centre air one last time. "It'll be nice to be back after the Solstice."

"You say that now. You'll be whinging the eve before lessons start again," Avelynne said.

"I'm quite sure we all will," Sabina replied while tucking her compass into a pocket of her coat. "It'll be rougher work next term, but there's nothing to be done about that. We'll get through the lessons best we can and unwind whenever we get a break."

"Wait, is that Sabina Rosenmarck with a... more relaxed attitude?" Eleksander asked.

Sabina's posture went rigid. "I'm trying to learn. I mean, death comes easily and swiftly, so it's best to make merry and unwind while you can, right?"

"Yes! Our Northerner finally learns that there's more to life than being responsible and sensible," Hale said, bumping her shoulder with his. "Does that mean you'll agree to go swimming more often when we return, older sister?"

Sabina blushed. "Aye. I didn't stop you before, did I?"

"No," Hale said. "I want to do more carefree things with you, though. Like, helping you take that stick out of your arse." He craned his head with a flirtatious expression, as if he was admiring her rear. She didn't laugh.

"Not funny," Sabina said in a tired voice, closing her coat and draping her arms around herself. "We all know you're not getting anywhere near my bum so don't leer at my body like that, even if it is for a joke."

Hale froze. "Shit. I didn't mean it that way. In fact, I'd smack any outsider who did that. I only meant that I want to help you stop carrying the world on your shoulders but that sounded pompous, so I made a childish, dirty joke instead."

"I know," she said, still sounding tired.

He rubbed the back of his neck as they looked at each other. Those knowing eyes of hers. He didn't want to disappoint them. For all that she and he were similar—physical, no-nonsense, fiery, warriors from a poor background—it was strangely hard for him to open up to her. Or perhaps it was *because* they were more similar than he was to the others?

He steeled himself. "Look. Ignore the fact that I act and

speak before I think and know that I respect you for trying to loosen up and grow. A-and I'm going to miss the shit out of you, Northerner. I've… been wanting to say something to you but not known how to phrase it."

"Just try. We'll help you if need be," Avelynne said, encouragement in her small smile.

He brushed the scar above his eyebrow as he tried to find the words. "Sabina, you feel guilty for killing Rete. I feel guilty for *not* killing Rete. So, I was thinking, maybe we should both try to lower our need to be in charge and to control things?"

She gave him a half-smile but didn't answer.

Shit.

Why had he thought that he of all people could analyse someone's behaviour? Or that he should give advice? Hadn't this term taught him to keep his mouth shut?

He scraped his foot on the ground, starting to sweat despite the cold.

Sabina gave a muted little laugh. "If you can stop to re-phrase what you said, express what you really meant, *and* end up sounding that sweet… I can certainly try to de-stick my bum. So, aye, we'll try to let go of our need for control together."

He blew out a held breath. They grasped forearms and he squeezed, trying to show all his affection and admiration for her in that simple gesture. She laughed, louder this time, and then pulled him into a long, rib-crushing hug. Stepping into her embrace, and her heavy coat, was warm and sheltering. It felt so natural and comfortable to hug her.

Hale released a happy sigh. *How did I get to have friends like these?*

"Splendid," Eleksander said when they had let go. "Hopefully, you can both aim to stop working yourselves into exhaustion while you're at it." He gave them a mischievous smirk.

"We shouldn't let you feel left out, Sander. What will be your homework?" Avelynne asked.

"Hm, I suppose I'll try to work on upping my confidence. Maybe also on my overreactions to things, the silver beasts in particular, although I'm not sure I can change that. What will yours be, Ave?"

Her reply came right away. "Like I said in the library, standing up to my parents. And all of you," she locked eyes with them all in turn, "have taught me that I am strong enough to do that."

That didn't sit right with Hale. "Hang on! Give yourself the credit, not us."

"He's right," Eleksander said with a smile. "You've become much more self-reliant than I think you realise."

Ghar came out and added his training mat to the pile of his and Hale's belongings. "Ha! Listen to you lot. Clapping yourselves on the back for your improvements. You're all still little nippers. Just wait to see what you'll have to learn for the rest of your time here."

He didn't let them reply but instead went to bid farewell to one of the guards he'd become friends with.

Hale watched him slap the guard on the back so hard the man reeled. "Ghar's right. We have a lot to tackle when we get back."

"Mm. Lots of change ahead if we're to survive and outsmart those who want to use us," Sabina agreed while crouching to pat Kall.

"Well," Ave said. "We won't be used. No matter what they try to teach us, no matter what the king wants us to do when we get to foreign shores, we shall act in accordance with our conscience."

Eleksander chewed his lower lip. "Perhaps we should liaise with the first wave? They're set to sail in six months. We must ensure they will rebel against any immoral orders too!"

"First of all, *we* might sail in six months too if the king really has tired of the slow pace of our indoctrination," Sabina said, standing back up. "Secondly, we don't know if we can trust the first wave. We decided that night after the... incident, that we could only trust each other, remember?"

Ave stared pensively at the icy morning sky. She didn't look cold, though. Hale wished he also could be sheltered under her thick cloak. "Do you think we should inform all of Cavarra of King Lothiam's plans?" She asked, gaze still on the horizon. "Spread the word before he sends us off into the great unknown?"

"Perhaps," Sabina said, with a hint of scepticism. "If we found a way to make people listen to a group of eighteen-year-olds and take our word over the people in power."

"Yes, and a way to ensure that the shit we call king won't lop our heads off right after we spill his secret," Hale said.

Sabina winced. "Exactly. Either way, it'll have to wait until after Solstice."

"Mm," Ave said, lost in thought. She ran her hand through her hair, sending the nightblossom scent of it towards Hale, making him lose equilibrium for a moment.

The sound of hooves and wheels outside the gate rang out.

"Whose carriage is that?" Eleksander said.

"I don't know but it sounds big, so it can't be mine," Hale replied.

Outside the gate, Myllie shrieked with joy. "Mine by the sounds of it," Ave muttered.

They all stood motionless. Then Ave threw herself at Hale and Eleksander and drew them to her, catching Sabina in the middle. In this quite uncomfortable, crushing embrace they all laughed together.

Hale tried to memorise every sensation, every sound, every scent.

Then Ave let them go, picked up her bag, and hurried off with a shouted, "See you in eight weeks. Happy Solstice!"

"Don't forget to write, little Countess," Sabina called after her.

"I won't. Farewell for now!" she replied, hurrying away as fast as she could in that weighty, impractical dress.

A fleeting moment and more hooves and wheels appeared.

"Now that sounds like an *ostentatiously* large carriage," Eleksander mumbled with shame. "Must be mine. Happy Solstice, you two. I…" His gaze flitted back and forth from them and down to the ground.

Hale put an arm around his shoulders. "Go on, big lad, get whatever sappy comment you're holding back out of your system."

Eleksander grinned and then softly said, "I merely

wanted to say that I've come to love you both and will miss you. Please be careful and write if you can."

"Try stopping me, my friend," Sabina said. She stood on tiptoe and kissed his cheek. "Now get in that carriage before your sister drags you away by the ear."

He nodded and hurried off.

Then there were two. Three if one counted Kall, who was stalking around them as if herding them. Hale petted him, enjoying the thicker winter fur. Kall licked his fingers and then let Hale pet him some more.

Sabina shoved her hands into her pockets. "Well. Goodbye for now. Don't get into trouble and, um, have yourself a good Solstice."

"I can't promise I won't get into trouble, but I'll certainly have a brilliant Solstice. Make sure you do too."

"Mm. You know, now that we're alone, maybe I should mention—" She stopped, shifting her weight from foot to foot.

"Oi, no secrets between us, Northerner. What?"

"I… doubt either of us is ever going to be in a relationship with Avelynne considering her stance on romance." She paused. "However, if I'm wrong and she chooses to be with you instead of me, at least I'll know she's with someone who has the fiercest of hearts. Someone I've come to, well, love and admire in the last six months."

Hale was lost for words and lost in general. This strong, smart, kind person who had their life in check and so much to offer… actually admired him? *Loved* him?

He pulled her into another embrace. "Not as much as I admire and," he stumbled before the word but made his embarrassed mouth say it, "love you. You're one of a kind, older sister. Anyone would be insanely lucky to give their heart to you."

They stood like that as long as they could without the embarrassment chafing too much. Then they parted with awkward smiles, pats on backs, and mumbled disparagements about sappy cuddling.

There was a melodic call in the distance, mixing with the sound of heavier hoofbeats.

"The sound of Northern horses and my father's halt call," Sabina said. "I better be there when he comes to a stop, or he'll have Kall herd me to him."

They laughed and waved goodbye. Hale snuck in one last ruffle of Kall's fur before the snowtiger joined his mistress through the gate.

When she was out of sight, Hale slumped. He had to physically force his body to straighten again. He wouldn't succumb to the loneliness, though, instead he thought about their earlier conversation. Yes, they had all changed. *He* had changed. He was more considerate, and his emotions were easier to control. Out of the blue, he remembered nearly being undone by the smell of Ave's hair a few moments ago. His heart fluttered. Fine, maybe some emotions weren't under his control at all.

Still. He'd found people who wanted him. Friends who forgave his mistakes and helped him grow. Three remarkable people who made him feel respected and loved even if he wasn't the best at everything. He'd still try to excel at everything, of course. Anything else would go against his nature.

He touched the weight in his pocket. His compass. He was Hale Hawthorn, Mapmaker and part of the second wave! He was going to explore the unknown one day. Travel far and wide. Find new people and lands. Probably fight dragons and wyverns. He could handle a crush on a charming lass. Especially since she'd still be a great team member and one of his best friends even if she never loved him the way he did her.

Ghar came back to fetch him. "Come on then, lad. Our carriage should be here any moment. Let's head home so the others can mock you for losing your tan and going soft in the belly."

Hale scoffed out a laugh. "You're one to talk! Let's go."

Chapter Forty-Three

AVELYNNE'S RETURN TO IRONHOLD CASTLE

Avelynne found the journey a lot faster on the way home than in the other direction. She slept well, without many nightmares, at the various inns. She sketched while practising what she would say to her parents and chatting to Myllie. She recalled golden memories from the Hall of Explorers: the evening swims, the cosy library study sessions, the interesting lessons, the bonding over training, and modest but delicious meals.

Currently, her mind wandered to other delicious things and she bit down to hide a smirk. Hale's array of corded muscles, Sander's crooked and ever so charming smile, Sabina's flirtatious eyes with that secret sliver of purple. She tried to draw her wonderous friends but never caught their likeness well enough; ink couldn't do them justice.

Either way, the journey flew past.

They were by the gates of Ironhold castle when she caught Myllie staring at her from the other side of the carriage.

"Is anything the matter?"

Myllie cleared her throat. "I've been meanin' to ask, Countess, but didn't know if it'd cause offence…"

Avelynne smiled. "Go on, Myllie. Speak your mind, you know I shan't be angry."

"Are you really goin' to stand up to your parents?"

The smile fell off her face. "Yes."

"What if they say you can't go back to the Hall of Explorers but must stay 'ere and marry some nobleman?"

"Then I shall run away. Back to the Centre."

Myllie scrunched up her nose. "Even if you lose your title?"

Avelynne smiled again. "When have I ever cared about my title?"

"Fair enough. What if they reveal how you got into the academy, tho? Get you expelled?"

Avelynne remembered that Rete had mentioned knowing the secret. Who already knew? What would happen if her secret came out? What would happen if her parents didn't protect her? Didn't agree to shelter her anymore?

She took a deep breath. "Then I'll handle that when I must. I can make my own choices and live with the consequences. I am self-reliant. Or I'm becoming that at least."

"If you're sure," Myllie said with raised brows. "I'd pick the easy way—marry some dishy nobleman and stay 'ere. No deaths or mysteries. No moral problems to mess with your bonce. No sea monsters or trolls loomin' in your future."

"I think I'd rather have all those things than what I had before. I think my new life suits me better, don't you?"

Myllie laughed. "Yes Countess. I believe it does."

The carriage stopped. Avelynne was helped out by a footman and saw a slew of familiar servants bowing to her. She waved at them in a complete lack of respect for social hierarchy.

Standing farther back were her parents. They looked particularly menacing with the backdrop of their forbidding castle and heavy storm clouds above.

Avelynne touched her necklace, then the compass in the concealed pocket of her dress. Afraid as she was, she didn't let that stop her from acting anymore.

She lifted her chin and smiled.

Today, Countess Avelynne Ironhold kept her nerve.

THE STORY CONTINUES...

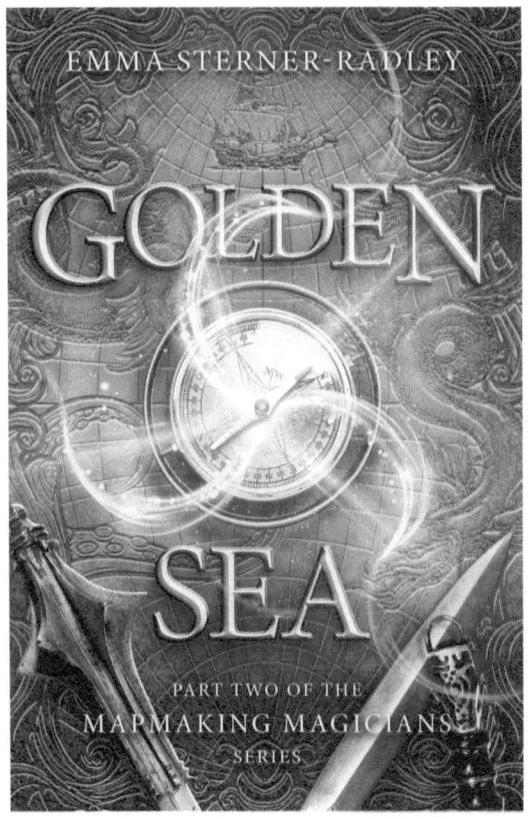

Read more on the next page…

GOLDEN SEA

Our four mapmaking magicians are back at the Hall of Explorers. As they continue their studies, their journey to find new lands is brought forward following a calamitous event. However, seafaring and exploring turns out to be even more dangerous and complicated than they expected.

Soon they have to battle not only the perilous waves, the king's evil plans, sea monsters, but also their emotions. Eleksander pines for Hale, who in turn joins Sabina in having feelings for Avelynne. Meanwhile, Avelynne is realising her lack of romantic interest may run deeper than she thought. Meeting new people on their journey make things even more complex.

Feelings will however have to take the backseat as the ocean brings new surprises, some wonderful, but far too many dangerous beyond measure. And the sea doesn't show mercy.

REVIEWS

I sincerely hope you enjoyed reading Silver Beasts.

If you did, I would greatly appreciate a short review on your favourite book website.

Reviews are crucial for any author, and even just a line or two can make a huge difference

SUPPORT ME ON PATREON

Being an independent author writing LGBTQIA stories you don't always get the exposure and financial support that other authors achieve.

Because of this, many of us rely on support from the reading community through sites such as Patreon.

As a patron of mine you will receive exclusive behind the scenes news, updates, my latest book releases for free before anyone else, and even free audiobooks!

If you are interested in supporting me then I'd be extremely grateful.

https://www.patreon.com/emmasternerradley

ALSO BY EMMA STERNER-RADLEY

MAKING A TINDERBOX

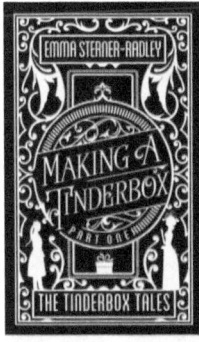

All the societal rules are different. The fear of unrequited love is the same. Will these two women find both love and freedom?

Fiery Lady Elisandrine 'Elise' Falk doesn't want to follow conventions and marry the boring prince. Nessa Clay, an introverted farmer's daughter wants to chase her dreams and leave her safe village.

Calling to them is the dangerous city of Nightport, brimming with new innovations in clockwork and steam power.

Circumstances bring Nessa and Elise together and different as they are, they find themselves magnetically drawn to each other. But will that magnetism be enough to make them overcome their insecurities?

Furthermore, what secrets does Nightport hold? Who are those men searching for them? And does magic exist after all? With the help of some new friends, Elise and Nessa start to unravel the mysteries — and their feelings for one another.

Steam towards love and adventure today, buy the standalone first part of The Tinderbox Tales – Making a Tinderbox, a gaslamp fantasy romance by Emma Sterner Radley.

ALSO BY EMMA STERNER-RADLEY

TINDERBOX UNDER WINTER STARS

When being captured is a likely outcome, which cage is worse – the one in your mind or the one behind a locked door?

Lady Elise Falk and Nessa Clay have happily taken on new identities as a married couple and boarded a steamship to Storsund, a land of frost faires, sprawling cities, and corrupt organizations.

As they settle in and make friends - some funnier than others – are Nessa and Elise safe under these frozen winter stars? And will their relationship survive, while they must check every shadow to gauge what is paranoia and what is real threat.

Under the old stars, but never far away, the villainous Queen of Arclid has her own threats to battle.

As events unfold, Elise and Nessa must overcome their personal issues and challenge themselves. Because now, it is not only their fates that hang in the balance, but also that of two nations.

If you enjoy romantic fantasy with a dash of steam and magic, Tinderbox Under Winter Stars, part two of The Tinderbox Tales is waiting for you.

Board the steam train by buying Tinderbox Under Winter Stars, the second part of The Tinderbox Tales by Emma Sterner-Radley.

ABOUT THE AUTHOR

Emma Sterner-Radley is an ex-librarian turned fantasy writer. Originally Swedish, she now lives with her wife and two cats in Great Britain.

There's no point in saying which city, as they move about once a year.

She spends her time writing, reading, daydreaming, exercising, and watching whichever television show has the most lesbian/sapphic subtext at the time.

Her addictions are reality escapes, coffee, protein bars, sugary snacks, and small chubby creatures with ridiculously tiny legs.

www.emmasternerradley.com